# BEYOND DESERVING

a novel by
Sandra Scofield

THE PERMANENT PRESS
Sag Harbor, New York 11963

**Library of Congress Cataloging-in-Publication Data**

Scofield, Sandra Jean, 1943–
    Beyond deserving / by Sandra Scofield.
       p.    cm.
    ISBN 1-877946-07-9 : $21.95
    I. Title.
    PS3569.C584B49   1991
    813'.54—dc20                     90-42707
                                          CIP

"Trespass" appeared in slightly different form in *Ploughshares* and in *The Ploughshares Reader: New Fiction for the Eighties.*

**Manufactured in MEXICO**

THE PERMANENT PRESS
Noyac Road
Sag Harbor, NY 11963

In memory of Al Scofield,
and for those who loved him

For Judy Griswold

And for Bill and Jessica,
who make it possible.

The support of the National Endowment for the Arts is
gratefully acknowledged.

I'll be home soon. Will you understand
if not forgive
that I expect to be loved
beyond deserving, as always?

   —Stephen Dunn, "Letter Home"

# ONE: TRESPASS
# 1978

—1—

Katie had already made plans to go to Texas with the baby. Her going didn't have anything to do with Fisher hitting her. On the other hand, she wouldn't change her plans, even though her eyes were black in the morning; even though he cried and said he had sat up all night in remorse, thinking about killing himself (he had slept the sleep of the dead drunk—she had heard him snoring); even though she'd have to lie to her mother, and her mother wouldn't believe her, so that Katie would end up defending him the way she always had, when he didn't deserve it anymore.

It was the first time he had hit her, unless you counted a couple of shoves. Once, in 1969, long before they had married, they had been visiting a navy buddy of his in Sausalito, and Fisher had given her a push, out on the deck of the buddy's houseboat, because she was yelling at him not to go off drinking and leave her with the buddy's super-Christian pregnant girlfriend. The push shut her up, scared her, out there in the dark; it almost made her mad enough to get on a bus and go home alone. But the buddy's girlfriend, who had been an acid freak before she tuned in to Jesus on the Christian radio station, said it was just that the guys were still coming down from all those killing vibes, and praying and loving were sure to bring them back. She said they had spent most of the war in shallow water, and real life seemed awful deep. She said Jesus would keep them afloat.

Katie worried about being out on the water without the rowboat; when she thought about it, she realized that the other girl had been thinking longer term. If Katie had had a longer view, she might have made the bus, but common sense told her Fisher wouldn't leave her floating a hundred yards offshore from a disco, once he had had enough of whatever he'd gone off to get. Sure enough, he had made it up to her. He arrived near noon with croissants and eggs. He made her an omelet, and pleaded temporary insanity. He took her out on the deck again—she could remember still the smell of shingles and the water and gull droppings at her feet—and shyly offered her a fat joint. "I'm better with gestures than words," he said, a grin plucking at the corners of his mouth. She gave in to his awkward charm, wishing there were more of it, and that it were real. She smoked a little with him, and then went back inside, her heart a caught bird thumping against the back of her ribs.

The next time he struck her wasn't that long ago, which made things seem really bad, because now she could see a connection between what had happened then and what had happened this time, an escalation of violence she would have to think about before she would know what she ought to do.

He had come home from a bar where, over a pitcher of Oly, he had heard some real straight-arrow assholes saying the soldiers in Vietnam must have been chicken, and now half of them were turning out nuts, too. Some guy had shot his wife and then himself, and the paper ran a series on the syndrome that was supposed to explain it. Downtown, in a seedy neighborhood near the Burnside Bridge, some vets had opened a center for their own kind. Katie and Fisher passed it whenever they went to their favorite restaurant, run by Thais. "Fucking everywhere," Fisher grumbled as they walked by. He was eight years home from Asia then. Those guys in the bar had been in junior high when he was bobbing around on the Mekong Delta, jumping on and off junks, hundreds of them a day; when he was checking bamboo wharfs that might blow his balls off. "Baby fascists, still wet from their first dip," Fisher said. Katie wanted to sympathize, to try to feel whatever Fisher was feeling. She hadn't been in junior high, she had been in outer space when the war was going on. She had never even voted. She had fled Texas to the west and then the north, and never looked around, as though she had lost her language in some foreign territory. Demonstrations she recalled dimly, like old Rose Parades. Pictures from the war were surprisingly clear, and recently recalled: burning, screaming children; the little guy wincing

as the bullet hit his brain. Those had been famous photographs or she wouldn't have noticed. She hadn't thought
about politics; she hadn't had time in between classes and
waitress jobs. She only dated once in a while, guys who asked
her out after work when she was too weary for talk. The war
meant more to her now, because of what Fisher had brought
home and held on to for so long. She wasn't so out of it, not
really. She had read in *Time* that it took years after a war for
the good books and movies to come out. Fisher's sister-in-law
Ursula, who kept up with everything, said that they hadn't
even started making hay of Vietnam yet. It took a long time
for some people to make sense of it, while others got
nostalgic. It hadn't been a good war, Ursula said. Katie took
that to mean that sympathy might have been hard to come by
at first, and she tried to feel bad when Fisher did. She felt his
pain in her welling up like some boiling dread. But she
already had such terrible indigestion from the baby in her,
she didn't have room for more agitation inside, and so instead of saying something right when he came home that
night, she belched. That was when he shoved her. She fell to
the floor like a beanbag, big belly down, and then rolled over
with a moan in time to see him out the door. She thought, *I
better not tell Ursula.* Ursula's job was looking out for people
who didn't have the sense to look out for themselves. Ursula's
job was giving advice, and Katie could see she was in need of
some, but then her mother had always said that advice was
wasted on her, and in this case she didn't want to hear it from
anyone.

   This time, though, Fisher punched her, plain as that. She
had been sitting on a high stool near the stove in the kitchen,
nursing the baby, and he came in late and loud and stumbling. She knew well enough not to say anything, not to ask
where he had been or what was the matter, not to ask why he
was drunk when he had said he wouldn't be, when he had
been sober for almost three weeks, ever since the day the
baby was born. She looked up and said, "Hi, Fish," trying on
her understanding wife-and-Madonna pose, and she tried to
smile, although she was very nervous. It was late, and she
didn't want him to break something and alarm the neighbors
or the baby. Once she had yelled at him, "Turn your fucking
drunk down, Fish," and he had thrown a pot off the stove

right through the kitchen window. She did smile at him, and
he turned and snarled at her. "What are you grinning
about?" he demanded. She was self-conscious, with her
heavy, warm breast exposed, and so she smiled even more, to
compensate, the way she had in school when she was bawled
out for reading ahead. Then he hit her—smack!—right between the eyes, with his fist. He wasn't standing very far away,
and he didn't pull his arm back or take aim or anything like
that. His arm shot out like a rubber band released from
tension, and her face just happened to be in the way. Later
she wondered if he had meant to hit her in the mouth, to
wipe off the grin. *My God,* she thought, *he could have knocked
my teeth out.* But her memory was clear. He had stuck his arm
straight out like a robot, just above nose height, just between
the eyes, and she was exactly an arm's length minus two awful
inches away.

—2—

"I'm tired," she said as she came through the gate. Her
mother, June, was there with her Aunt Christine. Katie had
not been home in years. The sight of the plains from the air
had been a shock; she had forgotten how flat the region was.
    She remembered from some grade-school lesson that these
plains had once been a blanket of buffalo. The buffalo had
all been hunted and killed, there were only people now.
    Both women looked different from the way Katie remem-
bered them. Her mother, in Gloria Vanderbilt jeans and a
nubby teal-blue sweater, was pretty. She had had her hair cut
in a skater's precise style. She looked fortyish, instead of fifty,
while Christine, who was younger, looked sixty. The sisters
had been widowed within fifteen months of one another;
they had taken their losses in quite different ways. Christine
had had the sour husband, the tight budgets, the blank
loneliness of no children, yet she had always been per-
petually cheery, a maker of fancy cakes with frosting. Katie
had thought Christine might have brightened as a free
woman, taken up jogging, perhaps, or classes, but here she
was, her hair ratted and her stomach bloated, wearing a smile
like a ribbon on a crutch. Katie's mother had been devoted to

her husband (never Katie!), and Katie thought June would wither without him, but no, she was brisk and attractive, as though it had been an amicable divorce instead of a heart attack that had parted her from Katie's father. Katie looked at her mother and saw how much a stranger she was, her life a mystery. Katie had no idea what her parents had really felt, or been, for each other. She only knew there had not been much left over for her.

In the car Katie told them how she had been going out the back of the house to call Fisher for dinner, and she had gone around the corner just as he came the other way, carrying a two-by-four. "It was so stupid of me," she said. Aunt Christine wailed in retrospective horror. "Thank God you weren't carrying the baby!"

"Seems to me he might have been a little more careful," said June, her hands tight on the wheel.

"Stop at intersections?" Katie asked tartly. "Honk at corners? It was unusual for me to go outside to call him. It was raining. Now that I think about it, I can't imagine why I went out." She felt her cheeks flush with conviction as they always had when she argued with her mother. The story fell so easily into place. "The baby was dozing. It seemed I had been indoors ever since I got home from the hospital. I guess that's why I went out, a little claustrophobia." She shifted the responsibility from Fisher to herself. She felt a little smug, it had been so easy. For the moment, she forgot her dull anger at Fisher, though she had spent the entire day, in planes and airports, chewing on it. It was displaced by this more immediate clash with her mother. They had wasted no time! Her mother drove in silence, but the tension was palpable, waiting for words. If no new reasons came up, there were old ones to spark fires between them.

"So tired—" was the next thing Katie uttered when they got to the house. The baby was screeching. Katie sprawled on the couch and undid her blouse and bra to feed the baby. Her mother's old Uncle Dayton sat across from her in a Lazy-Boy recliner, smiling and nodding from behind his blind frailty. The baby sucked. Katie lay with her eyes shut. Her face throbbed. She knew she must have shocked her mother and aunt with her racoon face.

She thought about Fisher, but she hadn't the energy to

recall the decisions she meant to make about him. She had
brought him along like luggage waiting to be unpacked. If
she ignored it, she would take it back exactly as it came. But
when she thought of him he was as flat in her mind as a
photograph. Yes, exactly as a photograph, she saw him
perched on the roof on the long metal warehouse where he
was working. There would be drizzle in Portland this time of
the year. It would be so easy for him to fall; he was a careless
man. She saw him, like a feather from a pillow on a bed,
drifting toward the pavement.

She was falling asleep. Unconsciousness would bring her
dreams—brilliant, violent dreams that evaded her when she
woke. She had had them for so many months now they were
almost welcome. It was their predictability that made them
bearable, the lurch into sleep, as though she had stepped
badly off a curb; and then the dream sucking her in and
hurling her out again, exhausted, into consciousness. If she
didn't fight it, she could sleep again afterwards. She could
rest. How much she wanted things lately to be laid out in
patterns (good or bad): meals and sleep, quarrels too. Fisher
was unobliging. He planned nothing, and had no ruse for
the way he set her up to knock her down. She never knew
what was coming from him, because he did not know either.
Love was what you felt before the pain came. She was fast
assuming a victim's pose. Except that she was too smart-aleck
to be victimized. She was a collaborator in their script. Sometimes she provoked him, to get the hurting out. It had been
much better when Fisher (they, really) had smoked grass, but
he didn't like the game you had to play with dealers, and
once there had been some trouble with the law. He said wine
was just as good, which of course it wasn't. The wine shut
Katie out; she hated the smell, the taste, the sweet stickiness
of it. When they had been stoned together they had crawled
into a safe place, together. Sometimes he talked to her there.
He told her about Mekong water so shallow they had to
invent boats to skim it on a thin skin of air. She remembered
sitting on the bathroom floor while their friends laughed and
yelled at one another out in the kitchen. She and Fisher sat
with their knees up under their chins, eyes floating out toward one another, and he told her that the whole war had
drifted by on just such a cloud. Rain and more rain; bodies—

theirs and ours and those you couldn't be sure of; death all colloidal in the choking jungle stench; everything drifting, make-believe, while everybody watched and got old really fast. He had been upriver and into canals and tiny veins of waterways. He had been into the heart of the dream that was a river war, into jungles and ambush. He had liked to wear the black pajamas of the people they were wiping out. They were little people, he said, tensile and stealthy. Even the children were wise.

She remembered the way her throat pulsed while he talked, and how hot the small room was. She lay down on the floor and put her cheek against the porcelain of the toilet, and then Fisher lay down beside her and said, "Someday we'll be really old, and I'll have told you everything." She thought, *This would be a good time to die.* She was that happy.

Someone brought a blanket for her, and took off her shoes, and set up a vaporizer. Her mother took the baby. "I've got a crib all set up," she said. She came back in a few minutes and laid hot cloths across Katie's eyes, and then cold ones. Back and forth the cloths went. Katie felt as though she were dissolving.

—3—

They both had a little money when they met. She had become part of a circle of friends that had been his before he enlisted. His friends liked to spend time in the bar where she worked, where the owner said one day he was going to be mayor. They had helped Katie find a better room to live in. They had tried to talk her into staying in college when it got so hard (Ursula had old papers lying around in drawers, she said), but when she quit, saying it was pointless, she had no ambitions, they said they didn't care about that. Some of them did graduate, and went on to be social workers and post-office clerks, land-use planners and teachers. They took on houses and had children. (Later some did move to the country.) Fisher's twin brother, Michael, and his wife, Ursula, were like a planet to all their moons. If anybody knew where the others were, it was Michael and Ursula. They had a cache of stories to tell. Some, like Katie, drifted out of school. Burly

Winston, everybody's confidante (he had such enthusiasm
for your history), drove a school bus and went to Salt Lake
for half a year to trace his lineage. Katie got a better job, in a
fish and chips place with a big lunch trade, and she saved her
money to go to Mexico in the winter. That was when Fisher
came home. He and his brother came in for cod and beer,
and waited for her to finish her shift. Fisher told her he had
money left from his tour because there had been no place to
spend it except on the way in and on the way out. He was
living in Michael's basement. He kept coming by to pick her
up after work. He was full of tales, mostly funny ones, about
people he had met in the last four years. He didn't come on
to her, except to watch her a lot, while she was working. One
night he showed her he had two cameras and two radios. He
gave her one of the cameras. She saw they were finally going
to get somewhere. He sold the other camera. One of the
radios had been gutted and stuffed with hash. That he sold,
or most of it. Then he went downtown and got a drive-away
car, a Grand Prix. It belonged to a hockey player who wanted
someone to drive it to his mother. Fisher told Katie—they still
had not touched one another—that he had been thinking
what a good idea she had, to go to Mexico. She liked it that he
assumed they would go together. She had planned to take
buses all the way. Later she realized it was one of the boldest
things he had ever done. He never came on to women,
except in Asia, where the women were gentle and he was
special, being American.

They drove like idiots down the coast of California, in
someone else's car. They told each other stories about made-
up people, and made up stories about themselves. He said
his first fuck had been a fat lady and he hadn't been able to
tell if he ever hit home. She said hers was in some bushes
behind a frat house at Texas Tech. That was close to the true
story, but she laughed, telling it, and hoped he at least wondered. It was understood that this was a lark. What else could
she expect from a man just back from the brink of death? She
didn't mind being easy. It was better than pretending you
might not when you knew you would. She thought he probably wanted a lot of sex. That didn't make any difference to
her, one way or the other, except that she had the idea that a
man owed you a little for each time: a little conversation, a

little attention. A little remembrance, after he left, or you did. Most of her memories were sorry ones. She had not known any men especially well; she had always assumed they would treat her badly.

At the border of Mexico, Fisher went into a deep funk and would not talk at all. He saw her looking at him, and he said he was going to have to get used to being *here* rather than *there,* though he thought it would help to be in a foreign country again, one that wasn't stinking with war. They were on a Mexican bus then and her curiosity was building. "I'll recover when I see the ocean," he promised, and then didn't speak to her again for a day and a half. She forgot what she wanted to know about him. She was good at spacing out, herself. She bought them candy bars and beer at the places the bus stopped, and he took them without looking at her. She thought him exotic, his enervation a come-on. She had been anxious most of the time since puberty. She didn't know much about depression. The first night in Mazatlán, he snapped out of it. They got a room in a decent hotel and ate lobster and got very high. "Oh lady," Fisher crooned, two fingers in and half the night to go, "your flak jacket's open, dumbshit lady." She thought he was talking out of some dream station, and she didn't care. Communication wasn't very high on her list right then. Everybody wakes up, even from deep sleeps, she thought, thinking of dreams as events, not states. Never thinking that what you take out of a dream might work like erosion on the solid parts of waking. Knowing nothing about war underwater.

They took a bus to a village down the coast and rented a thatched *palapa.* They were there for weeks; she thought she was happy, for the first time ever. One morning they hiked over a hot hill to a lovely stretch of beach lying below a grove of orange trees. She sat on a towel while he waded into the surf. He had just shouted to her to come in when she saw the Mexicans at the edge of the grove. They made a line, squatting against the trees. Katie ran down to the water's edge. "Come back," she cried. "I don't like it here." Fisher mocked her, but she begged him to come out, pointing to the Mexicans who sat like stones. He told her she was being stupid, but he did go up the hill with her again. As they passed the point closest to the *campesinos,* there was an audible rush of sound along the line. Then the Mexicans rose and walked away. "What did they want?" Katie whispered. Fisher pushed her onto the hill. "Nothing," he said. She asked him again when the hill was behind them. "The water had a treacherous undertow," he said. "They were waiting for us to drown."

She got diarrhea and couldn't get over it, so she took a plane out of Mazatlán and went to her parents in Texas. It was high season for her dad's tire store. As soon as she was well he put her to work on a phone. She called people who had bought tires from him a year to a year and a half or two ago. She let the Texan stream back into her voice, and sold a lot of tires.

Every night her mother made meat and mashed potatoes, and her father came home late. "If he gets home this time every night, it's not really late, is it?" she said to her mother one evening. June burst into tears, but she wouldn't talk about it. Then Fisher showed up in another car. Katie bought her mother a blender at the drugstore and left it on the kitchen counter with a thank-you card. They went by the tire store on the way out of town, but her father wasn't there, and they didn't want to wait. Katie never saw him again.

The next day it occurred to her that she and Fisher had no agreement. They didn't even know one another's age. He had hardly looked up to say goodbye when she left Mexico holding her gut. Now they were on their way to see some friend of his who lived maybe in Mill Valley and maybe in Sausalito. It was crazy. By then they were in Arizona, and there was nothing she could do except read the map and keep the radio tuned. In a roadside park, just past dusk, they made love on the back seat of the Oldsmobile. It made a wet spot on the dove-gray upholstery. She thought it was an awful thing to have done, a kind of trespass. Maybe nobody would know. But when you made love—or did hateful things, at the other extreme—some of you stayed behind. She didn't know how to explain it, she had never tried to put it into words. She didn't even know the word *karma* then. It was simply another of her ideas for which she had no vocabulary. She wondered if everybody who didn't watch television and didn't like to read had ideas like hers. If people filled up their minds or went around with them empty. What was important about this idea was that it helped her make moral decisions, when she remembered in time. She knew, for example, that she would never have survived a war. She would never have been able to keep it straight, them and us.

Back on the highway she kept on thinking, and she decided that if it was intensity that left your image, there must not be anything of her anywhere. She felt a kind of constant desperation, small and steady like the hum of a cat; it kept her moving, but it didn't make her interesting. She couldn't imagine what Fisher saw in her except accessibility, and though she could see that that might have appealed to him at first, she didn't think it was going to make much of a bond. What could two people have who were sure they couldn't have anything else? Yet for her, Fisher was made up of secrets, and she thought that inside him, his hum was louder. It wasn't just that he was a man, it wasn't that at all. It was that he had been somewhere that counted, somewhere she couldn't even imagine, somewhere he was making her think about when it hadn't ever before crossed her mind. When he said he didn't mind if they made love during her period, she didn't say that it seemed only fair, that sometimes she thought she could smell blood on him.

She finally got up her nerve to ask him, "What was the worst thing that happened in the war?" He said it was in an Oakland bar, right before he got out. Some drunk navy kid tried to get a guy to fuck him, right there in the bar, and before Fisher had finished his beer, there were cops and MPs both, beating the shit out of this wimpy kid. "Jesus, Fish, what could you have done?" she asked. She had waited a long time to get up the nerve to ask him, and she didn't like being put off. "What about the damned *war?*" She hated ellipses, metaphors, any lies that weren't up-front fantasies. And here she was, Miss Walking Ambiguity.

"I just watched," Fisher said.

—4—

Katie nursed Rhea toward morning. Someone laid the crying child in her arms and nudged her: Katie, Katie, the baby's hungry. Katie was in bed. She couldn't remember moving, or changing. She put her hand down on her hip. She was wearing a flannel gown, probably one of Christine's. Her mother wore pajamas. The baby was noisy. For a fraction of a moment Katie felt bothered to have her attaching herself so greedily. Then the gargled sucking shifted into an intense, rhythmic tug that Katie felt in her breast and neck and groin. Fisher had watched her nurse, but he had never commented. As the baby grew less hungry, she stroked Katie's breast, and Katie spread her free hand over the baby's fuzzy soft head. Though the urge was gentle, Katie felt the fine hint of hostility in her hand. The possibilities. She shuddered and drew her hand away. Her mother saw, and whisked the baby away. Katie slept again, not thinking, for once, about the territories of the bed. She slept beneath her dreams. When she awoke, she felt better, but she didn't want to get out of bed. To be a child again herself, the baby instead of the mother—how foolishly she craved that. Refuge, succor, regression: these were desirable things. When her mother suggested moving the crib into the living room, Katie agreed with relief.

Her mother came in and said there was a phone call. "It's Fish," she said, looking as if she were holding one. Fish spoke in a nearly inaudible monotone. He didn't have anything to say. Katie knew the call was as close to an apology as she would get, but it wasn't enough to acknowledge. And she would never assume the initiative. He had called. "How's your mother?" he asked, a silly question. "See me shrug," she answered. Her mother was across the room cutting mushrooms at the counter. "She's there?" he asked. The momentary focus on the third party—one Katie had betrayed in dozens of stories of minor malice—brought Katie and Fisher momentarily closer. "They're crazy for the baby," she said, relenting a little. She couldn't think of anything else to say. "Do you know how long you'll stay?" he asked next. This took some courage on his part. At the airport, she had refused to let him touch her. She told him that, after all this time, she finally admitted it was hopeless. He was a drunk and a beast. He stood docile as a lap dog while she hissed at him. She wanted him to do something vile, to fuel her journey, but he was too tired or too indifferent to her baiting. He stood with his shoulders slumped like a fruit picker at day's end. She was unmoved. She had every intention of leaving him. Maybe she had left him already. The trip was coincidence.

"We haven't talked much," she told him. "I don't know how much I'll have to take." The last words slipped out. Her mother looked up from her dicing curiously. Katie didn't know what she and Fish were talking about. Oh why did they always talk in riddles? "I'll write," she said weakly.

The next day her mother went back to her regular schedule. She owned a small dress shop. She went there around nine and came home around four. She said while Katie was home she would come home for lunch, too. Christine took care of the house and shopping, Uncle Dayton, and now the baby. Katie stayed in bed. She read old magazines and did her nails. She kept thinking she would go back over her marriage, her years with Fisher, and try to make sense of them, but then it would be time for lunch or a cup of tea with Christine, time for a nap or to feed the baby, and she never got started. She only got as far as that long ride down the length of California in someone else's car. She couldn't imagine what references Fisher had given, to make them trust him with a rich athlete's car. They had laughed a lot. She had put her head down in his lap while he was driving, to see if she could shock him.

Christine came in to talk. She had been quilting. Katie admired the intricate Texas pattern of the quilt on her bed. Her grandmother had made it. Christine said she herself had no talent for it—it was June who could sew however she liked, and Katie had taken after her—but Christine liked the feel of fabric in her hands, so she made quilts out of big squares, and tied them at the intersections. She was making one for Uncle Dayton, double-thick with batting because his circulation was bad.

June came home early and pulled a chair close to Katie's bed, like Katie was a patient in a nursing home. Her mother said she wanted to tell Katie about a time when Katie was an infant, and Christine had come over to help out. She said Katie had been terribly colicky and that she, her mother, had not managed well. One day she had slapped Katie quite hard while Christine was in the house. Christine didn't go home for a week. "And I went to bed," June said. "When I got up a week later, I was sane again, and of course I was mortified. It is a very serious thing to hit a tiny baby. I certainly never did it again." She stopped talking, and Katie waited for the moral. Her mother was full of admonitions. Maybe her mother meant to say she understood how Katie was feeling. Or she might be letting Katie know that one week was the limit. But Katie wanted to know how many times there had been when her mother might have hit her if there had not been the memory of that single harsh blow, struck too early. Neither of them spoke for several moments, and Katie saw that her mother wasn't going to clear up any of Katie's questions if she didn't ask them. Katie wanted nothing from her mother that required the asking.

"You know I never liked Fisher," her mother went on finally. Katie was expressionless. "It's not just that he came through her and collected you without a pause for courtesy—" Katie knew that was one of the reasons. "It's not that you haven't had a real home all these years, or that it was such a long time before the two of you married."

Katie interrupted her mother. "What was it, exactly?"

June looked at her oddly, with what Katie decided was distaste. "It's that your relationship with Fish has done nothing to change you."

"That's his responsibility?" Katie asked.

"I do think a good relationship helps you to grow up. Helps you to become a better you. Fisher doesn't seem to have been good for that. I assume the same is true the other way around."

Katie thought of leaping, cat-like, in an arch, to scratch her mother's eyes out. "While you are here, I want you to think about it," her mother said. Katie could feel her hands twitching.

"Think about Fisher's failure to mature me?"

"Think about what you want to be, and what you are."

"You're incredible!" Katie spat. She was crazy to have come.

"No, I'm normal. Many straight people are perfectly normal."

She didn't know that those categories were obsolete. Katie, who had risen stiffly from her pillows as her mother spoke, now fell back against them with a thud. Damn her! She struck the mattress with a fist. She had wondered what the price of her mother's hospitality would be. She had expected a little advice on mothering. But no, she was to consider alchemy. To be something she was not, when neither of them knew what she was.

—5—

The subject of marriage had come up when Katie and Fish had been together about a year. Not their marriage. His. She heard him talking to Winston about a girl in Bangkok, where he had spent four months. The two men were laughing about Fisher's "first wife." Paper Lady, they called her, and Blossom Juice, and Dragon Wife. Her name was Chee Sum (Chum See? something like that). Katie tried to ignore the talk but couldn't get it off her mind. She confronted Fisher with it. He wouldn't tell her anything. He said there had been a girl in Bangkok, yes, but not a wife. There had also been the best restaurants in the world, he evaded, with fish caught that day, and peppers that put your eyes out. She wanted to know what was so funny about the girl. Fisher said she would never understand. She hadn't been there.

She pointed out that Winston hadn't been there, either. But Winston had been in the army, stationed in Japan. "Eyes up, eyes down," Fisher laughed. "Forget it, Katie. It has nothing to do with you. Or with me, anymore." She did try to forget, but his mother forwarded a letter to him that came from Bangkok. She came on him as he was reading it. She cornered Winston and demanded to know what he knew. Winston said there had been a civil ceremony of some sort, to save the girl's face. Her father wouldn't let her live at home anymore any other way. Fisher had spent a lot of time with the family. Her father owned a bus line in Bangkok and lived very well in a nice house on the outskirts of the city. Katie wanted to know where Fisher had met her. Winston said in a whorehouse. The girl wasn't herself a whore, but one of her friends was. Fish had once told a story about a whore who sat in a plate of mushrooms on a bar. That whore? Winston became edgy. "Shit, Katie, how would I know something like that?"

Winston hated being put in the middle. Katie thought he owed her some loyalty because she had known him first. She had met him in the bar where she worked, and had introduced him to Fisher's circle of friends. But he was a *man*. He was Fisher's friend now. They drank together. They went to Hood River and picked apples together. They did finish work on sleazy tract houses together. Sometimes they were drunk and hateful. Katie went back to waitressing, to have someplace to go at night. She was ashamed to tell Ursula how lonely she was.

"Listen, Winston, a girl takes it seriously, and with a ceremony!" Winston said the girl knew it was for show. Fisher wasn't one to make false promises. But the girl had gone to the Americans, and that was when she found out it really did amount to exactly nothing. A joke on her, whatever her father had believed. Somehow she had obtained Fisher's home address. It had taken her a year, but here was the letter. Katie didn't think a girl could have managed that unless there was a baby. Fisher tore the letter up in front of Katie. "She wants a free ride," he said. "And didn't you?" Katie retorted.

Some days later—she and Fisher weren't speaking since the letter scene—Katie came home and found Fisher gone. That was the first time he went off like that, though not the last. Winston, who was now sober, was cleaning her kitchen. He had picked up all the little flimsy blue pieces of overseas letter paper, some of them stuck against the base of the cabinets, or under the stove.

"What are you trying to make up for?" she asked, but there was more affection than resentment in her voice. Winston said Fish had gone to B.C. to see friends, Nam buddies who had settled on Sechelt. Katie panicked. She begged Winston not to leave. He was uncomfortable. "I'm not asking you to sleep with me," she said. Men had no idea what women were about. "I need company."

They went out for hot Indian food, and washed it down with a lot of bitter beer. "I can't figure him out, I'll never understand him," she complained over the dirty table. "He contradicts himself all the time. I wish I had known him before he was in the navy, so I would know what is him and what is them. So I would know if he might change, when it all wears off."

Winston shook his head. "Man, I wouldn't count on that." He took her home and stayed with her. Maybe he felt sorry, or thought he did owe her something. He tried to help her understand. "There were those who thought you laid low.

Shadow grunts. Others said keep moving. Different schools of survival. Fish still hasn't figured out which way to stay alive."

That was when Katie realized how deep she was in with Fisher. She only cared what he thought so she could please him. She had to find out with delicacy, like a man on patrol. Only they were on the same side! It wasn't sabotage she had in mind. It was love.

If they could invent fast shallow-draft boats just for the waters he had patrolled; if they could send out cutters on barrier patrols in monsoon weather, there could be this, there could be love where there had been none before for either of them. Neither spoke of their parents. They came out of nowhere, needy in the way rootless people are, for touching without grasping. There was, in all the world, only each other, but they had never said that. "Someday I'll have told you everything." Fisher did say that, once when he was high. Later she asked him if he had ever been in love. He was drunk and slightly miserable. "Aw shit," he told her, "love is like the fucking Delta, man. You look down from the air and it looks so easy and open. So sweet. Then you get down on it and it's so dense it chokes you."

The next time the subject of marriage came up was four years later. She thought she was pregnant. Right away she said she would rather be married than not, though she didn't mean it as an ultimatum. Fish agreed as readily. They signed papers in front of a minister someone at Ursula's office had suggested. The minister, who was wearing purple beads on a gray turtleneck shirt, couldn't believe they didn't want him to say anything. "They even say things to launch boats," he said. Katie held her breath, waiting for Fish to say something. He would wonder what a minister who combed his hair across his bald spot would know about ships. Katie rushed around to get the minister a glass of Cold Duck. It was flat. Fisher had opened it and taken a big swig that morning. It turned out Katie wasn't pregnant.

Rhea was for real. Katie acted like it was a surprise, but she had been thinking about a baby since the false alarm. She had been careless. When she found out, she told Ursula first. Ursula bit her lip and said, "I guess I'll never have another one." She already had two. Katie thought it wasn't a very helpful thing to say. She had wanted a little reassurance. Even a hug would have been nice. The night Katie went into labor Fisher was drunk, and Katie, too embarrassed to call Ursula, took a taxi to the hospital. Fisher showed up early the next afternoon. The baby was bundled in a rolling crib by Katie's bed, and Katie was reading *Mother Jones.* "A divorce would be awful," Fisher said first thing. He hadn't even taken a good look at the baby. "All those papers, and a judge. You'd have to do it without me." Katie blinked. It took that long to figure him out. The marriage had meant more to him than to her. She had said she wanted to be married so he would know she didn't mind having his baby. He had thought marriage was full of promises—and he had meant to make them! Now he felt guilty. He was laying their marriage out like a pig on an altar. And he *was* guilty. She couldn't even depend on him for a ride. "Come on, look at her," she told him, placid as a cow, ignoring his contrition and anxiety. She was not going to make a neat trade, conscience for baby. She wanted both. Besides, he did look at the baby, and he cried. Like any other father, he cried, and made promises neither of them would try to remember.

—6—

"**I** do love you," she told him the next time he called. She had been at her mother's two weeks. She didn't have the courage to say she didn't want to come back. She did love him, she didn't want to go back. She could not explain it. She would write him about it. She would draw a line down the middle of a page. Write LOVE on one side, and THE REST OF IT on the other. Put it in an envelope and mail it. Hell, she could just put those titles down and he'd get the message. Getting divorced would be like that, all stamps and signatures and a great distance between them. She would stop talking to him. He would be humiliated. His worst doubts would be confirmed. He knew what he was really worth. He would go away from the people who knew them both, even Michael, and in a while she could go back if she wanted. She wanted

Ursula to be her baby's aunt. She thought it would make them closer. She would act like Fisher had never been there. If they talked about him, it would be like he was dead.

Rhea lay propped in an infant seat on the dining room table. Sunlight streamed across the table and across her fat legs. Next to her seat, a big Tupperware bowl of rising dough glowed yellow. The wind was blowing across the bare landscape outside. A norther was due, but who could complain? The sun had been bright every day. When Katie's mother came home for lunch, she opened the blinds in Katie's room and pulled back the curtains. She didn't like it that Katie wanted to be in the dark.

One afternoon her mother brought home another baby girl about Rhea's age. It was the child of a friend's daughter. Katie, lying in bed, heard the strange baby's cries. She went into the room and saw the two older women, each with a baby in her arms. The new baby was hungry. Katie's breasts began to leak. Katie's mother was trying to give a bottle to the infant. "Is she used to nursing?" Katie asked, taking the baby from her mother. Her mother said she thought the baby took milk both ways. "Usually my friend keeps her while her daughter works part-time, but she broke a tooth and had to go to the dentist. The little dear is all off-schedule," she said.

Katie took the baby over to the couch and undid her blouse to feed her. The baby took the nipple greedily. All Katie wanted to do was make the baby stop crying, but as the child sucked, Katie felt a wonderful sensation come over her. It was as if she lay in sunshine. She looked up contentedly, and saw her mother and her aunt staring at her. "Milk's milk," she said. It was amazing.

That evening, as Rhea was sleeping, Katie went and sat by the crib for a long time, leaning her face against the slats and making long red marks on her forehead. She tried to see what was unique about her child. What made her Rhea and not some other baby. Fisher had asked her, "Do you think she looks like me? Like you?" He said he wished they had taken photographs. Katie said Rhea looked like a baby.

In the morning, Katie woke to a terrible taut pain in her breasts. The front of her nightgown was soaked. She looked out the window. It was late morning. No one had waked her to feed Rhea. She went into the kitchen and found her mother giving the baby a bottle. She had gouged a bigger hole in the nipple, and was giving Rhea a pasty cereal. Katie saw, on the counter, a cereal box and a case of formula. It was that easy. The oozing cereal ran down Rhea's chin and over the front of her bib. Katie turned away and poured herself a cup of coffee. She poured the cream carelessly, the cup was too full. The kitchen was noisy and bright; things hummed and clicked and bubbled. Katie bent over to slurp from the cup.

Her mother came into Katie's room after lunch. The window was still dark. Her mother raised the blinds brusquely and stood at the foot of the bed facing Katie. The sky had turned the gray of a boat hull, and it was getting cold.

"I'll keep Rhea if you want," her mother said. Katie had been expecting a comment about the weather. "I'm not very old, I'm healthy, money's not a problem. I'm not desperate for someone else to take care of, I don't think it's a neurotic impulse. I think I'm thinking of the baby, though I must say a child is a sweet commitment in the early years."

Katie said nothing. Her scalp was on fire. An hour later her mother came back. "If you do leave the child, it has to be something legal, a guardianship. I won't take her for a while, and love her the way I would, and then have you come through on your way to Timbuktu and take her away." Katie looked at her mother with open, sullen hatred. "Think about it," her mother said gently. "For the baby's sake?"

The next morning, Katie was up and dressed by eight. Christine fluttered around her, pouring coffee for her, but her mother acted as though nothing were different. A day like other days. June was sitting on a chair by the kitchen table with the baby on her lap. "I bought a portable playpen for the shop," she said, more to Christine than to Katie. "I thought Rhea would enjoy being around people." Katie said maybe she could help. She heard how stupid that sounded. "I don't mean with Rhea. I mean with the shop."

"This wouldn't be a good week," June said. "Maybe next week. I'd enjoy showing you the store. I have a couple of women who sew up a few of my designs, did I ever tell you?" She stood up and handed Rhea to Katie. "So now she's been fed," she said, and went to get dressed. Katie dangled the baby over one arm and carried her coffee in the other hand,

and went into the other room. It seemed a baby wasn't much trouble, if there weren't other things to take your attention.

Uncle Dayton was in his place in the recliner. He was dressed in aged gabardine pants and a plaid shirt. "Morning there!" he bellowed. Katie didn't know if he could tell who had entered the room. All the vision he had was enough to see objects as blocks against the light. "Bring me that little one to pet," he said, and when Katie did, he was surprised. "So it's you this morning, is it?" he said. Katie saw how long the days would be, if she started them all so early.

—7—

The buddy with the houseboat was part Indian. He and Fisher were in the Rung Sat in '66. It was like being in a fraternity. The buddy's name was Jake. They had called him Kneebone in the navy. Fisher called him that when they got tight, and Jake gave a war whoop. He was Blackfeet, raised a long way from the sea. They threw stories back and forth. One was about another Indian, a Crow named Charlie-Bird-in-Ground. He had had his balls cut off and stuffed in his mouth, in a whorehouse in Saigon. "That was the war," Fisher and Jake said. They talked about it like pranks remembered from high school. Good old Charlie No-Balls.

There was a picture of Jake on the wall of his houseboat. He was wearing a headband made from torn black pajamas, and he was holding a submachine gun. His hair hung long and silky, as if he had had a shower and then put back on his dirty clothes. He looked a lot more Indian in the photograph than he did now. He was standing on a sampan. He had a smart-ass expression that didn't much resemble him now; except when he was drunk, he was soft-spoken, and never looked at you straight on. But he must have had some of those feelings still, or he must have remembered them, or wanted them, because there was the picture. And there was a Montana Indian on a houseboat in Sausalito.

Fisher studied the picture a moment and named a place: Can Tho or Ham Lo. Katie couldn't make it out. "Right," Jake, a.k.a. Kneebone, laughed. "When we got through, there wasn't a leaf left on a bush. We shaved the fucking shoreline, man." Fisher laughed too. "Three hundred junks a day. All mine were little guys with nets, scared shitless. You got all the cargo." Jake flicked the picture with his fingernail. "I could smell Charlie in their fish sauce."

"God, Fish," Katie whispered when they were in their sleeping bags, inches away from the couple's bunk. "I don't even know what you two are talking about, and it scares me. Even when it's over now." She could see Fisher's face in the glare of lights from a nearby disco, bouncing off the window above her head. The look Fisher gave her was the look you'd give a cat on your lap just before you put it off. "Don't try," he told her. "It was boring, and wet, and hot. You couldn't understand. Wait for the movie version." His voice cracked, as if he were talking over a radio. Across a paddy, maybe, or around a bend.

—8—

Fisher sweated all night, every night. He woke smelling sour and stale. All his shirts were wet in big circles under the arms. For a long time Katie changed the sheets every day, but it got to be too much. She lay on a dry place on her side of the bed. The cook at work said it sounded like diabetes. Katie nagged and nagged until Fisher went to see a doctor. He came home thoroughly peeved. The doctor learned that he was a carpenter, and he said, "Well, don't laborers expect to sweat?" There hadn't been a blood test. The cook said there should have been a glucose tolerance test. Ursula said Michael said his and Fisher's dad had something, maybe it was diabetes. Katie wept in frustration. "Don't you *know?!*" she yelled at Michael. Ursula shrugged. Michael wasn't unlike Fisher in many ways, she said. Fisher wouldn't discuss it, ever again.

He dreamed. Sometimes he groaned, or cried out, in his sleep. It didn't seem to wake him, only her. The dreams went on, year after year. She told him about them. "You should talk," he said, "the way you twitch in your sleep." He made an excuse of it, to take her from behind. "Go on, wiggle around and get your little ass in my face." Clearly, he wasn't going to discuss what was going on with him. She knew her own dreams drew from his, but she knew his were the real nightmares. The groans were too deep to ignore. She learned to sleep over them, like street noise, but she knew they were there, and she worried. The sweating didn't go away, either. Sometimes, to prove to herself that she loved him, she drew close to him, her thighs recoiling as they touched the cool, clammy space between his body and hers, where he had soaked the sheets.

But there were nights, dark, rich nights, plum and apricot, grapes and nougat nights, when they met and slid and plunged in the juice and acid sweetness. He lay sleeping, and when the sea of her chest was dry, she wiped her finger across the top, above the nipples, and licked it, to taste the salt he had left there. The bed was pungent with the smells they had made. There was no word for this. Love. Hate. Need. She lacked a word; it needed six, eight syllables, rolling consonants, resonance. A Russian word might do. A Bolshevik word, she thought, though she didn't know what that meant. She needed a word rich and thick enough to name what there was between them, some word complex enough, and sad, if spoken aloud.

He did wake up once and tell her he had dreamed he was firing into a tangle of thick green vines, and suddenly a bunch of gooks fell from everywhere, silently, like blossoms off a tree in a light wind. He saw that she was one of them, a body rising and folding over before him into the slime. She thought it a loving thing, his telling her, but once he had done so, he shut her out. He seemed to hate her for knowing about the dream. Sometimes he would lie in the dark with his eyes open, staring at her until she was the one to turn away. He wouldn't tell her anything else. "I tell it to my lady," he mocked, holding up a half gallon of burgundy and settling down for a night on the couch.

She began to have more vivid dreams of her own. They were black and crisscrossed with lights. They were damp, sticky dreams, in terrible places. She never knew what was going on. She woke disoriented. Sometimes she cried. He asked her what the hell was going on, and she said that it might just be fallout from his dreams; they had grown so big in him that they had crawled over into her. "What a dumb cunt thing to say," he said. She agreed, yes, yes, her lips slick with tears. Maybe she didn't have any right to his pain, but they were working on a decade together. There they were, two bodies side by side, wet and dry. Was it so strange that, after so long a time, she should start to share his night terror? She didn't ask for the dreams. She had never had patience with dreams, hers or anyone's, but these dreams—maybe she did welcome them. It was aggressive of her to walk into his secret place and steal from him. One night she woke with cold fright and called to him. "I don't know what I'm dreaming. Help me," she begged. He got out of bed and wouldn't sleep with her for days after. "Surrealistic dildo," he said, carrying the best blankets off the bed.

—9—

She found Uncle Dayton's company surprisingly agreeable. She spent most of the days with him. His face had two expressions, and he slid back and forth between them. Sometimes he was benign, listening to the baby gurgle, or to game shows on television. Because his hearing was poor, he had a radio that turned to the television stations. He put both the television and the radio on loud. Katie asked why he turned the television on at all since he couldn't see it. "If you only listen," he said, "you've only got half of what's going on." After that, if she was in the room, she would describe to him what was happening. She would tell him about the clothes people wore, and how the winners jumped up and down. This pleased him very much. At other times, Dayton sat in absolute silence, vulnerability sliding down over him like a fog. His paper skin looked ready to split. "He's scared he won't live to see ninety," Christine explained. Katie couldn't tell what that meant, so she asked her mother. "He's scared of facing payments due on his living," her mother said. Katie was fascinated. Here was this old, old man in a chair, so thin she could have lifted him easily. "What did he ever do?" she wanted to know, but her mother tightened her lips to a slit. "Remember it's your own history you're making," she finally said. "Look after that."

Katie watched her mother with Dayton. Spoon by spoon June fed the old man, catching the occasional dribble of broth before it ran off his chin. Her voice cooed while her face remained hard and resentful. Katie supposed she would never know what history her mother and her old uncle shared. Katie suddenly doubted all the kind things she had ever seen her mother do. She swore she would never act like that, as though she were generous when she was not. Katie asked her mother if she had a boyfriend. Both of them smiled at the silly word. "A friend?" Katie amended. "Why yes, I do," her mother said. He was a surgeon. "Can I meet him?" Katie asked. Her mother said she felt their hands were full. "I promise I'll behave," Katie said lightly. So her mother invited the surgeon to dinner. He was pleasant, and Katie saw that they liked one another very much. She saw something else. On the doctor's face she saw something she had not seen in a long while, the ripe open look of desire. She could not bear it; she left the table.

She went to her mother's store. A blouse caught her eye. It was of Chinese-red silk. Her mother insisted that Katie take it. Katie wore it as a nightshirt, with bikini panties. She thought she might look like a Chinese whore, and she wished Fisher could see her.

## —10—

She had been in Texas a little over two months when she saw the dream clearly, and could recall it. She had been trying all along to find herself in it. It came clear when she realized that she was there, but not visible. She had to look at the dream from the inside.

She dreamed of hibiscus flowers drifting like foam on water. She dreamed of shoals disappearing and reappearing. She dreamed of land underwater. She had grown up on the vast yellow plains of West Texas, and her brown-water dreams frightened her. There had been a woman from Mesquite whose husband had fallen from a derrick on a clear night. Afterward, the woman had had a healer's hands. People came to her from all over. Katie heard her mother talking about it, and begged to go.

"There's nothing wrong with you," her mother said, "and it's wrong to gawk." But Katie had longed to see the woman. To see sick people rise. Now, remembering the healer, she wished for her, even if only by dream. If the woman had touched her, so long ago, this terrible seed inside her, this thing Fisher had touched and set to bloom, might have withered and made her wholly another person. The thing was the pink of the hibiscus, but it was poison. It was love.

A sampan drifted toward a clearing. Fisher was there waiting. She could turn, back into the brush, but she could not take the child, because she did not know what was there. She could move out into the clearing, toward Fisher, trusting him not to be tired or angry, not to panic, not to fire. She could not do that with the child between them.

Either way, she could not risk Rhea.

She got up in the middle of the night. At first she felt hungry, but the light in the kitchen hurt her eyes. She went into the room where the baby lay, and looked at her for a moment. Then she went to bed. She put the night between them, waking alone in the morning, lying there in the cold dark, thinking of what to take, and what to leave.

# TWO: BECALMED
## 1987

Ursula must have known Katie ten years before she told her that she had once wanted to marry Fisher herself. Even as she said it, she wasn't sure it was the truth. Ursula had been with Fish a while before Michael and she hadn't been the one who wanted not to be together. That much was true. The rest was the stuff of memory, which has a way of growing sadder over time.

Katie looked startled, then quickly recovered. She showed hurt with little flickers of her eyelids, though she shrugged it off. "I always thought I was the first woman he ever loved—" she said. She meant, *the only one.*

"I didn't say that he loved me," Ursula added quickly. Probably, he had not. When he was there, though, when he was "on," he was almost giddy about love. Sex. You wouldn't have thought that, to see him most of the time.

"—unless you count the girl in Bangkok." Katie peered at Ursula. "Should I count her, Ursie?"

She had only asked what Ursula thought, not what was absolutely true or right. Ursula thought they should not call the Thai woman a girl anymore. Girls who fall in love and are abandoned are women.

Ursula said, "Certainly not." Why mix walnuts with cheese curds? A Thai girl—woman—in a setting as remote as the spicy food? The easy sweetness of young whores (who sometimes *were* just girls)? The absolute foreignness of the place? Ursula had tried to ask Fish about it when he got back. He hadn't made much of the love affair, though he mentioned it, anecdotally. He said he felt bad for the girl because she got hung up on her attachment to an American. Ursula asked if he was going to write her, and he turned sour. "Sure I am," he said, "right after I catch up on my correspondence with the Dalai Lama."

Why did she mention Fish to Katie at all? She can't remember anymore. They were driving home after picking thirty quarts of strawberries. Their hands were stained red and the car reeked. "I wanted to marry him." The words came out before she thought. Maybe it was that Katie was having a hard time, and Ursula wanted her to know that they all love him, as much as he will let them. He is their cowboy, challenging their comfortable, busy, straight lives, simply by not living them. Ursula understands the dark tug he can have on a woman, the sense of falling, and wanting to fall. The fear of the light. She remembers giggling and sighing, then waking utterly alone, as someone banished. It was all a long time ago—everything is different now, she is a different woman—but she remembers keeping her eyes shut tight to postpone the day. Now that she has been to graduate school she knows terms for the attraction (the compulsion), and such words make Fish less mysterious, make Katie pathetic, make all of them culpable. How much has Fish done for them all, acting out what they cannot bring themselves to do?

How much have they all used him?

"Fish never has been one to put out energy on a woman," she said.

Katie was astounded. "Fish is sheer energy! Why do you think it's so damned hard to live with him?"

Ursula would have said that falling, that despair. Maybe Katie truly knows him and Ursula doesn't. She doesn't believe he changed much in Vietnam, just that he has always been good at guarding himself, deep inside, though she has seen him knocked flat and defeated, too, in terrible, public ways. It is hard to say what really hurts him. She knows he is a man in pain, but she cannot name it. He refuses to recognize the norms of success or acceptance, even on the low scale that rose up out of their sixties slow dance. In the corner of him, whatever the weather, he is an immutable essence, which Katie that day called energy. Ursula thinks it might be the opposite, inertia, but in some compelling, negative way, a force with magnetic power. The grand suck of a collapsing star. It could make great demands.

Ursula said, "You're lucky to know that." They all think

Fish is special. Maybe it is time they outgrew that. What he is
is lost, like one of those nineteenth century Englishmen who
wandered around the Sahara instead of getting a job and
settling down. If only Fish had a Sahara! If only Araby.
They had been talking about how difficult he was. They
had been talking about whether Katie ought to leave him.
She did not and she didn't come again to Ursula for advice.
Ursula feels her guilt and pity tugged by the alliance of Fish
and Katie, but she works too hard at managing bad cases in
her work not to recognize the false seductiveness of *knowing
better,* and the futility.
There have been times Ursula wanted to yank Katie away.
There have been times she wanted to lecture Fish (or hit him
hard!). She did neither. She did not warn, scold or try to set
them straight, even when they seemed headed straight for
hell. She even learned not to vent her frustration by trying to
enlist Michael, because Michael said, annoyed at her litany of
concerns, that he was not going to abet any obsessions about
Fish. He has had his share of them. Ursula, wounded,
pointed out to Michael that he was wholly preoccupied with
his parents, but Michael cut her short, saying, "They're old."
That ended the discussion before she could also point out
that Fish, ever the little brother, if only by two minutes, often
got the benefit of Michael's interventions yet.
After so long, Fish and Katie seem indissoluble. Ursula
only wonders if they can survive themselves.
With Fish as the correlate, she observes her own husband
Michael and counts her blessings. Fate has moved her to the
right side of the Fisher coin. Michael has his faults (she thinks
of them as Fisher faults), but he is steady and kind. If only he
did not make her feel becalmed, like a boat on a vast still lake.
If only she did not have such a craving for little squalls, to stir
the water.
Fish is around again. He can provide a storm or two. Come
to think of it, they might just be counting on him.

—12—

Ursula wakes one May morning to the sounds of Michael's
snoring.

He disclaims such sounds when Ursula complains, but just last week, as he lay stretched out on the lumpy basement couch, his jaw a little slack, he made the particular sound that bothered her the most. They had been watching long-faced Sherlock Holmes on PBS for the third time, and Michael made this short, wet sound, a bubble-popping sound, through his mouth. "Hey, that's it!" Ursula shrieked. Michael was indignant. He wouldn't laugh even when Ursula doubled over laughing. She knew he had heard himself. He had a look. "What a dumb thing," he muttered, and went off to get a bowl of Almond Mocha ice cream. "It's just now the good part!" she called after him. He ate his ice cream in the kitchen and missed the end of the show.

The noises aren't so funny in the night. At first she was able to make him stop. He makes noises when he lies on his back, and stops when he turns onto his side. When he wakes Ursula, therefore, she lets him know, and he revolves compliantly. Sometimes he manages to say "Sorry" as he heaves onto his side. This used to touch her—she does love Michael—but eventually she realized he was not much disturbed by her nudge. Only she is bothered.

The snoring has been going on for about two years. Michael has developed a new version that sometimes overcomes the disadvantage of lying on his side. It involves a quick blowing of air, as though he were releasing pressure in his sleep. She regards this variation as an escalation. She wonders what twenty years will bring. Subtly, her reaction has been changing, so that where once she would have tapped him gently, she now sometimes jabs him with her outstretched stiff fingers and exclaims, MICHAEL, YOU ARE SNORING.

It is not quite dawn, the middle of the week, and the sky is a streaky gray, dry and soft, though it was drizzling when she went to bed. She knows she will not fall asleep again, and she minds. She hates mornings. She knows women who rise at 5:30 and go off to the Y to bounce around with weights on their ankles, all this before work. She doesn't care what such a regimen might do for her heart or weight or self-esteem. She craves oblivion before full sun. The best she can manage is to sleep until the exact moment the alarm bursts in her ear.

Now, though, she knows she might as well shut it off, since she is fully awake.

Resentful, and chagrined that she feels so, she pokes Michael with her knee, digging in his thigh and hissing, "Ssstop!" She falls back woefully on her pillow. All her life she has been able to sleep anywhere, to fall asleep in any position, on any surface. There have been second-class Spanish trains, church benches, the back seats of cars, and a line of beds, none very good and some hardly deserving the name, and she thinks, *This isn't anything that needs to change!* Why this, a blessing, when other habits and conditions rot in a compost of piled years, a swamp of established life? Tedious, awkward Christmases with the Fishers, pickle jars and milk cartons stacked any which way in the pantry, and a thousand extraneous things in the basement. Quarrels with her son about hygiene and English. The clacking and rattling of cars driven too many miles, as though a new one would be an act of treachery against some higher principle. She longs for a luxurious accounting, a sojourn in a kind of emotional fat-farm for midlifers. She knows she needs realignment, to remember what matters and what does not. Some days she feels sentenced to her life. Other times she feels it shudder, only a 1.5 on the Richter scale, but a warning that the plates beneath her can shift.

If only Michael would surprise her. Doing what, she can not imagine. Nothing bad, please, the way some of her friends' husbands have surprised them, pulling out of marriages that seemed like rocks. Adequate, at least. "What did he want?" Carol Beyers wailed the week before, standing outside the Red Lion Motel after a meeting. An insurance executive, her husband left for Gabon to work laying a pipeline. After that he thinks he may go to Texas.

Whatever I want, Ursula thinks, it's not that.

Michael crawls out of bed, goes across the hall to the bathroom, and blows his nose. He would wring it out if he could. Ursula plumps her pillow and puts the fat part under her neck, which had not relaxed through a whole night's sleep, so that she will go into another day with yesterday's tensions still biting the base of her skull. She listens to her husband's careful blowing, and she forgives him this vulgar aggravation. After all, she sometimes leaves pantyhose draped over the closet door for weeks at a time. She wills kindness toward him, her husband, who is never ill except for a cold, and that only once a year or so. He is her companion and helpmate, toward whom she feels enormous affection, and a certain steady admiration for his immunity to consternation. He is a rock. She, who belongs to so many people, who has to reach out every day to others, whether they want her to or not, she is a puddle.

She drifts. Their old cat Pajamas nuzzles her shoulder and settles in Michael's still warm indentation. Ursula strokes the cat's hip, but the cat wants only Michael's smell.

Ursula hears Juliette's alarm, far away and muffled, like the tinkle of a hawker's bell. Juliette, by nature as slow-starting as her mother in the morning, nevertheless rises at an ungodly hour to bathe and braid her hair, and to push herself through the day's first stretches, sighing and moaning as her legs part, as she leans her cheek against her thigh and strains to grasp her instep. This is Juliette's head start. It gives her an earned aplomb in her astonishingly early ballet class, which meets before school. Juliette calls school—a succession of academic classes required of high school freshmen—Slow Death. After school she dances again. She maintains a solid B average, but when it gets harder, as it must, Ursula doesn't know if Juliette will have any more to give it. Juliette simply thinks it unfair that she has to learn anything she doesn't need to dance. It is going to be hard to defend Algebra II-Trig, Biology, Personal Finance, and the like. You don't need those courses to get into a dance school, only to get out of high school.

Carter, named for Ursula's deceased father, who was a serious scholar, is certainly turning out nothing like him; his intellect is hot and quick and contemporary. Morning comes and Carter sleeps on. He goes to bed in his underwear— today's, if he bathed last night, yesterday's, if not—and rises at the last possible moment, after Ursula is already out of the house. He has only to pull on his clothes and spike his hair in the front to be ready. He doesn't really wake up until second period. He sails through math and science though. He has what the world wants. Ursula thinks that is at the heart of Juliette's dislike for him. That, and his mouth-breathing.

When kids ask Juliette if Carter is her brother, she says,

"You have got to be kidding." Ursula cannot remember the last time she heard her children speak to one another civilly.

Michael speaks softly. "Ursie, I've got coffee for you." She smiles in surprise. There was a time when he brought her coffee in bed every Sunday morning. It went on for years and years. She loved the luxury of slowly sipping the coffee, made from beans he would have ground fresh. Then one Sunday quite a long time ago, she came up out of a terrible dream and raged at Michael to leave her the hell alone on her days off. She wanted to sleep until she decided to wake up. He went away. Mortified, she listened to the rattle of the cup in its saucer as he took the coffee back to the kitchen. She wanted to run after him, not only to apologize, but to tell him about the dream, in which Carter—still inside her grossly distended belly, age four or five—was plucking at her flesh and gobbling it, eating her, inside out. All she managed was to pull on her robe and wander down with an embarrassed, amused, intimate acknowledgement of her bad behavior on her face. But Michael was already out of the house. Nothing was ever said. And he stopped bringing her Sunday coffee.

"So what's this?" she says as she sits up. Her flannel gown is unbuttoned, and her splayed breasts shine, pale between faded purple flowers. Without thinking, she clutches the neck of her gown together and buttons the last two buttons. She pats the bedcovers, to urge Michael to sit with her, but he ignores her gesture. He holds the cup straight out and says, "After you drink this, you need to call Katie back."

She glances at the clock. It is a few minutes after six. She did not hear the phone. So she did sleep a little. "What in the world does she want at this hour?"

"I wouldn't get up yet," he answers. "She said call her before you leave for work." And he is gone, probably to check on his oatmeal. Or to feed the cat, which follows him down the stairs. Or both.

Ursula savors the coffee. Michael's little rituals. One of them is fresh beans. She seldom gets to share the benefit of his grinding. Usually she gulps down a fast cup of tea (three dunks of the bag, two spoons of sugar) standing up, while everyone else is still upstairs. Juliette eats nothing before noon, a fact that nettles Ursula, though Juliette is the strong-

est of them all, with her incredible long legs and her 15
percent body fat, as tested in P.E. (P.E.! she shrieked. P.E.,
when she dances fifteen hours a week.) Carter buys donuts at
the stand by the bus stop and relies on his speedy metabolism
to keep him looking good. Only Michael has a proper breakfast, prepared and eaten, like most things he does, with great
absorption. He does nothing quickly. There have been times
when this drives Ursula mad for a moment, but it is a quality
she mostly admires. That self-care. It might even be what she
married Michael for: the sense that time does indeed pass,
with something in each moment, much of it under your
control or, at the very least, your fairly careful observation.

She gets up and sets the coffee cup on her dresser. A
jumble of jewelry, used tissues, little folded notes, and lists
clutter the top. Lately she has been feeling a keen longing for
a more orderly existence, but after twenty years of lax housekeeping (her mother, on a visit, had to tell her what to do
about the toilet bowl), how would she explain this to her
family? Theirs is a live-and-let-live house. The downstairs
gets wiped over once a week, the bathroom when she feels
inspired, and the rest of the house maybe once a year.
Michael keeps the yard. He putters and repairs and keep
things running, and usually has some project going to improve the place. There is no real reason to complain. Besides,
the clutter that is bothering her is her own. The children
keep their doors shut. Michael's mess is in the basement and
garage.

Impulsively, she lies back across the soft down comforter
and pulls it around her, shroudlike, burying her face in it,
dreaming of long-ago leisure days, of young adulthood and
the stasis of contentment and no ambition. She was very
happy for a long time in Portland. Moving there, for college,
felt like coming home. Dropping out of Reed for PSU had
been a matter of finding your own kind. Of course, people
grew up (some died, some got divorces, built seniority),
things did change. She loves life and embraces its surprises.
She thinks she is good at evolving. She has a good attitude
about certain inevitable encroachments: children fleeing,
hips dimpling, Michael's ardor waning (not much, not yet).
Actually she is already looking forward to "losing" Carter;

going up a size had been cause for new clothes; and Michael does not threaten to fade away anytime soon. She feels better, counting her blessings.

She pulls on her ratty purple chenille wrapper and goes down to the kitchen. Michael is eating oatmeal, as he does most mornings.

"You're eating early." The idea of that glutinous mass in his stomach turns hers. Yet there is a moment when she thinks how warm his body must be, through and through. The impulse to touch him is much like the one upstairs that sent her to the cloud of her bed for a moment's pleasure. Twenty-four years together, and it still happens like this now and then. (So why does she have to make a note of it every time?)

He says, without looking at her, "I'm not used to being watched."

She pours herself coffee in a clean cup and sits across from him at the round oak table in the breakfast nook. She rubs her fingers in something sticky on the table.

"I watched tv with Carter a while last night," he says. Their good television is in the basement with their lumpy old couch. "Fish brought a girl home. Young."

"Oh," Ursula says, feeling a knot come together in her chest. This is not the first time Fish and Katie have separated, nor the first time Fish has sought comfort with another woman, but Ursula feels a sorrow gathering in her, for Katie and Fish, for all the Fishers, for lovers estranged, and dreams lost.

Fish sleeping in their basement is a temporary arrangement, though familiar over the years. He was released six weeks early from prison, and his own house is rented until midsummer. Katie has taken tiny quarters downtown by the theatre, and she doesn't want to try to live there with Fish. "It's more like a dormitory than apartments," she said of her building. Fish, in turn, said he was put off by fruity theatre people. Katie came for supper a few times. She and Fish have spent some hours together downstairs. She still has not stayed the night, as far as Ursula knows, though who would want to? Fish sleeps on a foam pad on a plywood bench over storage cabinets they all think of as his.

There is something about Fish in the basement that pleases Ursula, as though Fish were in place under her protection.

All in all it is a thoroughly silly thought, as though no more bad things can happen.

"Is something wrong with Katie?" Ursula asks. "Is it Fish?" The urgency of Katie's call is diluted in that same moment by Ursula's sudden realization that she has not returned Mrs. Angstrom's call yesterday about Carter's English grade. *Urgent* the message said. Maybe Ursula doesn't want to hear about it! What if Carter doesn't graduate? A's in advanced placement Calculus and Chemistry, a semifinalist in the Merit Scholars competition, and he is fucking up in English! (She is sure he would have been a finalist in the tests if he could have been bothered to think about the language portion.)

"I don't keep track, Urs." Michael sets his bowl on the floor by his chair, for the cat to lick. Ursula tries not to show her annoyance. He goes to the sink and fills the oatmeal pan with water to soak. They have had many petty quarrels about the pan, until Michael, a fair man, began the practice of washing it as soon as he comes in the door in the evening, so that Ursula will not have to do so before making dinner. Of course, she often does not make dinner. Did the contract change? It is his oatmeal.

"Early as it is, couldn't you wash the pan?" she says, unable to stop herself. She realizes as soon as the words come out that she sounds nasty, and she knows it is really Carter who inspires her tone. She wonders where she put the note with the teacher's message. Ursula will have to catch her during her prep period. She thinks it funny when Michael refers to his "prep-period," as though teachers were surgeons requiring a harsh scrub. Ah, Carter. Mostly, she overlooks his adolescent eccentricities. She has had a lot of experience with strung-out, enraged teenagers, and she knows there is nothing basically wrong with her son that time will not cure. Failing to graduate, though, is not an option.

Michael comes back to the table and stands behind Ursula, bending over, putting one hand down into her gown. The warmth, so sudden and unexpected on her breast, sends a chill the length of her body. She reaches up to touch his arm. So what if he will not open up to her? There is this, and it isn't really rare. Sometimes it makes her a little indignant that he touches her so easily—she thinks him evasive, trying to distract her when she asks the wrong question, say—but she never throws him off.

She will not repeat the error of the refused coffee elsewhere in this marriage. Besides, to hurt Michael, she would be the loser.

Michael's parents have been married fifty years. A half-century of disappointment, guilt, suppressed anger, and—more recently—fiercely deliberate loyalty. Ursula wonders if Gully ever touched Geneva in this way, so easily. She has seen pictures of them, young, standing by one another, Gully's arm across Geneva's shoulders. Yet closeness between them seems inconceivable. Still, this is the couple who, newly married, drove to Mexico City in a 1932 Ford, and then traveled to Guatemala by train and bus. There must have been passion to spur such a brave endeavor.

"You know, that same thought occurred to me," Michael says, sliding away. She has forgotten what "thought" came before. He speaks in a faintly wry tone, one their friends think charmingly characteristic, never having been forced to weigh the burden of alternative interpretations. He pads in his sloppy sheepskin slippers to the stairs.

The pan. That was the referent. She is embarrassed.

Then Michael says, before he begins his ascent, "It's sure to do with Fish. What other topic is so dependable?"

Ursula feels her nipples grow pert under the flannel of her gown. "Michael?"

He stops, one foot suspended above the next step. She remembers, for no reason except the sight of his foot, a girl who was her client many years ago. The girl was very ill. She would stand in just such a pose for hours, rigid, as though she would never grow tired. In the end she walked out of her parents' home straight into traffic, and was killed. All the while, Ursula had been trying to get her institutionalized, and had failed. They weren't doing that anymore, she was told.

"Oh Michael," she says, back in the moment.

"Yo." He makes her laugh, but it isn't what she was looking for just then.

Michael's parents sleep in separate beds at opposite ends of their mobile home. Her own parents divorced when she was fifteen, Juliette's age. Do separations start like this, with snoring, or some other dreadful little tic? Or do people blow apart after an ignominious spectacle? Will the furniture one day shift in her house? Are they happy?

She knows that Michael will never leave her. The thought would never be a serious one for him, whatever turn their marriage takes. It is up to her to keep the marriage alive, because even if it were dead, Michael would not be bothered to bury it.

"I wish we had a little more time," she says.

—13—

She drinks her coffee slowly. She doesn't want to talk to her sister-in-law this morning. Life was calm with Fish in jail. The only personal crises, and small ones they were, have been with her children, who have a reasonable claim to her sympathy and occasional intervention. But it did not seem possible that Fish would survive a year in prison. They might have been locking him up in a trunk, for the panic she felt at his sentencing. He refused his brother's offer of bail. "You know I'm going to get it in the ass this time," he said. "I might as well get started on jail time."

At the moment of arrest—so stupid!—he looked amazed. Later he looked beaten and listless. He wouldn't see Katie until after the trial, and then he told her he didn't want her to visit him. He wouldn't write letters. Katie moved in with Michael and Ursula for a while. She couldn't stand the house out of town, with all its half-finished projects, its overgrown yard, its gloominess in winter. She couldn't sleep. She cried a lot. Ursula realized Katie had nothing to do with Fish gone. She told her to go find a job, something besides waiting tables. She knew idleness only worked for Katie when it was with Fish. Together they had amassed years of doing nothing.

"Damn him for being fucking crazy," Katie wept. "Damn him looking so goddamned *guilty*. He scuttled off like a—a sick *crab*."

Ursula was on the phone day and night, trying to find out

what was happening, what Fish was doing, where they had taken him, when Michael could see him. Michael said, "Really, ladies, where do you think he's going to get away to?" In fact, it wasn't long before the authorities moved him to a forest camp to plant trees. Prison was prison, even outdoors, but at least he wasn't in a little cell.

He wrote them once, a card. He said there was an Indian kid in the camp who went off where he wasn't supposed to go and got in trouble. Ursula wrote back to ask if that meant the Indian went back to Salem, but Fish didn't answer.

Freed, Fish appeared exactly as Ursula knew he would, out of the blue without warning, looking sheepish and sober, as if he had been caught with his trousers down. He didn't have Katie's street address—his one card had come to Michael's— and it was very late. Michael ushered him downstairs, carrying blankets and sheets and a pillow. Fish had slept down there enough times before. Michael had rented out Fish's house for the year, and moved his stuff for safekeeping to the basement, except for his guns, which were out at his dad's.

When Ursula saw Fish, she blurted, "But you're home early!" She thought he looked rather good, his eyes less bruised. All those months without booze, drugs, sex—had they been good for him? She wanted to wrap him in her arms and press against him, to bring some life back into his expression, but of course that was for Katie to do. Ursula said she would call her.

"Aw, don't bother her," Fish said of his wife. Michael went out and bought a half-gallon of tokay, and sat up and watched Fish get drunk and pass out content. Michael got mildly drunk himself. He came upstairs red-eyed, with a forlorn air. "Is he really okay?" Ursula asked sleepily. "Are you?" In the morning Katie asked the same thing, when Michael called her. Michael, tense and quiet, was, as usual, unable to say anything when it mattered.

Fish told them more stories about the Indian kid, who could whistle like thirty birds, and call deer and elk. He said there was an old prospector-type, too, who could speak four languages, including Athabascan. He told about the deer someone shot out of season, that ran up right into the compound and lay down on a bunkhouse porch and died. When

Fish is in a good mood he talks very fast, rat-a-tat, like somebody on speed. It sounded like he was ready to quit talking prison stories—he was winding down—when he said bitterly, "I really asked for it, didn't I?" He recovered quickly. "It could have been worse."

He looked at Katie, as if Michael and Ursula weren't there. "It wasn't like that inside, baby," he said, "not for me." He took a long swig of his bottle. "I'm too old. Not pretty anymore."

"What did that mean!" Ursula asked Michael as soon as they were alone.

"If you want to know, ask Fish, or Katie," Michael said. "I'd ask Fish, since he said it. Didn't he used to talk to you?"

Ursula blushed scarlet, surprising herself. She wasn't at all sure what Michael meant. She and Michael had never talked about her with Fish, anymore than if it was someone they never saw again. She never had said how lucky she felt, that Fish went off to Reno and threw his money away and enlisted, and she moved all her stuff downstairs to Michael's three weeks after. It was all blind luck, to have quick, silly choices yield good decisions. She had considered moving in with a graduate student named Delmore, but he was on a macrobiotic diet and she didn't think she could conform.

Days later Ursula realized Fish had to have meant sex. Everyone knew about rape in jail, she just hadn't let herself think of it. It made her sick to think of it, but Fish said it didn't happen to him.

Katie brought up the subject of divorce again, six months into Fish's term. "I guess I couldn't do it while he's there," she said. She was thinner, she didn't come over often. She said she was working long hours. Ursula wanted to ask her about her feelings, about the years with Fish, but she sensed there were things she wouldn't want to know. And she sensed a cooler Katie, as though the opportunities for intimacy might have passed. Had Ursula been looking the other way? Had she failed Katie as friend and family, to quiet her fears about her husband's brother?

There was no question Fish was easier to deal with absent, but to divorce him while he was helpless? It couldn't be right. Why now? Ursula thought. It wasn't like he had hurt anyone.

He had already been dealt a lot more punishment than he deserved. He had taken a little ride in somebody's double-parked Porsche. They were all going into the Chinese restaurant to pick up Hum Bows on a Saturday night, and there was that damned car. Once around the block. The problem was, it wasn't Fish's first such lark. The law made a big deal of it, like Fish was a threat to the fabric of society. Maybe the judge sensed incipient anarchy. The cops were their most arrogant with little people.

For years and years it has been Ursula's job to make recommendations about the disposition of human lives. Remove this child from this bad mother's custody. Place this one in a foster home. Choose these adoptive parents over these. Prosecute this abuser, and not this one. She tries to think the best of people (or not to have expectations), tries to forget them as soon as she files a case. Some stay with you, but most do not. A judge should certainly have had simliar experience, but the one who sentenced Fish said, "We could grant some levity to the young person who lacks judgment, but a man in his forties constitutes a threat to his community when he ignores its basic rules of property and decency." Property was the key word. They give suspended sentences for DUI manslaughter, for sodomy with children, but property! Ursula can still remember the helpless rage that poured through her. It was a scalding, inside. The judge hated Fish for having lived this long without buying in. He gave Katie a loathing look too; maybe he wished he could send her away with him. It was all no more and no less than Fish expected. He said that in Nam he had expected neither to live nor to die, and hadn't he been right about that?

Katie didn't ask Ursula's opinions at times she might have. She did not for example ask when she took her baby to Texas and gave her away. Ursula knows what she would have said. Give her to us. We're family. She has waked up many nights, grieving for that baby, as if it were dead, but she has never told Katie. She hasn't even told Michael. Well, Ursula has long ago forgiven Katie (knowing it isn't even her right to do so); Katie has no business with a child, and had the sense to know it. If only more young mothers made the same decision, early. Fewer infants would get underfed, left alone at night, fried in skillets, not that Katie would ever have done any of those things. There is still a tiny wedge between Katie and Ursula. Katie looking for approval. Ursula declining. Katie said this was the first time since she met Fish that he was gone and she wasn't looking at the door ten times a day to see if he would come back to her. It had cleared her head. There was peace in the certainty. But it was temporary. She had to decide.

And Katie has a new boyfriend, at her age.

Ursula doesn't think Fish knows. He has things to learn. He thinks the world in general is peopled by creeps, but he expects the best from his family. His wife. He has been living downstairs a couple of weeks, working most of that time. As soon as Ursula mentioned that he was home, her supervisor, Angela, said she was going to ask him to work on her house, a wonderful old Victorian above the boulevard. The idea made Ursula nervous. She did not want to end up with her supervisor angry at her brother-in-law. She warned Angela that although Fish's work was an artisan's, he was undependable. She recalled aloud the time he built them a fence but not the gate, and then didn't finish it for three years. (Michael wouldn't do it, either, it wasn't his project.) Angela, hearing all about the fence, didn't flinch. "Do you know what it's like, finding somebody you know will love your house because it is beautiful?" She gently chided Ursula. "I won't blame you, I promise. It's my decision. My gamble, if you will. I won't say a word to you." It went well enough. Fish has started a new project now, unrelated to Ursula. She can relax.

Fish says Katie needs time to wind up whatever she was into while he was gone. He didn't expect her to sit around the whole while. Ursula thinks it all bravado, and she aches for him. Fish is in jeopardy. There is no good resolution in the offing. The elder Fisher marriage is no model, and the Ursula-Michael union Katie dismisses as good luck. She has no idea how strong some Fisher traits really are, how they worm their way into the soundest beam. Besides, Ursula knows Katie has never envied her Michael. If Fish is the darker brother, Katie has no taste for the light. Through all the years, Katie has grown taut, a little brittle; there are pocks in her existence about which she volunteers no feelings (a true Fisher, if only by marriage), and she invites no questions. She has always seemed, at even the worst moments, the right match for Fish. And no one can deny the depth of her loyalty. Didn't it cost her a child?

—14—

"Katie, it's me," Ursula says. "I was surprised to hear from you so early."

"Sorry. I know morning isn't your best time. But Ursula, I've got myself in a mess—"

"What's wrong?"

"Fish. But you knew that."

"Fish," Ursula repeats. She would like to ask Katie if other things ever fail her. If everything does.

"I'm going through with it. For the first time in my adult life I feel like I'm getting it together. I don't think I can do it with Fish. I can't drag the weight any longer."

"I haven't got much time, Katie. Could you call me tonight?" Ursula knows it is terrible to pull away, knows she ought to respond to the message in Katie's plaint, but she doesn't want to hear it. And she is pressed for time.

"No, listen. It's important. My lawyer has been pushing me. She says if I don't let them serve Fish the papers, she is washing her hands of me and I can kiss the four hundred I've paid her goodbye. She says it has to happen. Shit, Ursula. she thinks she's my fucking shrink. My mommy."

"I didn't realize it was that far along."

"Oh Ursula, I told you. You know I did."

"Okay."

"Only not today! I told them today was okay, I just wanted to get it over with, and I told them he's over there, and to get there early, before he goes off, but I forgot about Saturday."

"Oh God." The anniversary party in the River Cove Grange. Fish will be a terrific guest. His parents celebrate fifty years of contract, and he greets the end of his own. What was it, Ursula wonders fleetingly, that he and Katie agreed to do?

"He'll go crazy. It could wreck things. What was I thinking? I've got these little papers all over the place. Reminders. Get the starter looked at. Get the strap fixed on my sandal. Take

Geneva to shop for napkins. Napkins. Ursula, could you get them? I don't want to drive. My car is acting up. And it's like only half my brain is in gear. Sometimes I wish Fish had—"

"What do I say? Katie? When they come?"

"Tell them to come back Monday. Say he's gone for the rest of the week. Monday is soon enough! Ursula. I still love him. That's not what this is about."

"I'll get the napkins. I don't see why Geneva has to go at all. What about you? Are you going to be okay?"

Katie groaned. "I don't know. I won't know till it's over."

Ursula goes upstairs to dress. A strange sound is coming from the bathroom. Not quite a groan. Something more petulant.

"Juliette, is that you?" Ursula taps at the door. When there is no answer, Ursula opens the door and sticks her head in. Juliette is standing in front of the mirror with her arms crossed over her breasts, her hands drooping off her shoulders. Seeing her mother in the mirror, she whirls and glares.

"I hate them!"

"What, baby? What is it?"

Juliette throws her arms out dramatically, baring the expanse of her white throat and the pink leotard she is wearing. She is a lovely girl. "They're getting BIGGER!" she says, horror in her voice.

It takes a moment for Ursula to realize that Juliette is speaking of her breasts. She has never progressed much beyond a pubescent pair of bumps, but now Ursula can see that she is right, they are filling, rounding, though you would hardly call them a bosom. Not on a girl who weighs a hundred pounds.

"Oh honey, they're nothing!" Ursula says, almost laughing. She remembers her girlhood chums weeping into their fists because they had little breasts instead of Ursula's full ones.

"If I turn out to have breasts like yours, I am going to have them cut off!" Juliette pushes past Ursula and out of the room.

Ursula washes her face and combs her tangled hair. She has no part. Her hair springs out in all directions. After an inch of growth, it begins to tighten at the ends, then to dry and break off. It is time for a cut. Juliette has inherited enough of Ursula's curly genes to have a mass of waves, and curls and wisps where she keeps pieces trimmed. Her color is better than Ursula's flat brown, with the russet tones of the Fishers.

In her room, Ursula puts on one of her nice-lady outfits, a jersey shirtwaist suitable for court or meetings. Michael is dressing with fastidious tedium, tugging and tucking to get his shirt set just so. He has his pants partway down his hips, the fly open, his hips thrust to one side to hold them up. She resists the urge to swat him. She eyes a pile of laundry in the corner, much of which will have to be ironed—a task she usually tackles during Sunday night's *Masterpiece Theatre* show. She sometimes wishes that Michael would wear polyester like other teachers, but it was she who taught him to love cotton. He could wear jeans these days, teaching, but he likes a certain quality twill.

She admires his flat ass. A Fisher trait. Carter has inherited her roundness and short waist. Though he is a good-looking boy, he won't wear so well as his dad.

"Shove that all down the laundry chute," she says. "I'll go down and put a load in to wash."

The door to the basement snaps behind her with a loud crack, like a gunshot. She insisted Michael install a spring-door because nobody ever closes the damned door, but sometimes it surprises her, it works so well.

In the basement she picks clothes up from the area below the chute, and hurriedly sorts them into piles of dark and light. She stuffs the light clothes into the washer, adds detergent, and hesitates for a moment. If Fish is asleep, he won't be when she starts this machine. She punches ON. There doesn't seem to be any sign of life, no sounds from behind the curtain that separates Fish's sleeping area from the rest of the basement.

Someone flushes the toilet in the corner and turns on the shower. Well, tough on that score, too, because the washer will pull off the water pressure, but she doesn't feel bad enough about it to turn the machine off. Besides, Fish knows about the water. And he has more time than she does.

She notices that the door to the outside is slightly ajar. Damn him! she thinks. She has a thing about doors, granted, but is it really too much to ask Fish to close the door when he comes in at night? They have been robbed; it is not just a theoretical threat. Once in Portland someone came in while they were gone during the day, and took their stereo, the only thing they owned of value, and a box of mushrooms. Then, here, the first year Carter was in high school, someone came in the unlocked front door early in the morning, and drove her Toyota away, while they were all upstairs, dressing.

She goes up the two steps to the door and slams it shut and locks it.

She is wiping off the breakfast table when she hears Juliette shriek. By the time she gets to her daughter's room, Michael is already there. Juliette's windows overlook the street on one side, and a row of wisteria on the other.

"He was peeing on our bushes!" Juliette says furiously. "Without a stitch on!"

Michael looks over his shoulder at Ursula. "Who else?" he says calmly.

"I thought he was in the shower." Ursula remembers she locked the basement door.

A car comes to a screeching stop at the curb. Michael sticks his head out Juliette's window and yells, "Better get your butt indoors, Fish!"

"Oh no!" Ursula yells. Suddenly she realizes that it was Fish's girlfriend in the shower, so Fish went outside rather than come upstairs to the bathroom. Before she locked the door.

Ursula races down the stairs to intercept the process server at the door, but as he reaches the steps, so does Fish, stark naked. Ursula throws open the door and cries, "You've got the wrong address!"

The process server, who knows a loser when he sees one, thrusts the summons into Fish's hand. "Looks like she's already got everything you had," he says, slapping his thigh and laughing.

Fish, bewildered, stands on the porch with his behind exposed for all the world to see. "Come ON," Ursula tells him. He darts past her, dropping the summons on the floor as he flees. Ursula picks it up slowly, as though it weighs a lot.

I'll tell Katie they delivered it while I was on the phone, she thinks. I won't say what happened.

But she will. Telling stories is one way to talk without too much intrusion. It's a way of creating and remembering their lives even as they live them. Sometimes, though, it is white noise.

She turns and finds Michael behind her. He puts his arms around her and pulls her close. "Poor guy," he murmurs. "Lucky us."

Ursula's heart flutters. Ahh, she thinks, like a heroine in a bodice-ripper. She can hear time ticking by; they are standing by an antique grandfather clock that runs but doesn't chime. "I've got to go," she whispers reluctantly. She runs and grabs her sweater off the back of a chair at the dining table, her purse from the kitchen counter. She yells goodbye to Michael from the front door. "See you tonight!" she calls.

In the car she begins to sing, only "La la la," tunelessly. Even Carter would not be able to ruin a lyrical line from Michael.

She drives off down the street, glad to get the day begun. Her work is filled with pathos, and sometimes tragedy, peopled with victims and villains, pitiful actors all, and still she goes at it, day after day, with enthusiasm. It is important not to stand too close. You can't help if you are a burn-out. People are mostly predictable, and you second-guess them. Sometimes you are shocked, and you collect those times into a repertoire. You bear occasional anguish as a wave so far from sea. You work quickly, without haste. You make good decisions and document them well. You do a lot, really.

You understand how precious your own ordinary, happy, pocked life is. Every day, you have some reason to be, some moment when you are, grateful.

—15—

The yellow sticky-backed note on the wall by Katie's phone says, "Geneva/napkins/W." Katie hangs up and peels off the note, crumples it and drops it in the brown paper bag by the refrigerator. Cautiously, she leans across the airspace above the bag and sniffs lightly. She accumulates so little garbage, she sometimes forgets to put it outside, and tuna cans, discarded bologna, stale bread, and crumpled take-out boxes have a way of festering and then erupting into full-blown stench. This bag is less than half-full, and holds only paper,

yogurt containers, and coffee grounds. She has not eaten at
home in days. She snacks on the leftovers brought home by
her neighbor Maureen, who is a cook in a vegetarian deli.
She nibbles crackers and dry cereal without milk. She goes
out with her lover, Jeff, and eats what he has chosen, agreeing always that it is delicious. She learned to eat anything,
without complaint, from living with Fish; Fish used odd food
to test her spunkiness. She has eaten sardines, sushi, several
kinds of game, black mushrooms, Chinese soup with chicken
feet, roots, berries and wild greens gathered while camping.
Whenever she has spent time alone, she hasn't known what
she wanted. Sometimes when Fish was gone, she ate nothing
except a meal once a day where she worked.

Her lover is an agricultural geneticist. He has developed an
orange baby cauliflower. A crop is growing right now, hydro-
ponically, at the agricultural experimental station. A few
years ago he helped develop a delicate, blush-red pear.
These pears are grown here, in this valley, but they must be
further modified, for a hardier fruit, to withstand shipping.
Since she learned about this exotic pear, Katie has looked
forward with increasing longing to the late summer harvest,
thinking of it at odd, inappropriate moments, such as during
lovemaking, or as she attaches braided trim to an officer's
jacket for the Chekhov production. She prefers thoughts of
the pear to thoughts of her lover. Meanwhile, Jeff's attention
has turned to grapes. He praises the conditions in the region,
saying they are just right for producing varietals as good as in
the Napa and Sonoma areas. Small wineries have sprung up
all over. A Frenchman has even gone into partnership with a
retired movie special-effects man to make a local brandy. Jeff
says vintners are interesting people. He doesn't comment on
wine drinkers.

It occurs to Katie that Jeff may see her as yet another
hybrid, perhaps a wild fruit brought into the station for
domestication. He professes delight in her somewhat out-of-
date personal style (the long, straight hair, usually in braids
or a ponytail; her "clear-washed"—his phrase—makeupless
face, her disdain for hose, bra, slip, jewelry). At the same
time, he brings her gifts obviously chosen to improve the
appearance he claims charm him. He gives her lacquered
hairclips and a straight linen skirt, a pale gray charmeuse

slip, a fine gold chain, and perfume. He asks her about prospects for training in costuming, as if he cannot perceive her contentment as a seamstress-lackey who presses seams, sews velcro in garments for quick strips, stitches decorative trims, and the like. She does not try to tell him how like a resigned stepchild she is, working among women who have college degrees in theatre, or certificates of design and garment construction, portfolios of fiber art. Even the few other local women who were hired purely as seamstresses have vastly more experience than she, and keen ambition. They buy their own copies of books like *Flat Patternmaking*, and *An Encyclopedia of World Costumes*, books that make Katie's eyes tear from the strain of reading them. She lets Jeff make what he wants of her modest position. She doesn't blame him; everyone assumes something extraordinary about people who work in the theatre, even if their jobs involve mailing brochures and selling tickets.

Though Katie only mildly wonders about Jeff's affection for her (whatever he says, she believes it is sexual), she is increasingly bewildered by her growing attachment to him, not so much emotionally as practically. He has begun to direct more and more aspects of her life. He takes for granted their coupleship, when she is still married to another man. She knows she has let this happen, that his behavior has intensified since Fish returned and she continued to maintain her own place to live. When she did not find a way to resume residence with her husband, she let Jeff assume a kind of authority over her, without ever deciding to do so, and lately it has begun to vex her. She especially minds the way he has begun to ask her questions about her life: whether Fish ever hit her, if she ever wanted children (he doesn't know about Rhea). He asks her questions like, "What worries you most in life?" She replies, "Earthquakes and spiders," trying not to smirk. In turn, he tells her about himself. He tells her how he used to be terrified of water, how hard it was to learn to swim, which he now does well. Late one night, he tells her about the time in graduate school when he stole the idea of a paper from an old master's thesis. He is quick to say it wasn't really plagiarism—in the end he wrote every word—but he feels guilty that he leaned so far that way. He says he thinks the experience has been for the best, that it has made him a more moral man. He talks about essays he reads in *Esquire* on friendship among men, sportsmanship, medical ethics. He seems to want her to prize his candor, but she is often bored and distracted, and cannot appreciate it when he says he talks to her more intimately than he has to other women.

She wonders how he can be so wrong about her, what need in him has invented her. She claims intimacy, in all the world, only with Fish, and it has come not so much from mutual disclosure as from years of accumulated, shared experience. From their shared dreams, now faded. From their shared debts, as to her mother, and losses, as Rhea. From the ways they have tried not to be the persons their parents shaped, using one another to fight history and habit and proclivity.

She has her own life to think about, and cannot envision revealing it to Jeff. She is weary with trying to analyze her own behavior, though she has yet to find any clear direction in the effort. She often feels a clutch in her thinking, like a case of mental cramps.

She cannot really remember making the decision to divorce Fish. The impulse was hers (and not Jeff's). It is not the first time she has considered it. She remembers Ursula suggesting it—tentatively, to be sure—years before. What Ursula said was, "You can decide how you want to live. You don't have to keep on like this." What crisis was she in then, to garner such advice from Ursula? She cannot recall, it does not matter, except that no one seems to understand why Katie has stayed with Fish anyway. Her mother is in a state of perpetual surprise that the marriage has "lasted."

This time, though, the idea came to her one particular evening last December, when it was rainy and cold, and she was sopping with self-pity and resentment that Fish was in jail and not with her. She tried the idea out on Ursula later—not long after she met Jeff, true—and something in saying it out loud gave it authenticity. "I could divorce him," she remembers thinking. "I've already got a boyfriend," a fact that, though it may have greased the wheels on which her notion rode, hardly gave it substantial argument. Then she grew piqued that Fish would not write her and would not let her come see him. "I'll show him." She may have thought that.

Besides, getting a divorce from a difficult man will please

the critics (only her mother comes instantly to mind), will appear as a "step in the right direction," when all along she has been bobbing in her life like a plastic duck in a tub of water.

Only this morning, as she moves around, dressing and making her bed, drinking coffee and picking at her nails, she is overwhelmed by the fierceness of her relief—almost elation—that she has intervened in time to stop the papers being served on Fish. It is as if some third party has set the divorce in motion, and she has put out her arm to stop the speeding train.

Relieved as she is, perhaps because she knows she will be seeing Fish on Saturday, she feels very much on his side.

—16—

It is after six when Ursula gets home.

She is surprised to find Michael in the kitchen, staring off in the direction of the back yard. The radio is on too low to hear. He is missing his beloved *All Things Considered.*

"Hi," she says. She sees that he has washed up from breakfast. She also sees that Carter has been through. An open peanut butter jar sits surrounded by crumbs, with a dirty knife alongside. She wants to sound chatty. Michael doesn't like to be probed. But she wonders what he is thinking, even if she does have a master's in counseling and knows people have a right to inner privacy. Space. Whatever you call it. Michael's seems so vast and pristine, and thus so alluring.

"Caught you idle," she manages to say.

"The back yard is shabby," he replies. "I was wondering if I ought to build some sort of patio out under the sycamore. Or a gazebo." He will be looking for a summer project, of course. "Or do you think the sycamore sheds too much, that I'd be brushing away seed balls half the year?"

"You already do." Ursula is pleased with this train of thought. Sometimes she is appalled by the shabbiness of their house. They can afford to fix it up. She ought to have someone in to clean it properly now and then. They have stuffed it and piddled at minor remodeling efforts, but it is a house in need of attention. Or a move. Could Michael be talked into a new house? She imagines expanses of bare white wall, water running through smooth new pipes. A shower.

"The porch is okay," Michael muses. Fish built it for them a couple of years ago. It is a wide, bare-wood affair with latticework along two sides, and a partial roof, and bentwood benches built in the shade. Ursula was thrilled with that project, too. She envisioned herself holding soirees in the late summer evenings. And not just social workers (Michael hates their talk), but people from the college and the theatre. Some of these transplanted hip California types, with their sound studios and art galleries. Of course she doesn't know those people, and she never seems to have any time. They don't even invite Michael's fellow teachers over. And last summer the family didn't eat outside five times. It was silly of them. All they need is a few of those cheap lawn chairs, already stacked up for sale like hats at K-Mart.

"It's going to be summer soon," she says softly. She always has hopes this time of year. She always thinks life will slow down. In some ways it does, because Michael is off from school, but the children spend their time with their own lives now, and her work goes on as always, whatever the season. Then many days are so hot you can't move until eight o'clock at night.

In a new house she'd have air-conditioning.

"We need a couple of trees with some color. Crab apple? Red maples? Something Japanese and expensive, like down at the park? We need more shade. And some perennials. It would be easy to spend a lot of money on the yard." Michael shakes his head and looks at Ursula. He isn't really inviting her comment; he has said what he thinks. "Juliette called. She's staying at Marina's to work on French."

She will call Marina's in a while. She likes to know where Juliette is. She has to call Katie, too.

"We can afford some new trees, Michael," she says.

Michael doesn't say anything.

Ursula pulls up a stool and sits down beside him. "Is something wrong?"

He is scuffing at the floor with his toe. He pulled up the old vinyl two months ago. They walk around on the plywood subfloor, waiting for him to put down the gray rubber he thinks will look and wear so well. "It'll cushion us while we

work," he said, as if they were gourmet cooks. The rubber is
in a roll in the basement. All of Michael's projects have this
kind of dead space somewhere in the doing. It is a Fisher
hallmark. Gully once housed his family in a garage for a
year, before he got around to attaching a house to it.

Michael sighs noisily. "Today at school Wilson told me that
next year I can't build crystal radios with my kids. Can't set
up electric trains, or put out birdhouses. No greenhouse. No
park maps. Just math, reading, spelling. The straight stuff.
He never got it. I thought we were past that shit."

He teaches junior high kids who can't get along in regular
classes. He gets along with the kids fine. Kids who couldn't
pass general math do all the measuring and cutting for the
birdhouses. And those birdhouses—scattered in the woods
for bluebirds as nesting sites—have brought good publicity to
the district.

Ursula sits up straighter. She is good at solving problems.
As her supervisor says, she has a practical mind. Chances are
somebody has been rubbed wrong because Michael's kids
have a better time of it in the school. (He often says they run
the place like a boot camp.) She can type up a memo for
Michael, if they work it out tonight. A memo to the principal.
Later, if need be, he can write the board. He can enclose
copies of the newspaper articles about his bluebird project,
which has gone on for several years now. There is a terrific
photograph of a seventh-grader with an officer from the
local Audubon Society.

"A memo," is all she gets out. He saw the gears turning. He
holds his hand up. "There are only three more weeks left of
the year! Nobody is going to settle anything in three weeks.
All they can do in that amount of time is dictate." He turns his
palms up. "See, I've let it go."

*Letting go* is not Michael's expression, it is hers. So is he
laughing at her? At least he seems to have relaxed. Maybe he
meant what he said.

"I see." She will bring it up later, if he lets her. Actually, she
is exhausted now. She runs her tongue along the ridge of
aggravated flesh inside her cheek, where she bit herself biting into a turkey sandwich at lunch. She wasn't able to finish
it. So she is hungry, too.

"Mom called. She thinks Pop is 'acting up.' "

Gully eats too much sugar, cuts too much wood, cultivates strange friends. He stays away too many afternoons. All that has to be balanced against the fact that he doesn't drink anymore, not a drop. Sometimes Ursula wonders if that isn't the problem for Geneva. Good Gully doesn't need so much taking care of.

She doesn't want to talk about Gully. He is seventy-three years old. "Never mind Gully, Michael. What about your son?"

"Carter?"

"The very one!"

Michael hops up and starts clearing things off the counter. He wipes up Carter's crumbs. He wipes the mouth of the peanut butter jar and puts the lid back on.

"Will you stop that?" she snaps. Michael always finds a way not to look at her when she wants to discuss Carter. *She,* not *they.* Michael knows Carter is just short of unbearable, but he can not bear to talk strategy. He likes for things to wind down in their own fashion. He is a great believer in the efficacy of waiting things out. Especially kids. However, social workers grow used to situations without that luxury.

"Put him in irons or let him be," he says.

"Carter or Gully?"

Michael scratches his head and grins at her. "Your pleasure, Ursie."

"My *pleasure* is to tell you that Carter's English term paper—the SENIOR PAPER—is totally unacceptable to Mrs. Angstrom, and he has the weekend—four days—to come up with something else. She told me that at first she thought he was kidding her. Seems he likes to joke at school. He told her he had been working on this paper for weeks. Daily, he said." Carter shows up at home for a short while after school, to change and gel his hair. Sometimes he eats. Then he is gone for hours and hours. "She wants to know, do we supervise his studies? What century is this woman from? What does she know about eighteen-year-old boys?"

"What did you tell her?"

"I told her he did his work late at night, and that most of it is over my head. She looked very superior. 'Oh, I see.' That sort of look. Michael, this woman could keep him from graduating!"

"And then he'll die," Michael says, as solemnly as though it were true.

"Goddammit, Michael, be serious. He'll have to go to summer school to graduate. This will of course fuck up his job at the produce market—"

"—the job you got him working for your friend Sharon—"

"—the job we are lucky he has, because we have to pay his expenses, with our two HUGE incomes." Suddenly she is lost. What was she saying, and how did she get so excited?

Carter's graduation. "What would this do to his acceptance into the university's honors program? How did he GET into the honors program? Did those people TALK to anybody about Carter?"

"Has Mrs. Angstrom told Carter all this?"

"She says so. Of course."

"Then why don't we let Carter figure it out? He has a word processor. He can write a paper in a weekend."

"Exactly the point. He turned in a bunch of dot matrix crap. Did you know what his paper was about?"

"No. Did you?"

"I do now. He says that aliens—we are talking outer space here—aliens came to earth and built the pyramids. He cited the evidence: positioning, relationship to the sun and to one another. Those damned doodles in Peru. I don't know what else. I only skimmed it. But you can read it."

"If it doesn't meet Bertie Angstrom's standards, why would I want to read it?"

"To find out if your son is trying to put his English teacher on, or if he is daffy."

"Carter is interested in that sort of stuff, honey. He reads books about unexplained phenomena. He opens his window at night and says, take me."

Michael reaches out and pats her hand. She jerks it away and picks up her purse from the floor. She takes out the folded term paper and thrusts it into Michael's hand. "I had to talk to her. At least you should read it."

Michael takes the paper and gently lays it down by the breadbox. "Okay."

"Oh Michael," she whines. "This woman." She hesitates. It is difficult to criticize educators, when you are married to one. It is like criticizing a Fisher.

Mrs. Angstrom looked at Ursula with her little ferret eyes and said, "I find that children of professors, social workers, and other teachers are often the worst cases. Parents either expect too much of them, or don't expect anything at all." It was clear where she thought the Fishers stood. Shocked, Ursula awaited further explanation, but the teacher simply rose and handed her a piece of purple-printed paper—the classic "ditto"—and Carter's paper. "Here are the criteria," she said. "I want his paper by Monday, or his F stands. And in this building, you don't pass Senior English if you don't pass Senior Paper." *Ergo,* graduation.

Ursula clutched the papers wildly. She didn't want this woman to leave her with all this to do. "What topic should he write about?" she nearly shouted. The teacher smiled and said (sly ferret! Ursula thought), "Something that interests you, Mrs. Fisher, wouldn't you say that would be best?"

As Mrs. Angstrom strutted away, Ursula took mean comfort from the size of her bottom and the shiny state of her pants. The teacher was younger than Ursula, but she was a lot farther gone.

Ursula can't tell all this to Michael. She will end up talking about it in the coffee room at work someday soon. The other caseworkers will sympathize. They will have their own teacher tales to tell. But Michael. He is a wonderful, gentle teacher, and she doesn't want him to think she doubts him. She doesn't want to upset him. Not that he would be upset. He would probably be perfectly sanguine—on the outside. But on the inside, she is sure, Carter is eating away at his patience, and Michael is involved with his own problems at work, his obligations to Gully and Geneva, his unfulfilled dreams. She is worried that his failure to vent anger, frustration, or sorrow means that his vital organs are undergoing constant erosion. She is afraid that he will one day die, and when they open him up, looking for the cause of death, they will find that, inside, he is completely gone.

"I should have talked to Bertie," Michael volunteers. He has had more than his turn at school conferences, dentist appointments, nights of flu misery. Now he leaves concerns to Ursula, or chides her to let the kids work things out for themselves, as though they have become autonomous adults, so early. He expects more of them than of his parents. "Bertie is as stiff as a starched wimple, because kids scare her to death. How would you like to look out and see boys with their hair bleached pink and mowed down the sides? Girls with dirty long-john bottoms sticking out from their tiny little polka-dotted skirts? Bertie can't see anything else. She's afraid of chaos, and face it, chaos rules high school. And then, there's the luck of the draw. Who you get."

"And if you get Carter—"

"You've got yourself a smart-ass," Michael admits. Something he has never been, and so admires? He moves to the refrigerator. "What's for supper?"

Ursula does not consider the discussion over, but she says, tentatively, "Spaghetti?" Once she was a constant user of her Julia Child and James Beard. On her shelf are cookbooks named for fashionable restaurants.

Spaghetti she can make by heart.

"Mmmgh," Michael says, so that she doesn't know what he means. "Why not? There's more sauce." He smiles at her over his shoulder. "But you knew that. I'll make a salad, how's that?"

Ursula feels better. She appreciates a joint effort.

"You go on and call Juliette," Michael says. He is standing on the far side of the refrigerator door.

He says, "You talk to Carter."

## —17—

Ursula stomps up the stairs and into Carter's room. The smell of dirty socks and rotting fruit assaults her. She spies an apple core under the bed. Although Ursula occasionally puts a clean fitted sheet on Carter's bottom bunk mattress, in no time at all it comes loose and ends up elsewhere, a dirty brown ball. He sleeps wound up in an old polyester comforter, pillowless. For years Ursula has insisted that he clean his room once a week by gathering up his dirty clothes, making the bed, closing his drawers, and vacuuming. It has never ceased to be a struggle worse than its worth. She knows all the maxims: Be persistent and consistent. Remain calm. She has made such speeches herself, to parents with fewer resources than her own, with children in genuine trouble.

Maybe Tough Love works on those isolated ranches where the delinquents have to get up every morning and shovel horse manure out of stalls before they get to eat their own breakfasts, but in this real life of theirs, Carter can outlast Ursula any week of the year. Like his father, he has learned the power of silence. Sometimes he loses his temper—which his father does not—but in general he is mild enough, if sometimes deliberately gross. *He* doesn't give a damn about his room. *She* does. Who owns this problem? her counselor-ghost demands. Now she washes his clothes if they are in the laundry. She insists that he keep his door shut, which he is happy to do. (One of his favorite teases is to stand at his door when he sees his mother upstairs, and open it a crack, then smell or cover his eyes, pretend to faint, and so on. Ursula usually tries to laugh, to make it stop.)

During the annual Big Clean, she and Michael scrub Carter's room ceiling to floor, clean out the closet, throw away mounds of garbage, and argue for two straight days about his character. Then Carter moves back in and starts over.

She wonders if he smokes marijuana. She isn't sure anymore just how it smells. She thinks he might, with Fish, in the basement. She would kill them both if she found out. The most trouble Carter has ever been in—and it was serious—was New Year's Eve, 1986. He got drunk with a lot of other kids at one of the kids' houses (while his parents were at another party), and somebody got pushed through a plate glass window. Everybody ended up in court. It was an embarrassing and instructive experience for Ursula. She had assumed the host parents would be home. They had assumed their child was at another party.

Carter is emotionally immature, maybe morally retarded. In recent years, since he has begun to return the longstanding interest of girls (who have been calling him since fifth grade), she has watched him from a distance, fearful that he will treat girls cavalierly. She can imagine the hysterical scene: parents again, this time with a pregnant daughter. She has been watching the girls, who come like patients at a clinic, for short visits to his room (how could they tolerate any more time in there?). It seems there have been dozens of them in the past year, though that surely exaggerates his attractiveness. The girls are all quite fetching. Sometimes they come in bunches, stomping on the stairs and jostling one another. She does not see how it could be possible for Carter to have *done anything* with any of them. She urged Michael to talk to him. They are modern parents. Both of them work with kids for a living, but Michael balked, even in the face of Ursula's blatant bullying. In the end she went to Planned Parenthood, took every pamphlet in sight, and laid them on Carter's desk, pushing aside clothes, books, Coke bottles, Big Hunk wrappers, magazines, and tapes, to make space for the literature. Month after month the booklets lay there, soon covered with more detritus, and month by month Ursula's need to mother her son (control? pry? Michael's silence accused) has bruised her until she feels pain under her skin, just thinking about him. To this day she has not managed to bring up the subject of sex with either of her children. She feels a great resentment toward Michael over this issue. She thinks he is cowardly. (She tells herself Juliette isn't ready for talk about sex yet; she still thinks boys are bogus.) Michael has wiped up spit and shit and vomit throughout the children's young years. He has repaired bicycles, rented skis, returned library books; yet he will not talk to his son about a "private matter."

Ursula argues that the children need guidance. Michael counters, "indoctrination." She says children have needs for intimacy. "With us?" asks Michael. "Well damn it," she cries, "they need advice *whether they know it or not.*"

"We've had our chance," Michael says. "Aren't you the one who made that sophisticated little speech at Nancy's Christmas buffet last year, saying you have your influence on kids until they are nine or ten years old and then it's up to the peers?" She cannot argue. He is right. She even believes what she has said, but she doesn't want it to be true. "Besides," Michael adds, "they get sex education at school, for the particulars."

Ursula can't sit still for that. "Oh yes. Umbilical cords and Fallopian tubes. Monthly cycles and swirling sperm." She cannot ruffle Michael.

"What's really bothering you," he says, "is that you want Carter to be *nice,* you're worried about his *relationships,* you want him to give for what he gets. Hell, Ursula, don't you think he's already drawn a lot of conclusions for himself,

watching the parade of people through our home? Hasn't he
learned about tolerance and affection and forgiveness?
Hasn't he learned about intimacy, if you think about it? If
you are willing to admit the intimacy implicit in friendships
with people we care about, people who live with us and go
away and come back, throw up in our rhododendrons, and
bring us presents from Mexico and England and Vietnam?"

Michael said all these things in a single evening. She can
remember just how he sat, his back curved in a way that was
terrible for his posture. He was in the yellow velour chair,
and Pajamas was on his lap. How he surprised her with such a
long speech! She leaned toward him, eager to get every
detail, not to miss any of the meaning, because she knew that
once he had said what he had to say, he wouldn't repeat a
word of it, or explain what he had meant, or—above all—
argue.

Michael is a man who once made maps, not voyages; who is
careful and thorough and loyal and uncritical. And if there is
a single central philosophy to his life, it is that we are all out
on the sea of life on inner tubes, so that fate becomes a matter
of luck and the currents, and maybe a bit of pluck. We're all
just flotsam. Some of us have drifted out, farther into the sea,
and others have ended up onshore, like Michael, who finds
that it suits him to have hard ground under his feet. But
Michael also likes a view of the sea, and he has a feeling for
the lost souls out there, who are welcome as anything to his
hearth, if they show up.

And he means for that to mean Carter, too.

It comes down to this: Carter is eighteen years old and he
has had all the making his parents can effect. If he fucks and
runs, it won't be because they didn't tell him about con-
traception. It won't be because Michael won't tell Ursula how
he really feels about things. It will be because of something in
Carter, some predisposition, as to fat or depression, and
because he has made his own choices about who he will be,
which might not include looking out for other people.

This is what Ursula most dreads: not that Carter will fail
English and embarrass her, not that he will lose his scholarships and cost her more money, not that his room will
spontaneously ignite, but that he will turn out to be someone
she wouldn't want near her daughter, a stranger to the values

she holds dear, to trust and compassion. It is easier to blame
Michael and take it back every time Carter causes them
trouble. Meanwhile all she knows to do is to watch her son for
signs of vulnerability and tenderness and, finding none,
begin sadly to sink into a bog of relief that, at least, he will
soon be gone.

She clears away some of the debris from Carter's room. She
fills trash cans from his room, hers, and the bathroom, and
lines them up in the hall where he cannot miss them. She
turns his mattress and puts on a bottom sheet, then fluffs the
soiled comforter and smooths it out, darker side up. She
kicks dirty socks and underwear into a pile with her foot, and
puts pop cans outside the door. Using one of his undershirts,
she wipes whatever surfaces show. She opens his windows
wide, then she sits wearily on the bed. From her perch she
sees that his Apple is the only neat thing in the room. It sits
on a small white iron computer table with a cover over it.
Sometimes Carter works at it all night. He is brilliant in math,
already far more than just a competent programmer. Supposedly on this machine he composed his thesis about extra-
terrestrial architects.

She notices a title on the spine of a book on his desk:
*Mysterious Phenomena of the*—She can't see the rest, and
doesn't care. Maybe her son really does believe in such
things. She hears that that is all teenage boys read, sci-fi and
fantasy. Maybe Carter sees himself in a spaceship, whirling
out into the galaxy, away from his ordinary world. Who can
say it won't happen?

Only, the Apple seems so much like Carter's brain, tidily
covered, while the rest of his room languishes in filth. Still, he
*could* do anything. He has his whole life ahead. That is why
Michael doesn't worry. He can remember being young.
Michael never had the chance for youth; maybe what he
remembers is how sad it is to grow up too fast.

She decides she will wake Carter in the morning before she
leaves for work, and tell him he is to spend every single
moment of the weekend at the dining room table writing his
paper, *in longhand.* Only after she approves it can he transfer
it to that machine. Or else—what? He fails English, of course.
Let him dwell on a summer of eight o'clock classes.

Of course he should go to the Fishers' party. And she will

be gone all day, unable to supervise. She will have to count on the power of natural consequences to keep him working.

Maybe Mrs. Angstrom is going to teach summer school. She could threaten him with that.

She looks up and sees Michael standing at the door, shaking his head.

"Go on and say it," she says. When he stays silent, she says, "I'm not mad at you."

"Why would you be?" He puts his hand out for her to take, and makes a big show of hauling her off the bed. She falls against him as she comes to her feet, then regains her balance.

"I decided against spaghetti, Ursie. That salad stuff died days ago. Let's walk down to the Thai Rose." The Thai deli, a few blocks away, has good hot, cheap food. Even Fish says it is "fairly authentic"; he orders in Thai.

"What about Juliette?"

"Call her. We'll bring her leftovers."

"I could leave her a note."

Michael nods.

"And Michael. Do you think Carter is—all right?"

"You've done just fine, Ursula."

"I didn't ask about me."

Michael kisses her cheek. "Right," he says, and then, "Let's go eat. I'm starved."

## —18—

They eat dishes with lemongrass and peanuts and hot peppers. The fish has a crunchy skin. They concentrate on eating, speaking little except to say this was tasty, this spicy, did you like it. Michael eats chili sauce on his fish, and smiles as tears pour down his cheeks. Ursula loves him for eating the sauce. He laughs at her when stray noodles hang out of her mouth.

Over a pale bitter tea, he mentions that his mother called. He talked to her while Ursula was in Carter's room.

"She was upset because he was out late last night."

"But isn't Tuesday his AA night?"

"And he went. But he brought somebody home, and you can imagine Mom let them both know what she thought of that." Geneva would have shut herself in her bedroom with the television on high volume, huffing loudly enough to be heard through a closed door. "So Pop gave this old guy a ride home to the VA domiciliary, and I guess they must have talked a lot. Evidently Pop's done this before. Got all caught up talking to some old fart. It drives Mom crazy."

"So how late was he?"

Michael didn't think to ask.

"Everything is relative, right?" Ursula says. "Gully usually goes to bed at nine, maybe ten on Tuesdays. So 'late' could have been ten-thirty."

"He was gone this morning before she got up. Without breakfast. That shook her up."

"Maybe he had two dollars in his pocket and went to the cafe."

"Maybe. He goes off in his truck, though."

Ursula gets a couple of cartons from the Thai girl lounging on a stool by the register, and scrapes food into them. To her dismay, she finds herself wondering if the girl is a good student, the way Asian children are said to be.

"You know, Michael, it sounds like your mother needs to complain. All those years she didn't. Why now? What's your poor pop going to do to get in trouble?" Geneva lamented to Ursula recently that Gully doesn't clip his toenails anymore. She says they will get ingrown. Ursula thinks she was hoping Michael would volunteer to hold his father down.

"He wanders off for longer and longer periods of time. Mom is worried he's getting senile."

"She's worried he's regaining a little independence!" Ursula says testily, and wonders why she should care that much.

Michael pulls out his wallet. "I haven't got enough cash on me."

Ursula pays.

It is dark outside but not cold. "I love this time of year," Ursula says. "The orchards have budded, they're so pretty now."

Two boys, maybe ten years old, are scuffling on the walk as Ursula and Michael go by. "Fuck you, asshole!" one of them yells. Ursula says, "Go home, both of you!" She hopes Michael won't scold her for her outburst. The instinct for authority in her does sometimes seem silly. But evidently he didn't even notice.

"Are you supposed to *do* something now, Michael?"

She thinks Geneva ought to find a group to join. Quilting. Herb drying. Some AA affiliated program. Anything. She needs to tell stories and get support. Or maybe better yet, *not* get any.

"I do wonder what's going on with Pop."

"It's spring. Gully has a little sap left."

"Don't be stupid." Michael is offended.

"Christ, Michael, I didn't mean women. I meant life."

"Mom's worried."

"Why don't you ask him what he's doing. Ask him what's on his mind these days? Why doesn't Geneva ask him? Don't they talk?"

Michael chews on his moustache as they walk. Ursula would like to take his arm, but he walks with his hands shoved down in his pockets, like a scholar weighing a mighty theory.

The whole dialogue could be reversed. If neither spoke for a few more moments, they could easily pick it up again, with opposite views. Sometimes she defends Geneva, and Michael stands up for Gully. Sometimes, like now, it gets off on the other foot. She tries to realize the incredible reality of Geneva's fifty years as Gully's wife. Her own twenty years as Michael's seem to have gone by so fast.

"Why do we talk about your parents so much?" she asks.

"They've only got me. I told you, Ursula."

So he has, more than once. So he did, when he moved his own family to the Rogue Valley so that he could take care of his parents.

Ursula was perfectly happy in Portland. She loved her work. She loved the people who worked with her. She loved the house her father helped them into. (She wouldn't like it now; it wasn't much of a house, but she didn't know that then.) Michael said. "Pop's falling apart, what will she do?" and they moved. There was never any talk of bringing his parents back to Portland. That would have been worse.

Poor Juliette, Ursula thinks. There would have been so much more for her in the city. But who could have known? She was a toddler when they made the move.

Ursula stops in front of a house she particularly likes, a rather ordinary two-story house, maybe forty-five or fifty years old. The owners have painted it turquoise and yellow, with panels of brilliantly colored fabric at the window. "What would you think of painting our house?" she asks Michael.

He runs his hands through his hair, pushing it back from habit, though it is short now. "Gray?"

Gray! "Oh when will you be done taking care of them!" she bursts out. What she really wants is to be young again, drinking wine and making love on Indian bedspreads. She wants a yellow house. Of course she has middle-class tastes now. She has china. And Michael has his parents. She respects him for his sense of responsibility; she hopes Carter will learn from it. She just wishes Geneva's needs were fewer. She hopes that what she senses is a delicate balance in the Fisher family will hold.

Michael answers coolly. "I'll be done when they die."

She wonders if he has always known that, or if he came to realize it over time. Maybe he minds but he can't do anything about it. He does what is right. Maybe it is fair. Maybe parents earn this by not pouring hot soup over your head, or beating you to death. And Michael has his brother's share to do, and his dead sister's.

She remembers sitting at her father's bedside in the house in Evanston as he fell away before her eyes. He had been a professor, an expert on certain Chinese dynasties. "Be sure you go," he told her. He meant China. She wonders what it was like all those years he couldn't see anything he longed to see, and then it turned out Nixon opened the doors. Pukey Nixon. Her father sent a photograph of himself his wife, Sheila, took outside the Forbidden City. Her father looked ecstatic.

She tried to talk to him as he was dying. She stayed a week that last time. She wanted to read him Sylvia Plath's poem "Daddy," and thank him for seeing her grown. She wanted to say, "I never had any complaint." She wanted him to know he hadn't taken her from her mother, and that it was nobody's fault she wasn't ambitious, as he was ambitious for her.

She managed some of those things. She said enough to understand that he already knew. "Take care of your mother," he said, and immediately amended the admonition. "Well, look in on her."

Clare doesn't need taking care of, but plenty of the world does.

"I'm going to take Juliette to France and Italy next spring, she told her father. Like her mother had done with her when she was fourteen. She thought her father winced, though it could have been the pain. She remembered sitting with her mother, drinking iced coffee in a cafe in Nice. Her mother asked her, "Are you terribly disappointed in the beach?" and when Ursula said the beach was fine, her mother added, as though it were an afterthought, "Your father and I are divorcing." Ursula was angry, terribly angry, and shocked (no, she hadn't seem it coming; her parents were so polite, and they cared for one another), and she screamed out at her mother, who was there to take the brunt of it. "I'm not going to live with you!" Her mother smiled and said, "That's okay, Ursula. I'm going to move back to Seattle."

Had her father minded? Bringing up that memory, with talk of a new generation's trip to the Louvre? He had a good second marriage, to a woman much better suited to the sweet dull ritual of an academic's life. Her mother has made a good life of her own in Seattle, full of the eccentricity of artists (she was an agent, and a gallery manager), and later, when she needed more security, in a position as a registrar of a fine arts college.

"Maybe you and Michael—" her father said. Evidently he still meant China. "There'll be money for you." She had assumed that was so, but she couldn't bear to hear him talk of it.

"That's wonderful," she said, because he wanted her to, but it sounded terrible. "China. Of course we'll go."

"I want him to have my maps," her father said next. Michael had once wanted to be a cartographer. Ursula wept. She didn't know if Michael would care, though he did, when he got the maps. Some are very old and valuable. It showed that her father had taken Michael seriously, more seriously than Michael. Michael has been happy to make a perfectly ordinary life, teaching kids other people didn't like. The maps nearly broke Ursula's heart.

—19—

**W**hen they arrive home Juliette is lying across her bed, crying over her French. Ursula looks over Juliette's shoulder at the book. The chapter is focused on the *passé composé* with irregular verbs, but Ursula knows that what is giving Juliette trouble is that she has never bothered to learn new nouns as masculine and feminine, and now they are piling up on her. A matter of *le* or *la* can ruin your life in French. It is hard not to say I told you so.

"If you want, I can look it over." Poor Juliette looks miserable. She suffers over small things. Dancing, she is radiant.

"Go away."

Ursula goes downstairs. Tears spurt onto her cheeks. She misses her father tonight, she is tired. She knows better than to get upset over a fifteen-year-old girl's tantrums.

Michael is putting away the take-home packages. "Juliette doesn't seem to be hungry," she says.

Ursula thinks he gives her a rather superior look. He has warned her that she is a glutton for punishment. Doesn't she know to steer clear of hot stoves, growling dogs, teenage daughters?

Michael goes into the living room, puts on a tape (with earphones), and settles down to read a *Natural History*. In a moment Pajamas comes along and noses the magazine out of the way, then settles down between Michael's thighs. Michael's hand strokes the cat's head and back idly. His eyes close. The magazine slides to the floor. His mind is probably empty of everything except the music. He can actually *not think*. He considers it stubbornness on her part that she does not have the same ability to escape.

Upstairs, Ursula runs a very deep hot bath in the old clawfoot tub. When they bought this house, which before them was owned by a chiropractor who practiced downstairs in what is now the dining room, Ursula had the nice fiberglass tub taken out. She drove all over the valley until she found an old tub. She thinks of it as hers.

She is soaking when Juliette comes in.

"Mother?" Juliette says in a little girl's voice.

"Hi, dear."

"When I try to be just myself, not to think about what I say before I say it, like you told me—"

"Be spontaneous," Ursula offers.

"Mother, I wasn't through!" Juliette sits on the rim of the tub. "I can't do it, that's all. I don't have any ideas. I want to say something so they will like me and I always say something *stupid*."

"You're so bright, darling. Who are *they*.?"

Juliette races from the room. Ursula lets the tears run down her face, dripping off below her ears, into the water. The tears are soothing and warm.

"Mother?" It is Juliette again. Ursula opens her eyes and nods. It is better if she remembers not to talk. "Can I get in?" Juliette looks very tried, and very young. All of Ursula's resentment (how can she act like that when she knows I love her?) melts in a glance.

"Will there be room?" Ursula asks, drawing up her knees. "With your big boobs and all?" She holds her breath, hoping she has not said the wrong thing.

Juliette laughs and undresses. As she climbs in she says, "Could you make it hotter?" She sits oddly, with her legs tucked under, and she knees forward, like she was about to play jacks.

Something about the water, their nakedness, the evening hour. They are companionable in the tub. Juliette says, "I've been thinking about Europe. Now that I know some French, I'd like to go back. Do you think we could?"

Ursula is surpised, but she does remember how impressed she was at her daughter's passion for the trip, her love of colors and the textures of walls, her delight at the sounds of people jabbering exotically. Juliette had an uncanny intuition for direction, and for the potential of cafes and *pensiones*. While Ursula struggled with maps and guidebooks, counting lire or francs over and over, terribly uncertain, Juliette took stride. "Let's go over there," she might say. "Oh, look, chocolate croissants."

Ursula thought her daughter so confident, and this just a year ago. It is painful and disconcerting to see her now downhearted. Ursula cannot deny the effect high school is having on her child; something in the very structure of it fails her. Carter jokes about it, makes it what he wants, and slides by on his mathematical prowess. Who values Juliette's grace and discipline? Who appreciates her need for time to do things right?

"Remember Madame Serault?" Juliette asks now. "I was so humiliated over that jam!" She laughs merrily, though she cried torrents the night she asked the Madame for jam to go with her bread at dinner. Madame found that hilarious. She was more Italian than French, with huge expansive gestures and a loud voice. Juliette had proven the silly taste of Americans, and Madame enjoyed it, not, Ursula thinks, meaning to be cruel. Juliette, mortified, cried herself to sleep. Now she recalls the episode dreamily, as though it happened in the youth of someone very old. "Rmember she put whole cloves of garlic in the chicken, and I didn't know what they were?" 'Oh, but Americans, they cook from jars, don't they?' she said. I didn't even know what she meant! I couldn't cook!"

"She exaggerated everything. She meant well."

"She was a great cook. Remember how those German boys ate like pigs? I forgot to eat, watching them."

"It would be nice to go again," Ursula says noncommittally. Actually she doesn't see the point in repeating herself, when there is so much world to see. She did a homestay in England in high school, and she went to Spain and Morocco the summer between her freshman and sophomore college years, and then met Fish and Michael and the others in the boarding house that fall.

"It's so nice to travel," Juliette says. They went the last six weeks of the school year, before the onslaught of summer tourists. "I'll never forget it.

"Mother," she says, climbing out of the tub, "did you know some girls at school talk about their mothers *awful?*"

Juliette falls again into a sorry mood as soon as she is dry and dressed. She has exhausted her affection. Ursula follows her into her bedroom for a moment, wrapped in a towel, and tries to begin a dialogue about travel again. "I wonder if we went again if we couldn't plan it around your dance interest, Juliette. Isn't it Bejart—do I have his name right?—who began a fabulous dance school in Senegal?" But Juliette gives her a withering glare over her shoulder and assumes an invaded-privacy look that sends Ursula to her own room.

Earlier she tucked and smoothed the bed and turned down the covers. She picks up clothes from the floor and then throws them down again. She puts on flannel pajamas—the evening has turned cool—and brushes her hair slowly. Then she looks in on Juliette one more time, expecting to give her a good-night kiss (whether she wants it or not), and then to tackle some of the reading she needs to do.

Juliette's light is on. Ursula switches it off. Her daughter

lies in bed, her head deep in her pillow. "Mommy," she
whimpers. She scoots over and makes room for her mother.
"Just for a little while, until I get sleepy?"

As Ursula takes her assigned place, she sees that Juliette
has been crying. Ursula wipes her daugher's cheeks. She
cannot remember seeing Michael cry, and she has not seen
her son cry since he was a small boy, not even when Ursula's
father died (she took the children to Evanston for the funeral). Of course he was never close to his grandfather, there
was never enough time for it.

She doesn't know what to say. When Juliette is sad or
frustrated, words are like tiny packets of potent explosive; it
is entirely too easy to say the wrong thing. Ursula is learning
that, if you wait, Juliette finally takes the lead.

"I just don't see how I can make it to the end," she says.
Awash in despair, Juliette does not say what end she had in
mind. Ursula chooses the best alternative because it is closest
and not so desperate. "There are only a few more weeks," she
says.

"But only dancing matters, and I'm tired all the time. I
worry I won't get to sleep, and if I don't I won't get enough
rest, and then I'll be tired in the morning. And Brian will say,
no, not on point this time. He's promised me a small part in
the second ballet on point, but I have to have my *all* for it.
And now, if I'm getting fatter, I'll be off balance. I'll be *ugly*."
She bursts into fresh tears.

Ursula thinks of Michael's hand on her breast this morning. She remembers that when she was young, her libido had
a life of its own, stirred by the way the sun hit a windowsill,
because of a song on the radio, or because her thighs brushed
as she moved in a chair. Now something else has to happen.
Some force has to be put in motion. She is especially touched
by surprise, and by gentle moments, by the sight of Michael
when she does not expect him. She doesn't know if he has
such thoughts himself. He is a good lover, much less restrained than in any other part of his life. He does not seem
to mind the places where she has gone soft, the inevitable
droops brought on by age and gravity.

"You're not listening to me." Juliette's voice is flat and
dismissing. She turns slightly, to give her mother the plane of
her back.

"Julie."

Juliette breathes deeply and noisily and lets the air out in a long whistling stream, through her mouth. "See!" she almost shouts. "I can't even breathe right! I can—not—RELAX."

Ursula puts her hand on her daughter's hair. She remembers when Juliette was small and so full of energy she could not let it go at bedtime. Sometimes she would literally fall over at the dinner table, straight into her plate, but she would lie rigid with wakefulness once put to bed. Ursula had a routine to lull her. "The roots of your hair are letting go. Feel your scalp melting—" she whispers. From Juliette a tiny whimper comes. "And the tips of your fingers, like jelly, melting away from the tightness of your hands."

Ursula pauses and wipes her face with her hand. She longs to get up at that moment and get her moisturizer. She read that you must put on cream at least forty-five minutes before bed, because if you lie down right after, the cream closes the pores and traps moisture in them and you wake with bigger bags than ever.

"That really helps," Juliette sighs.

On the stairs Ursula smells popcorn.

She turns into the kitchen and looks across it into the dining room. Her son has a pizza box in front of him, and a salad bowl full of popcorn. Fish sits on the same side of the table, swigging from a bottle of dark wine, talking, not just talking, but holding forth. He is saying something about search and seize missions, about a time they found weapons cached on a fisherman's boat.

"He was this big," Fish says, pointing to his midchest. "I had him by one arm, like a twig, but I could feel how strong he was. And stubborn. And scared." He takes a long drink, swallowing hard. "You couldn't tell, looking. They were so fucking little. But they were like steel wire. So I was holding him, and this other guy—our guy—was radioing for instructions, when my guy—the gook, the little fisherman—kicked me in the fucking shin and nearly knocked me in the soup. I went crazy. I had his neck in my hands, and over his shoulder I saw the piles under the nets. He was moving ammunition and guns, just like they'd told us we'd find, only I'd been doing this harassing of fishermen for four months and all I'd

ever found was fucking FISH!" He laughs hilariously. Carter
is snorting and cackling. Vietnam, for Carter, is a series of
Fish stories.

Ursula walks softly toward the other side of the kitchen
where it opens under an arch onto the dining room. Her son
looks up at her with his mouth full. His hair sticks up like a
patch of yucca. Fish raises his chin in greeting and drinks
deeply of his wine. Michael is bent over a yellow lined pad.

"So what's this?" Ursula asks.

"Listen, Mom, I'm going to have the greatest paper! The
first missions of the navy in Vietnam. Mom, Fish was *there*. So
I can have an interview as one of my research sources. He
was in the Delta. Everybody knows about grunts, all that mud
and guck and getting blown up and all that, but who knows
about the Delta, man?" Carter jumps up. "I am thirst*eee*." He
sweeps by Ursula on the way to the refrigerator.

"So you guys are helping. Granting interviews and all."
Ursula is looking at Fish, who looks back from hooded eyes.
She is surprised at his high spirits. She credits them to the
bottle. Michael puts down his pencil, and wipes his eyes with
the knuckle on one finger. "And you?" Ursula says testily.
"What's your role?"

Michael leans back, tipping the chair on its back legs, the
way Ursula asks them all not to do. "Hell, Ursie, we can
knock this out in two nights."

Ursula's ears are hot. When you come upon men together,
for a moment at least, they are always strangers. She is an
interloper, and wishes she did not come down. She does not
approve. She should have known Michael would take over
for Carter, despite all his talk of consequences. She should
have known, yet she forgot. Michael does not pull his hair or
grind his teeth. He does not bitch or demand gratitude. Saint
of all saints, he just does. You cannot make him do.

She feels foolish, and left out. Then she relaxes a bit.
There is something in the scene of the old days: Fish, helped
by alcohol, moving the moments along on a gush of funny
talk. His friends urging him on. Michael, getting something
done that needs doing. And Ursula? Waiting her turn, watching. Looking forward to bed.

"Just came to say goodnight," she says. As Carter goes by,
he offers her a swig of Pepsi from a can. She shakes her head.

"Don't worry, Mom," Carter says as he settles down. "Fish is really rád tonight, and he's got books, too, Mom. He's got sources." He grins hugely. "I can pick up a few more things at the library at lunch. We'll knock this out in no time."

Michael has gone back to writing.

"Which part are you doing, son?"

Carter thinks she is joking. He laughs, a happy, loved young man. "Oh you know, Mom. I turn it in!"

She tries to wait up for Michael. She takes a folder of papers into the bathroom to read. The topic is interventions on behalf of babies born of addicted or diseased mothers. She sits on the tile, because the cold floor keeps her awake.

She remembers feeling Carter move for the first time inside her. She had just read an article in a women's magazine that listed a calendar of mileposts in pregnancy, and she kept it in her dresser drawer, checking it secretly. "The sensation of quickening may be like a bubble of gas, a touch of indigestion—" But it wasn't that way at all. It was as clearly wonderful as the sun coming up. She felt the rest of her life ripening. She hadn't even wanted to be pregnant until then. Carter, Carter, he would die to think she had such thoughts about him.

And these poor women, the subject of dry essays—do they think of the life inside them, too? Do they notice?

At two in the morning Michael wakes her with his snoring. She wakes him gently. "Michael, Michael," she says, "you're making your funny noises." He says, "Mmm."

She puts her hand somewhere he will notice.

He turns and says sleepily, "Am I not to go back to sleep after a day's work and a long night's toil?"

"First you have to make it up to me."

"You're mad about Carter's paper?"

"Not now. It's the snoring. This is twice in twenty hours. It's not even morning yet."

He puts his hand on her nice round breast. "You make it awful hard on a man," he says.

—20—

Ursula makes herself a cup of tea and switches on the television to wait for the news on PBS. This television, a little

black and white, sits on their old highchair, against the wall
by the basement door. The Friday evening summary of the
financial news is on. Sometimes Ursula tries to listen and
learn. She has left her father's investments in his same funds,
just changing ownership, counting on her dad, even now, to
know what he was doing—and what she ought to do. But she
knows times change, investments should change, she will
have to know more to get more. Only an inheritance seems a
kind of free money, certainly a gift, and she trusts her father
to have remembered that she would have no head for it all.

Juliette phones. "Where are you?" Ursula sputters. She
hadn't realized that it was seven already. Michael has gone to
River Cove, to do his duty.

"*Mom,* Dad wasn't home either when I got home from
dance, and there wasn't a note or anything—"

"Answer my question. Where are you?"

"Other kids go places without checking in every fifteen
minutes. You act like I'm a baby."

"I'm waiting."

"The mall."

"The mall!" The mall is twenty miles away, in the next
town. "How did you manage that?"

"Kristi's mom picked us up and then dropped us off."

"Who's us?"

"Oh Mother."

"Juliette, you can't go off with anyone without checking."

"I tried! I didn't know where you were."

"Then you should have waited."

"And missed my chance?"

Juliette's high whine reminds Ursula that her daughter is
feeling cornered. And her complaint is at least partially valid.
Ursula did forget to make Friday plans with her daughter.
She didn't even mind until Juliette called.

"Never mind. When are you coming home, and what are
you doing at the mall?"

"It's too late for the bus, Mom."

"Where's Kristi's mother?"

"I told you she dropped us off. Kristi, me, Darlene, and
Brie."

This is not Juliette's crowd. (Why would anyone name a
child after a cheese?) Juliette doesn't run with a crowd. She

spends times with Marina, another ninth-grader, who also dances, and there have been a couple of other girls around now and then. Juliette has never been one for "spending the night," and she seldom goes to school events. Ursula has heard of these girls, though. They are "popular" girls. Within the last week Brie told Juliette her ends were split, and Juliette wanted to go to the beauty parlor as soon as possible. Ursula said their appraisal would have to wait until school was out, and Juliette seems to have forgotten.

"So how are you getting home?"

"Couldn't you pick us up? We probably would have come out here anyway."

"I could not."

"How am I supposed to get home then?"

"What are you doing?"

"Brie is looking for a prom dress. Kristi already found a bathing suit. I'm just—you know—. Mom, they're waiting on me, I've got to go. Aren't you going to pick us up?"

"I can't carry four of you in my car."

"Someone can sit in the middle."

"Not without a seat belt. Not in my car."

"Motherrr!"

"I will pick you up. *You*, Juliette."

"I told them you'd give us a ride!"

"You can't make commitments for me. I'm not happy about this at all. I'm going to listen to the news before I do anything. Hostages. National defense." She sighs. "Gary Hart."

"I'll leave here at eight, and I want you to be at the Meier and Frank bottom entrance at eight-thirty sharp. By the shoe department. Got it?"

"What am I supposed to tell them?" Ursula can hear tears.

"Tell them to call *their* mothers. Eight-thirty."

Driving to the mall, Ursula feels herself softening. She knows what happened. Her sweet Juliette was standing around when those girls were making their plans, and she got swept up in them. Going to the mall with the local Valley Girls. It is understandable. Unusual for Juliette, but not so unusual for an adolescent.

She tries to recall the faces of the girls Juliette named. All she can bring to mind is hair and glare, the standard teenage girl. So these are the desired companions.

She tries to imagine them prancing around the mall, looking at clothes, handling jewelry, scarves, purses, little stuffed doo-dads in the Hallmark shop.

She hopes none of them shoplift.

She tries to concentrate on the state of the world, but thinking about it makes it worse. Sometimes she wakes at night in the classic cold sweat, and realizes she has been dreaming about Chernobyl or Star Wars.

It is eight-thirty when she arrives, and there is no sign of Juliette. She waits in the car five minutes, then gets out and goes inside. That part of the store is almost empty. A very skinny sales clerk stands slouched against the frame of the arched entry into the storeroom of the shoe department. In Electronics, across the aisle, a much older man, tired and fleshy in a polyester suit, is watching the shoe clerk. Two women about Ursula's age sit on one of the mattresses talking intensely, their heads close together. They reach behind them several times to push against the mattress. Ursula walks past them, past the escalator, to look in Misses. Not a likely place, but if Juliette were early she might have wandered around.

With no sign of Juliette, Ursula goes up the escalator and walks through the store quickly, then looks out into the mall center to see if the girls are sitting somewhere, or coming toward the store.

By now Ursula is worried that Juliette will be at the agreed place, wondering where her mother is, so she hurries back. The couple on the mattress is gone. The girl in Shoes is straightening the displays and yawning, without bothering to cover her mouth. The man in Electronics is not in sight, and neither is Juliette.

Ursula sits in a chair in Shoes, facing into the store, and waits. Twice she gets up to look outside. Her unlocked car sits in plain sight.

I should be angry, she thinks, but already she is imagining horrible things. Small towns are not safe from monsters of madness. You have to move to another country—Canada, New Zealand, Japan—for that. Juliette is naive and vulnerable and dear. Ursula picks up a pair of forty-eight dollar huaraches, dyed bright blue, and examines the sole, the thickness of a crepe.

Juliette comes through the door from outside. Three girls come in with her. There is something formidable about them *en masse*. Juliette breaks from the others and runs to her mother.

I won't embarrass her, Ursula tells herself. It can wait. This is not a serious infraction. She forces herself to smile.

"I was worried, honey. Let's go." Ursula reaches for her daughter's hand.

Juliette jerks away and speaks in a hoarse, venomous whisper. "Don't you dare humiliate me!"

Ursula smiles at the other girls. "G'night," she calls. They smirk.

"Bye, Brie," Juliette mews as Ursula pushes the door. Outside, she says, "I hate you!"

Ursula keeps quiet as she pulls onto the freeway. Juliette is rigid in her seat, her face pulled into a paroxysm of anger.

"I will not be angry," Ursula says sweetly. One good whack is lurking in her hand, but she has never struck a child yet.

"How could you talk to me like that?" Juliette demands.

"Now you just shut up, Juliette. I am the one who ought to be mad here, after cooling my heels for half an hour. Where the hell WERE YOU?"

"You weren't there at 8:30. I looked everywhere." Juliette is unconvincing.

"That isn't so and you know it. You should have waited where we agreed."

"Where you said."

"I said. Right."

"They were going to go and leave me there by myself. I said, 'Can't you just wait until my mom comes?'"

"Where were you, honey?"

Juliette begins to sob violently. Though the energy subsides, she cries all the way home. Ursula, provoked but puzzled, bites her lip.

As soon as they are in the house, Juliette screams, "You don't CARE that I don't have any friends. You don't CARE that I look DUMB in my STUPID clothes and STUPID hair."

Ursula reaches for Juliette. She has always dealt with tantrums by touching and holding and waiting them out.

"I hate you!" Juliette runs to her room and slams the door. Pajamas scratches at the basement door in the kitchen, whining to be fed. Ursula opens the door and calls down into blackness: "Fish, you there?" Of course not, she didn't see his van. But she wishes for company in the house. That was something she liked when she and Michael were first married. They lived in a dump, but their friends crashed for a night, for a week. Carmen lived with them over a year. Not Fish, not then. He was gone those first years. By the time he got back, the marriage was real and solid, their lives had become stable, there was Carter.

She turns on the light and goes down to feed the cat. A spider floats in the water dish. Ursula washes and refills the dish. She squats down beside Pajamas. The cat attacks the food.

"Couldn't you be a little bit of a pal, huh?" Ursula says. The cat moves around so that Ursula is talking to her back-end. "Couldn't you nuzzle up to me when I feed you?" Sometimes at night Pajamas climbs on Michael's lap and rubs him all over with her head, pushing into his chest and his belly, then licking his hand or arm, finally settling against him. When the children were younger, Michael used to make them laugh by taking Pajamas' paws and making her "dance" as he "spoke" for her.

The cat is getting old. There is a bald place on her rear from a scrape.

Ursula goes back upstairs and through the living areas, turning on lights. She has read that light is a great balm for depression. She isn't exactly depressed, but she is a little lonesome. It used to be that Fridays were what you lived for all week. It used to be Ursula cooked great pots of stew or chili, and friends sat around listening to Bob Dylan and Janis Joplin, and talked about living in Alaska or Belize, as if any of them were likely to make such big moves.

Winston lives now in Seattle and drives a school bus. Two hours twice a day, this is his career. Funnier yet, he lives with Carmen, who always preferred exotic men from foreign countries before Winston. Harry Dayton is dead of a violent allergic reaction to some damned mushroom, in Mexico. The Lutters live in Portland still, in a much nicer house than this one, with their four kids. The Edsons have made country life work. In short, nobody is around anymore but Fish. And Katie.

They have friends, of course. But you call before you drop by. You make plans for dinner. You reciprocate. She can't imagine how she would get by, if not for coffee and commiseration at work. Social workers always empathize.

Carter has brought his computer downstairs and set it up on the old receptionist's counter, left over from the days when this was the chiropractor's waiting room. They meant to take the desk out, but it is oak, and they haven't got around to it. It looks silly, but there it is, a perfect place to type, too. Ursula keeps little potted begonias and ivy on top, and stacks magazines on the floor behind it.

One summer day she found a half-empty Coke can there. There were ants all over the top, all over the counter, running down the sides and into the corner of the walls. She yelled at Carter, who said blithely, "The ants were already there, hiding, Mom. I did you a big favor flushing them out." It turned out he was more or less correct. She began to see ants on the windowsills, upstairs and down. There were ants in her closet, in the pockets of her dresses. She called an exterminator in. The family left for two days. They drove to Newport and stayed in the new Sylvia Beach Hotel. Carter got the Edgar Allen Poe room, with heavy drapes around the bed. They had an expensive weekend, but a great time. When they came home, they left the windows open, even when a thunderstorm blew in. Michael said next time he would leave something out for the ants, that it wasn't necessary to poison the whole family, but after that there weren't any more ants.

In the dining room, books are spread all over the table. Wads of yellow paper litter the table and floor. It dawns on Ursula that Carter spent the day there rather than at school. She takes a sack from the kitchen and gathers up the discarded wads. Drafts? Notes? Whatever they were, he is through with them. All of his—and his father's—work is now on floppy disk. She carries the sack and the kitchen garbage out to the can in the alley. On her way to the bathroom she notes that the trash cans lined up outside Carter's bedroom are still full.

She washes and goes to her daughter's room. "Juliette?" she says softly, tapping at the door. When Juliette does not answer, she goes back downstairs, curls up on the couch, and tries to read a book review in *The New Republic*. In fifteen minutes, she is asleep.

When she wakes, Michael is sitting in his chair across from her, the cat on his lap. He has turned off most of the lights.

"What are you doing?" she asks.

He is petting Pajamas. "Watching you."

"That's not much." She is self-conscious, rumpled as she is. Whenever she lies down, the bags under her eyes puff up.

"I was thinking about the last few months you were pregnant with Juliette. You could not stay awake. That's why you finally took some time off. I swear, you only woke up to eat and bathe."

"And gained fifty pounds! Lots was going on. I wasn't always sleeping. I was gestating." She is pleased that he remembers, surprised he would bring it up. He doesn't often wax nostalgic. He took a year off after that, to take care of Juliette while Ursula went back to work. People thought it was a little crazy, but it worked fine for them, and of course now lots of people work things out that way. He had been teaching social studies in a Portland high school, and he was bored, and tired of policing large classes. So the next year he worked on his special education certificate and juggled studies with Juliette's babysitting needs. Ursula had had her turn with Carter. (Yet she feels closer to Juliette.)

"Oh, speaking of Juliette," she says. "Would you mind looking in on her? We had a spat."

"Really."

"She went off to the mall with some girls, and when I went to pick her up she was late meeting me. For some reason, that made *her* mad at *me*."

"Maybe you're the one who should go up."

"I don't know if she ate anything. I didn't."

"We could go get something."

"Did you eat?"

He makes a face. "Meat loaf and dilled potatoes."

"Sounds good. Too bad Geneva doesn't do take-out. How was she?"

"Comb your hair. I'll go ask Juliette."

Ursula wonders if what has just passed constitutes a conversation.

She wonders what Michael would say if she demanded, "Tell me something you never intended to tell me. Tell me one of your secrets." He would say he doesn't have any. He would say that if he did, he would keep them to himself. Otherwise they would not be secrets.

If you know what your husband would say, is it the same as knowing what he thinks?

As they go out to the car, Juliette takes her mother's hand and squeezes it.

While they sit in a booth waiting for their hamburgers, Juliette shyly tells them what happened at the mall.

"I hate them. I really wanted to have a good time with them, and I sort of thought I was having one, I was laughing whenever they did and all, but they went all over the mall making fun of people. They'd say, Look at that UGLEE woman. They made fun of a really tall woman with a short man. It did look funny, but I didn't think they ought to be mean about it. Then they were mad when I said you wouldn't take them home."

Ursula grinds her teeth. Her dentist threatens to give her a nightguard if she doesn't stop it. Oh I will stop, she said.

"They saw some boys from school last year and they went to ask them for a ride. Kids who graduated. That's where we were, when I came in from outside. We'd been sitting in their car."

"At least they were nice enough to wait until your ride came," Ursula says, wanting to make this easier for Juliette.

"Come on. They were in the boys' car smoking dope, Mom. I said I had to go, that you'd be there, and they—" Juliette's eyes brim with tears.

"I think we get the picture," Michael says gently.

Ursula is horrified. Not Juliette! "You didn't—"

Juliette shuts her eyes for an instant, and takes a deep breath. "God Mother, you can trust me. I'm not stupid."

"I'm glad."

"Then I saw your car and I knew you were in there looking for me. I said I had to go, my mom was there. The girls said, 'Well, we'll go tell her bye-bye.' I thought they were going to do something awful. They were stoned, Mom, couldn't you TELL?"

Ursula thought they seemed impolite.

The waitress brings their hamburgers on plates piled with fries.

"Forget it, darling," Ursula says. "Let's eat." She aches for Juliette. The awful thing is she was a lot more like those dippy girls than like Juliette at that same age.

Michael eats one of Ursula's fries.

Ursula says to him, "I think Carter cut school to work on his paper today."

"Well, he's got to get it done. At least he is taking the crisis seriously." Michael takes a strip of onion.

"You know how I feel about cutting."

"I wish I could stay home the rest of the year," Juliette says sadly. She is eating heartily, though. She gives Ursula a quick glance. "Sorry," she whispers.

As Michael juggles his keys at the front door, Ursula sees that the door is already ajar.

"Damn that kid!" she says. "He can't even close a door behind himself."

It is warm as summer out. "Think of it as leaving it open for us," Michael says.

They go inside.

"I'm going to bed," Juliette says

"I'm going to run the dishes," Ursula says.

"I think we've been robbed," Michael says.

Juliette calls from the top of the stairs. "What did you say, Daddy?" She creeps back down.

"You're kidding," Ursula says. They have *had* their turn!

Michael is staring at the cabinet where the tape deck ought to be. They can see the frame of dust around it. Juliette comes over and slides under his arm. "Oh Daddy," she whispers.

"The camera!" Ursula set it out on the highboy so that she wouldn't forget it for the Fisher reception. A Konica Fish brought back from Hong Kong and "hocked" with Michael long ago. Her two rolls of film are gone too.

They all run upstairs. Juliette throws herself across her bed and feels along the space between it and the wall. "My radio is still here!" she says happily.

Michael puts his arm around Ursula. "We don't have much, Ursie. And we've got insurance."

Ursula feels like someone has crawled under her covers, waiting to bite her toes. Theft is nasty. "HOW DID THEY GET IN?" She knows the answer as soon as she asks the question.

She shoves open Carter's door. Carter is lying on his bunk, earphones in his ears, sound asleep. He has found a fan and set it on his desk. As it blows across him, his hair lifts stiffly.

Ursula shakes his shoulder violently. "Get up!"

He comes awake groggily, surprised at the fuss. "What's going on?"

"You left the damned door open! You didn't empty the TRASH CANS outside your stupid door. They've been sitting there since WEDNESDAY NIGHT. Now GET UP. What did I TELL you about LOCKING THE DOORS?"

Michael tugs at Ursula from behind. Carter has managed to sit up and is shaking his head. The earphones dangle like a high-tech headdress, connected to nothing. Carter is wearing jockey shorts. His comforter is twisted around one foot. He looks up at his mother. "Dad?" he says.

Ursula yanks free of Michael's hand and goes out into the hall. "Oh God, what about the maps?" She has told Michael a thousand times they ought to be kept in a safety deposit box. He thinks they should sell them. Her father's maps. She runs into the bedroom, but she cannot remember where they put them. "THE MAPS!"

"Honey, honey, they're right here." Michael pulls all the towels and washrags out of the hall closet onto the floor. At the back are the maps, inside a sweater bag. He holds the bag up. "It's okay, Ursula. Calm down. They're right here."

"Yeah, Mom," Carter says from his doorway. "You're the one with a degree in crisis intervention."

Ursula stares at her son with contempt. How dare he put her down, when she's been robbed! Then she almost laughs. He has an uncanny knack for being right at the wrong time. It isn't funny, he would get entirely the wrong idea. "You slept through it," she says calmly. "They might have killed you."

"Mother," Carter drawls. "They just needed something to hock. It's not that big a deal."

"What do you know? Is that what that poor kid at the Minit Market thought when those punks shot him a couple of months ago? Not a big deal? And you in bed. LOOK AT

YOUR EARPHONES!"

Carter takes a moment to realize that his expensive tape equipment is among the missing items. "ASSHOLES!" he shouts. He flings the earphones against the wall.

Juliette backs into her own room, and slams the door. She lets out a terrible wail.

Michael crosses in front of Ursula before she can get to Juliette. He leans inside the bedroom, holding the door. "What is it, Julie? What did they do?"

"They didn't do anything. I haven't got anything to STEAL. I haven't got anything worth stealing."

"Then what is it?" Michael asks patiently.

"I'm going to bed and I never want to get up," Juliette wails again, and slams her door. Again. She opens it one more time. "Getting burglared isn't the worst tragedy, you know."

Michael tells Carter, "Go take a bath, son." To Ursula he says, "Let's go downstairs." On the stairs he laughs. "Burglared."

The little television in the kitchen is gone. Michael puts water on for tea. Ursula stares at the highchair. "Why do we still have that thing?" she asks. To hold the tv. She can't imagine not watching the news while she cooks. When she cooks. Michael is maddeningly calm. Ursula feels drained. "It was probably kids," Michael says. "This isn't exactly a high-crime area. It isn't Portland. And it isn't the Minit Market. Don't you wonder where they'll get rid of the stuff?"

"They sell it to each other, Michael."

"You'd know?" Michael smiles.

"Remember the year I did crisis intervention? Remember the mother who called because she found her son's closet full of stolen stereo equipment? Remember the boys who rented space in one of those store-and-lock places to stash computers?"

Michael says, "I'll pour the tea and then I'll call the police."

Carter lets out a whoop and bounds down the stairs, holding a towel around him. He sticks his head around to look for them in the kitchen. "You guys see my computer?"

Ursula puts her head in her hands. Michael goes with Carter into the living room. She hears Carter tell him, "I brought it all down here today to do my paper. I got it all on the disk. All I have to do is print it. WHERE IS MY PRINTER?"

Carter stomps around the rooms, cursing. Ursula is surprised at the variety of foul words he knows. Some are archaic. "My paper," he keeps saying. "My fucking paper."

In a moment he confronts his mother. "Where's my rough draft? What did you do with it?"

"I'll call Mrs. Angstrom," Michael says.

"What'll she care?" Carter says.

"What papers?" Ursula asks, to stall for time. She can feel a major headache coming on.

"We wrote it OUT. You said LONGHAND. Then I put it on the DISK."

"When you should have been in school."

"Not now," warns Michael.

The kettle begins to whistle shrilly. Michael goes to make the tea.

"I picked up your trash," Ursula says quietly. "I took it out to the garbage. The *downstairs* trash, that is."

"I'll have to do it over. Oh shit." Carter runs out the back door.

"Sugar or honey?" Michael asks.

"Whatever."

Michael uses sugar, measuring it exactly, a level teaspoon. Ursula wonders if it is a concern for calories or neatness.

Carter runs back in, clutching his towel up so tightly around his middle, his bottom isn't covered.

"Go put some pants on, son," Michael says.

"Mom! God, Mom! You threw the kitchen garbage right on top of my papers. They're all gucky."

"Have fun, Carter." Ursula sighs. She wonders if this involves friends of Carter's. Some of the rich ones, doing it for a thrill.

"Pants," Michael says.

Carter goes upstairs. Ursula sips her tea. Michael calls the police. When she hears them at the door, she goes up to look in on Juliette.

She can hear Michael speaking calmly to the officer. Someone comes to the top of the stairs, pauses, then goes down again.

Ursula sits down on Juliette's bed. The room is dark except for the spill of outside light through the blind. Juliette is crying, flung across the bed in her shirt, panties, and socks. Her discarded jeans hang off the bed at the end. "It's all right, sweetie," Ursula soothes. "It's all very shocking, but I'm sure the thieves were disappointed."

"What do I care?" Juliette says.

"And I'm not mad."

Juliette moans.

Ursula considers going to a motel. She is exhausted. Even a cheap, dingy motel sounds good. She still needs to wash her hair, and she longs for a shower. She is due at the caterer's at eight in the morning. On a Saturday. And she still hasn't called Katie.

Juliette begins to cry in earnest. "There's nobody in the world who cares about me."

"Juliette!"

"Besides you and Dad."

"Marina?"

"We're in dance together. And French."

"That doesn't mean you're not friends."

"It doesn't mean we are. She doesn't care. She doesn't understand. Besides, we both want the same roles. How can we be friends?"

"Julie, Julie."

"Don't tell me about when you were young."

"I wasn't," Ursula says, offended, feeling caught. After her mother left Evanston for Seattle, Ursula went a little crazy. She did worse than sit in parked cars smoking dope. Ten of them got raided one Saturday night at a Holiday Inn. They had made too much noise. Fortunately, that was all they'd had time for, noise. And look, she turned out fine.

"You can't make friends doing things you don't really like doing."

"Mother, I am not some *poor* kid."

Ursula cannot make her children understand that kids have troubles in all sorts of families. They love to use her job against her. I'm not one of *them*, they always say.

"I bet Gramma Clare will come down from Seattle for your ballet opening. Let's call her this weekend."

"I hope so," Juliette says. She sounds seven years old.

"If I sit here, don't you think you can go to sleep?"

Juliette sits up and pulls off her tee shirt. She is wearing a skinny tank top underneath. Her little nipples press like buttons against the knit material. She pulls the sheet back and crawls under.

"I love you so much, Juliette. Maybe you haven't met the right kids yet. This isn't the whole world. Kids with your interests—" Ursula pats the sheet on Juliette's shoulder.

"I never will, here." Juliette says sleepily.

"Let's just close our eyes a moment," Ursula suggests, and lies down beside her daughter.

She wakes suddenly from what she thinks at first is a bad dream. Someone is being sick in the bathroom. She walks into the hall. It is Michael, vomiting.

Ursula doesn't know what to do. "Are you okay?" she calls. Michael continues retching. She goes and gets in their bed to wait for him. She expects him to come straight to bed, but he washes and goes back downstairs. She lies awake a long time, thinking about him getting sick. Why can't he just yell like her? Or cry? He was sick like that when they took his father away to the mental hospital. He wouldn't talk about it. but he threw up for days. He called it the flu.

If it was Carter, she would wet a washrag and hand it to him. If it was Juliette, she would be on her knees beside her, holding her until she was finished.

But Michael? On his knees, gagging on theft? Or whatever was happening with his parents? Or his job? The kids? Her?

He still has not come to bed so she goes to look for him. She finds him in the basement with Fish, watching stock car races on TV. "Lucky," she says. "They didn't think to look down here."

Fish is drunk. "It's Big Mama," he says. "Come to collect Daddy." He sounds almost affectionate.

"Goodnight, Ursula," Michael says without looking up. The couch he and Fish are sitting on has sprung its springs, and the two of them are at different heights, seated Mutt and Jeff.

"Come to bed?" Ursula pleads.

Michael reaches for Fish's glass. It looks like whiskey tonight. "Later," he says. "Not now." He leans forward, watching something on the television, then punches Fish on the knee. "What balls that Turk has," he says. It sounds so unlike Michael, so vulgar and insipidly masculine, Ursula imagines for the first time his fraternal conversations are secretive, scandalous, pulling out threads of Michael's character she doesn't see, doesn't even know about. She feels, suddenly, desperately afraid of her brother-in-law.

She goes back upstairs to call Katie.

Katie has already gone to bed. When Ursula tells her about the papers being served, she says, "I'm sleepy," and hangs up abruptly. Ursula is disappointed; she wanted to talk about the burglary.

Ursula goes into the bathroom and sits on the cool floor. She tries to read from a new book she borrowed from Angela that day. It is about family therapy. The author is an expert on failure to individuate. The writing is stiff with current jargon. Ursula supposes there is something to be learned from the author, an eminent psychologist, but she cannot concentrate. Family therapy is a luxury of the middle class, like orthodontia. She finds herself wondering why Juliette wore her socks to bed. It seems more like Carter.

—21—

Friday is a day all tumbled for Geneva. She is relieved when Gully says he is going to make a sandwich and go scouting for firewood. There will still be a little snow in patches in the high country, but he might also find morel mushrooms and wildflowers lower down. She wonders if he is still looking back over areas where they searched for the doctor who disappeared in February, on his way to Bend. He will look for good places to cut wood. All winter he feeds the stove on the porch. He puts plastic over the screened windows and sits out there in a lawn chair rereading old adventure tales by Richard Halliburton or Joshua Slocum. His only move for hours might be to fetch wood from the woodpile. Now that it is spring, however, he doesn't sit down all day. He always wants to be doing something. He doesn't know how old he is.

Geneva has an appointment with Aggie Kolvitz at Heads Up for a permanent, and between the mess and stink of that, and all the gossiping Aggie likes to do, no way is Geneva going to get out of there in time to make lunch. Besides, Michael is coming by after school. She is going to make dinner so he will stay longer.

One of the things that pleases Geneva about their lives now that Gully is retired is her authority over the schedule of their meals. She spent a lot of years baking bread and cooking pots of food for dinner on the dot of six, with all the mess to clean up after. Now she makes the main meal in the middle of the day, and they eat leftovers or soup around five. When Gully in summer goes fishing, with plans to camp for the night, she is happy as can be to have crackers and milk before bed, if she eats at all. Anybody knows this is a healthy way to eat as you get older and your bowels get crotchety.

She made meat loaf on Thursday and there is enough of it left for a meal, along with nice red potatoes sprinkled with dill the way Gully likes them. She has a freezer full of packaged vegetables. Gully sometimes helps out at the fishing lodge a few miles upriver, when something mechanical breaks down or there is mending to be done—fences, porches, roof gutters, what have you. The lodge manager pays him partly in frozen food, canned milk, and appliances they are replacing. Gully fixes up the appliances and sells them for a nice bit of pocket change. The other day he cleaned a mouse nest out of a dryer, and it ran like new. Now he has two washers on the porch. It wouldn't surprise Geneva if she found buyers by mentioning them to Aggie Kolvitz.

Gully is late. Michael arrives first, looking unhappy and tired. He says school is getting him down. She is surprised; Michael has never been a complainer. He takes after her in that. His slow, almost drawled expression of fatigue and discouragement pinches her, the way her ovaries used to do midmonth.

"I know I ought to think of them as cans of soup, going by me on the line, but Ma, I can't do enough. I just fill time."

He was such a good student. All A's and stars on his papers, then National Honor Society and a rash of small scholarships to help him go to Portland State. He wasn't always looking for a way to skip, like Fish, though both boys liked their outings, mostly together. Fish might have done more—he was smart as a whip, too—but Gully never took their education seriously enough, and Fish never listened to anything Geneva said. He wanted to be like his Pop, he said. Lord he might have meant a hundred different things by that. Gully had had his own rough times when he was young, but he had had more school than Geneva. To her stepfather, she had been a coolie; somebody, along with her brother, to hire out, often to farmers, sometimes to odd labor, like the time they tore down a tenth-rate little hotel. Two half-grown kids with a crowbar between them! Her stepfather hadn't been hard on Ruby, maybe because she was the youngest— nearly ten years between her and Geneva—or maybe because she was pretty. Ruby used to sit on the old fart's lap and sweet-talk him to get a nickel for ice-cream. She always went to school. She always had a lunch.

"It's a good job, son," Geneva tells Michael. When he was a boy he used to say he would live in the jungle and make maps of rivers. He used to pore over *National Geographic*. Geneva bought them at garage sales, and later by subscription. "Listen to this, Ma!" Michael would shout, and read about some remote tribe in the heart of the Amazon. Or Borneo, or the Congo. Fish would say, "I'll go too, and build us a boat." Gully would say, "Better that than this." Which hurt; he was talking about their lives. They all sat around the table one night looking at an atlas when Gully said, banging his fist on the book, "Maybe we can't go to New Guinea, but by gum we can see the country we're in!" That was when he went out and brought an old school bus and fixed it up. That bus was home to them for ten months. Gypsies. What a time they'd had.

She doesn't know what schools pay their teachers, but they give them insurance and pensions; good benefits. Teachers have unions. It gives Geneva a great deal of comfort to know that Michael is secure. Young people don't remember what it was like when you only had what you had and when it was gone you had nothing. Insurance still seems like a miracle to her. Why, the medical costs of the past fifteen years would have wiped them out entirely, without the union insurance. There was Gully's breakdown, and small crises after that: his angina, her bad feet and hiatal hernia. She wonders if she is working on an ulcer. Now they get a little pension from the union fund, and Social Security. With what Gully picks up fixing appliances for sale, doing odd jobs, and Geneva sometimes helping with the cooking for big dinners at the lodge, they do all right. Michael and Ursula have a lot more. Their big house, two cars. Clothes, tvs, video machines, cameras, skis. Well, that was what Gully and Geneva hoped for their children. When you grew up poor, that was how you kept going a lot of the time, by thinking of the lives your children would lead if you were strong and persevered.

Fisher is the worry. He will be forty-five the Fourth of July, just like Michael, and he is still rootless and unhappy. She hoped he would make the navy a career, but she should have known better. Too many things to go wrong. The service is, above all, an homage to authority. Fisher couldn't see the advantage in turning yourself over, that yielding decisions could be a release. He came to that rightly enough, from a double line of malcontents and drifters. Fisher has his father's dislike for folks in charge, and his suspicion of promises. He has his taste for wandering, too. All that, without Gully's iron spine that kept him on his feet through a depression, when his mother had to say she didn't have the wherewithal to feed him. Fisher talked about switching to the Coast Guard when his navy time was up—it sounded better suited to him, smaller and more interesting, and maybe, in a war, safer—but one day he was back in Portland in civvies. The Coast Guard hadn't wanted him. He never said where he'd been since his discharge. He was nearly a year getting home.

Gully and Geneva have paid cash for everything they ever had their whole married lives. The only thing was, Evelyn's sudden death caught them by surprise. Geneva had to take money from Ruby to pay for the funeral, though they paid it back, all of it, in three months' time. Geneva stood beside the open grave in a drizzling rain, watching her first-born, her girl-child, laid in the dirt, and she thought, minding it something awful, *I never thought I'd have to ask Ruby for help.*

"It is a good job," Michael agrees. "And by September I always feel up to it. I always like the kids." He grins at his mother and pats his belly, which has grown rounder in the last year. Fish's still looks like a board. "You put on a little weight, it drags you down," Michael says, as though he can tell his mother something about aging. "People think it is so sweet, summers off. But by the time you go to school, and you squeeze in extra jobs to make ends meet while your salary is so low, I figure it's summer keeps older teachers at it. They're worn out, and it would be too much if you didn't have that long break to look forward to."

"So now you're one of the older ones?" Geneva thinks her

sons are good-looking and sturdy. They have their father's strong will before any physical challenge. But neither of them has any real idea of what it is to work past the point where you think you can.

Michael takes a milk carton out of the refrigerator and pours himself half a glass of milk. "Don't you figure forty-five is some kind of dividing line?" He drinks and pulls the glass away to reveal a white moustache, which he wipes with his forearm, as he has done since he was three years old.

Geneva knows something about current thinking. She reads magazines, and an occasional book of popular psychology, if Mary Courter showed her a new title. "Don't tell me you're in one of those crisis things," she teases her son, hoping it is a joke. "I saw a show on *Oprah Winfrey* about middle-aged men who decided they would rather be women. Imagine that."

Michael laughs, and Geneva relaxes. "The way I figure it, son, life is an unpredictable series of jolts to the system, and God judges you by how high you bounce. Having kids, having troubles, getting old. I can't even tell you much about any of it, things change too fast. You have to do everything your own way now. Though it does seem it ought to be easier for you, with your education." She rinses Michael's glass and sits down at the counter that juts out at a right angle to the line of the kitchen cabinets and sink. Her foot catches the little plastic garbage can and almost knocks it over. She sets it upright before she speaks again. "Now don't take this as criticism," she begins. Michael's face is perfectly placid. He never shows what he is thinking. His father has a habit of blinking when he dislikes the way the conversation is going. It warns her, his eyes flapping. If she doesn't back off he will walk away. "But it does seem to me it *is* a lucky thing to have summers free. You have a chance to stoke the fire a little every year. Most people don't get that. The most paid vacation your father ever saw was two weeks in a year. You know what his idea of a vacation was? Changing jobs." Though he took off a few times. Once he went from work to the train station. He sent her a postcard from El Paso. He was only gone a month, though. Came back, said he didn't know what had got into him. Said he saw a lot of sights, then went back to work. "There were plenty of summers your dad would have liked some time off, but in Oregon you work hardest then, in good weather, if you're a laborer."

"I know, Ma. Don't you think I remember how hard you both worked when I was growing up?" She would think he would remember. He was always a help to her, a lot more than Evelyn, who should have been. Evelyn used to whine and fuss about housework. She didn't think she should have to get dressed on the weekend. She moved out the day she turned eighteen. Geneva said to her, the last time she saw her, "Please come home, darling. At least come stay a little while." Evelyn said. "Pop wouldn't like it. You don't know, Ma. He never liked me, and now he wouldn't for sure." She must have meant because she was pregnant, but Geneva didn't know that then.

She doesn't want to complain, it isn't her way. She is grateful not to have spent her whole life tied to one place, doing one thing, the way a lot of women do. She has never been bored by marriage. She fell in love with Gully's light heart and she rode it around the country twice, to Mexico and Guatemala, across Canada. She had a happy year in the shipyards during the war, before Evelyn came along. She lived in old BLM cabins, school buses, garages, the backs of trucks. She loved Gully's adventuresome spirit. The underside of it, the way he needs to be alone, to dig down deep to a place that hurts—that was a surprise to her. But they got through hard times and this is the reward, growing old together. It isn't boring anymore to have one place and a life that repeats itself day to day. And it is a bonus to have close-by sons.

"I think I'll help Fish this summer with some carpentry jobs." Michael speaks so quietly she isn't sure what she heard. She turns what she believes is her better ear toward Michael. "He's had several people ask him to work. Has to hire out like a handyman, by the hour, because he isn't bonded or anything. I might look into that." Michael shakes his head slightly as he speaks, agreeing with himself.

So that's it. A gush of pure pleasure goes through Geneva, as though to wash her bones. "You'd like that kind of work?" Gully always had those two out making something or taking something apart. They built boats, birdhouses, radios, cars out of pieces of other ones. There was an endless parade of

Fisher projects. Gully was proud of what he could do with his hands, of being a welder. He built ships for this country, and machinery that carved out roads in Alaska. He worked on dams (though he never mentions them anymore). He built every house they ever owned, except this one, and he improved it.

"I would like it, Ma," Michael says. He pops a knuckle and shakes his hand out.

Gully comes in, calling to her as he goes through the big porch. "Genny!" he calls. He is with some old coot he met in the woods. Homer. This one looks as bad as his dog-crazy friend Austin Melroy. Homer is wearing a plaid flannel shirt, a worn-out pair of wash pants, a Levi jacket, and boots. He smells to high heaven of sweat, liquor, and woodsmoke.

"Sure pleased to meet you ma'am," he says. He is respectful for a bum. Who talks like that these days? Maybe Gully rehearsed him, to cozy up to her. "My wife, she's a sucker for a sweet word," he could have said.

Gully apologizes for being late. "We got to jawing before I saw how low the sun had got."

Geneva stiffens. "You wash up outside." She has never liked it when Gully messed up her kitchen. There is a sink in the laundry room and another back of the trailer, where she has a table for potting, though she has let the flowers all go this year. If she wants to see flowers, she can look in the neighbors' yards. Her back hurts.

As soon as the two men are out the door she says to Michael, "I don't think he can sleep right if he hasn't preached a little. Dragging in a bum like that! You've seen those little books he carries in his overalls? He takes them out and reads them to anybody who will sit still for it. Sentimental dribble." Gully is a man who finds it hard to say happy birthday, let alone I love you. Yet here he is quoting poets, preachers, the Bible.

"He seems to be feeling happy, Ma." Michael takes the extra plate she hands him and sets it on his side of the counter, then pulls a chair over from the little desk with the telephone. "Really, he looks good to me. He's already getting some color in his face."

"There's something about it I don't like." She doesn't want Michael to misunderstand her. "Your dad always went by the Bible, mind you. He didn't go to church for a long time, but he knew the Word. He knew the Commandments. But this stuff eggs him on past all reason. He's got good advice all mixed up with nonsense, and there's *too much of it.* Who does he think he is? A missionary? Does he think he is supposed to save these fellows?" She turns and moves her head toward the screen door. She can't hear the men yet. "I bet you, right now, he's got him out in that yard telling him how *he* used to drink. How he doesn't anymore. Talking, while dinner's getting hard around the edges." It galls her that Gully uses the past like that. She thinks it ought to be a private thing. She thinks he makes himself out worse than he ever was, for the effect. After the treatments at the hospital he didn't remember things right. He used to get morose, and go off by himself and drink some, that much is true. But he never stumbled around acting crazy, and he never drank so that it interfered with his work. The meetings he's been going to for years now rile him. She thought they were a temporary measure, to tide him over after the hospital. Can't he see how much they disturb him? Why else does he need to get away so much, in the woods? *What is out there?* Couldn't he give up history for the sake of the present? It isn't fair. She never butted him around with his faults and lapses, when they hurt the most, *when they mattered.* She doesn't need to be reminded now. Sleeping dogs ought not to be yapping and growling. That's why they have a saying about them.

She rummages around in the refrigerator and comes up with a can of pears and half a carton of cottage cheese. She gives Michael the can with an opener. She spoons Miracle Whip into the cottage cheese and stirs it around, then plops it onto the fruit halves, two to a plate for the men and none for her.

Michael pushes his plate back toward her. "Take one of these."

"Can't stand the stuff," she snorts. She can finally hear Gully and that man clomping up the steps into the tiny hall.

"Bless the Lord and paint the rafters. Now we can eat!" she says.

Gully seems cheerful. "I worked up an appetite."

Homer says, "I had coffee and crackers this morning." He has a wily look. He takes his time deciding on one of the two available plates before he sits down beside Michael.

People who don't eat regular have to store it up when they

can. She remembers that from a long hungry childhood. It has been fifty years since she had that terrible gnawing in her belly. Gully always kept them all fed. He always knew she could stretch a dollar and a bean, and he counted on that, but the dollars were always there. He left her money when he went off to be by himself. She's been sad, and she's been glad, but in half a century with Gulsvig Fisher, she hasn't ever been hungry.

"Help yourself," she says pleasantly to Homer, and passes him the meat loaf.

## —22—

"Homer here worked the Tok highway," Gully says.

She must look surprised. Gully says, "Sure a small world, ain't it?"

"That so?" she manages to say. The "ain't" was for Homer's benefit, she supposes. A man who has read the Bible, William Shakespeare, and Herman Melville knows better.

"Yes, ma'am," Homer says with his mouth half-full. "Lived in this old tin-can trailer all one winter, burning scrap wood and green logs, waiting for the work to start up again. From the Canada border up above Tok."

"The highway went past that."

Homer laughs. "Sure did, but I'd heard about work farther north that paid real good and—well, it sounded like an adventure. I wanted to see the real north. It didn't work out so good." He takes a huge mouthful of potatoes.

"Think of the miles they built with my machinery," says Gully, with awe in his voice. She hopes he won't start naming places. He loves to look at a map and put his finger where he's been, where they have been as a couple, as a family. Best of all he likes to point where a ship has sailed that he helped build, or a road. One time in Guatamela, they saw a railroad engine he said was from Sumter, Oregon. He clears his throat. "A man takes a journey one step at a time." Homer swallows and says, "Sometimes it's that first step kills you."

Gully knows. "That's what friends are for," he says. He sticks one finger up in front of his nose, his way of announcing a quotation. He says, "The comfort of a true friend is an affirmation of life." He looks over at Michael. "Homer's got a dilly of a drinking problem." Geneva thinks Gully looks pleased.

"I never heard of nobody getting talked out of drinking," she says sourly.

"Oh yes, ma'am, I'm sorry but they sure do." Gully sucks at his teeth. "Somewhere, every night of every week of the year, and lots of noontimes too, that very thing is going on." He holds up his finger again. "Though, 'Let no one be deluded that a knowledge of the path can substitute for putting one foot in front of the other.' M. C. Richards."

"If you say so." Geneva clears their plates. Homer has sopped up the last streak of grease with his bread.

The silver maple outside the kitchen window rustles in the evening breeze. The tree sprang up all on its own after the fire. Gully said it was from the roots of the tall tree twenty yards away, on the Lewis property. He said the trauma of the fire must have let it loose.

"I could make coffee," she says unenthusiastically. She can feel all three of them getting set to run.

"I've gotta get home, Ma," says Michael. She doesn't comment. She has never asked a married son to give her time that belongs to his wife. She does wonder what they do on a Friday night, though, that he can't sit with her a little while, especially now that he can see how his father is.

"We'll set a spell out in the yard." Gully pushes Homer toward the door.

"Appreciate the chow, ma'am," Homer says. Geneva sets her mouth to keep from saying something she will regret. Homer seems to her the veteran of too many soup kitchens.

Gully fed that other fellow on Tuesday night, hauling him home after that blessed meeting. She stayed in her room. Three pieces of pie was all that was left. Gully said *he* ate most of it, but he couldn't eat that much in a sitting. He gave it away to hold that old drunk captive to his talk.

She lies on her bed with the pillows all propped and the tv on with no sound. She tries to read from a *Good Housekeeping*, but there isn't one article to catch her eye. Editors think women die at forty.

Off her little night stand (a fruit crate covered with contact paper), she picks up one of the invitations she sent out a few weeks earlier:

> You are invited
> to celebrate
> with Gully and Geneva Fisher

Fifty years! On the back she printed "An old-fashioned recipe for a successful marriage." Gully thought most of it up, though it had been her idea, and she set down the words. They had a good time figuring it out.

1. Get together one boy and one girl.
2. Set the date.
3. Get a blood test, buy a license.
4. Find two friends or hangers-on.
5. Do it.
6. Stick to it.

People will either understand or think it is funny. It is the truth, though, and more people could stand to know it. Young people expect too much of marriage. What do her own sons want? Michael has done okay, all things considered. He is a good family man. Ursula isn't the friendliest woman, but she does her share, and they have the kids. But Fish and Katie are a downright wonder. She didn't even know they were married for the longest time. She hardly saw them half a year at a time. She never saw Katie pregnant. Nobody brought it up. It was little Juliette who told her, and Juliette who said Katie went away with her baby and came back alone. At least Katie had it. At least she didn't kill it instead.

Geneva never asks Fish anything. She can remember times he said he was going out for cigarettes, and she wouldn't see him for a month. When he was in Vietnam he didn't write for so long it drove her crazy. She wrote his commanding officer, who sent the chaplain to talk to Fish, who wrote her to say if she ever did that again he wouldn't come home when it was over.

She knows what it is with Fish and Katie. They are too self-centered for a baby. Neither one of them has grown up. Though she can't speak for Katie's mother, she knows she did her level best. You can look at Michael and see that. Fish could have turned out better. Twins, like two sides of a coin. She thinks Gully had a lot to do with it. There was something he recognized in Fish right away, something Michael didn't have. Now he is sorry. He said just the other day, "Isn't it something? Fish buys a house on the GI bill, and here neither one of them lives in it!"

She will be surprised if she sees Fish or Katie either one tomorrow. She asked Katie to take her shopping for napkins, because she thought it would give them a little time together. She wanted to see how Katie was getting along. But Katie stood her up, no different than she might have figured.

She goes to Gully's room at the other end of the trailer and straightens up the bed. Every morning Gully pulls the blankets up over whatever mess he has made of sheets and pillows, and, every day, sometime before bed, she straightens it all up, tucks things back in, and pulls the blankets back up as if she has not touched it.

The room has the faint acrid smell of Gully. Socks on the floor of the closet, like a little boy. His wool sweater on a hook, stretching out the neck. She sits on the edge of his bed. The mattress curves in like a hammock. She told Gully they both needed mattresses last year, but Gully insisted on her getting one, and not him. He said he liked his bed as it was.

He has things stuck up all over his walls. Clippings from the newspaper (the dead doctor; a new find in Egypt; a couple of cartoons; a photo of Michael and some of his students with their birdhouses). There are drawings from each of the kids when they were little. The drawings are brittle and brown around the edges. It does tug your heart to see the charm of children's art. *Their* children. People the same size as the trees beside them. A lion with a curly red mane. Flowers with yellow moons in the center. The drawings were in an atlas during the fire, that was what saved them. There is a photograph of Fish, too, at the radio on board his ship, smiling, looking straight at you. His face is cleanshaven; he looks like a teenager. All the other photographs he sent home from Vietnam for safekeeping were burned up. All the school pictures and report cards, the certificates, merit badges, and ribbons. Evelyn's yellow afghan she made for 4H. It would be a comfort to have it now. There isn't anything of Evelyn left, except a few birthday cards that Geneva saved in a metal box from the fire.

Evelyn probably did one of those drawings, but Geneva doesn't know which one. She could ask Gully, but it would make them both sad. He has his own way with memories. She leaves Gully's room and shuts the door. It does no good to go in there. Her room is hers, and in there there is nothing of the past to cling to, except that one box. She lives in the present tense. She has Gully, that's what there is. Michael has a family. Fish has his ways. Evelyn is dead. They haven't even had a dog in ten years.

She stands at the screen door that opens onto the big closed-in porch where Gully has a wood stove, a shop table, and his appliances waiting to be fixed and sold. She has her laundry room, and the freezer.

Through the screens she can see the men's shapes against the back of the truck. She can hear their voices. They might talk all night. Then Gully will be worn out before the party. Whatever Michael says, Gully seems frail to her. She worries.

Every night of the week, Gully said. Every night, AA meetings, was what he meant. For a long while he was gone two, three, four nights a week some weeks, until she thought she would scream from being left. He needed to go; those people had something to give him that she could not. She didn't say anything, any more than she had said anything when he got drunk and set the shed on fire, any more than when he called Evelyn a slut for coming in late when she was sixteen and looked like a full-grown woman. It doesn't do any good to do battle with a man's needs. You put him in God's hands and go around cleaning up after. You are thankful for the good days.

Now Gully goes on Tuesday. Once in a while he goes out to the VA Domiciliary and talks to the fellows there, besides. And he goes out scouting, not so much for wood as for men who might need him. "What do you spent your time with old sots for?" she asked one night. Gully said he had to. It was something he had to do. "You have to reach out, to keep yourself steady." She hears him sometimes in his room, whisper-reading from the Bible. He keeps a little notebook too, scribbling in it while he sits out on the porch in the rainy months. Keeping track of his sin and misery, she bets.

"Why don't you talk to your own son then?" she said. What she meant was *All your little quotes don't do any good with Fish.* Gully looked so stricken, she regretted saying it.

"Don't I wish, Ma," was all he said.

She turns off her light before Gully comes back in the house. She knows he won't say anything if her light is out. He will respect that she is either asleep or wants him to think she is. But it is ten-thirty at night, and tomorrow they are celebrating their marriage, which has lasted more years than people used to live.

She pulls her robe tight across the front of her and ties the belt, then steps to her door, just as Gully goes into the bathroom. She goes in the kitchen and gets a drink of water. Through the wall she hears him splashing. There will be water all over the place.

"You want something?" she asks when he comes out. He takes a glass of water. She sits down at the counter and so does he, across from her.

"How did he get back?" she asks. She wonders where the old man camped. What a way to live!

Gully has taken off his shirt washing up, and has pulled his overalls back up over his bare chest. He looks like a bird with a scrawny neck. The upper parts of his arms are still knotty and strong, but his hands looks frail.

"I put him down in the truck," he says. He keeps a bed under a canopy for his forays in the woods and mountains. "He'll be on his way at dawn."

"I see." She doesn't, not really.

He reaches over and pats her hand. "That would be me out there, if there hadn't been you." Then he gets up and says good night.

Geneva goes back to bed and lies in the dark listening to the tree leaves. She thinks about the first time Gully touched her. It was a long, long time ago, but she remembers it very clearly. The last time she has long ago forgotten, but the memory of the first is with her forever.

—23—

It seems to Katie that the very ease of getting a divorce keeps a person from thinking it all the way through. She feels victimized by the system, as if she is being sucked through a vacuum tube, her life out of her hands, ever since she signed a paper her lawyer thrust at her in return for four hundred dollars. You used to have to show cause—adultery, abuse, mental cruelty. She remembers her mother talking about a friend of the family, saying, "He certainly gave her cause." If you still had to do it that way, she would never have gone past the idea. Of what could she accuse Fish? How could she build an ugly file of bitter reinterpretations of their past? She was there, too. She is entirely complicit. There have been minor infidelities, but they were only larks to wound her or soothe him, and they passed quickly. There were unscheduled jaunts taken without regard for Katie's feelings, but that was something in his blood. Once when they were in Berkeley, he got mad and left her standing in a Chinese grocery store and drove to Reno with a week's wages from the shipyards. She can't remember why he did that, but she does not doubt that she provoked him.

There was that time he hit her, before she went to Texas, but she already punished him for that, didn't she? She was gone for so long. She can think of more reasons for staying than for going. Fish is like a part of her she can't quite dig out. There are all the things he knows how to do—building, repairing, inventing—that she cannot manage. Once, in B.C., he took a woodshed on a hillside slope—he'd been hired to help the Turkish owner clear the hill to make an RV campground—and turned it into a cozy lodge for them. He brought water down from a tiny creek, made a wood stove out of a metal drum, built them a bed from scrap lumber. He read *The Sotweed Factor* to her by kerosene lamp.

There are all the places he had been before he met her, experiences he brings to her like an abandoned garden of perennials. He tells her stories, like a man plucking flowers.

Maybe somebody could make a case against him because he has so little regard for people in general. They could say he is antisocial. But Fish's attitude confirms Katie's own assessment of most of the world, and it gives her the comfort of a cohort. She knows that Fish dislikes a lot of people, most of them mere flickers of experience across his life, but he loves Katie. She stands out from all the others, with him. He told her her little breasts were perfect. He told her that her skin could be experienced as the organ it is. He said she has a perfect cunt. She remembers where they were when he said those things. She can remember the pile of dirty clothes on the floor near

the end of the mattress where they lay. She remembers everything about the times when he talked like that.

Katie's friend Maureen, who lives in the apartment across
the hall from her in a cut-up old Victorian house near the
theatre, and cooks in a vegetarian deli, says that relationships
are like mirrors shining your history back at you. You are
what your family has been, she says. You live out the family
myths. She talks about her "family of origin." She gives Katie
books to read that are full of case histories to illustrate the
impact of childhood on adult life. She also gives her smaller,
less densely written books designed for small, quick readings
at night, before bed, ones full of good advice about serenity,
self-esteem, assertiveness, and intimacy. The second kind of
book has a lot of white space, checklists, and bold headings. It
makes it easy for you, repeating every point a lot of times, in
a kind of literary mantra.

Katie isn't much of a reader, but she has burrowed her way
through a good many pages of Maureen's books. What she
understands from them is this: Your parents acted out a
design of living that was probably made up of their reactions
to their parents, and so on. In this manner you learned how
men and women get along. Then, too, each parent had a trip
to play on you, and all of that taught you how to act with
people when you grew up. Your mind got stamped, like visas
on a passport to unhappy states. On the one hand, no matter
what you thought of your childhood, you looked for ways to
bring it into your adult life. You opened presents on Christmas eve, if that's how it was done in your family, and if this
conflicted with your lover's ideas about Christmas, you
fought it out until somebody gave up. You looked for lovers
who could be what you had not been, strong where you were
weak, yin for your yang, or was it the other way around?

The notion intrigues Katie. She has spent a lot of time
trying to think what it means for her. Truthfully, she can't
remember much about her family. Her father was from
Mississippi, and his parents had already died before Katie
was born. Her mother's parents lived on the other side of
Texas, and she hardly ever saw them. And Katie's own parents seem vague, like people viewed through a mist.

She grew up in a house where no one had much to say,
except for her mother telling her what to do. Her father,

when he spoke, said things he might have said to anybody's child. Pass the potatoes. Here's the funnies. Pull the shade down, change the channel. He didn't notice when she cut her hair and outgrew her dresses. When she broke her arm he didn't notice the cast until it was pointed out to him, and then he only said, "Did it hurt?" and he turned away before she could tell him what a surprise it had been.

What Katie has figured out now, amateur that she is, is that her father was remote to her mother, too. He was an inaccessible man. It may be true that Katie married a man who isn't always there, but Katie has never attempted the kinds of accommodations her mother made for her father. She has not tried to pretend she and Fish are an ordinary couple. She wonders about her father, wonders if he was a drunk who stayed away on binges, or went to bars on the way home. She remembers that he slept on the couch frequently, and she knows he was late very often, but she cannot remember anything that suggests alcohol. She always assumed her father worked hard. She always thought it was because he was trying to please her mother.

Maureen is not willing to let go of the possibilities in this analysis, though. They have a lot of free time, and talking about childhood fills some of it up. Katie lounges in Maureen's apartment, which has better furnishings, left by a prior tenant. While they play old Donahue programs on tape, and are sometimes distracted into discussions about the problems Donahue has packaged for them, they tell one another their stories. Maureen's are richer tales. She says she has worked on the details. She is disappointed that Katie hits so many blank walls, but Katie's "amnesia" excites her, too, because, she says, when Katie probes a little deeper, and the walls come tumbling down, oh boy, watch out, Katie will break out, feel the pain, and break free.

All of this supposition is based on Maureen's premise that talk heals. Maureen says at first it doesn't even matter if anybody tells you anything in return, if they'll only listen. Later, though, you need a sponsor, and later than that, maybe a therapist, or a spiritual mentor.

Maureen used to be in Alcoholics Anonymous. She still goes to Al-Anon, because she keeps falling in love with guys who stay high, and because she worries too much. Lately she has also been going to a group for children of dysfunctional families, run along the same AA lines of twelve steps, anonymity, and sponsorship. Her mother was a drunk, and Maureen has learned how many ways her mother's dysfunction affects her, even now. Maureen has a sponsor in each group, and is a sponsor to several people, but she can't afford a therapist. She says this means it isn't time yet. Once or twice a year she goes to a workshop to help her growth. Her last one was about personal mythology; she learned new insights into her tremendous sense of being doomed. The workshop before that one was a Celtic ritual. Everything feeds your transformation, she says. Her favorite step is number twelve, a spiritual enlightenment. She says next she is going to read Hildegard of Bingen.

Maureen tends to use a lot of catchy phrases and words from the books she reads, and Katie thinks maybe Maureen takes a little too much for granted about what Katie is able to absorb. Katie wonders if, when Maureen says "Talk heals," she isn't really talking shorthand for a more substantive process Maureen hasn't quite got a finger on, or can't quite describe. Or it may be that there is a formula for transforming yourself that doesn't translate outside of twelve-step groups. It's like, Coke isn't Pepsi.

Maureen says, "Anybody as strained in her relationship with her mother as you are has something she hasn't worked out. Including a lot of anger, I bet." She hastens to add that you cannot change the past. You have to change yourself. Katie protests that her mother isn't especially important to her anymore, that her mother has no power over her. She knows how weak that sounds when you consider that her mother is raising Katie's daughter. This is a shocking thought: that Rhea is being shaped by a woman with whom Katie cannot bear to spend five minutes.

Still, when Katie gives the matter a little more thought, she finds it intriguing to attempt to create a structure for her past, one that includes Fish, and, yes, Rhea, too. She can see there are a lot of variables to consider. The past seems to be a giant homework assignment, almost as bad as trig and chemistry.

Katie went to a meeting with Maureen once. It was the group about having horrible parents. She was stunned by the emotionalism. She cannot imagine herself speaking up like that, telling old childhood hurts and present pains. Why would anybody want to know? And how would she ever find words? If she talked about her mother, June would probably sound prudent and generous. It is Katie who would sound petty and stupid.

Furthermore, she was embarrassed by the buckets of tears shed, the storm of howls, the displays of anger, and resentment, and self-pity. She was left shaken. "Yeah," some of the others said when someone finished. They said, "We hear you," and "Thank you for sharing."

The group seemed to be for people who have not worked out their adulthood and need the past to blame. The experience left Katie feeling defensive; she didn't think she belonged with such a group. She pointed out to Maureen that if she wants therapeutic talk, she has a sister-in-law in social work. Maureen cried, "And what good does that do you! You can't let it hang out in your husband's brother's kitchen. Those people are all invested in the same family lies!" As Maureen was talking, a grossly fat woman on Donahue started telling about being asked to leave a restaurant because she was offending other diners. The woman began to quiver as she talked; her arms and jowls shook, and then she sobbed, moving all over, like a huge caught tuna. Donahue asked if she was okay, he asked her how she was doing. She blubbered, "I'm hungry."

Katie and Maureen looked at one another in horror, and then burst out laughing. It felt better between them. Maureen said maybe Katie should come to Al-Anon. "It's a quieter group. They focus on the present, and on positive steps a person can take. They don't dwell on the hurts." Katie could only lift her shoulders slightly. She didn't know anything else to say. Maureen insisted, "First you start to talk. Then you start working the steps. Then you start to heal. You'll see, Katie. The things that trouble you don't belong to you like a treasure. Other people have been where you are, and moved on."

Maybe that was what Katie didn't like, the way Maureen and her groups threatened Katie's sense of uniqueness. She really doesn't see how strangers could understand. She doesn't think even Ursula understands. And she doesn't feel

sick, she feels confused. The impulse for the divorce has
become faint, and old, and wavering. There was a moment,
clearly, when it seemed the right thing to do. She can no
longer put her finger on that moment. She is no longer so
sure.

Maureen says that Katie has her feelings all locked up,
which, Katie understands, is another way of saying, "You're
kidding yourself." Katie doesn't answer, but she actually has a
good idea what Maureen means. She has a good idea what
could happen if she let go.

—24—

Because Jeff is out of town, and Friday night is lonely,
because there are no good movies in town, and she isn't
hungry enough to go out and eat alone, because Maureen is
going to Al-Anon and doesn't make a speech to Katie about
it, Katie decides to go, too.

She is surprised at the turnout on a Friday night. Most of
the people in the group are married. All of them are women.
In a little while Katie realizes Friday night is probably not
very different from other nights of the week for them.
Maureen finds a seat across the room, and Katie sits near the
door. She does not sense the tension of the group, the electricity that threatens to burst with sparks of pain. There is a
young woman, probably not yet twenty, and an elderly
woman with a cap of lovely white hair, and Katie and
Maureen; the other women look like housewives (if there is
such a look, which Katie still assumes there is).

Taking turns, the participants calmly read the principles of
the group, the twelve steps, and then several homilies or
"thoughts for the day." The special topic of the night, chosen
by this week's leader, is "One day at a time," which, it turns
out, is the general slogan of Al-Anon. The readings are all
variations on the basic idea that worry doesn't do any good,
that you really ought to focus on getting through the day in a
way that's best for you, that you shouldn't let other people get
your goat and so on. The simplicity of the passages makes
Katie uneasy. She finds them just slightly less challenging
than the slim paperbacks Maureen has been lending her.

As she listens to someone reading, she tunes out and starts making up silly little sayings of her own. She thinks, for example, "No one eats an apple whole." She catches herself smiling. You can say anything about anything, she thinks, and if you say it in little short sentences, strung together on a page or less, with a quotation at the bottom, you will have suggested something profound, especially if the quote is from *The Prophet*.

One woman does weep. She says she has moved here lately and has delayed joining the meetings because she is so caught up in worrying about her new job, getting her apartment in order, wondering about her grown daughter who lives in Portland. Somewhere in there she begins to cry. Katie likes the way the other woman speak up encouragingly. "You should have come sooner," one tells her, "but it doesn't matter, because you are here now." They say, "We know how you feel."

Katie has a strong urge to speak up. She considers telling them what is going on in her life, in order to see if they say, "We know just how you feel." That would be funny, since she doesn't know! She has begun a process that changes everything.

There is a woman in the group who works for the theatre, too. It isn't until the end of the meeting that Katie remembers what the woman does; she is a hostess in the members' lounge, a very pretty woman with delicate hands. She smiles at Katie, but Katie thinks since anonymity is a principle of the group, it would not be okay to speak to her afterwards. The woman's name is Joyce. She says she has had a hard time because she wants to take care of things right away. She hates having her life in suspension. She says, "My alcoholic is thinking of moving away. He thinks his problems have to do with a lack of meaningful work, and that he can't do any better in a small county. I want to rush right out and find him a job, or, failing that, get myself a better one!" She smiles ruefully. "The only thing that saves me is reading my literature. I wrote something down yesterday that I especially liked—" She digs in her shirt pocket and brings out a crumpled piece of note paper. " 'There is nothing I have to do. There is only someone to be.' " She bobs her head, as if the line she read tipped her off-balance a very little bit and she is settling again. "Thanks," she says, and the others say, "Thanks, Joyce."

Although she knows it is silly, when the spiral notebook makes its way to Katie, she writes her own name down, and copies Joyce's name and phone number onto the back of a brochure she puts in her purse. She studies the name a moment, thinking something in the way it is written will help explain who Joyce really is, but all Katie sees is a round pretty hand, the kind high school girls often work to develop, with circles for dots above the i's, and fat capitals. The J is perfectly symmetrical above and below the line. It looks like a bow lying sideways.

At the end, they all stand in a circle, holding hands. "Keep coming back!" they all say cheerfully. "It works."

She has the distinct impression that Joyce is looking straight at her. Maureen is watching Joyce. The women who are holding Katie's hands squeeze extra tightly before letting go. Although Katie does not think these women could ever understand her tie to Fish, or the complications of letting go, still she senses that the community of the group is a lot like a safety net under a high-wire walker.

Maureen says something to her as they walk out. Katie looks at her, not really hearing what she says. Not knowing what to say. She is thinking how it scares her, thinking of how she will feel when she falls.

—25—

Geneva is standing near one of the long draped tables in the River Cove Grange Hall. Her back is to the punch bowl and, large as she is, it looks as if a loss of balance might make her bring the whole thing down. She is talking to River Cove's librarian, Mary Courter, whom Geneva counts as a close friend, since Mary always calls her first when a new book comes in she thinks Geneva would like. Geneva is wearing a new outfit, all bought by mail from Penney's and Spiegels' catalogues. She wears sky blue polyester stretch pants and a blouse of gray sheer georgette with a rounded collar and peplum waist. She wears beige felt bedroom slippers slit at the sides to ease the pressure on her bunions, corns, and hammertoes. Her fresh permanent has taken well, and with her hair short and tight and up off her face, you can see how smooth and clear her skin really is. She is by no means a fat woman, only a big one, taller than anyone in the family, her generation or the next, with broad shoulders and hips and long legs that are a little bony below the knees. Good as she looks, she is hot. Polyester holds its shape but it doesn't breathe.

"I guess you can't blame the caterer," Geneva says wryly. She and Mary are both a little shaken by the appearance and rapid disappearance of the *hors d'oeuvres*. They did not take a bite before the food was whisked away. "It's not her fault the weather went hot when nobody expected it this early in May." Mary Courter shakes the silvery mound of her curls in agreement, and the two women talk on of hot spells they remember, and wet Junes, of sweet false springs that sometimes come in an Oregon February.

The punch, concocted of 7-Up, ginger ale, and two shades of sherbet, was set out too soon, before the food, and the sherbet has melted to froth, and then settled into scum. Iced tea or lemonade would have hit the spot, but Geneva left all the arrangements to Ursula, who wanted to be festive.

Ursula, standing at the other end of the table like half a pair of bookends, is nervously working the tablecloth between her fingers. She gave up smoking eight years ago, but sometimes she has to find something to do with her hands. She has pulled off many a button, picking at threads. Her coworkers tease her and say that one day she will stand up after a day of nerve-wracking court proceedings, and her clothes will fall right off her, every thread pulled free.

Ursula paid twelve dollars to rent the heavy white tablecloth, and another thirty-five dollars for the two uninspiring bouquets that adorn the center of the table. The net effect depresses her. She decides it is the damask cloth, so out of place in the Grange Hall. She would have done far better with a length of bright paper.

She glances around the room, wondering if this is the acme of the party, so soon. If so, they are in trouble. There is nothing to do but talk until the food is ready, and most of these people see one another every day as it is.

She no more than set down two trays of food than she saw

that they would lose their center of gravity in this heat. She took them right back to the kitchen cooler, where the cake is stored. The cake is a pretty thing, a sheet piled high with lardy frosting and emblazoned with FIFTY GOOD ONES, in green and yellow. She hopes Gully will have the patience for a bit of ceremony. Geneva cutting the cake, having her moment. She hopes the inscription is not too casual.

Geneva now looks as though she has backed away from the room and found its limits at the table's edge. Guests do not seem to have noticed her isolation, or else they do not want the responsibility of cheering up the guest of honor. Now that Mary Courter has moved on, Geneva looks positively grim, her mouth shut tightly as though taped. Of course she could go up to any one of her twenty or so guests—she has never been shy, and she loves to talk—but she stands her place with a stolid look. "People came," Ursula thinks of going to her and saying. "Give them that."

The cloth between Ursula's fingers is starting to feel hot from friction. Important people aren't even here yet—son and sister—and Gully has fled to the yard.

"It's not like she asked you to do it," Michael said that morning as Ursula, sleepy and resentful, was loading the car. Saturdays are for sleeping in. Why is all this rah-rah her responsibility? All Geneva has ever done for her is pass on envelopes of clipped coupons and recipes, and insult her at Christmas with gifts of control-top pantyhose.

"Didn't ask!" Geneva talked about her anniversary for months. Her hints had the subtlety of a broad board. It was her topic of the day at the Christmas table.

"Nowadays people break apart at the least little thing," she commented. She had been watching Gully as though he might have fled, too, if not for the strength of her attachment. Gully joined in, his voice tremulous. (He seems smaller and smaller these days.) "We've done good," he said. "Stuck it out, Ma and me." Nowadays Gully often mentions Geneva's will and loyalty. He speaks of AA and Jesus, both credited with his salvation. He speaks like a man at the end of a perilous journey, grateful and still weak. One day he came to his senses and there was Geneva, waiting. He owes her everything. His softly gruff, self-deprecatory manner embarrassed the children. Michael asked Juliette, who was staring off in the direction of the kitchen, to please pass the yams. Carter announced that he was never getting married. Juliette said, "Boy is that obvious. Nobody would have you." Michael, with unusual grace, asked his mother what she had been reading lately. She had been reading a book about the Irish civil war (surprise! thought Ursula, who would have thought it more likely to be a romance), and her talk about it left the rest of them free to eat. She didn't blink when Carter belched. "Belfast women know something about endurance," she said, as if she were one.

Ursula is waiting for Michael to come back with the ice. All those miniature crab quiches, delicate cheese puffs, and crackers with salmon paste threaten to erupt with amoebae in the heat. Ursula let the hip young caterer talk her into the menu. The woman wanted to show off. (She cooks in the basement of a renovated church. Upstairs a cabaret theatre serves the desserts she makes.) "Don't underestimate their pleasure in a beautiful table," she said to Ursula, speaking of the celebratory couple and their plain folk friends. They would have done better with chips and dips, crackers and cheddar. Ursula prevailed only in the matter of a cake, white, with frosting, as Geneva requested. Ursula now thinks the caterer conned her into a more expensive menu and had spotted Ursula's uneasiness a mile away. Ursula's sensibility quivers with guilt where the Fishers are concerned. The food is lovely to see, though, if it will hold up. The hall windows are open and the double doors propped out, but the air is as still as in a closet. The river, which lies across the road, down a short bank, gives off no coolness.

Ursula realizes that she has simply made too much of the day. Half the fun had already happened when Geneva mailed out her silly card with its "recipe." Ursula asked Michael what he thought of it and Michael said, "There's something to be said for keeping your rules simple." Michael does not douse fires where none are burning. He does not probe wounds. He does not worry about whether things could be better, if they are not too bad as they are.

All Geneva really wanted was for people to show up and congratulate her. Both she and Gully came from families rent by death and abandonment. Half a century's fidelity is their lives' achievement. And look, the pharmacist is here, the librarian, the grade-school janitor who sometimes fishes with Gully. The minister is here, of course, with his wife. Fish is conspicuously absent. Geneva's sister Ruby has yet to arrive from Spokane. Katie has not shown up, and Michael's children refused to come. "Better dead than wed," Carter stupidly intoned. Juliette asked, "How is Brian going to choreograph a *pas de deux* with one of us gone?" She said "Bree-ahn," in that nasal French manner. At least neither of the children said what Ursula knows they know, that Geneva has never especially liked them, though now she says she can see the Fisher nose on Carter, and her own long legs on Juliette. She likes to count the children once in a while: two in this generation, both surviving.

The string quartet from nearby Canyon High School is playing Mozart, if not with zest, at least with a sprightly tempo. The pretty girl on viola had the good sense to wear a sundress. Her shoulders and back glisten with perspiration. Ursula can hear herself later chiding Carter, telling him how pretty the violist was, how her skirt fell down from her knees to the floor like a sheet of flowers. Carter likes girls who wear earrings up in the gristly part of their ears, and fatigue pants or men's boxers, with baggy shirts and Chinese shoes.

The other three musicians, two violinists and a cellist, are boys. This surprised Ursula when she heard them the first time, last February at a wine-tasting fundraiser for the battered-women's shelter. Ursula's Carter, eighteen and supposedly poised on the edge of manhood, listens to heavy metal through earphones, and cannot himself play a note on any instrument, though he has had a run of lessons on two horns and the guitar. The only common cultural ground he has with his parents is a liking for the Grateful Dead, and that has been distorted by the cultish skulls and bones on his shirts, on his door, and on the bumper of the car, before Ursula made him scrape them off. Recently Michael commented that he remembered when the Dead had hair and considerably less girth. Carter laughed, cawing like a crow.

The musicians move their bodies gently with their bowing, watching their music with slightly drooped eyes, as though they are enchanted. They play for themselves and Mozart, seemingly mindless of the guests, who give them clearance, like a hot fire.

Michael staggers into the hall with two big bags of crushed ice. His lower lip, sucked in by his concentration and effort, disappears under his moustache, pulling his chin up so close to the moustache his face seems too short. One game old fellow sticks his arms out in an offer to help, but Michael nods his head and picks up speed on the way to the kitchen. Ursula follows him out of the room, talking as she walks. "Do you think Katie is coming? She said she wanted to bring a tape-player and some Windham Hill music. She could borrow it from that woman Maureen, her neighbor. We met her, remember, at the movies when we went to see that rerun of *Martin Guerre?*"

Michael bangs the ice down on the counter and rubs his arms vigorously. He is wearing a shirt Ursula bought for him last winter, a good-looking forest-green brushed twill, and she sees that he trimmed his moustache that morning. It is close and neat with a fine crisp edge at the bottom. When they make love after his grooming, Michael's bristly moustache sticks her in the nose and makes her sneeze. Sometimes it is quite wonderful, laughing in those first moments of making love.

She thinks of the frustration of last night. They did not speak of it this morning. Michael seems clearheaded and not too tired, just a little grouchy. He never drinks too much, yet it bothers her when he drinks with Fish at all. She long ago accepted that Fish was going to pickle himself whatever they all did, but she feels uneasy about Michael, who has never even misbehaved under the influence. It is foolish of her, yet she thinks of the drinking as a bad gene that might suddenly take over. It makes her nervous when Carter drinks a beer in their own kitchen. It is her inexperience; neither of her parents were drinkers. Actually she likes the buzz of half a bottle of wine herself, but she is growing so careful lately she will soon be taking her own damned pulse.

She moves closer and puts her hand on Michael's. He is cold from the ice. "I said, 'Katie, these people are all old, what do they want with New Age?' Was I wrong, Michael? To hire a string quartet? Was I so far off?" Geneva and Gully will never say they didn't like the music; they will feel they ought to have. What if they all feel the same way, wishing for a fiddle instead?

"Pop's out in the yard, looking acoss the road at the river," Michael says. "I bet he wishes he was out fishing." He pulls his hands free and sticks them down in his pants. "He says the women are all talking too loud and he can't breathe indoors." This is all said without a hint of humor, just the dry truth of it, Fisher men hating a social occasion. Now that the weather is fair, Gully will only come inside to eat and sleep. In weather like this he likes to park his truck in the woods and sleep there. Geneva doesn't like it. She says he comes home smelling like sour leaves and fish. She likes to have Gully close by, though not under foot. It is fascinating, the way Geneva exercises control, or thinks she does, while Gully finds ingenious ways to assert his independence.

"The kids should be here," Ursula says. She is sure Michael is bothered by their absence. He thinks they could be better behaved in numerous ways, but he has never been a disciplinarian. He never loses his temper, though he can wear Ursula down with silence, while the kids are more impervious. When Michael talks about children he speaks of the whole population and not just his own. He sees nothing contradictory in saying that boys who drive their parents' cars should work to pay for the insurance, and failing to impose such a condition on Carter. He is also opposed to Carter going away to college, since there is a college a mile away downtown, but Ursula says she has spent the last two years living for the day she would see Carter off, and that has settled the argument. She *has* imposed one condition, that Carter work all summer for her friend who owns a fruit and vegetable market on the old highway. She wants Carter to get up and be somewhere every morning, and she wants him to learn a little about the value of a dollar.

When Michael does not say anything, Ursula says, "Carter would have upset Geneva with what he wore, or with his hair pulled straight up like a cock's comb. She told me Gully had refused to cut his."

"Such a little hank back there, you'd think she could leave him alone," Michael growls. He only cut his own hair short within the last few months. Fish kept his shoulder-length mane even in jail. It seems to Ursula that the Fisher men have peculiar ways of asserting themselves: Gully refuses to wear any socks but white, and there are those overalls of his;

Michael insists on pepper from a grinder at the table and changes his toothbrush twice a month; Fish wears his tee shirts until they hang like rags.

"Don't worry about Mom," Michael says. "It's her party. Fifty years of hanging on. Isn't that what it's for?"

Ursula does not know if Michael means the party or marriage, and if marriage, his parents' or everybody's. There have probably been times when he has been unhappy with Ursula and has thought of himself as "holding on," though Ursula cannot think offhand of when those times might have been. She herself has never been seriously unhappy with her marriage, though she has been angry with Michael and, especially in the early years, has yearned for sweeter attentions. She has not worried about Michael. He isn't one to back out of his commitments.

"She has endured," she says. It is Geneva's own word.

"There have been times," Geneva has said, "times when I thought about marching straight out the door." They all know what those times were: when Gully went from work to the train station and rode all the way to Guatemala; when Gully drove a truck into a tree on purpose because it had a cracked block and he couldn't fix it. Ursula supposes this rather frail old man has, in his own way, been a tyrant as well as a drunk, at times unreliable, maybe even mean. Ursula is sure of none of these things. Geneva makes veiled references to "hard times" and "those days." Michael says his father always worked hard, but sometimes took off, usually only overnight, to escape the family and wrestle with his demons. Nonetheless, the two boys always looked to Gully and never to Geneva. Geneva's comfort was a daughter, a year older than the twins, but Evelyn turned out dumb and wild and, finally, mortally foolish, the victim of a botched abortion, when it is so easy now.

"Fish sure as hell ought to be here, though," Michael says. He surprises Ursula. He seldom states expectations of Fish. He is more likely to say, "What did he do now?" when Fish's name comes up, though he has never refused to rescue Fish when Fish was rescuable. He does not now elaborate, and there is little expression in his mild voice, but Ursula is certain she detects resentment. It must have been hard, forty-five years the good son while everybody worried about the other one.

Katie does appear, breathless and scowling in a bright yellow leotard and an Indian print skirt. She often looks like someone left over from the sixties. She buys her clothes secondhand, or makes them. "Voilà!" she says now. "I know I'm late. My damned Datsun. The starter. I had to find a neighbor to give me a push. Nearly seventeen years living with Fish and I still don't know anything about cars." Fish, like Michael, often has a car or truck in pieces. "You know, I bet I haven't even filled my own gas tank ten times in all these years, unless Fish was out of town." Katie gives Michael and Ursula a weak smile.

Out of town? Fish has just spent a year in jail! Once he went all the way to Kansas to harvest wheat on Winston's brother's farm. He has been to Canada, Mexico, Idaho, Utah. He has spent time in rented rooms, and in Michael's basements. Katie calls all that "being out of town"?

"I hardly used that car last year," Katie says. "I was right downtown, you know? Then when I signed all that stuff to start the divorce, it hit me: I don't even know how to change my oil."

Katie has a boyfriend, a pear geneticist. You would think he would be smart enough to advise Katie. Katie hasn't mentioned him in a while—Jeff, wasn't it?—and never to Michael, only to Ursula. Ursula couldn't be enthusiastic, though the truth is she thinks Katie has the right. Besides, Katie deserves some regard for trying to live her own life, after so many years of abetting Fish. She is a stitcher for a repertory theatre company. She has friends now that Ursula doesn't know. "Stitcher" is a new word to Ursula.

Ursula begins digging out roasting pans and platters from the cabinets around the big kitchen. It isn't the right moment to let herself feel, or Katie know, what she thinks about Katie's fruit scientist, or Katie's years of dogged constancy, or Katie's decision to cut Fish off at last. It just is not the time, not because of this reception, but because of something going on inside Ursula that she has not yet named. You cannot be married to a twin without looking at the other one now and then. Ursula wonders if Michael has more of Fish in him than he lets on, something much more significant than a propensity for moustaches and taciturnity.

"Here," she says to Katie. "Pile these with ice, and we'll lay little tidbits in them, and go around and urge everybody to

eat up before the ice melts and the food floats and sinks.
Then when Ruby gets here we'll bring out the cake." Ursula's
table is going to look like an emergency food station in a
dusty third world country. All those pots.

"What about the punch?" Katie asks. "I saw it, coming in."
She makes a face.

Ursula feels a twinge at the base of her spine, and she puts
her hand there to press it out. She says "I'll try to find
something for water." Michael meanwhile has been crawling
around on his knees straightening out the chaos Ursula has
left in the cabinets. She is habitually messy. By the time she
gets up in the morning, the bedclothes are usually on the
floor. She cooks all over the kitchen. Michael is slower with
his messes, which accumulate over time. He often comes
along behind her, tidying.

"I don't know what I was thinking, having those papers
served on Fish just now." Katie is standing at the refrigerator
with the door open, handing plates to Ursula. "Geneva will
think I am a real bitch for sure when she hears. Did you see
that stupid announcement they sent out? *Stick to it.* Who do
you think that was meant for? She held on, why can't I? She
thinks there's salvation in digging in your heels. I bet she still
thinks, *Evelyn could have had that baby.* God, what a life. Look
at her. Do you see me like that in thirty years? Do you see
Fish?"

"Do you have enough pans?" Michael says, slapping shut
another cabinet door.

Katie says plaintively, "My lawyer was on my *ass.*" She looks
straight at Michael. "I tried to stop it, didn't I?"

"I'm going outside to see about Pop," Michael says. He puts
his hands down in the ice in the pan Ursula is handling, and
shakes them above his head, his face turned up to catch the
drops. "Forest fires and family quarrels," he says, summing
up projections for summer after a spring drought. Then he
leaves. He isn't one to stick around to hear his sister-in-law
talking about divorce. Ursula doesn't know if that is because
he doesn't care, doesn't know how to help, or is bored at the
sound of two women talking. She doesn't know what he
thinks half the time. Half the time! She never knows what he
thinks unless he says, and from what he says, she still has to
extrapolate. He claims that keeping busy keeps his mind free.

Ursula thinks keeping quiet keeps him uncommitted; on some deep level she has always craved his commitment.

"Geneva won't know it until you tell her," she tells Katie briskly. "So tell her some other time. When this is over, when the divorce is over. You know she'll never ask what's going on." None of my business, that is Geneva's anthem, but then Ursula's mother says that too.

"If Fish doesn't show today, she'll want to know why, won't she?" Katie says this lightly.

Ursula sighs. "Geneva told me she used to cook supper, stick it in the oven, and forget about it. I supposed then she meant she never knew when to count on Fisher men. She doesn't expect much from Fish, does she? Who does?"

"Where's Juliette?"

"She dances Saturday mornings." Ursula catches herself before she sighs again. "They're rehearsing, getting ready for the dances in the park that start next month. You'll come? I'll remind you. Juliette couldn't possibly disappoint that little French pimp who directs them." Ursula bites her lip. She picks up a big roaster, now filled with ice and spinach tarts. It takes a moment for her to get her balance, with the roaster held up against her chest. Katie chooses that moment to catch her eye.

"I don't know what else to do, Ursie. I don't know how else to get myself together."

Was it the boyfriend? Or has Katie read something? Joined a group? Has she just run out of patience?

Ursula gestures with her head, back over her shoulder, at the pans on the counter. "Grab something, Katie. Say cheerful things to all the fogeys. Let's get this show on the road."

"WHO is going to eat all this!" Geneva says loudly as they start laying it out. People drift their way and take up the little white paper plates with primroses at the edges. Geneva bends over ingloriously, going in her purse beneath the table to get her camera. "Say cheese," she says to everyone when she straightens up. Her camera has a cheap little flash that will give everyone orange eyes. They should have given her a decent little auto-flash for a gift, Ursula thinks with a pang. She thought the reception was gift enough, but it isn't really tangible. There aren't any favors.

Geneva begins to move around, to get all the shots she wants. It seems more like a party with her in motion. She makes the musicians stop playing and pose, their bows on their instruments. They do as she bids. They are polite kids, and they are splitting fifteen dollars an hour.

—26—

Ursula didn't meet the Fishers until right before she and Michael married. First, she and Michael and Fish were living in a rooming house near Portland State, and the Fishers lived way east, on the river. The young people went all the way to Troutdale to swim, many hot spring Sundays, but only Michael went the few extra miles to see his folks. Before Fish went off for basic training, he and his father took a three-day hiking trip in bad weather. Later, when Michael and Ursula started living together, Michael went out there about twice a month, but he never suggested that Ursula go, and she wouldn't ask. When they decided to get married, he said, "I guess you'll have to meet them." She had not realized they were the reason he had come back from Peace Corps training, and not her. It was something Geneva said that set that straight; she said she had always been able to count on Michael to be there in a crisis. She said, "Don't parents need their son as much as those Africans do?" When Ursula, who had been prepared to wait out the two years, asked Michael if his mother actually wrote him during training and asked him to come home, he said she had. She said she already had one son in a godforsaken place; the Peace Corps could find someone else.

The first meeting between Ursula and the Fishers was stiff, and didn't last long. From after the wedding until Carter was born, Ursula only saw them two more times, at their house, and not in the dumps she and Michael had rented. Once they had Carter, she felt more obligated to act like family. Her own father had come for a visit, and ended up making the down payment on a house for them, and her mother came with wonderful, practical gifts. Geneva Fisher gave Ursula boxes of detergent and a rattle for the baby. She said Carter was a funny first name. (Gulsvig wasn't?!)

Ursula was relieved when the Fishers moved to the southern part of the state, even when Michael spent weeks of his
summer down there helping his dad build a house. She
didn't see them again until she moved, too, reluctantly, because of them. Fish and Katie had been moving around, and
when they finally rented a ramshackle old house not far from
Ursula and Michael, she was glad. Later they bought a house
eight miles out of town, cheap because it was in disrepair,
with a tangled, overgrown yard.

The summer the children were five and eight, Ursula
talked Michael into taking them to Disneyland. Disneyland
was dumb, but it was something all the kids their kids knew
had experienced. Maybe it was important to see it for yourself. Wasn't it what every foreign dignitary wanted to see?
And dying children? At first Michael thought she was kidding. When she insisted that she was serious, he gave in
rather easily. He admitted that they had never gone anywhere together as a family, except camping at the beach a
couple of times. Ursula said they ought to be making memories, the four of them. Everyone likes to be able to look back
later. She was glad she had childhood trips to Washington,
D.C., Montreal, and Barbados to recall (all before her parents split, all unmarred by discord of any kind). She could
hardly believe this was coming out of her mouth; she kept
waiting for Michael to interrupt her. When he did not, she
was disappointed. She had hoped he would challenge her
and that would cause them to talk about "what really matters." They had passed a year in which it seemed they discussed only their own schedules, menus, problems with cars
and the oil heater, the kids' colds, and, always, the vagaries of
Fish and Gully. Michael did not argue. He chewed on his
moustache and said he guessed they could afford it. He
didn't act martyred. Certainly he loved his children, and he
enjoyed time spent with them. In fact he spent far more time
than most fathers, and more time, increasingly, than Ursula.
He was a man who did what needed to be done, as long as he
saw what it was or had it pointed out to him. Though Ursula
thought he was critical of the children in ways she was not,
the kids were actually easier and more agreeable with him
than with her.

The Disneyland trip went well enough, despite a mix of

searing heat and several gusty rainstorms. The children whined by midafternoon, and they spent too much money, mostly on food, but it *was* fun to ride a boat through a fake game park, to see a thousand dolls decked out in ethnic costumes, to walk the clean streets and watch cartoon characters six feet tall waddle and prance, making the children giggle. As they were packing up the morning they left, Ursula said to Michael, by way of expressing her gratitude, "Once was enough, wasn't it?" Michael gave her arm a squeeze and said, "Once was fine, Ursula."

On the way home they stopped in a town on the coast north of Los Angeles. A festival was in progress. Streets had been blocked off with colored ropes and streamers, and people were moving about in a great mass, laughing and eating and jostling one another pleasantly. As soon as they moved away from one group of musicians, they heard another. There were jugglers and clowns. The Fishers stopped at a food stand under a bright purple and gold canopy, and ate saté on sticks. The kids were entranced and good-tempered, the sky was clear, and a nice breeze was coming in from the sea.

They saw a group in Elizabethan costume dancing in the center of a main intersection. The ladies put their hands to their waists and then, lightly, put their hands on the men's arms. They lifted their skirts to circle and kick up their feet, and they moved their heads so that their hair swirled like ribbons. The Fishers watched them for a quarter of an hour. The group stopped to rest. A violinist and flutist moved in to play for a while, and Michael said, "We had better get back on the road if we want to get home tomorrow." When they looked around for the children, they did not see Juliette. Ursula was so suddenly and fiercely frightened she almost threw up, but Michael said, "Look, she's over there with the dancers."

A woman with curly red hair was showing Juliette how to raise her foot daintily, toe pointed down, and give it a shake. Juliette caught on right away, her bottom lip tucked under her teeth in concentration. At five she was a charmer, with a cascade of wavy hair to the middle of the back, and a bold way of looking at people. Onlookers had gathered around, and were giving her encouraging hoots and spatters of applause, which she was relishing. When Michael stepped in and said they really did have to go, she said, "But Daddy, they're going to dance now, and I must be here for it." She was quite serious, not fussy at all, and Michael and Ursula only had to exchange a look to agree to wait for another set of dancing.

In the car, Juliette was still excited, but sleepy, too, and Ursula was afraid the two states would mix badly, make her cranky, and she would incite Carter, who had fallen asleep as soon as he settled in the seat, but Juliette simply said, "I'm going to be a dancer when I grow up. I am too." Then she lay down and slept, so quickly that Michael and Ursula burst into laughter, and embraced.

The incident with the dancers thrilled Ursula, not only because it was surprising and pleasant, and not because she saw a quality in Juliette she had not yet recognized—the ability to make people love her because she was performing for them—but because she realized that a host of things were suggested, having to do with the future, and she thought, Now Michael will talk to me about them. What will become of the children? What will become of us? These were his children, their lives an extension of his own. And, on a smaller scale, they had had a good time, and it was worth remembering. They hadn't bickered much, hadn't frayed as a family under the stress of Disneyland. And she and Michael had been so close in that moment in the car, brought together by their pleasure in their children. She imagined herself saying to him, "Wasn't that sweet of the redhaired dancer to show Juliette some steps?" She imagined them mock-fussing over what they had liked best at Disneyland, and the children crying out, "When can we go somewhere again?" (Maybe Washington, D.C.—the Smithsonian, the Lincoln Memorial?) She imagined Michael saying how proud he was of the kids. All of that would have been so much, more than enough; she could not imagine Michael talking about himself.

As it turned out, the weeks that followed were so jammed with tension and pain, and with hard work and the management of so many unpleasant details, the trip was never even mentioned between Ursula and Michael again. It would be almost a year before Ursula remembered to develop the pictures she had taken.

When they reached home, they found Katie there. She jumped up as they came in the door and helped them unload. Ursula asked immediately if something was wrong. She assumed Fish was in trouble. It wasn't quite sunset, maybe eight o'clock on a July evening, and Michael had been driving all day. Ursula thought Katie inconsiderate to be there like this, waiting with some sort of bad news that could probably wait. There never was much Michael could do about Fish anyway, though he had put up bail more than once for DUI and reckless driving charges, or gone to fetch him when some old truck broke down. Damn him, let him walk. Ursula remembered later that that was what she thought as soon as she saw Katie. It was a bend in the road in her thinking. Let him walk. They should have taken that as a precept long ago.

What Katie did say was that Michael and Ursula had to go out to the Fishers right away, and that she would stay with the kids. Michael said, so calmly Ursula felt like shaking him, "So what's happened, then?" (Later Ursula asked him, "Didn't you think one of them died? Weren't you *worried?*" Michael was baffled. "Why would I start worrying and asking questions, when she was standing there in front of me, about to tell me what I needed to know?") In the space of half a minute, Ursula had already considered a dozen possibilities, none of them close to the actual circumstances, though all of them close enough in character. There was trouble. Katie gave the kids hugs and sent them up to dress for bed. When they were out of the room she told Michael that his parents' house had burned down. She added quickly that nobody was hurt. The house was gone.

As Michael and Ursula drove into River Cove, they passed an ambulance on its way into Medford. The ambulance, they would learn, was taking Gully away to the hospital for the night, and after that—though they wouldn't know this for several days—to the state hospital, for months. He had been down by the river, drinking and fishing, and when he had returned to find the house engulfed in flames, he had gone berserk, even though the firemen tried to tell him nobody was inside. He seemed to have lost his sense of time—the year, his own age. He kept saying it was his fault, and what would happen to the kids? Where are the kids? he kept

asking. Geneva had been at the library, and it was this scene—
the house blackened, the flames dying down, the mess of the
firefighting everywhere, and Gully babbling and wringing
his hands as he stomped around—this she found when she
returned. As soon as Gully saw her he began to scream
hysterically. He thought Evelyn was inside the house. The
men had to restrain him from scrabbling in the mess. The
fire marshal told Geneva that these things happened to people in a crisis sometimes. "Not with most men, I bet," Geneva
said when she relayed the fireman's words to Michael. The
fire marshal shook Gully and made him sit down in a truck.
He sent a neighbor to call for an ambulance. When it came,
Gully fought and had to be restrained.

Geneva went to stay with Michael and Ursula. Her sons
cleaned up from the fire. Fish came through that time. He
worked day after day until dark, until he was black with soot.
Michael helped Geneva pick out a mobile home to put on the
lot after the house was cleared, instead of rebuilding. They
didn't need much room. Geneva didn't need the burden of a
house to keep, and they would save some money. There was
enough money left over from the insurance to put into CD's,
to draw interest for a small income. Geneva stabbed at brav-
ery, saying for once she could choose what she wanted instead of taking what she got. She missed Gully terribly, and
was afraid of what they were doing to him. Michael went up
to see his father, but talked Geneva (it wasn't difficult) into
staying behind. Gully didn't want her to see him or the
hospital, once he could think about it. Geneva talked for
weeks on end, manic. That was when Ursula learned some of
the family history. She kept telling Geneva that things would
be better now. Geneva said she had prayed for something to
happen to make Gully—her voice ran out, she couldn't say
what she wanted, but only cry. Katie and Ursula helped her
go through the burned photograph albums and boxes of
artifacts from her whole married life, salvaging a very small
portion of them. There was a fireproof box, which Ursula
supposed held important papers, but which turned out to
hold old greeting cards and mementoes. Geneva wept cop-
iously when she saw it was saved. "I'd have chosen that above
all else," she said. Well, hadn't she known that when she put it

in a metal box? Ursula didn't see the value of the items, but she didn't look closely, or ask questions. She was glad something was salvaged for Geneva.

Geneva told them Gully had once fallen asleep on the couch with a cigarette, and had set the couch on fire. It had scared him enough to stop smoking, but not enough to stop drinking. Another time he burned down a shed because he couldn't get its door to hang right. She thought he remembered those things, at the fire. "He never said he was sorry, you know, either of those other times," she said, "but he's sorry now."

Gully came back skinny, his shoulders curved toward the center of his body. His wispy hair had grown long enough to pull into a ponytail like his sons wore, and it was all almost white. He had a hard time remembering things. He could remember anecdotes he liked to tell about his boyhood, or about his children, but he couldn't remember where he had set his coffee cup down two minutes ago. Names slipped away; he was embarrassed to see people he knew, and stopped going down to the cafe for coffee for a long time. He never went back to work. He drew disability, and then retirement. "Thank God I'm a union man," he said. He had been building heavy equipment for road construction. He had once been very strong for his size. Now he said, "To think God had to do that to get my attention." Ursula commented to Michael that the shock treatments had altered his personality, but Michael pooh-poohed that. Gully went to AA meetings nearly every night for months. Wednesday nights he went to River Cove Christian Fellowship prayer meetings with Geneva. The young people were vastly relieved that he didn't talk about it much. He didn't try to foist Jesus off on anybody.

His mind eventually cleared, and he spent his days poking and puttering, fishing and visiting with his cronies up and down the river. He slacked off on AA, going Tuesday nights at the Episcopal church hall. He became a mild man, with a streak of stubborn anger against people responsible for large events: the CIA, United Fruit, the Army Corps of Engineers, the Pentagon. He called Geneva his good wife. He said he didn't deserve half as much. But he and Geneva lived in separate zones of a small life and came together only for their old-couple rituals. Fish wouldn't go near them. Geneva's feet got bad. Gully developed angina. These matters gave them something to discuss over breakfast. Fish gave them something to worry about. Michael gave them a little comfort. Somehow, they went on.

—27—

Gully and Michael are standing near the road with their backs to the Grange Hall. Looking at them through the open doors, Ursula thinks how much alike they look in the slope of their shoulders and their wiriness. They even stand alike, with their hands in their pockets. They look like boys who might kick rocks all the way to the river.

"Fish stands exactly like that, with his pants hiked up by his fists in his pockets." Katie has appeared beside Ursula. "He would hate to hear me say so. He doesn't want to be like Gully."

"Too bad," says Ursula, "because he is, in lots of ways."

"He can't stand his father's weakness. His meekness."

"Maybe he can't stand the thought of getting old."

"He says he'll never get feeble like Gully. I don't think he plans to get old. Surely he can scrape up a catastrophe to wipe himself out before that." Katie's voice is harsh.

Ursula takes a step away from Katie, toward the men. She says, "That gives him a good excuse for being crazy." Crazy isn't the right word. Katie could probably come up with something more apt, but she goes away without commenting anymore. It is never okay for anyone to criticize Fish, except Katie. Well, she has had the most of him. She would know what kind of crazy he is.

Ursula calls her husband's name softly. He turns and gives her a quizzical look, as though he cannot fathom why she would come to him right then. Gully hasn't heard her. She hears him say, "Somebody must have got to him." Ursula realizes he is talking about the podiatrist who disappeared. Some people suspected foul play, but could come up with no possible motive. The man's Jeep was found on a forest service road not far from River Cove, but there were no signs of him, though they searched when he disappeared in February,

and again in March after the weather cleared. Gully seems to
have known him. He refers to him as "Dr. Jim."

"So many possibilities, Pop," says Michael. Ursula would
like to dare him to come up with one. Better, she would like
for Michael to ask his father, What was Dr. Jim to you? Did
something happen that you're afraid of too? Do you know
something? She has heard Michael talk for hours with Fish or
Gully about the world at large, especially if it has to do with
hunting, fishing, or what they see as atrocities against the
environment, but none of the three of them ever discuss
anything personal.

"When should I bring out the cake?" Ursula asks. Her voice
sounds strained to her. She is tired, and afraid guests will
leave if she doesn't serve the cake soon, even though Ruby
has not arrived. She isn't expecting Fish. Avoiding Katie is a
convenient alibi. He hates sentimentality, crowds, or anything that places pressure on him to behave himself. It is such
a hot day, he may have driven to the beach.

"Come on Pop," Michael says gently, taking his father's
elbow.

"Now what's that?" Gully asks in a shaky voice. He points
down the road toward where he lives, a mile away. "See that
smoke?"

"Probably somebody burning trash," Michael says, but
Gully won't budge. The smoke is only a wispy plume, like
Gully's ponytail turned upside down. You could almost take it
for a campfire.

Ursula, now anxious, makes a face to Michael as he glances
her way, a why-can't-you-take-charge look that makes
Michael swivel away in annoyance.

"As soon as we're through here we'll go take a look,"
Michael says to his father. He crosses in front of the old man,
to turn him back toward the building. They have reached the
bottom step when they all jump at the sound of tires screeching on the highway. A logging truck has come to a desperate
stop as a shiny RV cuts left in front of it and pulls in to the
wide part of the drive by the hall. Ursula's hands are flutter-
ing like birds let out of a cage, taking all her energy. She
doesn't know what to say next.

"Let's get it over with," she hears Michael say. It seems a

mean way to look at things, but they are all making special efforts for Geneva's sake, that is no secret.

"Gulsvig Fisher! You've gone and shrunk up!"

Ruby Hammond's voice hangs in the air like the lowing of a cow. She steps down from the Marauder, livid in turquoise knit, but a good-looking woman who has had a much better life than her sister. She is widowed and well-off. As she comes toward the men, Gully turns and sprints up the stairs, suddenly spry.

Michael follows his father, brushing past Ursula without a word. Ursula waits for Ruby and awkwardly exchanges kisses, not quite on cheeks, not on mouths. "We were starting to worry," she says.

Ruby tosses off their concern with extravagant waves of her arms. "I thought I had all the time in the world. I was only coming from Salem this morning, but the highway was an endless parade of poke-ass drivers. Oh, come on, where's that sis of mine?" She holds Ursula's arm tightly and starts up the stairs. "Fifty years! How has she stood it?" Ruby is half a foot taller than Ursula, and the effect is that Ursula feels like a schoolgirl in for a scolding. As soon as Ruby spots Geneva she lets go of Ursula and, with the same long braying as outside, calls to Geneva.

"Come and see my slick Marauder!" she says as she and Geneva unwind from smacking kisses and great hugs. She sees that a number of guests have turned to stare at her. "Anybody else want to come?" she says rather grandly, and indeed, as she turns, pulling Geneva with her down the stairs to the camper, she is followed by a small parade of the curious. In the yard, everybody stands around while the sisters go in and out of the fancy camper. Geneva pauses at the door of it to say, "It's so tidy, and handy, and *cute!*" She steps down, and speaks directly to the minister's wife. "I'd give anything to have a little house on wheels like that. You could go anywhere you wanted." The minister's wife kindly agrees. Geneva does look yearning.

They all troop back inside and eat in a frenzy, jazzed up by Ruby's arrival. Ruby keeps Geneva close by her, but drags her around the room, demanding to be introduced to everyone. The volume in the room is way up, a good sign. Ursula starts around with a big bag, picking up abandoned spinach

tarts and plates. Katie has found several pitchers and has set
out water. Here and there, cups have overturned and made
puddles. Ursula sees that the musicians are exhausted. A
violinist takes out a handkerchief and wipes his face. Suddenly everyone has that semi-desperate look of readiness to
depart.

"Okay, everyone!" Ursula announces. "Come around the
table and have some cake!" They all do as she asks. A lot of
the guests will be up for similar celebrations, if not for their
own funerals, soon enough. Ursula resolves on the spot to
see to it that her July Fourth picnic will be a real bash. She
won't care if everyone gets falling-down drunk, as long as it is
lively.

Gully has been gathered in like laundry off the line. Guests
crowd in to offer congratulations one more time. Ursula
rushes into the kitchen for the cake. Katie has found a big
butcher knife.

"That'll do," Ursula says firmly, and, cake balanced on her
hands, she prances back to the party.

Geneva takes the butcher knife and applies it with a flourish to the cake. She is good at making do. Gully looks mortified, caught between his wife and sister-in-law behind the
table, but at least no one is holding on to him anymore, and
he has not bolted.

Mary Courter says, "I say fifty years is reason to cheer!" All
oblige, bringing tears to Geneva's eyes. She takes the first
gooey bite. She offers the next to Gully from her hand. His
eyes are wild, but he takes one small morsel, with the enthusiasm of someone eating a sock. Ruby guffaws. "This cake is a
gas!" she says. Geneva doesn't seem to notice, or mind.
Guests come in to get their servings, then back away to other
parts of the room. Ursula, amazed, realizes she has tears in
her eyes. Michael comes to stand beside her, puts his arm
around her waist, squeezes, and slides away. For him, it is a
large gesture.

Still buoyant, Geneva calls out, "Goodbye, goodbye!" to the
first couple out the door. They have a slightly guilty look, but
when they make an easy escape, others follow. Ursula rushes
over to Geneva to tell her she looks radiant. "Have you still
got film?" she asks, taking Geneva's camera and urging Gully
in close beside his wife. Gully says, "She's worn real well for
an old gal, ain't she?" Geneva, pleased, makes a face at him

and rolls her eyes. This is the expression Ursula catches, and then she realizes it is Geneva's last shot. Michael and Katie are making the rounds to pick up trash. A few guests linger, licking their fingers and chatting.

In walk Fish and Juliette. Fish is wearing the shirt Katie bought him for court last year. (He chose to wear instead the clear shame of jail garb, green coveralls.) The shirt is white with tiny red stripes; Fish looks like a stick of peppermint. He is fresh-scrubbed and combed, his hair still damp from washing. He has his head tucked, not looking at anyone. Juliette is in her dance garb, a black leotard with a black gauzy skirt that hangs in a swoop around her legs and flares as she moves.

Geneva stops in the middle of a word as Fish enters the hall. Her face falls. Ursula thinks, *But he came!* Then she looks at Fish and sees what Geneva sees, his uneasiness that can turn sullen and swollen as a flash flood. Juliette, with her hair caught up in a loose French roll from which long curling hairs have escaped, looks quite pretty. She has none of her bad mood left today, or at least she is not showing it.

Ursula has the sudden uncontrollable urge to escape. She turns and runs back to the kitchen. At the door she runs into Katie, both of them gasping at the impact which is, fortunately, a glance and not head-on. "Oh God!" Katie says, looking into the room, and "Oh!" again. Ursula reaches for Katie's hand and presses it. She is facing the kitchen. With her eyes she hints at escape, but Katie takes a step forward, moving Ursula backwards in the same move. "I'm the one who doesn't belong here," she says. Her chin quivers.

"It's okay, Katie," Ursula whispers. "He knew you'd be here. Don't worry."

Katie moves past Ursula and walks up to Fish. She reaches him, with Ursula behind her, as he says to his mother, "I'm a nonperson now. For a year I was a number. Now I'm nothing." Geneva is bewildered. "Not a father, not a husband, nobody's breadwinner. NOBODY. I can't even live in my own house because it's rented." He bangs a fist into the other hand. Geneva's face has crumpled. Her collar is crooked. The button at her waist is undone, setting the scoop of her peplum askew. Katie bursts into tears. "This was going fine!" she half screeches. "Why didn't you stay away?!"

"Whose party is this?" Fish asks sarcastically. "Whose par-

ents are these?" He is clenching his hand so tight the veins
stand out. "Have you given Ma your little present yet? Your
news?"

Ursula looks around for Michael. Both he and Gully have
disappeared. Everyone else has gone, except for the musicians, who are gathering up their music stands and loading
their car. Ursula considers fainting, but she doesn't think she
can pull it off. She can see what is coming, and it makes her
sick: Fish, wilted and self-pitying (his anger will lose momentum in a while), desperate and bitter, will be beaten by
Katie's mounting hysteria, her accusations, all the things she
has not said to him before he went to jail, or after he got out.

"What would you know about marriage?" Katie screams.
"When did you ever keep a promise? When did you pay any
attention? I had to take a goddamned TAXI to go have a
BABY because you were DRUNK!"

Katie's anger hangs in the air. Geneva's face shows that she
knows Gully is gone, that love does not work out, that Fish is
in for a sorry fate. The cake, mostly gone, lies in a mound of
slimy frosting. Ruby looks aghast, though she still looks full
of energy. She does not retreat, as Fishers do. She is all
attention.

Juliette runs out of the hall down to the musicians. Ursula
sees her gesturing and talking excitedly. Fish says to Katie,
"You did this with a lot of class. You really thought it over,
didn't you?" Ruby takes charge of Geneva, putting her arms
around her. Katie pulls Fish away to the corner of the room.
There is a buzz in the room, but Ursula doesn't think anything is really being said. She watches Fish and Katie, wondering if Fish might lunge at Katie and hit her without
thinking. But Fish and Katie move together, against the wall,
like high school sweethearts in a crowded hallway. Katie is
talking in rushes, punctuated by her crying. Ursula sees her
punch Fish once in the chest. He doesn't move. Geneva is
sobbing. She sees what Ursula sees, her son's defeated posture.

Fish reaches up and touches Katie's hair. Ursula holds her
breath, afraid Katie will begin to scream again. Instead she
bends her head close to Fish and, finally, with a sigh, leans
against him.

The two boys with their violins come back in, followed by

four or five of the guests who have not driven away yet. The
other musicians stand outside, fanning themselves with
sheets of music.

The boys begin to play a lively and sweet gavotte. Their
violins are tucked under their chins, their necks are curved
and long. Their bodies—they are standing—quiver slightly,
like reeds in a breeze.

Juliette begins to dance. At first she takes only a small
space. She moves, almost like the musicians, in a flutter.
Then her arms move out from her like a flower unfolding.
Her head rises and her face, sweet and pale, is sad and
yearning. She turns gently, once, and again, venturing out
away from the music, into the center of the hall. Her arms
wind up and pull her heavenward, beyond the building, away
from their quarrels. This is unlike any dance Ursula has seen
her daughter do. It is fragile and strong at the same time,
lively, in the 4-4 beat of the song, and at the same time it is
tender and sad.

The music changes tempo, suddenly faster, and Juliette
twirls and dips. Katie peeks out from around Fish's shoulder.
Geneva is sagging against Ruby, one hand on the table in
front of her for more support.

For fifty years the Fishers have been saying wrong things,
or nothing at all, or pretending to talk while they speak
riddles and small deceits. Here, though, is a Fisher who with
a few deft moves has rescued them from a day's spite. Fish is
grounded. Katie's fury and embarrassment have leaked away
with her tears. Geneva is still on her feet.

In the instant the music is over it seems the musicians and
the odd guests vanish. Juliette moves quickly past Ursula
and, across the table from Geneva, she curtsies. They are all
frozen. Ruby breaks the silence. "Did you see that? An angel!" She claps her hands for a long moment, all alone.

Juliette, suddenly shy as a child, rises. Geneva has never
known how, or wanted, to love Ursula's children; her own
children burned up all the fuel of her love, singed away all
the affection and sweetness. Yet Juliette has given something
of herself to this grandmother, whose face is splotched with
tears, whose mouth is sticky with the residue of cake; has
given as children never do when they are asked. Unless, of
course—and Ursula does not want to think this true—

Juliette has simply learned the power of performance. Whatever her reason, Juliette has saved the day.

Ursula runs from the hall and stands in the yard and bawls. If someone demanded to know whom she loves best just then, her husband or her daughter, she could not say. If someone condemned them all, a family of trees with no branches, she would defend them.

To the north, around the curve of highway, she sees smoke again, feathering above rooftops and trees, a gray curl against the sky. Around that same curve, she sees the small figures of her husband and his father, walking along the road toward her.

She cannot help herself. She runs to meet them.

—28—

Fish pushes Katie's car to get it going. He follows her back to Michael's in his snub-nosed Econoline. Katie tries not to look in the rearview mirror; having him behind her makes her nervous. She knows she isn't driving fast enough and he will be back there, slapping his steering wheel and muttering, telling her to get on with it.

Juliette rides with her. Her parents are behind in River Cove, closing up the hall.

"That was something you did back there," Katie tells her as they hit the stretch of road outside River Cove, before the heavy equipment, hardware, fast food, storage buildings, and junk yards. Where there is irrigation, there are green fields, but already there are patches of dry grass, too. Or maybe it is always like that. Katie has no eye for the great outdoors all the Fishers love so much. She is like a child in kindergarten. She knows a generic landscape of hill and mountain, river and creek, tree, flower, road.

There have been summers she and Fish drove through the eastern part of the state to camp and hike. They came upon whole fields of white and purple flowers. Then, south of here, over the mountains into California, they used to drive where the sides of the road were thick with clumps of bushes, orange-red, as though they were already on fire. They took drives in the relentless summer heat, following a river, looking for a secluded spot with no campers or dredgers.

They always got along in the country unless something went wrong with the car.

Along here there are only yellow-headed weeds, ugly things. The beauty is in the horizon of blue and violet hills. In winter, they disappear into fog or haze.

Juliette stares out of the window on her side. Her face has a long grieving look to it. Hot wind whips through the car.

Katie says, "I thought there would be a disaster. I thought your grandmother had her hopes too high. Then Fish showed up and I thought, Oh boy. But you, too. You saved the day." She glances at Juliette to see if she is pleased. Don't teenagers like to be praised?

Juliette says, "It was just a stupid dance."

"I never saw one like it."

"It's not like it was choreographed."

"Not a ballet, you mean?"

"No."

"I never saw a dance until I started going with your mother to your recitals."

"You don't call them recitals. God."

"Oh?"

"I'm not a little girl. Petunias and fairies and that stuff."

"What do you call them?"

Juliette gives her a withering look. "Concerts."

"I remember you in tutus, with your tummy sticking out." Is she sounding like an old lady talking to a kid? Is she so far gone?

Juliette sighs audibly. She hangs her hand along the windowpane and looks out. Her hair blows loose from its roll into long wavy tendrils. In a moment she slumps back against the seat again. "I'm so tired of Brian and small-town dance. I want to do modern, for one thing, but Brian says it makes your butt muscles clump up, and wrecks your line. I don't know. He's not God. Ballet's not all there is."

"You don't have to dance, do you?"

"What would I *do*?" That look again.

"See that little hamburger stand over there?" Katie asks. "A worker there had hepatitis, and nine hundred people had to have shots."

"We can just ride, Katie, okay?"

Juliette turns her head to lie against the seat, looking away from Katie. Katie is sorry she doesn't know anything to say. She thinks of Juliette as a little girl, when she isn't anymore. It is hard for her to talk to Rhea now; what it will be like in a few years can be imagined. She will be mute, stuck between her mother and her child in stupid silence.

Katie sees Fish behind her, coming close as they near the freeway entrance. He sees her look in her mirror, and he grins. She never doubts him when he looks like that, never doubts the moment's pleasure for him, or his desire to please. He is incapable of pretense. He can't be bothered.

She wonders if she is doing something foolish by letting him repair her car. If she takes it to a garage, it will cost her money, and besides, Fish wants to do it. Fixing cars is in his repertoire, something he is good at.

They go onto the freeway, and a car comes between them.

"Will you go to Texas now?" Juliette asks.

"I might go see Rhea this summer. I haven't made plans."

"I mean to live."

"Why no."

"Will you still be my aunt?"

"When I'm divorced?" So that's it.

"Yeah. What'll you be when you're not married to Fish?"

His ex-wife, she thinks. It sounds fakey, like a character on a soap opera. "I'll be Katie Fisher, same as ever. I'm not going to disappear, or stop loving you guys. I'll still want to come to your *concerts*." She tries to smile at Juliette, but she feels a terrible wave of sadness come over her. She didn't really consider what it would mean, the possibility of not seeing Fish anymore, let alone Ursula, Michael, their children. What did she envision? Maybe it is as simple as this: not having Fish to worry about, his not being *her* worry any more than anybody's else's. Will a divorce accomplish that? Will it change her so much?

She hated him today when he started in on Geneva with his little poor-me rap. Then he took her aside and whispered things to her, Katie, just to her. Her anger dissolved. She felt his breath on her shoulder as he bent to speak, not looking at her.

"Did you talk Fish into going?"

"I got home from dance rehearsal and he was hanging around the kitchen, so I said I'd go if he would."

"Did you practice the dance?"

"It was just a dumb dance! I saw everybody getting all worked up. It was supposed to be a party! But people were mad. All that glowering. Besides, then they all looked at me, didn't they? I was solo. I was the star."

"Sure." Katie wonders if, when Rhea is this age, Katie's mother will understand her. June certainly did not have the slightest idea what was going on with Katie, who at fifteen had already learned you could get a boy's time and attention if you weren't too prissy about where he put his hands. Maybe it will be easier for June the second time. Maybe Rhea is easier to love. Probably she is.

Katie pulls up in the driveway. Fish motions for her to go up to the garage. He parks at the curb. Before they get out, Juliette says, "On our way out to River Cove, Fish told me he might build a boat and sail around the world. Do you think he will?"

"I'd say that is very, very unlikely."

"Do you suppose he's crazy? Like, he can't help himself?"

"Depends on what you think a person ought to have control of."

Juliette is baffled.

"Don't think about it," Katie says. "It's for Fish to figure out." Saying that, she thinks she might have put her finger on something important, something those women in Al-Anon would understand. She can almost see them nodding, smiling, giving her their approval. "There's nothing that has to be done," she hears Joyce saying. "There's only someone to be." Why does that seem like such a fresh idea?

What else has she been doing all these years?

—29—

They are hungry. "It looks like dead people live here," Juliette complains, examining the contents of the refrigerator. A dank odor emanates from it. "My mother doesn't seem to think anybody eats in this house anymore."

Fish laughs.

Katie, rummaging in the cabinets, finds a can of boned chicken, and another of green chiles. "Is there cheese?"

Juliette comes up with a very hard chunk of cheddar about

two inches square, with a crust along the edges. The waxed paper has crumpled and fallen away from it. "I can cut the dry part off," Katie said. "How about an omelet? There are eggs."

Juliette puts her finger in her mouth and makes a gagging noise.

"What about those enchiladas you make?" Fish asks.

"With no *cheese?*" Something in his easy familiarity bothers her. As though, after all these years, she should not be reminded that she has cooked for him.

Fish throws both hands up in surrender. "I'll go to the fucking store."

"Cheese and tortillas, that's all I really need."

"Sour cream," Juliette adds. "Salsa."

"Salad," says Fish.

"I am NOT cleaning lettuce," Katie says.

Fish plunks his keys and a ten dollar bill down on the table. "You go, Katie. I'll take a look at your car."

"Me?" Katie's heart gives a peculiar thump. She hasn't been in Fish's truck since last summer.

Fish gives her a steady gaze. "You stop driving in the past ten minutes?"

"I'll take a shower." Juliette flees up the stairs.

"Okay, okay," Katie says. Fish goes down into the basement. She goes out the front door. She approaches the van with trepidation. Getting in Fish's lair is too personal. She sits in the driver's seat a moment and tries to clear her head. All over the dashboard are Fish's penciled calculations: mileage, gallons of gas, mpg. A couple of phone numbers with initials. She doesn't know how he makes sense of it.

In the rider's seat is a beat-up pink tape player and five or six tapes. She picks some of them up: Janis Joplin, Jefferson Airplane, Dylan. Carter would say, You guys are living in another century. A wave of nostalgia sweeps over her. The music goes with times and places, miles and miles in this van. She punches ON. Mick Jagger wails, "High and dry . . . up here with no warning . . . What a way to go . . . She left me with no warning—" Oh perfect, Katie thinks painfully. She glances at the back of the truck. Fish built a bed there, a wooden frame latticed with rope. She has spent a hundred nights in that bed, or more, in this van or the one before it.

Now the bed is littered with scraps of lumber, manila folders, paper sacks. That helps. It isn't so much a bed as a surface for piles of Fish's *stuff.*

She realizes she was nervous because of an instinct not to be moved by something so stupidly nostalgic as a bed that has to be tightened every couple of nights to fight its sag.

One summer they lived in the parking lot at the pier at Honeymoon Bay while Fish worked on a salmon trawler leased out by a nervous college professor. She went out with Fish every day (what else would she have done?) but she wasn't any help. The most she ever managed to do was to make tea, and once in a while yell at sea lions as they came up to the boat and bit salmon off the lines. She was sick every day. Her weight dropped below a hundred pounds. But she wanted to be with him. She was scared of the fog, for him. She thought if she went along, nothing would happen to him, or if it did it would happen to her, too, and it wouldn't matter.

She can only remember one really pretty day, with brilliant sun. It warmed enough for bare shoulders, which were burned by late afternoon. The professor went out with them He swore he saw a whale. He ran from one side to the other, tossing them around with the movement of his heavy weight in the small boat. Neither Fish nor Katie saw any whale.

She wanders around the Safeway store like a visitor from out of town. She keeps forgetting what she is in the aisle for.

By the time she has thrown together the enchiladas (Juliette takes charge of the microwave), Fish comes in and announces he will have to buy parts. "It's too late today, and I probably can't get them on Sunday. I'll take care of it Monday, though, the latest. It's not a big thing, Katie. You should have done something about that starter a long time ago." He is confident, chiding. He seems happy to have her there. He seems to have forgotten what hangs between them.

"You shouldn't miss your work," Katie says weakly. "I can take it in somewhere." The starter suddenly seems too intimate a thing between them. She doesn't think it should make him happy to work on her car.

"How would you get it there?" he teases.

They sit down to eat, but she only picks at her food. Fish

asks Juliette when she is going to get her learner's permit and start driving.

Juliette perks up at the suggestion. "Nobody's had time to help me," she says.

Katie has her doubts about Fish as instructor (though he more or less taught her to drive, trucks being far out of her limited experience with vehicles), but he is fond of Juliette. Maybe he will draw on reserves of patience Katie has forgotten, or not known how to tap. Both Fish and Juliette seem cheered by Katie's modest effort with the food.

Ursula and Michael burst in. "Never again for fifty more years!" Ursula says.

"What do I smell?" Michael asks enthusiastically. He picks up a plate on the way to the counter. Ursula gives Katie a peculiar look. Katie can't tell if it is critical or not; she thinks it has more to do with Fish than with cooking in Ursula's kitchen. Ursula has never minded that.

"Spinach tarts didn't do it, huh?" Ursula sits down without taking any food. She taps the table with the tips of her fingers on her right hand.

"Fish was looking at my car," Katie says.

Ursula looks at her but doesn't say anything. Her left hand joins in the rhythm of her right.

"Say, Ursula. Could you take me home?"

Katie says how hard she thinks it is going to be to avoid Fish, unless she avoids them all.

"Maybe it would be easier if you left town," says Ursula. "Though I suppose that's not practical."

"The costume shop closes soon. I'd like to work wardrobe on one of the shows, but I could get away if I needed to. The shop doesn't open up again until after Christmas."

"You could go see Rhea."

"Maybe." The thought brings a lump to Katie's throat. Sometimes she misses her daughter in a vague, wistful way. It is like thinking of a trip to the Himalayas, something read about in a book.

"You need to call your mother, Katie. She called our house last night after I talked to you. I didn't give her your number, but you should. You've got to get along with her, for Rhea's sake."

"I suppose," Katie says. She gazes out of the window, down the picturesque street, with its Victorian houses and showy gardens. Like a movie set. On Michael and Ursula's street the houses are funky, but no one looks poor. Poor people live farther down, in the basin of the valley. "Do you know what Fish said to me today? He said, 'Does your new boyfriend love the taste of you?' "

"Meaning something gross?" Ursula doesn't seem to make much of it.

"He doesn't. Jeff doesn't."

"Oh Katie."

"I'm not saying he wouldn't. But some things are still—they still belong to Fish."

"Not your sexuality, Katie. Not if you get a divorce."

Ursula sounds neutral, like a social worker. She is probably thinking of her bath. She has a thing for baths, with bubbling lotions and loofahs, a radio in the bathroom, a little plastic pillow she leans back against.

"I'm not divorced yet, though, am I?" Katie says.

"Not yet. But as I understand it, you're on your way."


—30—

The professor who owned the salmon fishing boat came out every week to see how they were doing. He seemed nostalgic about his own sessions on the sea, but when he once went out for the morning with Fish and Katie, it was hard to believe he had ever known which end went first. Several times he brought them hash, good stuff, bestowing it on them with great self-importance. Another time he brought a bottle of expensive wine. He obviously expected them to drink it with him—he had brought a corkscrew with him—but Fish got a laugh out of sending him off disappointed, and then slugging the wine down as if it were two bucks a gallon. The man had a thing for Fish (and not Katie, as they naturally thought at first). Katie assumed it was admiration, Fish doing what the professor would like to be doing if only he weren't so responsible and straight.

He quizzed Fish about Vietnam. Fish always answered in short noncommittal ways, not encouraging any questions.

But he was getting a very good deal on the boat, because the professor was busy with a special grant. He was a sociologist with an interest in "the alternative culture." He often quoted books he assumed Katie and Fish knew when they didn't and he quoted verses from rock and roll songs like someone pulling out his Shakespeare. Eventually Katie and Fish realized that he considered them good specimens. Fish started leading him on. For example, Fish told him about going to Altamont (which they had), and seeing the Angels kill that poor kid (which they had not). Fish could really talk when he got wound up.

The professor came by one Saturday in August, and said they had to come to his house. There was a barbecue, a rock band, all for his daughter's seventeenth birthday. The people from Sausalito who did bubble tents were setting them up in the yard. "Gosh, we don't have a thing to wear," Fish said. The professor took him seriously. "That's okay," he reassured them. "We'll tell everyone you're from my boat. Come as you are." *That* wound Fish up. He smeared his hand across his shirt. "A little fish guts? Bait in my pocket?" The professor joked and laughed and hit Fish on the shoulder. "Be sure to wear your moustache," he kidded.

When they got to the house in the wasteland development in Fremont, the guy took them out in the back yard, behind his hideous fake-Tudor tract house, and showed them his daughter's playhouse. It was a modified replica of the big house, with electricity and windows that opened and closed. He punched Fish on the shoulder again. "She used to come out here to have tea parties with her little girlfriends. Now she comes out with her boyfriends and wants a lock on the door." Hah hah.

He put his hands on Fish's shoulders hard and peered at him. "Listen," he said, his voice cracking with earnestness. He was leaning so close Fish was cringing. "If the revolution comes—" He looked over his shoulder. "When it comes—do you think they'll take my house away?"

Fish wriggled out of his grasp and took the boat keys out of his pocket and handed them over right there. "Absolutely, man," he said. "I hadn't realized what danger we were in, fucking around with you. What a fucking near miss!"

In the truck he drove eighty on the freeway, so that the

metal shuddered. He screamed a long scream, a kind of war whoop Katie imagined they used to psych kids up in Vietnam before an attack. He leaned out the window and screamed, "AAASSHOLE!"

Fish has told that story a lot of times. Katie has heard Ursula tell it too, though a long time ago. She told it to Jeff, herself. She was trying to make him understand about Fish and her and the times in which they had come together. She was a little self-conscious because, halfway through, she realized Jeff had been in high school when this was going on. Jeff said, "I really don't want to hear about him. Why are you telling me stories about your crazy husband?"

Of course it wasn't "stories," it was one story. Katie told Jeff to get the hell out and not come back. She was an artifact from the sixties. She was embarrassed. She had had all that to say (when she seldom said much), and it had come back at her like that. A few days later Jeff showed up again like nothing had happened. He teased her about her braids, and tickled her hairy armpits and called her "my little hippie." She knew he was covering up for the fact that he'd discovered things about her—a *part* of her—that he didn't like. That part had been with Fish, eating Saltines and joshing a puffed-up academic. Maybe it has become too difficult with Fish, but she has not become another person altogether. She still hates arrogance and people who have to be "in," and she still takes pride in never having joined anybody's club. Maybe that part is only a sixth of her, an eighth. But if Jeff doesn't like it, it doesn't mean she can throw it away.

She told Maureen about the quarrel, if you could call it that. She doesn't think Maureen would know zip about the sixties, if John Lennon hadn't been murdered and everything dredged up to make money on that. Maureen isn't yet thirty. What she said was that no man wants to hear about a former lover, especially a husband.

"But everything I've ever done my whole adult life has been with Fish!" Katie wailed. What history would she have if she eliminated him?

Besides, Fish knows her, and Jeff doesn't.

Maureen insisted. "Didn't you ever hear of a clean slate?"

Katie thought that sounded like she was the one who had

gone to jail. "Shit," she said. "What's Jeff going to think when he hears about Rhea?"

—30—

Jeff comes at six-thirty and takes her to a new Mexican restaurant not far from her place. It is run by a couple from Southern California. They put black olives on everything. Katie doesn't want to say she just made enchiladas, so she claims to have overeaten at the reception. She nurses a Coke while Jeff eats fajitas. She picks something green out of his dish. "I like that," she says. "What is it?"

He says it is cilantro. "You should help me cook," he says. "You can help me make chutney soon. I'm putting it up for next winter."

They each have a beer, and he tells her about the conference in Eugene where he has spent the last three days. Agricultural geneticists living it up at the Riverside Inn. He is twisting in his seat. "I really have something to tell you."

She has to fight a yawn. The day has been exhausting. His excitement is not contagious. Actually, there doesn't seem to be much that excites him, except for his fruits and vegetables, and a certain way she touches him in bed.

She just cannot stop thinking about Fish. "I'm sorry for any way I ever hurt you," Fish whispered to her in the corner of the Grange Hall. "I wish I could be a better man." That was a lot for him to say. She was embarrassed. Men make her feel responsible for their vulnerabilities. She learned that from a book Maureen lent her.

Jeff suggests they walk. He isn't pleased with her sleepy nonchalance, but on the street he can't help being happy.

"The grape-growers are sending me to France!" They are standing beside the duck pond in the park. "I'll probably visit pears, too." Visiting pears sounds silly.

What can she say? "That's nice."

"Nice!" He squeezes her hand and marches her up the street, up the steep hill to her back entrance. "Nice, the lady says! I'm going to France, and she calls that nice!" They go into her apartment, and he puts his arms around her and kisses her. "Did they serve him the papers?" he asks, leaning against her the same way Fish did in the afternoon in the Grange.

"Oh yes, they did that."

"Good."

"He came out to his parents' anniversary party all worked up. I shouldn't have done it."

Jeff pulls away.

"I should have waited until next week." Her mind is suddenly full of Geneva's forbearance, the sister's good-natured brazenness, the awful food that should have been good. And Juliette with her arms above her head. It would be too much work to explain all that to Jeff. He wouldn't be interested. It makes her tired even to consider talking through all that.

"Now it's started. Nothing can happen until that's behind you, Katie."

"Fish," she says stubbornly. "Fish is not a 'that'."

"That tie, I meant."

She doesn't ask: What happens then? She hasn't thought ahead and doesn't know if Jeff has. He is closer to Maureen's age than hers. He was surprised when she said she was forty. Besides, she doesn't have much curiosity about him, or about the future in general. If there is anything she believes in, it is fate.

Jeff blurts out, "And there's no way we can plan a damned thing while you still have him around your neck!"

She doesn't like the idea that he knows how things might go but she has to pass a test to hear about it. What does he think he is planning? She doesn't have any plans, with or without him. She is thinking about buying a little air conditioner, to get through the hot months of July and August, and that is about it for plans and Katie Fisher. Even the divorce remains tentative; it's not like she has a court date set, is it?

She goes over and sits on the cushions on the floor, and Jeff pulls one close and sits down beside her, facing her. The room is pleasantly bare. A rectangle of glass sits on two wooden blocks near the cushions. There is an old director's chair and a baby spotlight on a slim, long stand. These things came with the studio. The floors are bare shiny oak. The little kitchen has a table that clips up against the wall when not in use. She sleeps on a futon in an alcove, and keeps her clothes in baskets. It is the neatest she has been since she stopped living in June's house. She doesn't feel like she lives here. She feels she is visiting. She thinks about their house. Jeff reaches over and runs his fingers along Katie's neck, then leans way over to kiss her. "Kate," he calls her. He wants to go to bed, so she gets up with him. He walks behind her, a pale slim shadow. She doesn't especially like his fairness, though she has gotten used to it. She does like the long corded muscles of his legs, and his long fingers. She likes his broad shoulders edging out over hers when he lies on her, instead of meeting her, bone to bone. She likes it that he feels so different from Fish.

They make love on top of her pale green down comforter. Pistachio Ice, the package said. Ursula gave it to her at Christmas, as if she needed something special while Fish was away. Katie was made uneasy by the expensive gift. She blurted out once, when she and Ursula were alone in the kitchen, "I've got a lover." Ursula immediately got busy slicing cheese and laying out Wheat Thins on a platter. She didn't say anything. Later Katie thought, maybe all I really said was, I've got a boyfriend.

"I thought you might go with me," Jeff says. He is urgent after three days away. He jogs, plays racquetball, makes love. A well-rounded fitness plan. "You can carry the phrasebook." He runs his hand along her spine. She feels disconnected, but she feels she will eventually be able to sleep, and sleep will release her from thinking. She is just about sick of thinking.

She touches Jeff at the back, pushing her finger up against him in the way that delights and embarrasses him. "When?" she asks. She is asking about France.

"Now," he moans.

"Where's your car?" He is standing at the kitchen door, looking out onto the little lot behind the house where he is parked.

"At Ursula's. There's something wrong with the starter. I had to get pushed today."

"We can go get it tomorrow."

"It's okay." She can see he doesn't like it. She can't think when he has gotten so possessive, or whatever this is. Probably since Fish got out of jail. The first time he came home with her she told him, "I don't want to pretend I'm free when I'm not." Hearing herself, she burst into nervous laughter. She felt like Katharine Hepburn. They made love, and he had a terrible nosebleed. They laughed some more and said you did what you could when you could, and who ever expected more than that? She threw away the pillow where he'd bled. Later he said, "I never have gone with a married woman. Of course I didn't know you were married at first—" She said she had never had a ring. He went on. "But I thought it over and it feels okay to me. Like he isn't around for more reasons than just where he is. Like you weren't feeling married." She said, "It's okay, really. It's okay." He sounded like he wanted to be forgiven for spending time with her. She didn't think he would like it if she said she didn't think Fish would care. It wasn't like she could be with Fish instead.

"I'll pick you up at five," he says now. He likes to cook for her, likes to take charge of her days off if his are free. "Or we could have a late breakfast and spend the day together. You can keep me company while I do my bachelor things."

"I've got things to do myself." They have never discussed it, but neither has suggested sleeping at the other's place. Maybe that's what could change if she got a divorce. Only she has never thought of it as something she'd like to do.

She ponders the word *bachelor* a moment. It is a word you never hear anymore except on old tv reruns. Where did Jeff pick it up? She knows nothing about his family. He is from the Midwest. Maybe he has said other things, but she wasn't listening. Such things don't make much difference to her. She does know that people can see the world in very different ways. She would never ask him personal questions. Besides, he will probably get around to telling about his parents. So far he has told her about former girlfriends, boyhood pranks, and several college tales. She has no idea why he talks so much, except that you have to do something besides eat and make love. It is a problem that never came up with Fish. Fish has never bored her, though she has often worried about saying the wrong thing to him. All in all, being quiet seems safest with men and mothers.

"I feel like sleeping in," she says.

He kisses her on the cheek.

It occurs to her that if she is getting a divorce for Jeff she might be making a mistake. Divorce better firmly have to do with her and Fish. They are the only two she knows who will for sure have to live with it.

—31—

She bathes and heats water for chamomile tea. She is just reaching for a cup when she hears a noise at the back door. She glances at the clock. It is only eleven, though it feels later. Someone in the parking lot, she decides.

She pours the tea and sits at the table with the cup between her hands. The night is cool and pleasant. She can smell it through the window above the sink.

"Katie." It is Fish at the back door. The tea she drank rises up in her throat.

"What are you doing here?" she asks through the screen. The door isn't locked, but he doesn't try to open it.

"I saw you had somebody here. I waited to be sure he wasn't coming back, not just out for beer. I wouldn't mess you up, Katie."

"Go home." Just what she felt like saying to Jeff, though she doesn't know why.

"I've never seen the inside of your apartment."

"There's nothing to see. It's practically empty."

"We need to talk."

"It's late." About fifteen years.

"Not for us. I know you. You don't go to bed early."

"I have new habits. I work. I get up earlier."

"They got me up at five in the morning, but that doesn't mean I have to do it now."

"You've been drinking," she guesses. He has to have worked up his nerve. She is worried he will laugh at her herb tea, that he will say it is "dandy," something picked up from the arty people she now knows. He should see Maureen's apartment, with aphorisms stuck up all over the place.

"I haven't, Katie. Honest to God." He leans his face against the screen. The light hits his face. "Smell," he says.

She opens the door and lets him in.

"There's not anything to say," she tells him. They remain near the door. She thinks she should be cool, detached. If they talk she will only get emotional. He will confuse her.

"I learned a lot in jail. There was a lot of time to think."

"You were in jail before. What did you learn those times? What good did jail ever do you, or anyone?"

"Those times were before you." He is leaving out two overnights for tickets, thirty days for DUI, forty-five days until he plea-bargained a dumb possession charge in Napa. He is only counting hard time in Miami, and Oakland, in the navy. "All I learned was to be mad and not to trust anybody. Not to be a stupid dick."

The first time, in Miami (he'd borrowed somebody's car that time, too), he was grateful to this big black guy who gave him a cigarette. As soon as he turned around with it, the dude pulled his pants down and clamped his hand around his mouth before Fish could take a drag. That story plagued Katie when Fish went to jail this time. She kept remembering the sound of Fish's voice as he talked about it, the pain, and how she had wanted to make it up to him.

"So what do you know now, Fish?" She feels as if a heavy fluid is being poured into her veins. She wants to go to bed.

"I'm converting the top floor of this big old house into an apartment. A neighbor wants me to do a fancy screened-in porch. Hell, there's work all over, Katie. Michael says I should get licensed, legit. He's going to look into it. I like working, Katie. It feels good to have money in my pocket."

"I know."

"Should I give you money?" What a pathetic question. He really doesn't know. But neither does she.

They don't give June money for Rhea. It is part of the agreement. June has Rhea. She has the say, and the costs. Katie and Fish have their freedom. Katie can't help wondering, lately, if she would be happier if she had her daughter instead.

"I get an okay salary."

"Sewing, right?"

Tears are working their way up from a well deep in her chest, into her nose. "Jesus, Fish, I'm not going to stand here in the middle of the night and tell you about buttons and zippers and basting threads!"

She walks into the main room. The glass table top is splotchy with fingerprints and smears. She has a strong urge to find something to clean it.

"Don't do it, Katie. Not yet. Give me some time."

"I can't."

"Because if you do, you might not?"

"Or because I've made up my mind."

She sits on the cushions, not looking at him.

He moves quickly. He kneels and puts his hands along her hips. He has always been a good lover. If he ever shut her out, he shut her out that way too. He hasn't used her.

"Oh God don't leave me Katie baby." The words come out in a fierce gush. "What have I got without you? How will I get through the years?"

The blood of her flesh rushes to the places where his hands lie. He said something once to her, long ago, about growing old together, and she was thrilled by it.

She has only gone to bed with him once since his release, in Michael's basement. He reeked of cigarettes and wine and sweat, and the smells made her sick. She put him off, saying she was working overtime, saying she needed time to read-just.

"Just tonight," he whispers. He has showered again and put on a clean shirt, a faded yellow plaid. She bought that shirt at a flea market in Astoria.

She jumps up, startling him. "You've got to go home. I want you to go home." She doesn't know how else to accomplish this, except to put a distance between them. She should go to Texas, and find out what her daughter's favorite color is. "I just went to bed with another man, goddamn you, Fish. Go home."

He has moved onto a cushion. His legs are apart, his elbows resting on his raised knees, his head hanging. "Shit," he mumbles. "Aw shit."

"Listen, listen to me." She stands a few feet away, uncomfortable lording it over him, but not daring to come down to his level. He is contrite and sad and pleading. He would come to her tenderly, he would make her cry out. "I don't hate you or anything. I'm not mad. It's not a stunt." That's all he would know about, stunts. He does not know about resolution. "I've made up my mind, that's all. I've—turned a corner."

"It's that guy. Somebody you met while I was in jail. Some-body you fucked while I was locked up with nothing but squirrels to diddle." While he talks, he stares at the floor.

Maybe he is right. Maybe it is Jeff who gave her courage. Maybe she is using what she can find for strength.

"It's like, I ran out of gas. All the energy all those years. When you got busted this time, it used up all I had left. I cried. Then I got sick of sitting around Ursula's watching daytime tv, and I got this job, and my own place, and that gave me new energy, but for something new."

He looks up. "What the fuck have you been reading?"

She smiles tightly. It is aggravating of him to put his finger on it like that. She is starting to sound like Maureen's books. But if you are going to stop rejecting the whole world, you need something to hold onto, you need a bridge. And books are better than a lot of things, better than nothing. They give you a vocabulary. They give you ideas to mouth when you can not come up with something on your own. And some-times they are bound to be right.

"I haven't had a drop to drink all day," Fish says.

"I don't care!"

"I could stop drinking. Like you always wanted. I *have* stopped. What if I stopped drinking altogether? And I worked steady? What if that?"

"I guess things would be better for you."

"Isn't that why you want a divorce? To make me be *good?* You think I'm a fucking alcoholic, but I tell you, Katie, I am not. You didn't see me shaking and moaning in jail with nothing to drink, cause it didn't matter."

She doesn't look at him.

"How long does it take for the divorce to happen?" he asks.

"Ninety days."

"What if I'm sober the whole three months? What if I leave you alone but I'm a fucking saint? Would that make any difference? Would it convince you?"

"I don't think so."

He finally gets up. "Cunt," he says.

She goes out the front door, slamming it behind her, and knocks on Maureen's door across the hall.

Maureen is in her robe, but her lights are on. "Come in," she says. "Quick, honey." Katie thinks she will start bawling, but she doesn't. She takes a deep breath and she says, "Fish is at my place. Saying he'll straighten up."

"Let's go to bed, you look beat." Maureen turns off the lights. Katie follows her to bed and crawls in without saying anything more. Maureen snuggles close and wipes Katie's hair off her forehead. She smells of sesame oil.

"Jeff is going to France," Katie says wearily. "He thinks I should go."

"Oh to hell with Jeff," Maureen says.

Towards dawn Katie wakes up. She thinks about going home, but she is lying on the inside of Maureen's bed, near the wall, and she doesn't want to wake her.

"Worrying?" Maureen asks.

"I woke you."

"I'm a light sleeper."

"I was thinking about selling my car. I can't stand having it to worry about. I was trying to think of all the times I've driven it in the past month. I could do without it."

"Is it going to be expensive to fix?"

"I don't think so. It's only the starter. I'm silly."

"Look at me." Maureen doesn't own a car.

"This is the first time I ever had a car on my own. I never drove until I met Fish."

"I thought all Texans were car nuts."

"Myth. I took driver's ed in high school but my father always had the car. My mother said I couldn't bother him with it."

"Want to hear how I started driving?"

"Sure."

Through Maureen's filmy curtains Katie can see daylight.

"I started driving when I was twelve."

"You didn't!"

"We lived in Prineville, you know where that is?"

"Sort of. Eastern part of the state."

"Right. We'd need things in Redmond. There was my mother and me, and two littler kids. She had a boyfriend for a while. He teased me, said I was big for my age. Now I think he probably had something in mind, but he never made the move. He didn't stick around long enough. He said I ought to learn to drive, *the way my mother was.* The way my mother was, was some mornings she couldn't get out of bed. Some of the time she worked at a cafe. Some of the time we were on welfare. Anyway, he taught me to drive. Good thing, too. Once I took one of my sisters to the hospital by myself. She broke her arm on a swing."

"Where are they now? Your sisters?"

"I'll tell you another time."

"I should go home."

"Give me half an hour and come back for coffee."

"You do too much."

"Come back. I hate Sunday morning." Now that Katie looks at her, Maureen does look teary-eyed.

Katie reaches for her friend's hand. "Did I upset you? About your sisters? Are they okay?"

Maureen shakes her head. Which question she is answering, she doesn't say. *No*, she says and puts her finger to her lips. "Another time," she adds.

When Katie comes back, dressed in loose old khaki pants, Maureen has put blueberry muffins in the oven, and made coffee. Katie reads a pink card on her refrigerator. It says, "My past is finished and I am free of it."

"You know," Katie says as they wait for the muffins, drinking the first cup of coffee, "you don't seem like a girl with a hard-luck background. You seem like, well, like anybody."

"I was trash."

"I wasn't much, either."

"How old were you, you know, the first time?"

"My senior year. Seventeen. It was dumb, nothing awful."

"I was fourteen. I was mad at my mother because she said I was acting slutty. I wore makeup and went around with older kids, but it was all put on. Then she made me mad. I brought a boy home, maybe nine o'clock one night. She was out cold on the couch. We went into my room. The next day I told her, before she was all the way awake. She acted like she didn't understand. 'Now, Maureen, when you bring a boy home, you introduce him to me. Wake me up if I'm napping, now.' Napping!" She takes out the muffins. "Okay without butter?"

"Who needs butter?" They break apart the muffins, releasing the sweet smell and steam.

"What I hate," Maureen says, "is that my little sisters were there too, in the living room watching tv, while I was in my room screwing. Like, I was doing to them what my mother was doing to me."

"You were fourteen. They weren't your responsibility."

They eat in silence. Shyly, Katie says, "I can't believe that I can talk to you about—I hadn't thought of that boy in a hundred years. It was in a park, behind some bushes, and I'm sure he thought I was wild and experienced, and he was upset when he found out I wasn't. He said he was sorry, and made me cry. I never talked to him again. Now, all these years later, I can see him. His short buzzed haircut and his nice big shoulders, and tight jeans. And I remember I wanted to tell my mother, too, I wanted to taunt her with it, but I knew it wouldn't hurt her, it would hurt me. What was better was having it secret from her. Having her ask where was I going and what was I going to do, and having curfews, while all the time I knew I could do whatever I liked. God. It comes back."

"See? Memory's not a hole your life falls into. It's all there. You could get into it. We've got everything in this town. You could get into rebirthing, that far, or farther."

Katie finds that funny. "I don't think there was a birth," she says. "I don't think my mother had me. I think she spit me out."

—32—

Katie, dressed for dinner at Jeff's, is standing with him in the driveway of Michael's house. They arrived to find Michael buzzing the lawn with edge-clippers. Michael turned the machine off and is now amiably listening to them.

"I don't understand this arrangement of vehicles." Jeff says. He insisted on going for Katie's car. He has made arrangements for a friend to work on it in the morning.

Katie's car is in the front of the drive, by the garage. Behind it are both Ursula's car and Michael's pea-green pickup. "How are we going to get in there to give your car a jump?" he asks Katie.

Katie says nothing. Michael drawls, "I don't think a jump will do it."

"I told you, it's not the battery," Katie says. Her jaw aches from clenching her teeth. To please Jeff, who invited another couple, she is wearing a dress she bought a few weeks before, a mauve rayon print in a modified forties style, with a wide waist and buttons all the way down the front. She feels awkward in front of Michael, with Jeff, in a new dress.

"What it would need is a push," Michael says blandly.

"A push!" Jeff explodes. "How the hell are we supposed to push a car that's between the garage and another car!"

"I don't think Fish figured on giving it any more pushes. He's going to repair the starter. The rest of us will be at work, and he can back right out."

"If you move your cars now we can push it backwards into the street," Jeff says. Katie is mortified. She can't imagine what Jeff is waiting on. Maybe he is starting to see how stupid he is being. Until today, Katie would have described Jeff as a calm and polite human being, not provoked by minor irritations, and predictably intelligent. A scientist. She seems to have brought out the worst in him.

"Ursula!" Katie calls out brightly as Ursula comes down the front steps.

Ursula looks rumpled and sleepy. Katie makes hasty introductions, which Ursula and Jeff barely acknowledge. "We've come for my car."

"Fish has gone round to Bi-Mart. He'll be back any minute. Anybody want a beer?"

Jeff marches over to Katie's car and peers in. Katie says to Ursula, "Feels just like summer, huh?" She feels stupid.

Michael is winding the cord neatly around the handle of the edge-cutter and tying it with a length of wire. "Beer sounds good," he says, and takes the edger down the basement stairs.

Fish pulls along the curb. He comes up the drive carrying a large brown paper bag of cans. "I thought since I couldn't work on the starter today, I'd change the oil and plugs and filter," he says to Katie. He pretends not to see Jeff.

"We'd like to take the car," Jeff says stiffly, coming closer. He glances at his watch.

"That'd be a real dumbshit thing to do," Fish says to Katie.

"I've made arrangements." Jeff is telling this to Katie, too.

"This is ridiculous!" Ursula snaps. Her glare takes them all in. Ursula's eyes narrow. It is unusual for her to be ill-tempered.

"There's plenty of help here. We just push the car into the

street and get it started." Jeff speaks as if they are all small children. "After the cars are moved." He goes to his own car.

Katie sees Fish go from angry to hurt to perplexed, and back through again. He clasps the cans to his chest. "What is this shit about?" he asks Katie.

About MY business, Katie thinks angrily. About Jeff, whose business it is not, telling me what to do.

He was so insistent, rational, and cool. She should not be depending on the man she has just decided to divorce. She should learn to manage her own affairs. (And who is managing them now?)

"I've got to go," she says.

"I'll push the fucking car down the drive," Fish says. He throws the sack to the ground and the cans roll in the yard. "I'll push it through the fucking YARD—"

Ursula reaches out and grabs Fish by the shirt. "Hold on."

Katie turns and walks back to Jeff's tidy little Nova. Standing in the street at the door, she smiles tensely at Fish. "Sorry," she says. She doesn't know if he can hear her, but he is looking her way and he must get the idea. He picks the cans back up and stomps off toward the car.

Michael comes down the front steps with beer bottles. "Forget it," Katie hears Ursula say.

"Hey thanks!" Katie calls inanely. Michael and Ursula are attending to some other matter between them It is a relief to slip away.

"What is going on?" Jeff demands as he slams his door. "This is the craziest damned divorce I ever saw."

She is looking past him at the Fishers in their yard. Carter has come around the back and taken a beer from his dad. Ursula begins to talk intensely, shaking her hands at Carter, who looks, as he usually does, like he is about to laugh. Juliette is hanging out of the second-story window, waving toward Jeff's car. Her hair hangs loose, a Rapunzel's cascade. A year ago she was a child.

"I want to go!" Katie says.

Jeff starts the car.

"There are two ways to get through this evening," Katie says. "Take me home or forget this scene."

"I have a rack of lamb in the oven and good friends coming to dinner." He looks at her glumly. It seems almost funny to hear him say, "I like your dress."

A block or so later he says, "So that's the famous Fish."

Katie ignores his contempt, though she feels defensive and angry. She says quietly, "He's a plain person, like me."

Jeff's friend Oatley is a specialist in grains at the experimental station. His wife, Jane, is pregnant, just starting to show. They are at least ten years younger than Katie. Jeff puts on music that Katie doesn't like—something jazzy but quiet, muted, and dull. He and Oatley begin to discuss things she can't follow, while she and Jane sip their Chablis and smile now and then. Jeff's duplex is furnished comfortably. Katie sinks back into the big soft cushions of an armchair. Jeff says he has to see to the food, and Oatley follows him into the kitchen, talking about durum wheat.

"Do you—" both women begin at once, and laugh. "You first," Katie says. She has been thinking that Jane's hair is expensively cut, in a precisely casual way that makes her look as though it isn't necessary to spend any time at all on her looks. Such easy beauty has always awed Katie.

"I was wondering if you have something to do with the station, too."

"I met Jeff at a party. I work in the costume shop at the theatre festival." Katie is sure Jane knows everyone who works at the experimental station. Why doesn't she just say, Who are you?

"How wonderful! How fascinating."

Katie doesn't know whether to ask what Jane does. *She* did not do anything at all while she was pregnant. Maybe Jane is waiting for Katie to say more about her job. People think anything that has to do with theatre is exciting. In its way, it is. She does humble work, but she is fast and dependable. She sees the designs go from paper through all their hands to the stage. It is the only interesting work she has ever done. To think she learned what she knows from her mother!

Would Jane be interested in any of that?

Or would she want to talk about herself?

At the shop, Katie listens to the women talk about babies. Friends and sisters, one of the cutters, all expecting. They talk about whether the baby was planned or not, whether there will be a midwife or a doctor. They talk about prenatal yoga and bonding.

Jane, apparently cued by Katie's silence, says, "I do children's books. I think of myself as an illustrator, but we're so far from anywhere, I have to do the stories, too. I can't pair up with anyone from here."

"That sounds like fun."

"It is, though I don't do as well as I might, financially. I need to get to New York and make some contacts. Once people know me I can do a lot by phone and mail. I was thinking of spending some time there this winter, but now—" She pats her stomach.

"New York will always be there," Katie says. It is the last place she would want to be.

The conversation, such as it was, dies. Katie offers to get them more wine but Jane pats herself again and declines. "I'm trying to do all the right things. After all, I'm married to a biologist."

Katie supposes that was a witty thing to say, and she smiles at Jane, but she is starving, and she wonders if Jeff will stay angry at her. She hopes their tiff has not made Fish angry too, so that her car will still be sitting there tomorrow. She hopes Jeff will be himself again, but not amorous. She wants to eat and go home to sleep. Alone. She feels she has walked straight into a conflict not worth having, and she wants to forget it. She doesn't care if she ever sees Jeff again.

She is happy to see the food the men bring in: lamb and crusty peaked potato puffs, and the orange cauliflower she has been hearing about. She utters praise. She answers their questions briefly, and by the time the plates are emptied, she realizes the three of them are having quite a good time without her. They are friends, and they go easily from topic to topic, to which she has nothing to add. Most of the time she doesn't even know what they are talking about: old-growth forests, land-use planning, airline safety, a new museum site. She cannot stifle her yawns.

She and Fish used to talk about things they had seen that day that were dumb, things that made them mad at the stupid way the world was run. They told one another the plots of books they were reading. They talked about Ursula and Michael and their kids, about what to make for dinner, and maybe about someplace to go next winter or next summer or next year. It didn't really matter what they said. They occupied the same space. They were companions.

The others begin speaking of the baby. Jane's mother will come first for two weeks. Oatley's will come next, and then he will take a few weeks' leave. They will decorate the back bedroom in yellow and white. They will use a birthing room at the hospital. Katie floats. Surely they will not ask her opinion. In her own pregnancy she did not so much as read a magazine article. She assumed someone would tell her what to do at the hospital. She was glad she hadn't fooled herself about who was in charge. She was glad she hadn't had any idea how humiliating and painful it would all be.

If they look at her she will say, How wonderful.

The wonder is that Jeff is so intrigued. He is enjoying the talk of babies and breathing lessons. He hasn't ever brought up those prospects for himself. Maybe only women speculate about babies. Maybe, for all his rambling revelations, he thinks she is too odd to talk about babies.

Oatley and his wife are hardly out the door before Katie jumps on Jeff. "You could really get into that, couldn't you?" He is an ordinary, hard-working, successful young man, with a strong ego, and every reason to want a normal life, a family life, which she has never assumed she would have. Which Fish has guaranteed she will not have.

His eyes flash with aggravation. "We must have covered fifty subjects tonight," he says.

"Babies."

"They're my friends. I'll be the godfather."

"You'd like one, too, wouldn't you? You'd like to be a father?" She is growing angry, with no time or inclination to wonder why.

"Well of course I would!" He looks away. She takes a breath and calms down. She feels doltish. She feels, as she has for days now, that things are out of her hands. She did not mean to pick a quarrel. His very defensiveness is full of warning and hints of perspectives she has not considered. His private life. His future. For all his intimate discussions, he has never said anything that really matters.

She collects her wits. "I only ever had one real lover and that was Fish. I never dated. I don't have the experience to figure out where we are, you and I, Jeff. If I'm supposed to understand something, you have to tell me. It's probably not a good time to bring it up." She tries to think why he would be attracted to her. She must seem so uneducated and out-dated, though he once claimed she was intriguing.

"Christ, I asked you to go to Europe with me!"

"And then?"

He is exasperated. "I'll pay for it. I want your company. I thought you would be thrilled, Katie!" At least, excited, he calls her her own childish name and not the alternative one he has imposed on her without asking.

"I never said I wanted to go to Europe."

"Everybody wants to go to France."

"Everybody wants to have children, too. You should ask someone else. You don't have me in mind for that."

"I'm not going to Europe to have a baby! Why are you trying to pick a fight? Christ, Katie, you are crazy."

"I want to leave." He said *crazy*. And maybe he is right.

## —33—

They drive to her place in silence. After Jeff drops her off without apology (what does he have to be sorry for? why did they quarrel?), she sits in the apartment in the dark, sipping her own cheap Chablis until the bottle is empty, and so is her mind. All she thinks is, What was I thinking?

How did she ever forget that she is an outsider, and that only another outsider would ever understand?

She changes into her scuffed Reeboks and walks down the hill and across the boulevard, over to the Fisher house.

A single light shines in the front room, but she cannot see in the window. She imagines Michael reading. Or maybe Carter working on something.

She sees no light through the tiny basement window. She walks down the steps and stands there dumbly, still not know-ing what she is doing. Did she expect Fish to be sitting on the curb waiting for her?

When she thinks back over all the years with him, all the anguish, the separations, the quarrels and silences, she re-members how there were perfect moments, too, when they understood that a bad time had passed, when they came together without explaining or dissecting what had hap-pened before, just came together because it felt right and there were the two of them against the world, and there was nothing they needed to say.

She leans toward the door and hears the low murmur of a radio. Fish's truck is on the street. He has to be inside.

She aches, though she does not know just where.

The door opens and she jumps.

"I heard you on the stairs." Fish slips out of the basement and closes the door behind him. He is wearing jeans and no shirt or shoes. He puts his hands on her shoulders.

"I'm sorry about this afternoon," she whispers.

They are so close on the stairs she can feel his body heat. He is tan and strong, his arms ropy, his hands rough from his work.

She realizes there must be a reason he didn't want her in the basement. She feels a flush of embarrassment. "I'll go."

"No." He moves a hand to her waist. He touches the top button of her dress with the other hand. "Pretty," he says.

She slides away and moves up the stairs to the yard, slowly, with effort.

"Let's sit in the van," he suggests.

She turns back to him. "Who's inside?"

"Never mind. She's asleep. I was coming out for a smoke."

She follows him to the truck and slides in on his side, across to the other seat. The stars are out. People are supposed to be happy. Somewhere nearby someone plays a melancholy song on the saxophone, not well, too slowly.

"What do you want me to do?" he asks. He takes a cigarette and match from the dashboard, lights the cigarette, and inhales deeply.

"I want you to tell me about it."

"Jail?" She feels closest to him when he tells her things that happened to him when she was not with him, things he would not tell anyone else, things that will never be a story in his repertoire.

"Yes." She waits while he takes several more drags off his cigarette. He flips the butt into the street.

"We planted trees."

"I know. But before that, in the prison. Did they hurt you?"

"No. They hurt younger guys. Kids. Pretty boys." He scoots closer to her. "Fresh meat."

She makes a sound in her throat. "But not you."

"I lay on my cot at night and listened to them scream."

"And nobody came."

"Nobody."

"But not at the camp."

"There wasn't that. There were two men who had their way, but they wanted it and nobody cared." He touches her top button again. He undoes it, and touches the base of her throat with two fingers.

"And the Indian?"

He takes his hand away and stares forward. "Indian?"

"You wrote about an Indian." How could he forget? It was his only card. ("He can do bird calls.") "Did they send him back after he broke the rules?"

"They put him to work in the kitchen."

"Oh."

Fish crawls past her and begins moving things off the bed. Her heart is pounding so hard she thinks he must hear it. The loose button of her dress seems to flap against her pulse. He shakes the shabby quilt and smooths it over the bed. She made the quilt from scraps in a cabin they rented one winter in British Columbia. She felt so clever, like a pioneer cat.

"Come here." He is sitting near the end, on the edge. She moves to the bed, not quite next to him. She notices the horn again, playing the same tune again, something she knows.

"There were deer." His voice is sweet now, and it touches some place deep inside her. "There was a little fawn whose mother must have been shot. We heard it bleating in the brush and took it up to the cabin. They got us bottles so we could nurse it. I fed it from a bottle."

She touches Fish's hand. He is warm. She is nearly shivering.

"It wasn't so bad," she says. "Long, but not awful."

"Not so awful." He kneels in front of her, kicking things out of the way, and he puts his face into her lap. "It was half my life," she thinks he says. Slowly, he pulls her dress up to her thighs and lays his face between her legs. "It was forever. It changed everything."

She moans and lies back on the narrow bed. Her head pushes against the wall of the truck. She smells wood and the cold metal of tools, a mustiness in the quilt. Fish is kissing and caressing her. It is an old Nina Simone song, she's sure of it.

"But the Indian was okay?"

He moves onto the bed with her, shifting her to its length and to his. "The Indian put his head in a bread bag and suffocated. The Indian had the last say."

"Fisher," she says. The song says, 'I see my life come shining . . . Any day now, any day now, I shall be released.'"

It grows cool in the night. She would have been cold but for Fish lying next to her. At the first tinge of gray light she wakes with a start and feels herself clutch with panic. Fish is awake, too.

"Katie," he says, in a rare, throaty voice.

She sits up. "I've got to go. I've got to go to work in a while."

"I'll drive you."

"No." She puts her shoes on and tries to smooth her hair. "That's silly."

"I want to walk." She crawls over the seat and slides down out of the van. Fish follows her. He pushes her against the side of the van. He leans against her, his face along her cheek. "I do love you," he says. "You're the only woman I've ever loved. You're the only person who ever understood the pain."

"Shh! Don't talk, please don't talk." Talk was what she wanted. Now she doesn't know. She remembers a story in a magazine, years ago, about a woman from New York on vacation. The woman fell in love with a Laplander. She went off with him to herd deer and she didn't know a word of his language.

"What's going to happen, Katie?"

"I don't know!" she cries out, pushing him from her. Quickly she walks away, down the street. She knows he will watch her until she is out of sight. She is glad she wore the dress.

What would he think of her silky slip, her linen skirt?

—34—

Gully wakes about five that same morning. He knows it is too early for Geneva to be up. He pads into the bathroom and back to his room, and sits on the side of his bed in his boxer shorts and shirt. He speaks quietly. "Yesterday don't count for nothing, tomorrow will come soon enough. Now's the day I'm going to make it, good or rough." It is his own poem and he says it every morning. He believes it.

Then, because there is time to kill before Geneva gets up and makes coffee, he takes out a little book of reflections and reads for a while. He doesn't try to ponder what he reads, or make too much of it. He just reads, though he does tend to read a page two or three times before he moves on to the next. There are things he needs to be reminded of, like counting on a Higher Power, and knowing that, helpless and worthless as he is, he can get through the day cold sober and maybe useful to somebody for something, as long as he isn't too wrapped up in what *he* needs, what *he* wants, in what he wishes he'd done different, way another time ago.

His mind wanders from his reading. He has been dreaming of his boys, and bits of the dreams stay with him, happy thoughts. There was the year the Columbia River was so high it backed up the Sandy for several miles above them and made a lake. Fish went into what he called his gyppo logging business (and sure enough that's what it was), enlisting Michael and their dog Sprout, who would never be left behind. The boys scouted logs that had been stuck along the river bank by earlier floods, and took advantage of the high water to get them down. The hard part was leaving the slack water, to go into the flooding Columbia, with a twelve-foot boat and a 3 1/2 horsepower motor. At that point everything turned hind-to, and it was all the boys could do to keep the logs aimed to hit the log buyer's boom out in the river, but they never lost a log. What good boys they were, and smart to figure all that out. Fish, especially, had his wits about him, and a real go-to attitude. He always liked doing something nobody else had thought of or managed before him. He must have been good use to the navy, seeing the kind of boy he was. Gully remembered a time Fish told him about, when his boat challenged a North Viet freighter in the moonlight, goosing it to make it fire first so they could fire back. Of course there were lots of young men involved—it was a big Vietnamese boat, one of the biggest destroyed in the war, and the boys later got citations—but Gully always thinks of it as Fish in his Sandy River boat, fighting his way to the buyer's float, riding on the thrill of a challenge.

There is no shade on Gully's little window, and the room is brightening. He wonders if Geneva has had a hard time getting to sleep. All day Sunday she and Ruby talked and talked; he went stalking in the woods to get away from their rattling. It isn't like her to sleep in past six, though she sometimes makes coffee and goes back to bed again. He can wait. If she is still in bed, it is because she needs the rest.

He wishes he knew what else to do for her. He knows he has not succeeded in making amends to her, though he has come back to that step again and again. You never finish a step. You work in a cycle, finding new ways to be a better person, or—more likely, in his case—to hold on the best you can. You learn things about yourself and find new faults, remember wrongs you've done. You are never finished. Dr. Jim told him something important though. He said you could get puffed up with your own importance if you dwelled on your past sins and mortifications too long. It is a delicate thing, to remember and be sorry, without wallowing. One way or the other, there is Geneva, popping up in his daily ruminations, not only because she is there—God bless her, and what would he do if she wasn't?—but because there is a prickly bush between them, they are always reaching across.

For a long time he thought that if he could help Fish, that would make her happy. He even said so in an AA meeting, but as soon as he spoke the idea out loud he knew what a fool he was being, and arrogant, too, thinking he had all that power. You can't deliver people, or save them, or make them "be good," the way you want them to be. You have to look to yourself, and if you are humble and happy (and humble is important), other people can do what they need to do, *if they want to.* Even if it is your beloved son, and you can see plain as day the deep carved lines of pain and shame and hopelessness in his face, you can't take hold of it, you can't *tell* him. That is such a hard thing. *Help me accept,* you pray. He prays it in the morning and a hundred times a day. Oh how he prayed this past year, with Fish in jail! Help me accept. He doesn't pray for Fish. He prays for his own serenity. God will see to Fish. Eventually.

Geneva is another matter. She is his wife. She is there every morning with his coffee, with his meals and clean clothes and a house to live in, with her boxes of mementoes and rented movies and library books. He knows he has to do for her if he can. And he does try. He puts up new shelves, he trades his labor for a better washer at the lodge up the road. He sat down with her and humored her through that blasted anniversary "recipe" she wanted. He puts up with her sister. He admits he would never have lived this long without her. He brags about her. But she is a furious woman and he cannot fix that. It isn't in his power. It isn't his anger.

He cannot bring back Evelyn.

He does better with strangers than his own family. It was Dr. Jim who taught him to reach out, that it is the twelfth step that fuels all the rest. The doctor had his name down to be called, and the time came when Gully needed to talk. Getting Dr. Jim was sheer luck and God's intervention. They found they both loved to stomp around outdoors; the talk came easier that way. It is a hard thing to think of the doc gone, and not to know what happened. Well, now he is the one to offer a lifejacket now and then. The men are his own kind, except for the difference in luck. "I'll give you a ride, brother," he'll say. "Let me tell you what I did a hundred times." Or "What's on your mind?" Mostly the men slip away after getting warm and fed, after a little company, and sometimes a place to sleep at night, but sometimes they carry away an idea, the germ of their own salvation, because they learn that there are other people in the world, and those people care. Maybe they don't want to be sober yet, but they will know where to go when they do. "Now you remember," he always tells them. "It isn't me you need, it's AA." He doesn't say Higher Power, because it takes a while to get to that. He just wants them to know there is help, anywhere they go, even if it is jail, a flophouse, a detox ward. "Don't worry about what you'll do," he'll say. "Worry about the first step." Surrender, son.

He has never been able to make Geneva understand. Once he suggested that she go to an open meeting with him, and she just about died. "Me go listen to a bunch of drunks tell horror stories!" she cried. In fact she got good and mad. She said *he* didn't have any business going, either. He wasn't a drunk, and he didn't need a crutch.

"I'm not a drunk anymore, that's the truth, Geneva Fisher," he said back, "but I sure am an alcoholic wretch, and that's never going to change until you lay me in my grave."

Geneva retreated. "Never was as bad as that," she muttered, but she knew it was. It was worse than she pretended to remember.

Maybe she has never forgiven him. You can do all you can to make amends to people, but you cannot make them forgive. No matter how many years he is sober, once he was a drunk. That will not go away between them until she lets it go. And what keeps it going is, she holds on. For some reason, she wants the new Gully, but she wants some of the old one too, no matter how many times she says he never really lived.

At six he drinks a full glass of water, and takes a can of orange juice out of the freezer to thaw. Twenty minutes later he stands outside Geneva's door, not knowing what he will hear. Often she sleeps all night with her radio on, but it isn't on now. He stays several minutes, and thinks he hears her turn over, so he goes back to the kitchen. The whole weekend must have worn her out. Both nights, he went to bed while she was still out in that RV thing with Ruby, so he doesn't know what hours they are keeping.

He will have to make his own coffee. Finding the pot is easy enough, because it is in the dish drain upside down in parts. He opens the cabinets in search of coffee. The first one is the wrong one, he should have remembered she has her Crisco there, and little tins of powders and dabs of this and that for sauces. On the second try he opens the right cabinet, but the coffee can has teabags in it. Next he takes down a Nestea jar full of rice, and behind that a Malto-Meal can with pinto beans in it. He sees baking powder and soda, salt and pepper, another jar of tea, and powders he can't identify and doesn't want anyway, but he cannot find the blasted coffee.

He puts his shoes on. He will do what he should have done in the first place, go out in the truck and get his Nescafe and make a cup from the tap.

He meets Ruby at the door. She has a pot of steaming coffee in her hand and Geneva right behind her. "Go on now and sit down. Sis says it's past time for your brew, Gulsvig." He has no idea why she wants to call him by that name anymore, but he isn't going to make a fuss and give her pleasure. She will get tired of it too. It isn't even his name. He is Michael Fisher, though he once was Michael Gulsvig, till he took his stepfather's name, out of respect and gratitude to a decent man. But his mother called him Gully, and then so did everyone else, even on jobs where other men were called by their last names. Then, out of a long moment's sentimentality, wanting to keep something of history alive, when anybody knows it is only today that matters, they named the second twin for the blood grandfather, an undependable man who died young.

"I thought you'd died!" he blurts out to his wife.

"I slept in Ruby's camper," Geneva says primly. She is wearing a blue and yellow striped robe that isn't hers, that makes her look like an Arab's concubine, and her tight new hair is bushy as Austin's dog Rowdy. Those pouches under her eyes that swell up every night are puffy and soft-looking, but she looks rested. She hasn't been turning over in her bed at all! And she sure didn't die.

"So you were worried, were you?" Ruby asks as she pours him a cup of coffee. He is grateful for it, even coming from her, and it is fine coffee, too. He says so, not being a man of mean spirit.

"It's a Mr. Coffee coffee-maker like I've been telling you I wanted for six Christmases in a row, Gully Fisher," Geneva says loudly. She slams down a can of condensed milk in front of him. He has already taken one drink of coffee black, though it is not his preference, and now he stirs the milk in carefully, thinking how he seems to be in a spot without having done anything to bring it on.

"A coffee maker in a camper, think of that," he says. He thinks he ought to do his part to keep the conversation moving. "That's nothing," Geneva says. "She's got a microwave, a tv, a tiny vacuum cleaner, the most comfortable little let-down bed for a guest, and she's going to get an itty-bitty satellite dish as soon as she gets up to Portland, on the way home."

Gully can't think why a person would want to haul things around that you don't need at home. People have too much stuff.

"That's nice," he says, though. The coffee is perfect now that it has milk and sugar, and he is starting to get hungry.

"What has been going on in my kitchen!" exclaims Geneva

when she turns around and sees all the cans and jars on her counter.

"I was looking for the coffee."

"Oh you know perfectly well I keep it in the frig," she says, and opens the refrigerator door and takes out of its recesses a yellow can with silly flowers all over it. "Coffee," she announces, holding it practically in front of his face.

"Next time I'll know," he says, though he knows he will never again wait more than fifteen minutes before going straight out to his truck or—this is perfectly possible—down to the diner on the riverfront highway, where there would be plenty of other old men up before their wives.

Geneva does some rummaging and comes up with three silly little doodads from the back of another cabinet.

"I'll soft-boil us some eggs," she says, "and use those darling egg cups you gave me two Christmases ago, Ruby." She sets up a clatter of pans.

Ruby sits down beside Gully to drink her own coffee. "You don't get a morning paper, I don't see how you can stand it."

Gully shakes his head irritably. They have never used those cup things, and he is wondering how he is supposed to know what to do with one.

"I don't know how an egg would set on my stomach this morning," he says. "I could use a piece of toast, though, and maybe some cereal."

Geneva grabs a box of Wheaties and the milk carton and slams them down in front of Gully. He gets up and finds his own bowl. If he doesn't eat, he will be sick in an hour, but his stomach is a tight knot and he just wants to get out of there. He doesn't have to ask what is wrong with Geneva. She is always mad when Ruby is around. She compares herself and then blames him that he didn't die and leave her well-off, like Ruby's poor old Gordon. They sit around and talk about things that make them mad, and that is their idea of a good time.

He has already finished his cereal by the time Ruby takes a knife and neatly whacks her egg while Geneva watches. "Oh do mine," he hears his wife say, as he heads for the door.

Geneva jumps up and grabs the door before it closes. "Where are you going today, Gully Fisher? I'm going to make plans of my own, you know." She sounds downright nasty.

"I'm going to do some work on the truck," he grumbles. Then, just thinking of it, he adds, "I'm going out to see Austin Melroy, he's been feeling bad lately. I'll be home for dinner. You have a good time."

"We might not eat 'til six," she says tersely, and goes back to her headless, neckless egg.

—35—

You can't see Austin Melroy's place from the road. It lies in a small creek bottom grown thick with alders and tall cotton-wood trees. The slopes are covered with oaks, and on two sides, his property is bordered by BLM land. Starting at his property lines, the blackberry bushes have grown so tall and thick that Melroy's one and a half acres wouldn't be more private on the moon.

The place has the look of a movie-set tenant farm, with heaps of scrap metal, a broken-down chicken coop and a few scrabbling chickens in the yard, and dirt, lots of dirt, that turns to mud in the winter rains. It smells bad.

Then there are the vehicles. He has a rusting butter-yellow '52 Buick that looks like it might have come with the place. It is the dogs' favorite place to sleep, and both front doors are always open. Melroy's red 1954 GMC pickup is the model that runs. It is parked behind some blackberry briers near the creek, as if it were being hidden. He has two other cars, an old two-tone Chevy, and the completely rusted hull of a vintage Willys that might be worth something in better condition. The two dilapidated cars are used to store items for Austin's flea market enterprise. A back seat overflows with pots and pans, the front seat with old kitchen appliances. The Willys is piled with Bibles, old dictionaries and encyclopedias, cookbooks, and the odd book of etiquette or aphorisms thrown in. The back of the pickup is piled with bicycles, and there are parts, pumps, and oil and paint cans on the trailer porch.

It is late morning, and the heat has already sent the dogs to shade. A huge animal, maybe part St. Bernard, lies under the trailer steps, its nose sticking out one end, its tail out the other. Two coon hounds sprawl near some blackberry bushes, one with its nose in the other's belly. Melroy has more than a dozen dogs, mostly mongrels he rescued from boredom or death at the pound, with a stray or two that wandered to his place as if the word were out. He and his dogs made the papers late last year when he rescued a Pomeranian stranded on an overpass. The dog had been trembling and defecating while folks drove by. It was not wearing a collar, so Melroy took it home with him. He was eager to find the owner—the dog was a blasted showdog type, nervous and yippy—so he called the radio stations, and the story made the evening paper. When the dog's owner, a banker's wife, came to collect her sweet pet, she was so outraged at the chaos and neglect she thought she saw, she went straight to the pound, and then, for good measure, to the district attorney's office. Officials at the pound knew Melroy and thought him an admirable character. Nevertheless they did investigate, making two visits, once with a reporter at their heels, and later, a cameraman for the late night tv news. The director of the pound appeared briefly to say that most of Melroy's dogs would be dead if he had not rescued them. He had to repeat his statement when the banker, goaded by his wife, insisted on a proper review in court. Over the course of the hearings, Melroy's dogs were taken to the pound and fed at taxpayer's expense. Three veterinarians came forth with offers of care for free, and a discount food store contributed a hundred pounds of generic dry food, which Melroy's dogs won't touch. The dogs' homecoming rated a quarter page spread in the "Lifestyles" section of the paper.

Melroy spends most of his time with his dogs, except for the time he spends foraging for their food in cafe and grocery store scraps, or catching small game. When good weather comes and he has to get to flea markets, he often takes a couple of dogs with him in the back of the truck.

You couldn't call the work he does with the dogs "training." He doesn't use a leash or a chain. He talks his dogs into everything. He says he wouldn't force a dog any more than he would a child, and if you get him started he can talk on and on about the coercion and deceit, the fear, in child-raising and dog-training both. Melroy uses a beer can with beans in it to get his dogs' attention. It is his fiercest ploy for scolding bad behavior. Geneva was incensed, reading the articles about Melroy. "Just what business is it of BANKERS?" she raved, and Gully loved her like a girl again for her righteousness on a good man's behalf. Her affection soon faded, though. She resents Gully's visits with Melroy, and suspects the old man is smelly, wacky, and a drunk. She is more or less correct on all three counts, but neither her grumbling nor Melroy's bad habits can dissuade Gully from a friendship with him. He likes Melroy. Besides, he has taken him on. The old man is gray as a bird feather, feeding his dogs and neglecting himself, and Gully feels sure the moment is at hand when he can guide Melroy out of the thicket of his own making (what with rhubarb wine, home brew, cheap whiskey, and bad nutrition).

He plans to work on Melroy today.

Melroy is in the center of the yard, tossing a stick with Rowdy, his tight-haired little part-terrier.

"Hey boy," Melroy yells, and the dog brings back the stick, slobbering with pleasure and pride. "Hey boy," Melroy says again, watching Gully approach, with sidelong glances away from the dog. He bends to one knee to give the terrier a brisk rub, and endures a drenching of his arm from dog kisses.

Melroy loves an underdog. To him, a mutt has rights effete pedigreed dogs have no claim to. When you were a Depression-era farm boy, and then spent thirty years on oil rigs before heading to the Northwest, you appreciate the dog in the street. You identify.

"You tell me," Melroy once said to Gully, "how a mutt differs from a Borzoi when his intestines tell him squat?" He can remember dandy bankers, engineers, and journalists from the East, strutting in boomtown bars and streets, feeling high and mighty over the roughnecks and drillers. Melroy always felt more kinship with the whores and bootleggers than the fancy men, and a man who came from oilfield trash knows which animals deserve his attention.

Gully and Melroy first met behind the Cove Country Cafe. Melroy was at the back door, sorting through a bin of garbage. Gully was driving through the alley as a turnaround. Anybody would have misunderstood the case. There was Melroy in red longjohns and baggy denim pants, a watch-cap

and knee-high rubber boots. Gully pulled the truck around
to the side and came back on foot. It was a dull day so far,
and here was a man in need of a hand.

"I'll buy you coffee," he offered. "And a donut—" With still
no reaction from the old man, Gully added, "—and an egg."

Melroy began to laugh. It didn't seem he would ever stop.
Gully followed him back to his trailer and spent most of that
day with him, missing lunch and causing himself grief with
Geneva later on. "I did live on beans and cornbread once for
two weeks," Melroy told him. "A driller left town without
paying us, and all I had was a sack of pintos and one of
cornmeal. Can't stand the sight of pintos ever since, though
I'll still eat a white bean." He listened with interest as Gully
launched into a story about dissipation and madness and his
great good fortune to come to his senses just in time, but had
nothing to comment in return. As soon as Gully wound
down, he took him out in the yard to feed the dogs and talk
about the difference in the game of Northwest and Southwest, which led to livelier tales of drenched hunting trips,
wily deer, favorite shotguns. Such talk fed friendship.

Gully calls out a hello. The dogs set up a howling. Melroy
yells at them to mind their manners. It is too hot for much
movement, so they settle down. There is one fat wienie dog
that runs as fast as her stubby legs will carry her, up to
Melroy. She pushes herself up against one of his legs, takes a
stand between his ankles, raises a back leg, and pees.

Melroy steps wide away to avoid the spray, and shakes his
head. "That Haggerty. I named her for my son, who was
named for his mother's brother, all of them shy dogs. Course
there's nothing mean nor little in Haggerty, only those dumb
sawed-off legs, whereas my son learned early on to be sneaky,
to make up for what he don't have nerve enough to do up
front. Come in, Gully. Good to see you."

"I brought lunch." Gully carries a paper bag from the cafe,
with chicken sandwiches, two fat pickles, and two silly sacks
with about five potato chips in each. He had his thermos
filled with coffee.

"Will you look at that," says Melroy when Gully lays the
food out on the table. There is hardly room for it. Melroy has
bottles lined up two deep on the side along the wall, a fresh

batch of his home-brewed beer. There are newspapers, a
Farmer's Almanac, a dictionary so worn the cloth binding is
frayed white at the edges, socks brought in from drying and
not put away, a needle stuck in a card wound with thread,
and other odds and ends.

Melroy's half-retriever, half-something-smaller, Bounder,
has been sleeping under the table. True to his name, he
jumps all over both men, slathering and nosing them, whap-
ping his tail around, knocking over a cup and a glass on the
floor by a chair.

"I made a mistake with Bounder," Melroy says. He pats the
dog until he lies back down. He opens up his sandwich and
lays chips on it, neatly overlapping. He closes it back up and
sits down in his rocker. "I got him young, last winter. Bad
timing. Long rainy days. Cold. You stay inside, and a silly
pup like that crawls all over you, licks and laps and climbs,
and then the durned thing is set for life. It's habitual. Thinks
this trailer is his. Thinks I'm his pet. Doesn't give a hoot for
the other dogs."

Haggerty has come to the front door and is whining loudly.
"And that pest!" says Melroy in mock exasperation. He still
has not had a bite of his sandwich. "Scared to be by himself,
scared little turd of a dog. That's why I let him sleep inside. I
had raccoons all over the place last year, till I finally moved
that durned dog food over to the other side of the creek.
Haggerty liked to collapse when they came rummaging
around. Course they were big as polar bears, don't you
know?"

Gully moves to the door and lets the dog inside. Haggerty
runs around in a circle, then huddles in a hump between
Melroy's legs. Gully sinks into an old green easy chair with
wide, flat arms.

In a moment, Haggerty waddles over and jumps to put her
paws on the edge of the cushion. "She wants to show you she
can say her prayers," Melroy says. "We've been working on
that. You just tell her to. Go on, you'll see."

"Well, then, say your prayers, Haggerty." Gully has had
dogs of his own. He has thrown sticks, played hide and seek,
done a little jumping. But his dogs never said prayers.

Sure enough Haggerty moves her front paws together and
bows her head. She makes a squeaking noise.

"Good dog," Gully says. Haggerty slides away, down into a lump again at Melroy's feet.

The men chew contentedly for a few moments. Gully is relieved to see Melroy eat. He knows that if Melroy could open to a spiritual connectedness, and eliminate destructive behavior, he could become whole, healthy, and serene. It might take a while, but Melroy is a good man, garrulous but mild.

"I forgot the coffee," Gully says. Melroy motions for him to stay put while he washes two mugs and fills them from Gully's thermos. He takes a long noisy drink as he sits down, then another which he sloshes around his mouth before swallowing.

"My first cup of the day," Melroy says. "Just never got around to it this morning. I fed the dogs and exercised them, shoved a little dung aside, and then there you are. Life goes fast at my age." He says this as though he were talking to a kid, instead of a man within a few years of the same birth date. He pulls his boots off and Bounder nestles closer, putting his side to good use as a foot cushion for Melroy. Gully watches Melroy work his toes in Bounder's fur. If Melroy didn't have his dogs, he'd hardly have a reason to get up of a morning. Only, he does have them, and you have to admit they all get along.

Peace of mind can have eccentric definitions, Gully thinks. Melroy is not an unhappy man. If he set about inventorying his life, making amends to others, who would he need to make amends *to*?

All of that being Melroy's own business.

"I don't believe there's a dog you wouldn't have, is there?" Gully asks. "Except the fancy ones."

"Don't want no mouthers," Melroy answers. He puts his half-eaten sandwich on the table. "I don't mind a tug-of-war now and then with an old sock. All my dogs like that. But when I see a Doberman or a Shepherd, I look close for that mouthing habit. That kind of dog's likely to have had an owner who called it Fang or Killer. You can tell right away if you know what to look for. I don't want no part of a dog like that. Too hard to undo, and I've got my other dogs to think of. Other problems you can solve. It'd be boring if they came to you neatly trained like goldarned cadets. When I first got that little beagle out there, say, he was a shit-eater. That was a hard one to break, but you wouldn't know it now unless I told you. I can see him now and then looking at a crap pile in a studied way. I just shake my bean can at him real hard. I think he does it to tease me. To keep his place in line, don't you know?"

Gully, full and comfortable, feels like never moving. He is used to the dog smell already. He wonders if Melroy ever thinks about making a little visit to Texas again. He has always had a mind to see the Big Bend park, maybe float down a river.

He wishes Melroy would finish his sandwich.

"I don't believe in a dog's spite," Melroy says. He likes to chat. Gully doesn't know who else visits him. "I had two wives, and both of them spiteful as a lemon is sour, but a dog does what it has to when it's cornered. I'm not talking Marine Corps dogs, Nazis, drug sniffers. I'm talking mongrels. What does a mongrel know about politics and spite? I had the cutest little spaniel once. We was living in Blanco, Texas. I called her Sugar. She was yard-trained as good as any dandy dog, but my wife would ignore her wanting out, till Sugar would find a corner and let it plop, whining and feeling so goldarned bad about it. Wife said it was spite. One night I was working, and the wife went to the movies without letting Sugar out. Wife got home before me and found the dog had done her business right in one of the wife's shoes. When I got home, wife said, 'That goddamned dog don't like me, Austin. It's me or her.'" He grins and scratches his head. "That was my second wife."

"I've been married fifty years," Gully says. It sounds exaggerated, spoken plain and bald like that.

"That a fact?" Melroy says mildly. "But no dogs."

"Not right now," says Gully. He is embarrassed. When you think about it, life isn't all there if you don't have a dog. But their mongrel retriever died years ago, and when Gully mentioned going to the pound to look for another dog, Geneva said the trailer was too small, her voice entirely final on the subject. Gully would keep a dog in the shop, or with him when he is out in the truck, but he didn't argue. He hadn't really wanted the dog all that bad, had he? He can't think what he has wanted very much in a long time.

"I've been considering it," he says now. This is news to him, but it rings true.

"Pick of the litter," Melroy says, and guffaws. He swings his arm around to indicate the yardful. "Whenever you get serious. I mean it, Gully. Bounder'd keep you good company. Or Haggerty. You could bring her out."

Gully is staring at the beer bottles, and Melroy catches him at it. "Want to try one?"

"Not me," Gully says. "You know me, Melroy. I can't drink. I'm, you know—"

"Yea, yea. But this is home brew, mild as mother's tit. We could split a bottle and it wouldn't be half the kick of a spoon of cough syrup."

Gully never thinks about the taste of beer or whiskey. He never really thinks, I wish I had a drink. But he feels bad, turning Melroy down. It seems impolite. It seems stiff. Maybe Melroy doesn't lead a fit life, but he is an easy man to like, and he sure is an independent one.

"Nothing like what I learned to drink when I was still a kid," Melroy says. "What hootch that was! I ever tell you?"

Gully shakes his head. He doesn't think he ought to encourage this line of talk, but he is interested. Men their age have a broader experience with liquor than kids today, despite all those foreign beers in fancy bottles.

"It was in Van Zandt County. Little bitty town. They had a Texas Ranger lived there, and lots of Bible belt believers. But they had dance halls and hell-raisers too, like any boomtown. I was a dopey damned farm kid, thrilled to death with the company and the money. My folks were about starving, and here I was making decent wages. The guys called me "Shortstop," and "Weevil," and "Kiddo." They called each other stronger names than that. I had been drinking home-brewed beer with them when one night we got hold of some of the bad piss got sold around there, this one batch was made of denatured alcohol. Some men died. Some got this jerky walk we called Jake-leg. You'd hear about it on rigs ever after. Everybody knew about Jake-leg. Me and my friends had got full on beer, we didn't drink much of the rotgut. We got sick and recovered. We didn't get Jake-leg."

"I've heard what moonshine can do."

"Dishonest moonshine. Those fellers are probably all dead

now. Weevil. Hah. 1930, it was, or '31. Where were you, Gully?"

"Making my way, same as you." It only takes a moment to remember clearly. The past is like a fruit tree for plucking. He had a job with a railroad survey party for the Bureau of Public Roads, courtesy of his stepfather's position. He smiles, remembering.

"It's a stingy man who recollects in silence, Gully," Melroy says. He opens one of the beers with a flourish.

It must be warm, Gully thinks. He says, "One of the other young men and I set off on a Sunday on a hand-pump car, right up into the wilderness, with a picnic lunch and a cadged bottle of something my friend called whiskey, a word it did not deserve. We had a good time and got a little juiced, and then set off downhill for the ride home. We got sick of pumping, and realized that, going downhill, you could let the handles go. What neither of us thought about was that you couldn't get the handles back once the speed picked up. We had to bail out, and the hand-car went airborne and flew right into camp. It was a near disaster." Suddenly self-conscious, Gully feels his face flame. He is acting like an old man, Geneva would say. She doesn't like to hear about exploits that don't include her.

"If I had the patience with a pencil, I'd write my memwars," Melroy says. He passes the bottle to Gully, who takes it without thinking. "It's a good thing to have youth to look back on. Makes you glad you didn't grow up stiff and sober like a goldarned preacher's kid. Makes you glad you did a little living back when, don't it?"

Gully takes a long drink. It takes a moment for the taste to register, the funny yeasty tickle at the back of his throat, the long lick of liquid down his gullet. He feels it spread to the back of his head, behind his ears.

He sets the bottle down on the table and stands up. "I need to get outside, it's too hot in here," he says. He stands up too fast and he is dizzy.

Melroy sticks his legs out straighter and belches. "All a hot day's good for," he says. He winces. Something hurts.

Bounder gets up suddenly and runs back and forth from one end of the trailer to the other. Then in a long leap, he lands in the chair where Gully has been sitting.

"He thinks you warmed it up for him," Melroy says. "He thinks you're wonderful." The dog tucks his paws and closes his eyes.

"You gotta watch it, Melroy," Gully says weakly. He meant to tell Melroy about the fire and how it changed his life. "That stuff will kill you."

Melroy snorts. "My beer? Not likely."

Gully meant to tell him how bad it was before God intervened. He wants Melroy to go with him to a meeting one night. He thinks he might propose it as a kind of social event.

"Hell, Gully, I ain't a married man. My son don't have nothing to do with me. I don't drive when I drink. There's just me and my acre and my dogs and my recollections. Now, don't a man have a right to seek a little bliss? To have a little fun? Drinking is a pretty short route to a good time."

"I never saw it that way. I always thought of it as getting away."

"But now you're older, and the bogeyman's gone to bed." Melroy stands up and winces apologetically. He hitches his pants and cranes his neck toward the back of the trailer. "Don't run off," he says, and goes to the toilet.

Gully stares at the closed door for a minute, then shakes his head to clear his thoughts. He reaches down and scratches Bounder's backside. The dog wiggles and moans, his eyes still shut. Then, still for the moment, he looks at Gully raptly.

"I can be no man's salvation," Gully says to the dog. "I can't teach a man tricks with a bean can." And he heads home.

—36—

Gully goes to bed soon after supper, but he isn't sleepy, so he reads a few pages from a book Fish left at the place a few years back, Joshua Slocum's account of sailing alone, feisty old bugger. He knows this is Fish's fantasy, to lose himself somewhere on the ocean, and though Gully does not share it—he does not think he would like the openness, or the lack of steady balance—he would do anything to help his son sail away.

Geneva goes out to the RV with her sister, but Gully is still

awake when she comes back in about nine. She takes a long
time getting ready for bed. She fusses around in the kitchen,
and then the bathroom. He hears her switching tv stations
back and forth in her bedroom, and then turning on the
radio. Down the length of the trailer, he thinks he hears her
make a noise, a sigh, or cry of some kind, and it worries him.
If she were ill, he wouldn't know until morning.

He goes to see. Her door is closed. He taps lightly and
opens it. She is sitting on her bed with her keepsake box
spilled out beside her on the covers. Little homemade Valen-
tines with cut-out hearts and white doily trim; he remembers
Evelyn making them; and other cards, store-bought, now
faded and a little tattered, with shiny foil fronts, Be Mine,
Love Me, I Do; and Christmas and birthday cards; he recognizes them, anyone would, but he didn't realize that was what
she saved in her blackened metal box. Except for the ones
their daughter made, they are all cards Geneva gave the
children. He remembers sitting down to breakfast on Valentine's Day, a card at each child's plate. Evelyn would read hers
and smile shyly, and say, "It's sweet, Mama," but the boys
would set the cards aside and eat cereal and toast without
ever opening them. He has never wondered where the cards
went when those breakfasts were over.

Geneva starts gathering up the cards, without haste, her
long and slender, blotched hands moving with grace and a
kind of sadness. He wants her to look at him, but he has no
idea what he ought to say. It is pathetic to save mementoes
you gave away that nobody took, or kept, or wanted, and he
feels bad for her, and worse that he didn't know. Of course
she could not have told him, she could not have shown him
when she gathered up her silly verses and tucked them away
for some undefinable reason; he would have mocked her, he
realizes with a pang. There are probably some school photographs in the box, maybe a letter or two from Fish in the
navy; those things you can understand keeping. If he asked
her, would she show him what she had? Would she say, You
never gave me a Valentine's card, your sons never did, no one
ever said Be Mine?

He sits down on the bed, with the box and a few cards
between them. Her mouth is tight; he thinks she will tell him
he came in without her permission, that it is none of his

business (he knows it isn't, and wishes he had not seen her like this), but she stops figeting and just sits, her hands on her lap over a faded red paper card.

"Genny," he says in an old man's voice. He could curse, to hear it croak and quaver on him now.

She puts the last few cards in the box, fastens it, and sets it on the floor away from him. "I'm going to bed now," she says.

He puts his hand lightly on her wrist, and when she doesn't pull away, he feels relieved, and braver. "I'm glad Ruby came."

"She wants me to go with her."

"To Spokane?"

"No. South, next winter."

"Well." He shouldn't be surprised, he thinks, but he is. He never thinks of one of them without the other anymore. He wouldn't go off without her, not now.

"It's been a long time since I've seen anything of the country."

"I'd think it might be a disappointment," he says. "The way things are built-up and paved-over."

Now she frees her hand, and pats her hair, bouncing her fingers on its wiry fluff. "Still, a person ought to know what's going on past the edge of her yard."

"Why, you ought to go." He tries to sound hearty, but his voice betrays him, or perhaps it is only the hour, late for him. Slocum sailed, to leave a wife behind.

"I'll decide," she says. She stands up suddenly and makes him feel foolish, perched on the edge of her bed like an old buzzard on a tree limb.

On his feet now, he takes a long leap of faith and says, "I wouldn't mind another fifty, Geneva, in the next life if not in this." He means to comfort her, to give her what she wants.

She shakes her head. "Go on," she says.

Now she'll tell what her sister says about me, he thinks.

"I set your coffee on the stove," is what she says. She crawls into bed while he watches her. She wears an old soft pair of flannel pajamas. When it gets hot she changes to cotton "shorties," she calls them. "All you have to do is turn it on and let it perk, if I sleep in." She shuts her eyes.

He nods, and leaves her, feeling foolish and bewildered. He thinks of a time Geneva went out after supper, to go to a meeting. She was working on a raffle sale for the church. The girl was supposed to do the dishes, but she whined about it, and then when he yelled at her, she ran the water and began, leaning hard on one foot, her other hip higher, her posture slouched and slutty. Right away she broke a dish. And he hit her. He remembers watching her, disliking her; he remembers seeing the plate slide out of her hand and drop to the floor. He remembers his hand hard against her ear. At the time he forgot it, drinking.

When Geneva came home and Evelyn ran to her, wailing, and Geneva stood across the room from him, glaring, hating him, he had already forgotten. The girl was always unhappy, was always complaining, always trying to get out of things she was supposed to do, or into things she wasn't, and this was just another time, something between mother and daughter, that he did not need to understand. When he stumbled to bed that night, Geneva made a wall between them, out of rolled blankets and extra pillows, but he didn't care, he hardly noticed before he was asleep. Only, the wall was there a long time after, and when, weeks later, she made the bed in the old way, so that when you pulled the covers back there was the bare smooth expanse of sheet, and no reason he could see not to reach for her, or roll to her side in the night, he had forgotten that too. He had forgotten so much. There was only a blur between the time Evelyn broke the plate, and the day she lay in her coffin, looking pale and pure. He remembers Geneva whispering to him—there were people around, and when he looked at her, astonished, she had already turned away—"Now she can't do anything more that you don't like." And after that things blurred again. There was the fire, and the hospital, moments when he knew it was his own voice he heard shrieking, and then this new, better life they have, the pieces put back together, except for the girl. And over everything, a haze of pain. It isn't that he ever wants to drink, and it isn't that he needs to forget, because he still cannot remember; it is that he knows Geneva remembers everything, and the wall is all around her, as though she is her own estate.

In the kitchen he goes to the stove and picks up the coffeepot, sets it back down, and commences to weep, as quietly as he is able.

## —37—

Katie calls her mother. June answers the first ring. She sounds neither surprised nor pleased to hear Katie's voice. She sounds like a doctor's receptionist.

"Did I get you at a bad time?" Katie asks.

"I've got a pot of soup on the stove, and I'm sitting at the table reading. I've got a quarter hour till I go get Rhea at practice."

"What's she practicing?"

"Gymnastics."

"Oh," Katie says. She should have remembered. "Ursula said you called. I've got my own phone now." She gives her number to her mother, blushing deeply, whether ashamed, or frustrated to do so at all, she isn't sure.

"I've wondered how you're faring."

"I work, I eat, I sleep."

"You wrote that you were seeing a lawyer."

"Oh that."

"Katie, really. 'That'?"

It must please her mother, Katie thinks. She feels a wave of defensiveness for beleaguered Fish. "It's all in motion, Mother. The end of Katie and Fish." She is repeating herself, she realizes, or was it Jeff who said that?

"Is there a chance you'd want to come down here, dear? Rhea asks about you."

"I'm working. I can't get away right now." When her mother calls her "dear," it affects her exactly as does the scrape of nails on a chalkboard.

"Then I don't suppose I can do anything."

"Do anything?"

"To help."

Katie feels her throat tightening. "You already do a lot, don't you? Like take care of my daughter?" June does not throw that up to Katie; it is Katie who keeps it in the air between them.

"She's a sunny little girl, Katie. I don't know where she gets her disposition. She puts us in a good humor most of the time."

"I'm glad."

"She's been asking about you lately. And her father."

"What do you tell her?"

"I try to answer questions in a straightforward way. I say, your father is a carpenter, he lives in Oregon, where there are lots of trees. Your mother works for a theatre. I tell her it's an office, is that right, Katie? Selling tickets?"

"You don't tell her that I worked as a waitress for twenty years? Or that her father was in prison?"

There is a long silence. June says, "It's not a rare thing anymore, for a child not to live with her parents, especially not with both of them."

"Lucky for all of us, to be in style."

"Nobody's being criticized, Katie."

"I hope not. Since it's my call."

"I'll write. That won't cost you anything."

"Sorry Mother. Sorry, sorry."

"I think she wants more of you, that's all. She's not unhappy, Katie, but she's growing, and she has questions."

"Maybe it was a mistake for me to come and go, to see her at all." There always is a bad moment, every visit, but not with the child.

"It's too late to think that. And it's not like you were dead. I didn't want to trade you for her, you know. I didn't see it as an exchange."

Katie thinks, but that's exactly what you wanted, Mother. You got Rhea, Fish got me, I got off the hook. "I don't know when I can come again. I just don't know." She wonders which step would have to do with her mother. She wouldn't know how to make amends. She didn't make her life by herself; her mother has always had the upper hand.

—38—

Katie went to Texas at Christmas.

Her trips to Texas are nothing like going home. Though it is the same house, it looks different, it feels different. Of course it holds a different family, only June being constant, and, all these years later, she seems in many ways younger and happier, a relaxed mother to Rhea.

There is the real difference: the attitude of house and family toward child, the place of the child. Sunny Rhea.

The house has been improved by paint and wallpaper,

tasteful furniture, a new large sun porch in recent years. There is an easy feel to the rooms, a brightness. June cleared away old pictures and left the walls bare. She replaced the heavy furniture of the fifties with spare chairs with slung seats, a chintz-covered couch with fat pillows, an old chaise lounge upholstered in polished cotton.

Rhea has a bedroom with twin beds. Christine has the third bedroom, so Katie shares Rhea's when she visits. It was once her room, and for a couple of years, Uncle Dayton's.

She lay on the bed in the middle of the night and tried to recall the room as it had been in her childhood. There were twin beds then, too, a blond wood set. (Rhea's are white iron, with firm mattresses and feather-stuffed pillows.) There was a dark dresser with drawers on two sides and a large oval mirror in the middle. Katie can remember sitting on the cushioned stool in front of that mirror, an adolescent anguished at the sight of her own image. Rhea has a long sleek wall of laminated cabinets, and a little desk built in at the window. Above the cabinets are wide open shelves, filled with the paraphernalia of a contemporary girlhood: a boxed set of *Little House on the Prairie;* a dozen paperbacks all called *Babysitter's Club;* some old volumes of Katie's, with fairy tales and Bible stories, myths and legends, a book of narrative poems; modeling clay, and small fanciful animals made from it; drawings; airplane models; a working paper clock; origami birds; a dangling God's eye.

Katie lay in bed and remembered the few books with red and brown spines, and the spill of her schoolbooks on the unoccupied bed, clothes on the floor, her hairbrush and mirror on the dresser, but nothing more, and all of that seemed so impersonal to her, devoid of character. What kind of child had she been? There was nothing left of her in the house to tell. In her mother's room there was a portrait of her done at five or six, with color retouching to give her apple cheeks and lemony hair. That was all. It seemed strange to Katie, that portrait, because the child in it was not recognizable as herself. She thought she would have recognized photographs of her, past age twelve, say, but not before. There had to be a high school yearbook somewhere; she would get it out and look at it, she thought, though the next day she forgot the intention.

Katie remembers that when she came into the house after

school, she entered quietly, speaking if her mother was in the room, or if her mother called out to her from the kitchen, and otherwise going to her room silently to read or brood. She spent a lot of hours staring at the ceiling. When she was about Juliette's age she went through a long period when she slept too much, or badly; she would go straight to bed after school, until her mother called her for dinner. Then she was awake through long hours of the night, and after that, sleepy and reluctant in the morning.

Rhea wakes up cheerful. When Katie opened her eyes in the morning, her daughter was watching her, and as soon as she saw that Katie was awake, she broke into chatter about anything—the day's plans, the upcoming breakfast, a dream she'd had.

June is a mild presence these days. Katie remembers her sterner (as she can be, still, with her). On the whole, June treated Katie delicately, as she might treat someone recovering from what used to be called a nervous breakdown. She didn't pry. They all did best when they kept busy. Rhea had a game she loved that was played like Monopoly, but was about farming. It was endless and boring and silly, but it took up hours, especially if Rhea could talk Aunt Chris into playing too. On another card table, on the sun porch, there was a "Schmuzzle Puzzle," a jigsaw of what looked like baby lizards, difficult for Rhea and not very easy for Katie, either. Besides that, Rhea loved to play card games like Go Fish, Hearts, and Old Maid. Sometimes she helped her Aunt Chris make elaborately decorated cookies while Katie sat at the table and watched. "We sold these at our school carnival last year," she told Katie, "for fifty cents apiece!" Christine smiled fondly. Katie said that didn't surprise her.

It was strange to lie near Rhea at night in the dark room, surrounded by fuzzy animals and Japanese boxes, under a spread decorated with printed pandas. Katie tried to guess what Rhea might dream, but she could only suppose there were fantasies provoked by movies, and, whatever the dreams, that they were not nightmares, because Rhea never seemed to stir.

One day Rhea said she had something to show Katie. Katie followed her to her room and sat down on one bed while Rhea looked in a few drawers until she came up with an old flat gift box like a scarf might have come in.

"I've saved them all," she said. "See?" She seemed pleased with herself, or pleased that she was able to show Katie. She had dumped some greeting cards onto her bed. She stirred them around, then handed one to Katie. "See?" That's yours from Christmas when I was six."

Katie looked at the card quizzically, not remembering it, and then Rhea gave her another card and said, "And this one was from my father." The child kissed the card and passed it to her mother. "I've saved them all."

Katie managed to utter, "That's nice." She felt guilty and embarrassed, and desperate to be somewhere else. The cards became instantly familiar, and as she looked at them dutifully, one by one, she remembered choosing and buying each one, and taking some of them to Fish to sign. Hadn't Rhea ever realized that all the cards were addressed in her handwriting? Hadn't she guessed? The cards that were supposed to be from Fish said, "Merry Xmas, from Fish," or just "Fish." One was scrawled completely illegibly, and Katie could instantly recall the scene where she screamed at Fish that all she was asking him to DO was to put his goddamned NAME on a goddamned CARD for his KID.

Ursula, apprised of the birthday/Christmas deception, advised Katie that somewhere truth would catch up with Katie's good intentions, and Rhea might be hurt more than she would have been otherwise. But even Ursula admitted that a ruse once begun was difficult to end, so Katie kept on with the cards, even that same Christmas, signing Fish's name herself, sending another lie into the pile of lies. And Rhea saved them all.

Later, lying in the dark, Rhea asked about Fish. She asked "Is he a hippie?" and Katie said, "I don't think so. I don't think you would call him that," wondering furiously where Rhea had heard such a thing. She wanted to know, "Does he build nice houses?" and Katie patiently explained that he worked on old ones, to make them nice. Then Rhea asked, "Where do you live?" When Katie named the town, she said no, she wanted to hear about the house, and so Katie painfully described their house, a little shabby, in need of paint, but surrounded by lots of trees and vines and bushes, with a nice bright kitchen (well, it did get lots of light) and a fireplace in the living room—speaking slowly, until Rhea was asleep and did not move when Katie said, "It's a house in a hollow, perfectly chosen for the couple we make, with an old chicken house in the back full of empty bottles put there, day by day, by your father, Fish the fish."

June now runs what amounts to a small factory, which produces her own designs. She specializes in comfortable clothing for working women in the 12 to 16 size. Katie wonders if women ever mind that June is herself a tidy size 10. She also produces a line of accessories, scarves and satin rosettes, ribboned clips. On Christmas Eve while Katie was there she had a benefit for one of the hospitals. Although she didn't put strings on her gift (she had been doing this for four or five years), she was pleased when told that her funds had helped in the new preemie ward. June the baby-helper, Katie thought. She wondered what had happened to the passionate doctor-lover of so long ago. June didn't go out while Katie was there. Katie couldn't bring herself to ask Christine about her mother's personal life, largely because she knew she was being stingy with the details about her own. She noticed books by C. S. Lewis and Thomas Merton lying around. Though she had never read either writer herself, you could not exist in the environs of a "hip" community without hearing of both. There was even a C. S. Lewis study group. She had seen the notice on bulletin boards, along with study groups for feminist mythology, dreamwork, and A Course in Miracles.

"Have you thought of going to school?" June asked one evening, a few days before Katie was returning to Oregon. June was knitting an elegant sweater of mohair and silk. Rhea had fallen asleep watching television, Christine was in bed. Katie was pretending to read *The Ladies Home Journal.*
"I haven't," Katie said simply.
"There are so many career opportunities these days," her mother said. "In business, health—"
"I hadn't noticed."
"You're a bright young woman, to spend your life serving food."
"I haven't the money or disposition for school, Mother."
"I wish I had spoken sooner. You might have stayed here and gone to Tech while Fisher was—away."
"Too late," Katie said, appalled at the thought.

June put her knitting down and looked directly at her daughter. "I'm not interfering if I say I want the best for you. I still want you to have a good life."

"Still? After I don't deserve it?"

"I didn't mean that. I meant, you're forty years old, and I might not concern myself with your welfare. But you still seem rootless and unfocused, Katie, you still seem unsettled."

"I've lived in Oregon nearly twenty years. We have a house."

"You're not going to let me talk about this, are you?"

"Mother, lots of people get by. Most people, maybe. Everybody doesn't have a career. What did you do for years and years?"

"It was different when I was young. If you were lucky enough not to be a poor woman, you thought it was your job to take care of the house and the family. Now, I must say, that seems a luxury fewer and fewer women have."

My, Katie thought. Mother the Feminist.

"But you could still choose something. You could still make your life mean something—"

"I marched for hunger last year." Actually, she had walked on the sidewalk alongside the group as they set out from the plaza toward the next town, carrying placards. It had been a beautiful spring Saturday, and she had gone for something to do, and because Fish had mocked the effort, and her interest in it. She had spent days thinking about hungry people, in this country, maybe even her town, and God knows, in Africa and Asia. It had soothed her, to think about emaciated women with their drooping, flaccid breasts flapping over the cheeks of their starving babies. She had thought: So many people are desperate. So many people die young. She felt lucky, being who she was. She gave forty dollars to the hunger walk.

"Good," her mother said, and picked up her knitting again.

Katie hated her, as she always did, not for interfering, but for being right. Katie's life was mostly very boring, especially with Fish gone "away." She got by on the vicarious experiences of Ursula, mostly, hearing about children abandoned in junkyards, or found wandering naked in a house full of far-gone users, and about Ursula's children, whose lives were good and sometimes funny, especially Carter's.

"There is something I want you to know," her mother said in

a moment. "If something should happen to me before Rhea is grown—" She paused, to let that sink in, Katie supposed. In truth, Katie had not considered the possibility of her mother's death. June was in better shape than Katie. "If that happens, you should know that there would be plenty of money for Rhea. Christine would have the house until she died, but there's money and the business. But there would be strings."

"Of course."

"I didn't want you to worry."

"You didn't want me to look forward to a free ride!" Katie exploded. "It never crossed my mind! I've always assumed you are IMMORTAL!" She threw the magazine from her lap across the room, nowhere in particular. "Why don't you fucking BILL me for my visit here?" Rhea, asleep on the floor, moaned.

"Katie, Katie," her mother said. "You know I'd pay your way if you wanted. I'm glad you came, for your sake as well as Rhea's. For all of us."

"Why? So that on some quiet evening you can slip in the knife? Usually it's my nutritional standards."

Christine appeared in the doorway. "Don't, June," she said quietly. At least she knew not to admonish Katie!

"It's all right, Aunt Christine," Katie said. "I was just about to tell my mother that I have a new job, as soon as I get back. I'm going to work for the theatre festival. I'm going to have a GOOD JOB."

She stormed out of the room and left the two women to commiserate about Katie's bad manners and temper. Goddamn her, Katie thought. There'd be strings. Big surprise.

Of course she had done a small mean thing, bringing up the theatre job just then, and not telling her mother what the job was. She might have said anytime, Mother, you'll never guess, aren't you glad you taught me to sew, did you know I learned so well? I'm going to be a stitcher in a costume shop. I'm going to like working for once.

She knew she had withheld the information because it would have pleased her mother.

She went to bed. In a little while Christine helped Rhea to bed. The child didn't seem to have waked. Christine sat on the edge of Katie's bed and stroked her arm. "Your mother never seems to find the right way to say things, Katie, but she means well. She loves you. She's a good person, good to Rhea, and to me, and if she knew how, she'd be good to you, too." Katie turned over sullenly, like a bad child. Rhea was the good one. Oh, wasn't she a sad case? Katie thought of herself, wallowing in self-pity and jealousy. Oh to be a child again! Of different parents, in a different life!

To be Rhea, even.

In the morning, Rhea's sweetness and enthusiasm assuaged Katie's bad feelings, and June acted as if nothing had happened. Whatever June's efforts to make Katie feel guilty (and Katie would have had a hard time remembering them, but one was surely last night!), Rhea's disposition and health relieved Katie of the burden. She only felt sorry that Fish had missed out completely. A sweet daughter might have been good for him. But that had not been the child's function. Katie had not used her.

Of that much she was glad.

—39—

The week goes by, and Fish does not return Katie's car. In the middle of the week Katie calls Ursula to ask what is going on over there, and Ursula acts thick-headed and makes her ask about Fish specifically. Ursula says he is pushing hard to start a new job, a big one. He is working until dark every night. "Oh, it's the car," she says. "He didn't call you?"

"To say what?"

"He didn't call to say it would take longer?"

"Nope."

"It's still sitting in front of the garage. Are you okay without it?"

"Yes," Katie says. And it is true, she is. She walks to work. She has spent the week sewing velcro in vests and jackets, so that the actors in heavy Shakespearean costumes can change in a hurry.

"Should I tell him you called?"

"I guess. No, no, don't. He said Monday. I won't give up until next week. It has a Monday in it, too." She laughs and hangs up. She tells herself it is a good sign. Fish isn't acting out of character. If he were prompt, it would bother her.

Getting her car fixed right away now seems a cool, dispassionate act she is glad he has avoided.

On Saturday she goes with Maureen to the park in the early afternoon, before Maureen goes to work. On the way, they walk a block in silence and then she tells Maureen that she is feeling shaky about the divorce. Maureen says maybe Katie is going too far too soon. Maybe she is using the divorce, instead of walking away from it. Before, Fish messed up her head, and now the divorce is doing the same thing. "Don't kid yourself," Maureen tells her. "The divorce won't solve your problems, because Fish isn't the problem. The problem is inside you."

"Great. Thanks a lot."

"You need to go to group. You need to listen to what other people have learned. Learn to work the program."

"It sounds like a sprinkler system."

Maureen is unruffled. She takes Katie's hand as they walk. "Have you read the steps?"

"I heard them read the other night."

"The first step—you have to start there. Maybe you are avoiding it. The first step is surrender, kiddo."

"Surrender what?"

"The idea you can control it all. Fish, your pain, your life."

"If I stop believing that, I might as well give up."

"Oh no, Katie, You've got yourself blown out of proportion. Lots of people have a time when they make a turn, or don't. Before that they're shit. Like me. I was a drunk, I fell in love with drunks. I got drunk with my own mother and sister and sent them off in a car that way. See, you don't have so far to go. You're functional."

"As long as somebody tells me what to do." She thinks of her mother, and of Jeff. Maybe Maureen now. "Not that I follow advice all that well." Maybe she just wants sympathy. But from whom?

"Nobody can tell you what to do. You have to find out."

"You talk in circles."

"Look inside yourself. Talk about what you find. Pretty soon you'll hear what you're saying."

"Sure. Who wants to hear it? Who would care?"

"Me, for starters. Or take a name in group and call someone. When you're ready to start, I promise you, you can get the help. You have to take the first step."

As they come to the park, Maureen explains that she is meeting her nephew Ricky and his foster parent. The foster mother has things to do in town, and Maureen can spend an hour with the child. It is the first Katie has heard about Ricky. It is a relief to have the subject changed.

"They live way out in the country, there's no way for me to get there, but once in a while the foster mother calls and I go over on the bus to the mall and meet them. It's been nearly two months since I saw him. He doesn't seem to care, one way or the other, he's only seven, I guess he takes it as it comes."

"Am I not supposed to ask about his parents?"

"You don't think I'm going to hold secrets, do you? You don't think I'm going to repress?" Maureen laughs at herself. "Besides, I told you I'd tell you about my sisters. One at a time. This one is Rochelle, she's two years younger than me." She looks at her watch. "We're a little early, you want to go in the shops?"

"No, I want to hear this."

They sit on a low stone wall in the shade.

Maureen speaks softly, staring at the grass. "Your sister-in-law would know Rochelle. Everybody in that work in the valley does. She was a big case last year. She had Ricky, and a toddler, Summer. And she had this boyfriend who was talking about moving in with her. She was very crazy about this guy. The kids' father had been gone since she was pregnant with Summer. She was living on welfare, drinking some, she was depressed, and then this guy came along and cheered her up.

"Last spring, this is a year ago, there was a really sunny day, and they took a ride out to the lake. Rochelle had packed sandwiches. I guess they had a little picnic, with a blanket spread out on the grass above the lake. Sometime in the afternoon Rochelle went behind some bushes to pee—" Maureen's voice breaks. She looks at Katie. "Nobody believes that. I don't, but I told her I did. She's my sister."

"What happened?" Katie has an idea she knows. She has the faintest memory of something Ursula told her.

Maureen takes a deep noisy breath. "They say she went

back behind the bushes with the boyfriend. Rochelle said they'd been dozing on the blanket, she went back to pee, the boyfriend was asleep, the baby was asleep, Ricky was playing with some toy trucks—"

"Oh shit, Maureen, I do know about this."

Maureen goes on anyway, doggedly. "The baby woke up and went down into the lake, quick as anything. When Rochelle came back to the blanket, the baby was gone. Ricky was down by the water's edge. Summer had gone into the water and drowned." She grips Katie's hand. "Is it really worse if they were both in the bushes? Is it worse if the guy was back there instead of on the blanket? Does it change how drowned Summer was?"

Katie remembers Ursula raving about the case. They didn't do anything to the man. He wasn't the parent, he wasn't responsible. Rochelle they took to court for neglect, she got a county jail term.

"So Ricky is in foster care until she's—on her feet again?"

"Oh, she's on her feet. She's out and gone. She said they'd take Ricky away, what was the use of fighting it?"

"I remember Ursula saying they probably wouldn't be able to keep Ricky from his mother. The state wants kids with their parents. She yells about it all the time."

"I couldn't take him, you can see that, can't you?" Maureen says. She speaks so softly it is hard to hear her. "All my energy goes into staying afloat. I'm still putting one foot in front of the other." She gets up and rubs the wrinkles in her pants, smooths her hair. "Do you still want to go? I thought I'd get him a corn dog or something and take him to the swings."

"Sure, I'll go," Katie says. They walk to the stretch of parked cars. Maureen spots the boy and his foster mother by the bridge. She waves, and the woman waves back. The boy watches Maureen and Katie approach, his face placid and inexpressive. His foster mother kisses him goodbye and says she will be back in an hour. He doesn't say anything. He watches her until she drives away.

Katie thinks of Rochelle behind the bushes. At least I'm better than that! she thinks. It is hardly comforting.

She sticks her hand out for the child to take. He walks

between her and Maureen. He raises his arm limply and allows her to grasp his fingers. He doesn't look at her.

Suddenly ashamed, she squeezes his hand lightly. They cross over the bridge, and catch sight of the pond. A duck is crossing the stone walk. Ricky breaks away from the women and runs to the duck. Maureen, coming up behind, says, "Don't scare it, Ricky." The duck waddles up the grassy slope and back onto the walk. There is another pond farther up the park, away from the congestion. Ricky stays right behind the duck, pacing his steps to the duck's stops and starts. Maureen and Katie follow.

Maureen says, "He was standing by the water, watching where his sister had gone. I asked his foster mother if they were getting him any counseling. She said he was too young, he'd forget about it. She's a nice lady, but—too young? What must he remember? He never mentions his mother. I used to, but what could I say?"

Katie says, "I'll go get something to feed the ducks and meet you at the upper pond. We'll have a good time." Feeding the ducks will be something to do. Maureen nods gratefully and moves closer to the child. Katie watches them take a few steps, and then turns and flees.

Katie finds Maureen at home another evening. Maureen is unraveling a failed knitting project, winding a ball in her lap. She says hello without smiling.

"Are you not feeling okay?" Katie asks.

"It's a mood. I guess it's from seeing Ricky. Thinking about my family, my life."

Katie doesn't want to know any more. She feels cheated. Maureen has been giving her advice for months. Now, when Katie feels impaled on her own indecision, when she desperately wants to do what Maureen says to do—hear herself think aloud—Maureen is full of her own trouble. One thing for sure, Katie wouldn't know how to console Maureen.

The only person she comes close to understanding is Fish. That means only that she knows better than to predict what he will do; his unpredictability has become familiar over the years. It is she who has broken the pattern, done something to shake his teeth. He is driven by an energy unique to him.

He cannot be bullied, and does not negotiate, unless he has already decided to yield.

The only real question now is how long it will take him to come around. She thinks she knows what she will do. It isn't even a decision anymore; it's fate.

—40—

Katie comes home and finds her car in the lot. The keys are on the floor. She runs inside to call Fish, but only Carter is at home. "Tell Fish thanks," she says, a little out of breath, but she doesn't think she can count on Carter to deliver a message, so she calls back later. This time Michael answers. He says, "Carter said you called," and she feels stupid, like a pining girlfriend.

This is an evening that Maureen works at the delicatessen. Katie wishes she was home with her for company. They could watch Donahue tapes and chew on other people's problems. She could find out what happened to the other sister.

She is undressed and ready to shower when someone knocks at the back door. "I'll be a minute!" she yells loudly, and pulls back on some clothes.

It is Jeff, not Fish. She hesitates for a fraction of a moment before she tells him to come in, and he asks, "Are we friends? Are you mad at me?"

The disappointment is palpable. She feels like someone who opens a present and finds a mixer, or a book of synonyms.

"I'm not mad. I thought you were."

"Would you like to go somewhere for a drink, or dessert?"

"Not really." She brushes at her old jeans and shirt. Jeff is obviously waiting. Like it or not, she is cast as hostess. "I could make tea."

Jeff leans against the door jamb as she prepares jasmine tea. In a navy and white baseball jersey and crisp canvas pants, he cuts a handsome, stylish figure, dressed for a casual visit. She feels sloppy. He is looking at her, really looking, and she feels her body, naked under the jeans and shirt. Lately there have appeared on her body spots of sensation the size of elongated quarters, at the side of her left breast near her armpit, on the outside of her arm just above the elbow, and a larger area on her right hip, high. Sometimes the spots burn slightly. Sometimes they prickle, and she twists and strains to look for signs of a rash, but there never is one. She feels a slight burning now. She feels her nipples, irritated by the cotton of her shirt. She thinks of him touching her— of someone touching her—and she feels a stab of pulsation along the creases of her labia.

"I should have called," Jeff says. She shakes her head to show he didn't need to bother. She honestly hasn't given him much thought. She has been waiting to hear from Fish. "I should have come sooner," he says, and she shakes her head again in the same way. She concentrates on the tea. The pale flowers puff in the water and rise, then sink again. She hands him a mug and steps past him.

Settled in the front room, she holds the steaming cup near her face.

"You've been working hard?" she asks. It is the only thing she can think to say. The week since she last saw him seems a long time.

He smiles. "My work is often intense, often tedious, but never really hard. I like it too much. Plants confound you, but they don't play politics." He stops abruptly and glances behind him.

She realizes that she has been staring over his shoulder, and that he can see she isn't listening. Her cheeks burn. She looks at him with determined earnestness, and sees that he has changed his hair. "What have you done?" she asks, brushing at her own forehead.

"I've let the front grow more. It's not really new, Kate. It happens like wheat growing, a little at a time. Only you just noticed." He leans toward her. "Do I look too ragged?"

"I like it."

"I'm sorry if I bullied you."

"I'm sorry if I overreacted."

They look at one another shyly and sip the fragrant tea. When, in a few moments, they both set their cups down on the glass at the same time, they laugh. She thinks, he's a nice man. He likes me, and the more he shows it, the worse I act. It is mystifying. I am a bitch, she thinks. It doesn't bother her to know so, she just wonders when Jeff will see it for himself.

"I bought tapes," he says.

"What group?" He likes jazz, singers she never has heard of. Maybe they are contemporary, and she isn't.

"French tapes. I started listening to one last night. *Comment-allez vous, Je voudrais,* that elementary stuff."

"Is it coming back to you?"

"Perfectly. I remember how in high school I used to memorize everything, and then the teacher and the tapes went too fast and I never recognized anything as it went by."

"You have to have a gift for it, like for music. I don't."

"I'll be in the Bordeaux region for the September harvest. Then maybe I'll stay on and go to Italy. I bought Italian tapes, too, on impulse. Now I'll be incompetent in three languages. I thought--maybe you'd like to come over later, at the end of the summer. When all the college students go home. You could use the tapes if you want." He shrugs. "It was just an idea."

Katie doesn't say anything. She doesn't remember anything about Italy, except for martyrs and lions in the Coliseum, and a picture she saw of Mussolini hung upside down.

"There's something I came to tell you," he says. He has the resolute look of a teacher. He takes a deep breath. "I had a girlfriend once, this was some years ago, when I was first out of college. She smoked, and I hated it. I nagged her about it. Finally she said, 'Look, smoking is a habit, I'm really hooked, and it would be hard to give it up. If you want me to, then you have to give up something and suffer, too. You have to know what I'm going through.'

"So I gave up sugar. I didn't put it in my coffee, I didn't put it on my cereal. I even started making my own bread, and not putting sugar or honey in it, and if I bought bread I only bought French bread at the bakery, flour, yeast, water, salt. I worried if the little bit of sugar they use to start the yeast counted."

Katie fidgets. The spot under her arm is on fire. She knows that he means to tell her something, but she is completely lost as to what that is. He seems to feel it is for her good.

"I could get more tea," she says. She reaches for the cups on the glass table, and one of them rocks noisily against the other. He puts his hand out to stay her gesture.

"Wait. One weekend we went somewhere with another

couple. They were giving me a hard time about my sugar fetish, they called it, and she kept watching us, hearing their remarks, looking on coolly and not offering any support. I wanted to shout—it's all for her! She made me do it! As if I'd done something wrong, instead of only something I didn't want to do.

"That morning we were driving back. I woke up early and she wasn't in the cabin. I thought she might be putting her things in the car. I went out to look for her. It was windy and damp. I found her standing out by the car, smoking. When I saw her, I just about went nuts. I started screaming at her. She laughed at me, and she said, 'Well, now you can eat whatever you want, can't you?'"

"So it didn't work." Katie thinks the girl sounds cool.

"It most certainly didn't work. I'd become obsessed with her habit, as if she didn't have a choice in the matter, and she had worked me so that I was doing something I didn't care to do, didn't care about. I wasn't fat or diabetic, I didn't eat too many sweets. I'd have given up eggs, or listening to the radio, I'd have done sit-ups. She was the one who came up with sugar.

"I swore I'd never again get wrapped up in other people's decisions. I'd never try to be in charge. The other day, that was what I was doing, though. I wanted you to get on with it, according to my schedule. I'm sorry, I had no right."

Katie feels a rush of relief and sympathy. She could tell him he isn't the first person to make her angry, trying to tell her what to do, something she seems to invite.

"Whenever I minded something Fish did, whenever he saw that I minded, he did something worse. He had to let me know I couldn't make him start or stop anything." She remembers that her other story about Fish led to a quarrel. "Never mind," she says wearily. She hopes they won't analyze old scenes.

"It's okay, Kate. Katie. Go on. Really."

"Once we went up to a mountain lake to fish. It was spring. We were high on the nice weather. It was the middle of the week, so nobody else would be up there, and we felt great about that." It has always been important not to go where other people go. She wonders what they missed, avoiding anything that had a trail. "When we got out of the truck, we saw that all along the shore of the lake, way up past where we'd parked, there was this groundcover of baby frogs. Everywhere you looked, a mass of wiggling, tiny frogs, hardly more than tadpoles. It was fantastic! Fish bent down to look closer, and I made a noise, *ugh,* you know? He looked up at me, all excited, and when he saw my face, he was disgusted with me for being so squeamish. 'When did you ever see anything like it?' he asked me, and he lay down right on the baby frogs, spread-eagle on his back, his arms flung way out, laughing and yelling at me, lying on this blanket of frogs.

"What will I see in Italy to top that?" she asks.

Jeff turns red across his cheeks and nose. Before he says anything, she touches his hand. "I'm joking. I know about Italy. Florence, Venice. It'd be nice to see them, to be able to say, I saw this church, I saw that statue. Michelangelo. Spaghetti." She feels heady. He is at one end of a line and she at the other. Sometimes he tugs, and she follows, or does not, but sometimes she lets the line go slack entirely, and then jerks it like a kid with a trout on the line, and he does not let go! She feels clever to have thought it; the pleasure of metaphor is new to her, like *al dente* pasta after a childhood of overcooked spaghetti. If everything has two meanings, your life occupies more space in the universe, because it is both life and a game of life. It is a show and a rerun.

Jeff reaches up to brush back his new, longer hair. She can see his impatience. He reminds her of her mother. "The good part," he says, "is doing it, not talking about it later."

"That's how you see it," she says pleasantly. She thinks that at the door, when he says goodbye, she will say, Have a nice trip. She picks the cups up, and this time they touch with a single bell-like ring, like a tiny, graceful signal at the end of a round.

—41—

She draws on an old cotton kimono she bought in a thrift store in Vancouver, B. C. Its blue flowers have faded to pale gray. It was rainy the day she bought it, and she felt happy. The memory stirs her. It also reminds her how little she has

demanded to be happy. If it rained, and they found a place to
be dry. If they were hungry, and they found cheap food. If
she spent the day with Fish, and her chest didn't ache with
trying to say the right thing. On a day like that, she was
happy.

She towel-dries her hair and combs it, and looks at the
clock to see if Maureen might be home. She has some books
to return, they could talk about them. There is a whole new
language of terms to learn, when you start looking into
psychology. It seems that if you learn them, you take on
power. You learn better ways. If you speak a different life,
you can live it. What else do all those therapists do, but help
you see that? Why can't you do it by yourself?

She is at the front door when she hears a knock at the back.
It is Fish. He stands looking at her through the screen until,
with a sigh, she opens the door and lets him in. He is carrying
a bottle in each hand, and wearing a bright blue shirt with an
ASPEN logo.

"I thought you gave it up." Where did he ever find such a
silly shirt? Aspen. The last place he would ever go.

"Guzzling, getting shit-faced, drinking alone. I have, I
swear I have utterly rejected such asshole behavior. But this
stuff is nice—" He holds up a bottle of pale wine. "I thought
we could share it."

"Share it?"

He grins. "I read up on what to say."

He makes her laugh. Adrenaline gushes in her, making her
head feel full and her heart race.

She has two cheap wine glasses. Fish pours the pinot noir.
He holds his glass out for her to tap. "To us," he says. "To
clean water and air, steady employment, benign moles—"

"All right, moles, then," she says, and drinks. She feels as if
she has been on springs, and they have suddenly come undone beneath her. Once she settles, she will be on firmer
ground.

"I haven't eaten," she says. "This will hit me in the head." It
is a nice wine.

"And then will you seduce me?"

"I'll probably fall asleep."

"I'd feed you, if anything's open."

"There must be something here." She opens a cupboard

door, revealing mostly bare shelves. There is a package of Ritz Crackers. She eats a cracker and drinks more wine. "I shouldn't be doing this."

"Lawyer's orders?" he says bitterly.

"Why no, I don't think it would occur to her that I'd want to be with you."

"You must have laid on a lot of shit."

"I said I wanted a divorce. I gave her money." She hopes they aren't going to descend into hostility, or even a large distance between them. She likes being with him. She doesn't have to pass a test. If anyone has to prove anything, he does. And to her. She tries to remember what she learned about detachment in the Al Anon meeting. You are not supposed to create a crisis, but you aren't supposed to prevent one, either. A recipe for living life as it presents itself. She feels like trying out her detachment. It doesn't mean you have to be unfriendly.

"Give me a cracker," Fish says. He is studying her. He can see something different in her. If it makes him wary, he will throw it back at her. If it only teases, he will look for the promise behind the tease.

I survived while you were gone, she thinks. That's really all there is to say, except, Now I'll decide if you can stay.

She holds a cracker between her teeth. It sticks out of her mouth. "Come get it," she says giddily.

When he is close enough, he puts his hands along the sides of her breasts. His thumb grasps her at the tender spot on her skin. "I can't figure it," he says, and bites off the cracker.

"Me either." They make a lot of noise, chewing.

"What do you want to do tonight?"

"I want to move around. Walk, maybe."

"You don't want to—?" He looks away.

"I do," she says, and feels her face flush. "But not until later, not until I've wanted to for hours."

He looks back at her. "To taunt?"

"To anticipate."

"Should I open the other bottle?"

They drink. Every few moments Fish reaches over and touches her somewhere. Each time, her nerves jump, as if he has shocked her. She thinks he looks much better than he did when he first came home. He already has a tan on his face and arms.

She hears Maureen calling her, and a tap-tap-tap at the door. She talks to her through a partly open door. "Someone's here," she says.

"Someone?"

She only mouths the word. "Fish."

"Really," Maureen says.

"Why not!" Katie snaps.

Maureen seems to lean away, as though Katie has slapped her. "You do what you're ready to do."

"Don't we though?" Katie says. Her head is spinning.

"Do you want to come over when he leaves?"

Katie shakes her head. Maureen would never understand. "You're drinking."

Katie pushes her head forward from her neck. "You have a one-track mind, Maureen."

"It makes a difference."

"It matters to you, but not to me. Don't come over and try to make me be good."

Maureen is hurt. "That's never what I'm doing. I come over to look after my own good. I come over to help myself. And I thought we were friends."

"So do you want to come in?" Katie says stiffly. She hates to make Maureen mad, or hurt her feelings—Maureen's face is far away, its contours fuzzy—but she only has so much energy. You can only ponder your life for so long a time; then you have to jump back in. For her, that means Fish. At least tonight.

Maureen smiles slightly. "No kiddo. I can see that wouldn't be helping anybody."

"I'm hungry," Katie tells Fish. She feels queasy all of a sudden.

"Shit, everything's closed by now," Fish says. He is comfortably sprawled on the cushions.

"The Safeway's open. We can buy some cheese or something."

"I know! Let's go to the house where I'm working. I'll cook you an egg." He pops up so quickly, Katie blinks.

"They let you cook?"

"I usually make breakfast there instead of at Michael's. This woman is completely cool, Katie. Being laid-back is on her list, along with wearing hand-woven clothing and belonging

to Amnesty International. She digs having me as her carpenter. Besides, she isn't there. She's in San Francisco, and
her kid's in Hawaii."

"I'll throw on some jeans," she says.

The night is balmy and clear, and she can smell grass and
new leaves in the air. They leave his truck parked at her
apartment and walk in long strides on the avenue. They pass
three kids in pajamas, sprawled on a lawn. One is looking
straight up at the sky through binoculars. Behind them, the
house is completely dark.

"This woman has good taste," Fish tells her. "She's a retired
anthropologist. Another Californian looking for cheaper living."

A man Katie often sees on the streets comes toward them.
He wears a too-short ragged sweater over his shirt, and a
watch cap. He carries a long stick, whittled on the end. They
pass him as he stops to spear something from the edge of a
yard. He carries a McDonald's bag, which Katie supposes is
full of paper and butts. Fish doesn't seem to have noticed the
bum, nor does he seem to have noticed the moon. The moon
is huge and full and straight ahead, as if at the end of the
avenue. Katie takes Fish's arm, but before she can think of
what to say, to make him look up, he starts talking again.

"She said she looked first for a cottage. Of course all she
could find were dumps—I could have told her that, except I
didn't know then, did I?—" He is talking very fast. "And
those duck-pond jobs east of the high school, with those
teensy-weensy yards, French doors, and fucking toy bridge
over the creek. So she bought this big house, and she's going
to do the bed and breakfast number. I'm going to do a
basement apartment for her kid, she's got the first floor—I'm
putting in a cedar-lined shower—and upstairs for guests. It's
great, Katie, she wants the best of everything. She says, take
my time. She's a fucking money wheel."

She tugs his arm, to make him pause. She points at the
moon. She feels a swelling of emotion, something in her
chest and throat. She thinks it has to do with the sky, and the
children back on the lawn. She has an urge to run back and
join them. Fish waits, as if she has stopped to scratch an itch.
She feels suddenly deflated and foolish. She does not know

how to pass her feelings over to him. She can only do that when they make love.

He leads her up a side street and a driveway, then onto the back porch of a large tan Victorian. "She's thinking about painting it purple, but I told her, I don't paint purple. Job it out. Purple, Jesus." He takes a key out of the porch socket and lets them in. It is hot inside. "They're putting in the heat pump day after tomorrow. Then I get to work in air-conditioned comfort. Great, huh?"

He raises a kitchen window and props the door open, then leads her upstairs and gives her a quick tour. Downstairs again, he heads for the refrigerator. "Eggs," he says. "Sundried tomatoes. Greek peppers, black olives. what did I tell you? And here we have—" he holds it up— "balsamic vinegar." He stoops and moves a few things around. "No butter. Can I cook eggs in olive oil?"

"I think the Italians do," Katie says. She has found a stool and is watching Fish with pleasure. "Just enough to slick the pan." She bursts out a quick loud laugh. "That looks like a Fast Eddy pan."

Fish grins. "The ultimate dipshit."

They rented a cabin from Eddy and his wife one rainy winter, on the Sechelt Peninsula. At nine o'clock one night, Eddy showed up from Vancouver to reclaim an iron skillet his wife needed to make an apple pancake. He jumped around and spun right out of there, to make it back on the last ferry. Whenever they saw anybody uptight over something stupid, after that, they called him Fast Eddy.

Fish slides the egg carefully onto the warmed skillet, humming a Dylan tune. "Lay lady lay, across my big brass bed—"

"Lo." A girl in a short black polka-dot skirt, yellow tank top, and pink Birkenstocks appears beside them. "Hey Fish, you put on one of rich son's thousand and one shirts. Think he'll miss it?"

"Carol Lee," Fish says. He finds a saucer for Katie's egg.

"Fork?" For a moment Katie tries to act like the girl isn't there. She is a tall leggy one, with hair halfway to her waist.

"My brother was playing bigshot host, I didn't want to go home. I've been asleep in the kid's room. I saw where you put the key."

"Oh well," Fish says. Katie eats her egg.

"Sometimes I help Fish out," Carol says to Katie.

"Sometimes I do too," Katie says.

"Aw Katie," Fish says. "She's just a kid." Katie rinses her plate off at the sink. He comes up behind her. "She lives up the street from my first job. She hangs out, you know? Sticks her legs out in the sun, heats up coffee, holds the other end of a board—"

Katie turns around, drying her hands on her jeans. "Don't mind me," she says to the girl.

"I've got a couple of joints," the girl says. When neither Fish nor Katie take her up on her offer, she pouts and says, "It'd be easier to stay here, you know? I mean, my brother can be a real jerk when he's entertaining. He's okay otherwise, but—"

"Don't go on account of me," Katie says. Seeing the girl out of sorts makes her relax. She doesn't think Carol Lee has too big a claim.

Carol sits down on the floor in the center of the kitchen. "I wondered what you looked like."

"It's cool," Fish mutters. "Hey it's okay," to no one in particular.

"They sit around at night and watch tv," Carol says. She crosses her legs in a yoga-like position. "He sits in his chair with the throw that has ducks on it, and she sits on the couch with her legs tucked under a lap robe she crocheted. She's a bank teller. Every night she says, 'My legs are aching, Joey,' and he says, 'Would it help to massage them?" He rubs her calves a few minutes and then he gets out the vibrator from the basket where she keeps magazines. She turns the vibrator on, while he turns up the tv. In a little while she hands it to him and he rubs his neck with it. Sometimes I hear his teeth clicking."

"The American family," Fish says. "Huh, Katie?"

Katie shrugs. Obviously, this is a little act of Carol Lee's.

"She used to be fat," Carol says. "Then she joined this group where they have meetings, and weigh in, and tell each other about the candy bars they sneaked during the week. She comes home and tells us what everybody said."

"And now she's not fat?"

"Not fat. She cooks these vegetable dishes, and baked potatoes. She goes to exercise classes. She nags Joe about his gut. She says he should come to the group, that he'll get better if he does. Like he's sick or something. She says a gut on a man is a time bomb, especially when he overworks. Joe's a CPA."

Katie laughs. "So what?"

Fish says, "Pop talk. Crystals, channels, Alcoholics Anonymous. AA people came to jail and tried to lay it on us. Ex-addicts and drunks, really full of it. They said they knew where we were at. Shit. When the meeting was over they went home. That's not where we were at. My pop got sucked into that shit. They turned him into a pipsqueak, that and frying his brain."

"Do you think it's stupid, Fish?" Katie asks. "People talking to each other, if it makes them feel better?"

"Shit, I don't care," Fish answers magnanimously. "Whatever gets you through the night. But not me. I'm not getting brainwashed with anybody's group think. And I'm not telling about the fuzz in my navel and how I used to fuck my mother."

"Silly," Carol says.

"You sure?" Fish says.

"I like to hear stories," Katie says. "As long as they're funny."

—42—

They smoke Carol's dope and go for Fish's truck. Katie suggests a drive. They stop at Safeway so Fish can buy another half-gallon of Chablis. He holds it up for Katie to see as he gets back in the truck. "White," he says. He likes red wine, but he knows she doesn't.

"Our house is out this way," Fish says when they reach the edge of town.

"Have you been there since you got home?" asks Katie.

"Nope. Michael's taken care of it. They're supposed to be out the end of June."

"Ooh, I'd love to live in the country," Carol coos. "Someplace with lots of trees so people couldn't see what I'm doing."

"Sounds like our house," Fish says. "And a yard big enough to build a boat in someday."

The first lawyer Katie went to said she should make Fish

sell the house and split the money with her. "Not on your life," she told the witch. She doesn't want Fish to spend the rest of his life in Michael's basement because of her. And child support! It isn't Katie's mother getting the divorce. Katie found another lawyer and didn't even mention the house or child.

Fish slows on a long dark curve. "We're not far," he says, and Carol says, "Drive by." Katie says, "Yeah, Fish, drive by." She has been trying to imagine living there again. She rides with her window down, the air blowing in her hair. They come up on the house, which sits far back at the end of a long drive, hardly visible from the road. Fish cuts his lights and rolls onto the drive. Katie can see, in the flash of illumination, that the grounds have been tidied up, trash hauled away, bushes clipped back. The grass is neatly mowed. She doesn't think Fish will like the new look.

"I guess they're good tenants, huh?" she says. Fish is opening the wine. She crawls down out of the truck and closes the door quietly. The driveway surface crunches under her shoes. There are lights on in the house. She takes a few steps away from the drive, and sits on the grass. Fish and Carol make their way over to join her, and they pass the wine around in silence. In a while, Carol produces another joint.

"It looks okay," Fish says. "What the hell, the grass got cut."

"I heard Michael say the woman's pregnant," Katie says.

"Yeah?" from Fish.

"I had a baby once," Carol says.

"Yeah?" Fish says again.

"My folks kicked me out when I wouldn't have an abortion. That's when I started living with my brother. He's okay, you know, for somebody 32?" Katie and Fish laugh and lean toward one another. Carol, oblivious, says, "I was sixteen. She's four now. I just saw her for a minute. God, it hurt." She lies back on the grass. She says, "It'd be different now. It'd be great to have a little kid to be with all the time."

Katie feels almost cozy with the girl. She reminds her of her own younger days, though she never was silly about babies. She turns to Fish. "Are you awake?"

He moves closer and puts his arm across her shoulder. He says, "I was thinking about the time Michael and Ursula and I went to a concert in a park in Portland. We brought four people home. One of them was Carmen. She lived with them for fifteen, sixteen months after. She was about Carol's age."

Carol appears to have fallen asleep.

"Fish, look at the fucking moon," Katie says. Just then someone comes toward them with a flashlight, startling them. "Who's out here? Who is it!" a man's voice says.

"Oh shit," Fish says, jumping up. The light is on his face. He puts his arm up to shield his eyes. "Hey, don't do that, man," he says. "We're nothing to get excited about. We were just driving by."

"Well, get out of here," the man says. He isn't very old.

"Listen," Katie says, moving toward him. "It's our house, see? We just got back into town, and we drove by, that's all. It's our house. Katie and Fish. It's our house."

"Who is it, Sky?" A fat woman with a light girlish voice stumbles through the darkness. As she comes closer, Katie sees that she is pregnant, and it is only her belly that is so large.

"You go in, Prudence," Sky says.

By now Fish and Katie are on their feet, and Carol has come up to a sitting position. "Like, when are you due?" she pipes up. Prudence drops to the ground beside her. "Anytime," she says. "They're kicking me to death!"

"Hey man, sorry if we scared you," Fish says, extending his hand. Sky hesitates, then shakes it, and says, "We didn't want people camping on your property."

Prudence groans, trying to stand up again. Carol and Sky help her up. "You guys could come in, I was going to make some tea," she says. "I can't sleep."

"Naw," Fish says.

"Like, what kind?" Carol asks. "Do you have spearmint, or rosehip?"

"Oh sure," Prudence says, stumbling ahead of them as they troop toward the house.

They enter through the front room into the large kitchen. Katie is dazed for a moment. The kitchen is bright, like an operating room. They have added a row of fluorescent lights, and they have painted. The ceiling and walls are stark white, and the cabinets are pale yellow with stenciled flowers around the edge. Someone has put in a lot of time. A gleaming black kettle on the stove starts to whistle.

Prudence has a dainty face, one you might call heart-shaped, with a pointy chin and round eyes set out so far you can see all the lid. She has long delicate arms, stuck out from her swollen body like twigs on a snowman. When she stands it looks like two people could sit on her belly. She has to lean out over her distension to get the kettle off the back burner. She motions toward the table. "You guys sit down. What's your names? I didn't hear."

Katie does the introductions. Fish looks uncomfortable. "I'd like to look around the back, if it's okay," he says. "To remember the place, you know? I haven't been here in a year."

Sky takes a couple of beers out of the refrigerator and opens the back door. He has the sort of baby face that takes a long time to age, and then gets soft all at once. He might be thirty. It is hard to tell.

Carol pulls out a chair and sprawls at the table. She is wide awake now. "Are you using a midwife or what?" she asks Prudence.

Katie rushes to follow the men out the door, though they pay no attention to her. Sky has turned on the back light.

"Here Fisher," he says, handing Fish a beer. "That what they call you? Your last name?"

"Fish," Fish mumbles.

"You understand we can't move before we're supposed to, end of June? Pru's due any time, and the house we're supposed to move into isn't ready. Actually, we're moving into the house of Pru's mother, and it's her new house that's not done. Everything's logjammed."

"Yeah, it's cool," Fish says. He guzzles his beer and starts walking around the yard. "Did my brother pay for all this shit?" he said.

Sky coughs, and says, "We worked it out, reimbursement. I hope you like what we've done." They have cut back some bushes, cleared a space, and laid a circle of stones. Around the stones they have dug a narrow dirt bed where small flowers are poking their heads out. The back fence has been propped and repaired.

"I dunno," Fish says. "I wouldn't have done it myself."

Katie sits down on a bench near the back door.

Fish stops in front of the shed. She can see that Sky has replaced the stick of wood Fish used for a handle with a real door knob. She wishes fiercely that only she and Fish were here, that time could move back, or forward, and give them another chance. When they bought this house she thought, we'll have a real life after all. Just like she thought when Rhea was born. A real life seems a wonderful and possible dream, if only she did not smash it. One of her eyes begins to throb.

She thinks what Fish would probably want is to turn out the light, find a stool, sit in the dark, and get drunk. She knows he is eyeing all the "improvements" with disgust, wanting to pile his belongings where he wants, to paint over those sweet little stencils, and spill grease on the stove. He turns around with a wild look on his face. Only she sees it.

The last night he spent in this house, before he got busted, she made Poor Pizza, with pork and beans on top. They laughed until her sides hurt, eating it. It was awful.

He opens the shed. Even in the dim light, she can see that it has been swept out, and the odds and ends rearranged. There are still boxes of bottles. "Didn't get to these?" Fish asks.

Sky comes closer and peers in. "I turned in all the beer bottles out of there and from the yard. But the wine bottles— we do recycling, of course, and I could haul them—but I thought there might be some reason you were saving them. Maybe you make your own." His voice is strained.

"Don't haul them away," Fish says. He shuts the shed door and whirls around, nearly nose to nose with Sky. "And don't paint anything else, or fix anything else, either."

"Sure man, whatever you say." Sky backs toward the house.

"I'm living in my brother's fucking basement, *man*."

"Yeah, well. July 1, it's yours, I guess, huh? I was hoping we could get an extension—"

"You know July 4th? Fucking Independence Day?"

"Sure, what about it?"

"It's my birthday. Forty-five, man. And I want to be in my house, *man*. I want all my bottles to be here, too."

"What are you so uptight about, Fisher? There's no problem here. We've got a lease."

"Yeah, don't I know it." Fish stomps into the house. Katie follows. They walk straight through the house, ignoring Prudence, who calls out, "I've got tea—"

Fish scrambles into the truck and starts the engine. "Wait," Katie says. "What about Carol?" He turns the ignition off, and leans back hard against his seat. "Creeping hippies," he says.

Katie crawls into the space behind the seats, over to Fish's side. She reaches up to rub his shoulders, and he moans. She says, "Carol and that girl hit it off, couldn't we wait and let her finish her tea?"

Fish turns, kneels, and, over the seat, puts his hands in Katie's hair and kisses her.

"Mmmm," Katie says, pulling away gently. She lies down on the bed. Fish sits on the floor beside her and reaches for the wine. He hands it to her. The wine is still slightly cool, and tart. She feels like she is floating in the van, like a goldfish in a tank.

Fish pulls her shirt up and puts his hand on her belly. He props the bottle up against one of the seats. "You're warm," he says.

"It feels like summer," Katie says.

"It really pissed me off, seeing them in my house."

"Sure," Katie soothes.

"I feel okay now," he says.

She rolls onto her side and props herself up on her elbow. "Do you remember the little frogs that time at the lake?"

It takes him a moment to answer. "The little wiggly ones."

"It was this time of year. Do you think we could find them again?"

"It was probably a freak thing."

"Probably." She lies down on her back. "I don't think they'd spook me now."

"Why's that?"

She laughs. "I'm older."

He moves up onto the edge of the bed. "You're prettier."

"You're sillier."

"You're sexier."

"You're hornier."

"I am." He kisses her.

"Hey guys," Carol says, opening the door. "Guess what, I'm going to stay."

"Do what?" Fish says.

"At least tonight. Sky needs to go to bed, and Pru can't sleep. I said I'd sit up with her. Maybe I'll help with the babies when they come."

"Babies?" Katie asks.

"Oh yeah, didn't you hear her? She's going to have twins. I told her Fish and his brother are twins, and she said maybe it was something in the house. Your house, you see?" She slams the door and runs off.

Fish and Katie burst into laughter.

"Where'd you find her?" Katie asks.

"I told you, she wandered along when I was working on that house on Primrose."

"She's cute. A little young."

"She's young," Fish agrees. He presses Katie back against the bed.

"I'm old." Katie whispers. "But sexy."

"That's right. Remember that."

Katie unzips her jeans. Nobody has ever liked touching her like Fish does. He has all the time in the world.

He slides his hand along her belly and makes her wait a long moment.

"Can you get your money back?" he asks. His face is on her belly. His tongue darts around her navel and then along the perimeter of her pubic hair.

"What money?"

"From the lawyer. Do they give refunds?"

Her stomach lurches and settles again. She doesn't answer him. They both forget what he asked. She can't tell where his finger is, and what is his tongue. It is so familiar, and so amazing.

"Where should we go?" he says. "Do you want to go to Michael's with me? Or your place?"

"Let's drive up to the lake," she says. They won't get back in time for work. It will be a long, dark, winding drive.

"Whatever you say," Fish says. "If you can wait that long." He gives her a wet, winey kiss. "Me, I've been waiting for most of a year." He turns on the Rolling Stones tape. He backs out of the drive and starts down the hill. "What do I do with those papers now, Katie? What have you done with yours?"

—43—

Sometimes in the past month, Ursula has felt that she is watching her children on video. They seem inaccessible.

Carter is well and cheerful, on a happy slide toward commencement, but he is as remote to Ursula as an exchange student, as if he had another life to go home to when the year is over. She thinks of the confusion and fuss in getting his term paper in on time—she ended up typing it on a borrowed typewriter, working until three in the morning to finish it—with a nostalgic ache. Normal life provides them too little intersection. He is seldom home. She thinks he cannot bear the silence of the robber-stripped house. Michael has been muttering about getting a new system for his music, and he mentioned that they ought to get Carter a computer for graduation, but neither matter has come up again between them. Of course he may have bought either or both, but they are not in evidence.

Recently Ursula saw Carter on the street downtown. She was driving home from the bakery and she saw him with a girl in a red dress. The girl also wore a short black jacket, trimmed gaudily, like a bullfighter's suit. Her hair was pale and glossy, and even in a glance from a distance, she seemed very well put together. Ursula didn't recognize her as one of the girls who have been through the Fisher house in the past year. This girl had her arm through Carter's, and she was leaning toward him as they stood at the edge of the park, near the pay phone booth. Ursula saw her son touch the girl's hair, and his gentle gesture with this strange girl, on the street in plain sight, sent a shiver of surprise down Ursula's neck. She saw immediately that there were Carters she had not yet met and might never know, boy-men he would reveal only to young misses, away from the constraints of his parents and home.

Juliette is as elusive, and troubling. She slips by Ursula as if the crossings were prearranged. She leaves the house many evenings just as Ursula's car pulls into the drive. Ursula assumes that rehearsals are taking much of Juliette's time. Juliette goes to bed as soon as she is home from them, sometimes quite early, and then she rises in the middle of the night to bathe and wash her hair. She nibbles before dinner is prepared, and so isn't hungry when it is. She is too busy, too tired, too full, to go with the family for spaghetti or steak, or the hot Cajun shrimp Carter loves at the Bay Leaf Deli. She says she doesn't need rides anywhere, she can walk.

Sometimes Juliette creeps out of the house after dark and does stretches in the yard. Sometimes she sits on the deck in a lawn chair, her feet drawn up close to her buttocks, her chin on her knee, and stares in the direction of the sycamore, behind which, in a converted shed the size of a laundry room, a Japanese graduate student plays a mournful sax.

There has been no more outright defiance, and no scenes of tears and childish comfort-seeking. Juliette is a phantom.

Ursula thinks about her children's upbringing, and laments the things she has left out. Where there was no church membership, why was there no visiting of different denominations? Where there was so little athletic emphasis, why were swimming lessons cut off at Porpoise level? Why no tennis, with college courts a five-minute walk away? And how has she so thoughtlessly failed to provide them a sense of family history? She condenses family stories to anecdotes three sentences long, makes jokes and doesn't bother to explain the context. They've done practically nothing to establish family rituals. (What is there to say about Christmas except that the elder Fishers come, dinner is always late, and presents have usually been negotiated to prevent disappointment, thus expunging any sense of surprise? Even Halloween is an embarrassment of neglect; Juliette remembers well first grade, when her teacher had to throw a sheet over her head, lest she be the only costume-less child.)

The years from babyhood through primary school seem in retrospect a time when the children were handed back and forth, their care like a baton in a relay, with only one runner on the track at a time. With a stab of pain—truly and physically located beneath her breastbone—Ursula realizes that Michael has spent hundreds of more hours, perhaps hundreds of more days, with the children than she. Summers off. The three of them have filled time she remembers only as days at work. They have gone swimming and hiking. They have built playhouses, birdhouses, scooters, and hand looms. One year they built a kiln and made a hundred pinch pots. Ursula, laboring for the past eighteen years on a bureaucrat's schedule, has organized the formal leisure. There were camps: Camp Fire, B'nai B'rith, YMCA, once a ten-day seashore botany camp from which Carter had to be fetched, raging with a fever that disappeared by the time they reached home. She took them to Chicago half a dozen times, to Seattle as many or more. And there was Disneyland; there they were all together.

She has tried never to think of their future lives as something she can mold. She has tried not to desire their careers, their ambitions for them. She feels too keenly, still, her father's disappointment in her, after the years of kindly discussion of the scholarly life, sustained by his hope of contaminating her with his ambition. But she also understands, though it has been little mentioned, that her mother postponed her intellectual and artistic life for marriage, and for Ursula, because she lacked the strength of conviction and the bolster of family support. Be what you like, she tells her children, but do well, because you have to *do* a lot of years. She wants them to see a large range of possibilities. Once, watching "Nature" on PBS, she asked Carter (he was eleven years old at the time), "Who do you think sits there and waits for the night flower to open?" He said, "Vampires come out at night," and, bored, scurried off to play something mindless on his first computer.

Michael does not talk with them about work. He does not share Ursula's conviction that a good life must include fulfillment, satisfaction, inner reward, in that arena. He says there isn't enough intrinsic reward to go around; somebody has to shovel shit. He acts sometimes as if he doesn't recognize that he is in the middle class. The professional class. Yet he has liked teaching, at least not minded too much the things he didn't do that he once thought he might.

Carter and Juliette have grown up faster than Ursula could see coming. They seem to have grown while she was away somewhere. This is especially true of Juliette, who was such a little girl two years ago. Now Juliette walks with her shoulders slouched, a very un-ballerina posture, and spends too many hours alone. Ursula never sees her eat, though she sees signs of it, and Juliette, although thin, is surely not gaunt.

Ursula would like to discuss the children with Michael, but he says you cannot talk a crop in. Wait and see, he ways. She wants to ask him if that is what his parents did. When was it that the boys became distinctly separate, were they boys or young men? When Ursula met them she sensed immediately they were uncannily bound, although she didn't know for months that they were twins. Fish seemed then to be on the front line of life, often in the way of people and events, stumbling against convention, while Michael moved quietly in the background, finding his way without disturbing anyone else, or asking too much. She remembers how disoriented Michael seemed when Fish joined the navy and disappeared from his life. She knows he dreamed about his brother, especially after Fish went to Vietnam. He woke Ursula frequently with his tossing, but he said it was indigestion, or a stuffy nose, or a little insomnia. He scoffed when Ursula said twins had ties across all sorts of time and space. He said they were not identical, implying that they were uniquely individual, bound only by family ties and a shared birth date, as if the years had diminished their likenesses rather than endorsed them. And when Fish came home from Asia, for a long time Ursula thought they were really different. They were finally divided by lanes of war and marriage, by Vietnam and Ursula.

She catches him one night in bed. He has been spending his free time with Fish, in the basement or yard, or weekend days at Fish's house project. She sees them poring over plans and pages of figures, photographs and lists, and she considers listening, to see what is going on, but they speak a different language, elliptical and specialized, and she always remembers the hundred and one things she needs to do, and leaves them alone.

On this evening, though, Fish is out, and Michael takes an unusually long bath and goes to bed, moving one of Ursula's pillows to join his two for proper propping, adjusting the light just so, and taking up the special *National Geographic* issue about a new archeological site in Peru, fabulous for its gold and quantity of artifacts.

She asks him if he thinks she should take Juliette to see a counselor.

"About her classes next year?"

"Don't be dense, Michael," she scolds.

"You mean a therapist, then."

"Yes." Immediately her face heats with embarrassment, exactly as it did when she first brought up the matter of Juliette's retainer in seventh grade. Michael called that "another middle-class American gouge," as if they should ignore her mismatched layers of teeth, leaving her to a crooked smile and awkward bite, when they had the means to urge her teeth into place. Of course Michael left the decision to Ursula, and Ursula, if she erred, erred on the side of luxury and caution rather than penury. And, for conscience sake, she contributed an enormous pile of clothing to the Nicaraguan Bus for Peace drive, along with twelve tubes of Neosporin.

"Do you see something coming?" asks Michael. The cat, reclining on Michael's torso, is stretched out full length. "Do you think she needs guidance in developing her *self*?" Sighing noisily, making it clear that he feels interrupted and put-upon, he tosses the magazine to the floor and pulls Ursula's pillow out from under his head. "Are we going to get her started early? Something like a training bra?"

She raises her head so that he can put the pillow behind her. "Of course not. We're too hip, aren't we?" This is a concept Michael despises. He says that bleached oak and odd vegetables are like piss on the corners of the middle class. Don't cross over here in your polyester, eating Twinkies, they say. He brings up a version of this argument (diatribe, really) anytime Ursula considers working on the house, buying a piece of furniture or a good item of clothing. It never comes up when *he* has a consumer-attack, but, she would admit if he pressed her, when he buys it is for his own pleasure and never for show. "And you know I never bought her a training bra."

"But therapy—you have an investment there. It's your field." Is she to understand that he *minds* her training?

"That's not fair. I'm not a therapist, though I could be. You know I've chosen to stay in this job, to work in the public—" She gropes for a word, retrieves "sector," and knows she would gag if she said it. "I work for the bureaucracy in order to help keep a few children out of the hot oil. I'm hardly in the therapy business, and you know so."

"I allowed myself an unworthy digression," Michael says. He has shifted into his slightly arch comic mode. She thinks he sees himself cast in a British movie. He leaves one hand on Pajamas's rump, and slides the other along Ursula's. "What's brought this on?" The cat purrs loudly and stretches even longer, looking, in the moment of extension, like a mummy cat Ursula saw in the British Museum.

"Don't you see her slouching toward depression? Don't you find her evasive and solitary?"

"She seems adolescent and sensitive and very much your daughter."

Ursula pops up from under the sheet to a sitting position. Michael's hand slides off her thigh. "I brought this on?"

"Indeed, Ursula, I don't even see anything to worry about, so I'm not attributing guilt. But weren't you the teenager who drank gallons of lemon water to purify your system, and then turned around and drank cherry codeine syrup to get high?"

"Teenage foolishness is not genetic. Besides, we're not discussing my etiology. Or Juliette's, either." Actually, Ursula has to suppress a smile. Michael tosses a bit of old history at her, and shows that he heard something she said, a long time ago.

How long ago was it they traded personal narratives?

How long since he asked her a personal question?

"Maybe it's girls," he says.

"Oh great."

"You aren't suggesting therapy for Carter."

"I wouldn't do that to a therapist."

"He doesn't need any help with his psyche. He just needs time and experience with consequences." He says this lightly, alluding perhaps to his own Carter rescues, and her disapproval.

"He needs a haircut." She hears her prim, tense voice and calls up an image of her son that makes her titter. "Admit it, Michael, he looks like a rooster."

"He has a beautiful girlfriend. Annabel."

"I think I saw her. At the park the other day. Has she been around? Have you met her?"

"A couple of times. She drives a Honda Prelude. New."

"Really."

"She's an heiress, says the son."

"Is that part of the sudden interest?"

"I don't think it's sudden. I think he hasn't wanted to bring her around in case if didn't pan out. I think he's rather proud of her."

"Because she's beautiful or because she's rich?"

"Because she breaks his trend. He's proven he's not in a rut."

"I didn't know there was a trend. There've been so many."

"Flaky girls, you know they were."

"That Kincaid girl got 1400 on her SAT's. I heard her mother going on about it at the cleaners."

"And how long did she last?"

"Or did he? Honestly, Michael, what has he done with girls these last few years? Where do kids go when they go out?"

"Movies, the mall. Games, dances. It doesn't change all that much. Little back roads."

"You think he's basically your average kid?"

"Somewhere in the middle of the curve."

"So cut him loose, aren't we about to do that? It's still Juliette who worries me. Not that Carter hasn't in the past. Not that I don't worry about his responsibility, and whether he'll brush his teeth next year, but Michael, stop diverting me, JULIETTE IS HURTING."

"I know. She's slipped away from you. You don't know what to say to her."

"Why yes."

"It's supposed to happen, Ursie. Children push their parents away so they can grow up. Child Development 201. Remember?" He speaks kindly enough; she chooses not to be offended. She wants to say, *I miss her.*

"My mother left town," she does say. "It was easy to make a break."

"My mother had her teeth clenched my whole childhood. There wasn't anything to break away from."

She resists a strong notion to say he has not broken yet. Instead, she says, "Keep an eye on her. You're home before me in the afternoons. See if you can spend some time with her. She's off mothers for now. Reassure me."

"If I can, if I can."

"You're not humoring me?"

"Of course I'm humoring you." He spends a moment adjusting his position in the bed. "If I don't humor you, you will lie there and agitate, and how will we ever get around to you-know-what, which we haven't done this week?"

"Michael. Are Fish and Katie back together?"

"Some other time, Ursie. Turn off the light." He has

worked his way down the bed so that his mouth is on her shoulder.

"All right, but there is one more thing."

"Ursula, Ursula."

"You've got to fix the kitchen floor. I want a floor for Carter's graduation."

"They're not holding it in our kitchen."

"I might have a party."

"Have you talked to Carter?"

"Not for him, for us."

"We're celebrating?"

"Not really. More like wallowing in reminiscences. I'd like to get out the baby albums, tell stories. I'd like to see some old friends."

"Don't they live other places?" She detects a sad tinge to his words. She feels her belly warm, then her knee jerks involuntarily. His mouth is quite hot on her collarbone.

"I'll tell you a story," he murmurs.

"I'm listening."

"Come closer."

He rises, whispers in her ear.

"You're perverted, Michael!" Delightfully so, she thinks.

"And that gets you a gray rubber floor."

"Deal," says Ursula to her husband. Juliette slips away, a shadow on a screen. Though somewhere in the house she sighs, there is nothing to be done about her. Not right now.

—44—

On the Sunday morning before Carter's graduation, Ursula meets a social worker from her office, Teresa, at the bakery. They order cappuccinos, and congratulate one another on getting up and out at seven-thirty in the morning. As they stir in the frothy milk, they plan a route for their long walk, promised one another Friday at the office.

Ursula is surprised that there are so many people out so early on a weekend morning.

"But it's so warm, so summer-like," Teresa says. "In a few weeks we'll be clogged with tourists. I love it now, when I still feel the city's mine."

They march through the park into the hills above. By then they have slowed to a mild canter. "God," Ursula puffs. "I seem to be running out of gas."

Teresa laughs and says, a little shakily, "Why don't we do this all summer and fall, right up until bad weather?"

Ursula groans. "I'll have to think about it."

They both stop, gulping air and laughing. Teresa puts a hand on Ursula's shoulder and says, "More immediately, would you want to go together on a yard sale?"

"A sale?" Ursula's mind is filled with images of heaps of clothing, chairs and tennis rackets, lamps in the back of the closet. "That's a terrific idea," she says. "When? Your house or mine?"

"I'm going to do some major repairs and painting, and buy new furniture, so let's do it in my driveway. I'll take care of the ads. Say a month, towards the end of June?"

"Sure."

"Maybe your husband's brother could come over sometime and see what I want done. Angela says his work is good."

"I'll ask him."

"Let's go back to the bakery. Let's eat something this time."

Ursula agrees. She swings her arms vigorously. "Do you think we've burned off a rugulach?"

She returns home feeling quite proud of herself. It's only nine in the morning and she's been out of bed for two hours.

Michael and Fish are on the front porch steps drinking coffee. Ursula holds up a bakery bag. "Scones," she says. The men follow her back to the kitchen.

"We're going to do the floor," Fish says, and bites into a scone.

"Right now?"

"I told you I would," Michael says.

Ursula goes upstairs to bathe and change clothes. While she is in the tub Juliette knocks on the door. "I'm dying to go to the bathroom," she says. "You can come in," Ursula says, and Juliette makes a sound of disgust. "Hurry UP."

Juliette goes in quickly as Ursula exits wrapped in a towel.

Downstairs Michael and Fish are banging around. The roll of rubber flooring has been brought up.

Ursula takes a cup of coffee into the dining room and calls her mother.

She hears water running upstairs. Knowing Juliette is occupied, she tells Clare how worried she has been.

"Is she actually not eating at all? Is she wasting away in front of you?" Clare asks in a calm, almost leisurely way.

"That's not it, but she's certainly not robust."

"She's a dancer. They want their bones to show."

"She's a child, still growing. She's terrified her breasts are sprouting on her."

"I never knew where you got yours." Clare is thin and flat and angular, a body type that ages very well. "Your father's mother, I suppose. She was all pillowy."

"It's not my figure I called to discuss," Ursula says. She should have known her mother would downplay her urgency. One of Clare's favorite expressions is, "I've seen worse."

"I'll be down for her ballet opening. Do you think Carter will mind very much my missing graduation Friday?"

Ursula laughs. "A bus load of kids leaves soon after the ceremony. They're going to Disneyland. He has a girlfriend. He thinks it's funny that I even want to attend the graduation. To him, it's already happened."

"Tell Juliette to call me. When nobody's home."

Ursula knows that Juliette will want to. She is stabbed with jealousy, and with gratitude, oddly mixed. "You think you can find out long distance if she's too shaky? You'll tell me if she worries you, too?"

"Don't underestimate your mothering, Ursula. You do very well with both of them. I have always admired your light hand."

"Of course *I* was crazy at fifteen."

A long silence tells Ursula that her mother is not eager to dip into the past. "I got out of it okay," Ursula adds.

"Without a lot of intervention, as I recall."

"You weren't there," Ursula says, surprised to hear the recrimination in her statement of fact.

"I was on the phone with your father, or with his wife when he was buried in his studies, several times a week, for several years, my dear daughter."

Now it is Ursula's turn to be silent, this time in amazement. "I had no idea."

"We all agreed not to make too much of your moods and antics. Your father said he could do so as long as you kept your grades up. He worried so about you getting into a good college. Did he tell you that, or did you just sense it?"

"I don't remember considering it. School wasn't hard, that's all."

"Your stepmother was the reliable one. It was her idea to send you to England the summer between your junior and senior years."

"I was hopelessly polite and timid in an excruciatingly proper British homestay," Ursula recalls.

"Her theory was the experience would distract you."

"And break my habits?" Like whole weekends in bed, refusing to come out. Her stepmother brought in two trays a day without a rebuking word. Then there were the beer binges, which her father certainly didn't know about.

Her mother says, "I wanted you to come to Seattle that summer. I was managing a wonderful small gallery, and we ran classes all summer. I thought you could work it out if I got your hands in clay or paint."

"Mother," Ursula says sadly, because that option was never discussed. She assumed her occasional one-week visits were all her mother wanted.

"I wasn't aggressive enough, and England sounded nice."

"Well," Ursula says brightly, wishing she could really "reach out and touch" her mother, "where shall I send Juliette now?"

"Let's see," Clare says, and then goodbye.

By the time Ursula hangs up, the activity in the kitchen has accelerated. Fish has brought in a battered tape player and put on Janis Joplin.

"Oh Lord, won't you buy me a Mercedes-Benz," Ursula sings along. She pulls her knees up to her chest and clasps them. She closes her eyes. "My friends all drive Porsches, I must make a—mends—" She really tries to match Janis's coarse cry.

"—Oh Lord, won't you buy me a color tv," Fish joins in. "Dialing for dollars is trying to find me—" They laugh.

"Ohhh!" Juliette cries as she speeds through the kitchen and out the back door. Michael doesn't even look up, Fish is still laughing, and Ursula goes to the window of the dining room to peer out on the yard. The window is filthy.

Juliette arranges herself on their one battered lawn chair, stretching her legs out to catch the mild morning sun. She is wearing a pair of shorts, a top from a two-piece bathing suit, and rolled-down anklets with sandals. Ursula wonders why in the world she keeps on socks to lie in the sun.

"I've got to make some calls," she says at the door to the kitchen. "I'm going upstairs so I won't bother you." Neither Fish nor Michael even look up. She finds her address book in the mess of her top drawer and sits on the bed to call Portland. She wants so much to reach old friends, the impulse is almost painful. She says to herself it is too early for this, then chooses the first number, and dials.

Carter stumbles across her vision, on his way to the bathroom, clad only in his jockey shorts, the ones that say JOGGER on the hip. He stubs his toe on the loose carpet near her bedroom door and grumbles, saying something obscene. "Carter," she calls, and he says, disappearing from sight, "Yo, Mom."

"This is Ursula Fisher," she says to Hank Lutter when he answers on the fifth ring. "*Ursula*, Hank," she says. "Don't you remember?"


—45—


"The Lutters are the last couple I'd have predicted would divorce," Katie says when Ursula tells them about her conversation with Hank. Katie seems completely unself-conscious, bringing up the subject of divorce.

The are sitting on the new gray kitchen floor, eating pizza fetched by Carter from two different establishments. Katie worked wardrobe on a matinee and showed up just in time to rave about the floor. "It looks so *expensive!*"

Michael says it wasn't. "I bought the flooring at a close-out sale. And except for the pizza, the labor was free." He punches his brother on his folded-up leg.

Carter appears from the living room where he, his girlfriend Annabel, and his buddy Joel have had their own pizza feed. "So what do you think? Which do you like best? What crust?" he burbles.

The adults stare.

"The one with pepperoni is deep-dish. They call it Sicilian. The other one is supposedly hand-tossed. I wanted to try spicy shrimp but they didn't have anything to use for spices. Wouldn't it be good with that Cajun shit on it? And instead of Canadian bacon—shit, that stuff is rubberized—I'd use that real Italian ham, I can't remember what it's called—you used it last July Fourth around melon strips, remember, Mom—"

"What the hell?" Fish drones.

"You did good, son," Michael says.

"What is this mad interest in pizza, Carter?" Ursula asks.

Carter bends down on one knee, to their level. "You'd think the pizza market would be saturated, right? Pizza Hut, Dominos, Pappy's— But where's the high-class pizza? Where's the REAL pizza? You know, on the streets in Rome they sell it cold. It's got a deep bready crust—sort of like that one—and they put olives and anchovies—"

"How do you know?" Katie asks.

Carter grins. "Annabel lived there a year, when she was thirteen.

"What are you trying to say?" Ursula asks. From around the corner Joel yells. "Caaaarter! The movie's gonna start!"

"I just think there's untapped poTENtial," Carter says, and is gone.

"Did Juliette eat?" Ursula asks Michael.

"Where *is* Juliette?" Katie asks.

"She's out back," Fish says. "She made a cheese sandwich and went out a while ago."

"What's her PROBLEM?" Ursula says, up on her knees.

Michael grabs her arm, to keep her from getting up. "There is nothing you need to do out there," he says.

Ursula slumps. "She's bugging me."

"Relax," Fish says. "It's the end of the school year. All that boring wind-down shit they do. She's sick of it."

"Moody," Katie says. "I was moody at that age."

"What about Hank Lutter?" Michael says. He gets them each another beer from the refrigerator and sits down again, leaning against the cabinet and stretching out his legs. "I suppose you got all the details."

Ursula, slightly flustered, says, "I was so shocked I said, 'What do you mean, divorce?'" and Hank *laughed*. He said Jane has a new job at the university in Santa Cruz—she's a therapist in the health center. He said she'll finally get to deal in intimacy all day. What do you think he meant?" She has a tiny hope Michael won't say he knows just what Hank meant.

"She's been doing something new since I saw her," Fish says. He grins. "Her idea of therapy used to be feeding you and then rubbing up against you in the hallway—"

"Go on, Fish." Katie flicks his hair with her fingertips.

"It's true," Michael says. Ursula stares at him. "Meaning what?" she demands.

"Just what Fish said. She liked to get a feel before you went home. I think she felt daring, without feeling compromised. We were all friends."

"She's the straightest friend we had in Portland!" Ursula says indignantly.

"Remember the time she and I took the drive to the Japanese flower gardens?" Michael says. "You took the kids to see Bambi or Cinderella or some other sappy movie."

"Vaguely." Ursula feels hazy herself. This reminds her of one of those novels where the author gives you fifty pages of "her" and then tells the same story only about "him" and it isn't like "she" thought at all.

"We never got out of the car." Michael starts to laugh. "She said Hank was working so hard, studying for his CPA exams, that he was neglecting her."

"I don't think I like this," Ursula says, but she is definitely interested.

"You fucked in the car?" Fish says.

"Naw. She talked for two hours straight. Hank this, Hank that. She had just found out she was pregnant again. She was starved to talk."

"You sat in a car and listened to Jane Lutter TALK for TWO HOURS?"

Michael, Fish, and Katie laugh, while Ursula blushes and blinks.

"Well, gee, yes," Michael says teasingly. "But we never did it again, honest. It didn't mean a thing."

Ursula starts to cry. "Oh shit," she says.

"You're kidding," Michael says. "Aw, Ursie, I didn't mean to hurt your feelings." He crawls over to her and pats her cheek and says, "I'm sorry, honey."

"Two HOURS," Ursula sputters. She runs upstairs, throws

herself across her bed, and weeps. Even if she did live in
Portland still, their old friends would be new people, just like
she probably is, too. She doesn't mind growing up; she just
never thought it would be lonely. She feels abandoned by
life.

Michael sits down beside her and strokes her back. "Are
you coming down with something?"

"Oh!"

"I know, Ursie."

She sits up. "You know what, Michael Fisher?"

"I know you wish we talked more."

"You do?"

"I never mean not to. I just always seem to see a shortcut to
the point. I could try, I guess. I do love you."

Ursula sniffles. "There was something about—about Jane?"

Michael smiles at her. "Now you're stirring up dust where
there's no dirt. Jane Lutter is not and was not an issue."

"I had this idea. I thought maybe Carmen and Winston
could come down from Seattle. I got Carmen on the phone
but she and Winston are going camping with friends, and she
didn't even suggest coming later. I asked Hank about the
Edsons. He said Tony Edson's diabetes is so bad he's losing his
sight—"

"That's awful."

"Hank says Tony says it doesn't matter, their kids are wonderful, their house, their land. He can go on, not seeing.
God, Michael, I'm talking about all this with Hank, and I
know I'll NEVER talk to Tony or Bea, either one. We haven't
seen them in so long, can you imagine how I'd launch this
conversation. Heard about your eyes—" These are people
Ursula loved.

"What did you do, Ursie? Who else did you call?"

"That's all. My mother, Hank, Carmen. I tried to get one of
my friends from work up there but nobody answered."

She lies on her back, and Michael stretches out beside her.
"Where are Katie and Fish?" she asks. Before Michael answers, she says, "Katie and Fish, hear that? They are back
together, aren't they?"

"Fish says he doesn't know. He says he isn't ever going to
bring up the subject of the divorce again, like he thinks Katie
has forgotten it."

"Why would she divorce him now? He's a saint."

"Listen, Ursula, I don't know anything more about them than you do."

"Fish talks to you. Katie and I haven't really talked in a year. Not since Fish got busted."

"Fish and I mostly are talking houses. Construction stuff."

A breeze rattles the leaves outside the window and gushes across them on the bed, creating a quick moment of dramatic feeling in Ursula. Like standing on a high bluff.

Michael says, "They went somewhere with Juliette."

"They did?" They would hear the ocean below. They would embrace. People have been swept off this cliff by the wind.

"Fish said they wouldn't be long." He runs his finger along the side of Ursula's breast. Her attention snaps back.

"Not now, Michael."

"What then?"

"I don't know."

He lies on his back, too, folds his hands on his chest. "I used to think I'd have lots of friends. I'd work and when I was off I'd drink beer and listen to funny stories, I'd hike and fish in season, you and I would make love every night—"

Ursula almost whispers. "But it hasn't turned out like that, has it? Not exactly?" She thinks of Friday nights in River Cove. Did he foresee that set of responsibilities? And the children?

"Remember that stupid tv show we watched a couple of times, about the old college friends? How they all fall in and out of each other's houses and problems, and they tell one another everything? It's bullshit, isn't it? I hated that show right away, it was like an ad for a certain lifestyle, an attempt to validate the *idea* of lifestyle, but now I don't think that's what it's about at all. It's a fantasy about how you hold up your life, how you have lots of support from friends if you're cool enough. It's about friendship, the way *Dallas* and *Dynasty* are about being rich. It's that *Big Chill* fantasy."

Ursula waits a long moment, and realizes that Michael isn't going to say anything else. She feels close to him, and surprised at him, and completely unsure about what she can say or do. Only she can't just let it lie. "I guess that's what you have family for," she says tentatively. "For support, and purpose? The kids, for fresh chances." Ideas about altruism and citizenship crowd her mind too, ideas her father hammered in with years of light taps, but it isn't the right time to suggest an overhaul of their life. Not even of her life. She votes. She gives. She's on the board of Planned Parenthood.

Michael turns onto his side, takes her hand. "Once when Fish and I were about Juliette's age, we went hunting. We hiked out five, six miles from the road, and this incredible storm came up, lashing wind and rain. We came to a little campground and it had an old neglected outhouse. We got in it out of the rain, till it let up. Only it didn't let up, all night it rained. And all night we stood crammed in that damned outhouse, telling each other stories and jokes, until we both fell asleep. I can't remember what we talked about. Kid shit. I wouldn't want to be stuck with him anywhere all night anymore. But sometimes, when he's a real asshole, I remember that stupid hike. We had a good time in an outhouse! It was an adventure."

Ursula turns on her side to face her husband. "If that was us, now. What would we talk about?"

"I'd finally be caught. I'd have to answer all your questions. Try me. Go ahead. Ask one now." He lets go of her hand and touches her breast again.

"Okay," Ursula says. "Here goes. If I have a garage sale in a month, can I sell your potter's wheel? Can I clean out your closet? Should I paint the cabinets to go with my new floor? Why are you and Fish talking so much about building? What don't I know yet because you haven't told me?"

She hears the front door slam. "We're back!" Katie calls out.

"Maybe we'll build a house together, to sell," Michael says.

"Who's going to get the loan for that? Who's got the credit?" Ursula knows what he's going to say.

"We should talk about that," he says, but he gets off the bed and goes downstairs, leaving her to sort out love, sentiment, and conspiracy.

—46—

Fish has bought Juliette a hummingbird feeder. They all sit outside until dark, whispering and being careful about their movement, watching for birds. Fish says the neighbor has a

feeder, and he has seen several birds nearby. They have just
about given up when the first bird comes. It has a throat that
is blue and then green, shot with gold. A second bird is
yellow and orange and gilded with green. The last bird is the
smallest, tiny, with a glowing red throat. Juliette is awed. She
sits between Katie and Fish on the grass, plucking idly at the
dry blades. Fish whispers in her ear a couple of times and she
smiles at him.

"Remember the crows?" Michael says as the evening begins
to turn cool and dark.

Fish nods. He says to Katie, "Go get the wine, could you?"
and though Katie hesitates for a moment, looking at Fish,
then at Ursula, she finally leaves and comes back with a half
gallon of rose.

"What about crows?" Juliette asks her father.

"We found a nest of babies, and the mother dead on the
ground," Michael says.

Fish takes a long swig of wine and passes it to Michael.
Michael asks Ursula if she wants a glass of it. Ursula shakes
her head. She is studying the two brothers, not sure what she
is looking for. What she ought to look for.

"The crows, Daddy," Juliette says. She sits with her feet
stuck up, her knees close to her body. She fiddles with her
toes through the holes in her sandals, rubbing and scratching
through her socks.

"We took them back to the house," Fish says. "And fed
them. We built them this wooden nest and set it up in the
yard. When they got a little bigger, and they could get
around, they started coming to the window of our bedroom
every morning, by dawn, and pecking like crazy at the pane."

"What a racket," Michael says. "It woke Mom up every
morning, and she got more and more annoyed with it. Finally she said that we couldn't have all those pet crows pester-
ing us. So Pop took us and the crows—we had them in two
shoeboxes—in the truck a couple miles away, and we let them
out.

"The next morning, there they were. Peck, peck, peck."

"So what happened then?" Juliette asks. "What did Geneva
do?" She makes a face, as if she can imagine it wasn't good.

Fish props up the bottle between his knees. "She never said
another word. We had those birds for months, then it got

cold and they went someplace better." He reaches up with both hands and scratches the front of his scalp. "Your dad always had a bird or two after that. We built nests for years. Simple little houses for wrens and swallows. A fancy nesting site shaped like a ship, for bluebirds; we took it out in the woods to hang, like your dad does now every year. We built birdhouses that looked like pueblos, and pagodas." He laughs a little. "I outgrew that shit, but not your dad. He must have forgotten hummingbirds, though. All they want is a little sugar water."

Ursula sees that Michael looks almost stricken, as though Fish's remark has wounded him. "I didn't think of it," he says.

"Thanks for getting it," Juliette says to Fish. She is quite cheerful and sweet-voiced. She hugs his arm. "As few friends as I've got, I'll get to know every one of those birds."

After Ursula bathes and dresses for bed, she goes about the house picking up towels and dishes, papers, books, balls of cat fur, shoes. It takes her half an hour to put the house in order. She should have cleaned it thoroughly, but there is to be no party, why bother? She'll do it top and bottom before July. She loves her new floor. It makes the room entirely new.

Michael is in the kitchen drinking a glass of wine and writing on a yellow pad.

Ursula pulls up a stool to sit beside him, and he turns the pad over.

"Something secret?" she asks.

"No. Just not important. I mean, since you're here."

"Have you decided about a present for Carter?"

"Maybe just money," Michael says.

"How much?"

"Depends."

She sighs. "We're going to be giving him lots of money for four years of college. I'd rather give him something specific."

"Something you want him to have?"

"Don't," she pleads.

"He wants to deliver pizzas for Pizza Hut."

"In what?"

"Your car, my truck."

"No way. I read the other day that those goddamned pizza

deliverers run down people every day somewhere—I mean, KILL people, to get a pizza somewhere fast."

"And that's why he can't?"

"He has a job."

"Ursula, he ought to be able to get his own job. It's better if he does."

"He can't use my car."

"I already told him that. And not my truck. But if he wants to work there—God knows why he would—I don't see that it's really our business."

"He better be letting Sharon know he doesn't want to work for her. Plenty of people do."

"I told him that."

"Why is it I keep finding out you know things I don't?"

"As soon as I get a chance to tell you, you know too."

"He's already in bed, asleep. The sleep of the innocent, I suppose."

"He's more innocent than a lot of kids his age."

"And Juliette? Where is she?"

"She just went out in the yard again."

"It's ten o'clock."

"It's safe, Ursula. Our back yard."

She heads for the back door. Michael says, "Why don't you just leave her alone?"

She answers, one hand on the door. "I'll see you upstairs."

Michael toasts her with his nearly empty glass. "In the conjugal bed, Ursula. Cheers." He sounds almost angry.

Juliette sits on the step down from the deck, her head bent over, her cheek on her knee, her hair falling down over her face and legs.

Ursula sits beside her, not close enough to touch, and says nothing.

"Did you know Marina's quitting dance?" Juliette says in a few minutes.

Ursula, truly surprised, says she had no idea.

"She isn't even going to be in the summer ballet. Brian wants to kill her."

"Did she get mad or something?"

Juliette raises her head and speaks, looking out into the dark yard. "She says she's sick of classes and hurting, and she wants to do speech next year. Debate, you know? She says she thinks she'll like the kids, and she'll get to go to tournaments out of town."

"Are you disappointed?"

Juliette looks at her. "God, you don't understand anything. Marina and I were always competing, Mom. Why would I CARE?" Ursula thinks she must, very much. "Marina's mother is really mad, though. Marina says her mother yelled at her and said the problem is Marina has no passion."

"No passion?"

"Can you believe it? Marina's barely fifteen, and her mother says, like, what are you going to do with your life? Does anybody fifteen know what they're going to do when they're OLD?"

"You've got a passion, don't you, baby?"

"Dance? I guess I do. But it doesn't mean I know."

"Kids don't know—"

"No?!" Juliette says furiously. "What about kids who are in the American Ballet Theatre School? They've gone to New York from all over the country. You think they don't know?"

"At fifteen?"

"Fifteen, sixteen. You have to know."

Ursula wishes desperately she knew what Juliette is trying to say. She reaches over and touches her lightly on the shoulder. "Darling," she croons.

"Everybody's supposed to have a passion, Mrs. Clarence says. Boy. She thinks selling real estate makes her special? I've been sitting here, thinking about it. What's anybody's passion? Famous writers, actors, politicians, and baseball players, maybe. But plain old people? Do they have a passion?"

"Some yes, some no," Ursula says weakly.

"Like Dad and his birdhouses? Fish and his wine?"

Ursula decides it's best to ride this one out.

"Then there's you, Mom. You know what your passion is? Other people's kids!"

"Juliette, what are you so damned mad at me about?"

"You know how at the end of class, we do all those jumps? *Changements?*"

"Sure, Julie, I've watched them." Saying so makes Ursula realize how long it's been since she visited one of Juliette's classes. She remembers little girls in tutus, Juliette at the barre, pumpkins and fairies. Lord, it's hard, she thinks, when they get big!

"That's my passion. Those jumps. Those tiny, tiny moments in the air."

"You're a fine dancer, sweetheart."

"I've had this dream a bunch of times lately. I'm doing the jumps, and then I do a grand jete, my arms out over my legs, my legs extended so far, I'm like a bird, I'm like a Russian ballerina. Then I look down, and I'm way above everybody, or where everybody was. Only everybody's gone." She turns toward her mother, her face glazed with tears. "Everybody," she cries.

Ursula takes her in her arms. "We're all right here, sweet Julie," she says. "Right here."

"I'm sorry," Juliette says against Ursula's neck. "I don't know what's wrong with me."

Ursula pulls away enough to wipe Juliette's cheek. "It's the price," she whispers. "For the passion. Because you're special."

Juliette almost smiles. She extends one arm gracefully. "In my dream I look like Natalia Makarova when she was a teenager. I'm wearing white and I look just like her."

—47—

It is Wednesday before Ursula has a chance to talk with Teresa and Angela about her weekend. They share cold pasta out of a carton and she says ruefully, "I just about died of sentimentality. It makes me think of old football players reliving touchdowns. I don't know what got into me."

Teresa licks her fork, then her lips, and says, "Your trouble is you think too much, Ursula. What you don't realize is that introspection is out of style. It's an artifact of the past decade. You should be thinking about your cholesterol and your aerobics—"

"And the addition on your house," Angela adds, pointing at herself. "Joking or not, Teresa's got a point. You have to look out, past your kids, in the opposite direction of the past."

"I thought about working in the presidential campaign,"

Ursula says, "but every time I look at the choices I get depressed. We'll end up with another Republican and I'll feel responsible."

"Guilt! Ding!" Teresa says.

"Look, Ursula." Angela folds up the carton flaps and discards the carton and their forks and napkins. "Neatly disposed of. You know all this."

"I'm not complaining about my kids, you know," Ursula says. "I'm thrilled with them, really. Look at all the trouble they never got into. And Juliette doesn't even like to shop."

"Let's take a walk," Teresa suggests. "We've got a solid quarter hour and we can march off a little of that pasta."

Ursula and Angela moan, but comply.

They walk briskly, in silence, to a little park near the railroad tracks. "Who got the idea to beautify this little spot?" Angela wonders. "It's stuck in this dismal neighborhood, it's great, isn't it?"

"Great," Ursula agrees, and sits down on the bench. "Give me a minute."

Teresa and Angela sit down on each side of her. "Let me tell you about something that happened to me," Angela says. "Even though I swore I wouldn't tell anybody.

"I went to the doctor to get a mole removed. It had popped up right along my bra line in the back. I think subconsciously I was convinced it was probably cancer or something. I'm sitting on the table in the doctor's office, in this paper towel gown open in the back, and the nurse comes in with the chart and sits down across from me. I hadn't been to the doctor in a year. 'You need a Pap smear, Angela,' she says. 'Fine,' I tell her. 'Whenever. You schedule it, but not today.' Then she runs down this list of questions. Any problems with my bowels, my bladder, do I have headaches. No, no. Then she looks right at me, and she says, 'Any personal problems, Angela? Any mood swings?' And I burst into tears! I mean, I begin to *wail*."

"Gee, Angela," Ursula says. Teresa strokes Angela's arm.

"I wiped my face with the paper gown and the doctor came in and took the mole off. He said he'd have it checked but it was symmetrical and a nice brown color and I shouldn't worry. He said he'd see me in a few weeks for a Pap smear. Then the nurse comes back. She's holding these different colors of paper. She says, 'You don't drink, do you?' I say no, and she tucks the green sheet behind the others. 'And you don't have a family history of violence?' I'm a little startled, but I manage to say no. The pink sheet goes to the back. So now the blue one is on top. She pulls it away and hands it to me. 'These are all books Doctor recommends, dear. I'm sure you'll find something helpful.' This nurse, calling me dear, by the way, is probably twenty years younger than me. I look at the paper.

"It's a list of self-help books. Books on depression and on anxiety, books on sexual addiction and on meditation. Books on adjusting to menopause. This whole goddamned list of books on *getting it together*."

"It's everywhere," Ursula commiserates.

"You know what I decided?" Angela says. "I decided crying when you're fifty years old is a perfectly sane thing to do. The world has turned out to be full of terrorists and thieves, my whole professional life has to do with dysfunction and neediness, and I'm on the downslide toward my own end. Why should I look for something to feel better? Why should I want to kid myself? And you know, I do feel better. There's good reason to be sad once in a while. Depressed."

Teresa says, "A helluva lot saner than worrying because you didn't make CEO, or you're losing your looks."

Ursula says, "I don't know how I'd get by if I didn't have social workers for friends."

They hurry back to work.

—48—

"I tried to talk to Carter about the possibilities in his original subject," Michael says. "Which is what a really good teacher should have done, instead of declaring his ideas contraband." Michael and Ursula are stretched out on the bed, drinking a bottle of modest champagne, a surprising gift from Carter on the occasion of his graduation. "You deserve this at least," he told his parents before Michael took him back down to the school to catch the eleven p.m. chartered bus to Disneyland.

"He could have gone in any direction. Anthropology, archeology, geology. It's not lunatic to wonder how such marvelous feats as the Pyramids were possible. To wonder why primitive people would lay out enormous monkeys on plains nobody could look down on. Astronomy might have suited him, since I think he thinks he was touching on it. Did you know that astronomers in the last century worked out the relationships of dozens of British stone circles and their outliers? That they were already analyzing the orientation of the Pyramids to the sun and the stars? He could have learned that prehistoric people knew a hell of a lot of cosmology, some of which we may not have achieved in our so-called modern times, spaceships or not. And of course he could have stretched his mathematical thinking."

When Michael pauses, Ursula says, "I can't really see Mrs. Uptight Fat-Hips Angstrom going for any of that, Michael."

Michael pours more champagne for them. "Pretty sweet stuff, isn't it?"

"Listen, from our son Carter, this is a fine vintage."

"He looked handsome in his cap and gown, didn't he?"

"He did." Ursula scoots closer to Michael. "They all did, pimples, rooster hair, raccoon eyes and all. Kids are beautiful."

"You sound downright tipsy."

"No, really! It's just sentiment. And relief that he made it."

"You didn't seriously doubt him."

"I did! I thought he'd do something outrageous at the last minute and get in trouble—"

"Pooh. He's more sensible than you give him credit for."

"Have you thought about when they're both gone? About just us? Have you thought about retiring and having all your time free? Do you realize you could retire in ten years?"

"Oh yes, I think about it. I'll tell you something I'd like to do. I'd like to walk some of those Nazca lines in Peru, and ley lines in Britain, whether they're real or not." He laughs. "At least get to the Southwest and see what's there."

"Aha, my husband the cartographer, making maps with his feet."

"I suppose it's a corny idea. I'd like to walk where—*they*—walked. I think it's something from Pop. He had such an urge. I wish I could afford to take him somewhere now, someplace he never dreamed he could go."

"But Michael, those things are possible! God, if there are things you want, and you can have them—"

"I don't think about things like that much, you know."

"I had no idea you thought about them at all. I thought you had a blank mind, the product of a naturally Zen character."

"You harass me about it. I have to claim something behind my brow. As mine, I mean."

They finish the wine and turn off the light and lie beside one another a long time in the dark, then undress and crawl under the covers. When Michael does not move again toward her, Ursula assumes he has fallen asleep. She lies with her eyes open, thinking about what he said. She thinks about her father's maps, about maps of all kinds, of a time when there were none, and man's mind was closed to the world for lack of a concept. Maps seem to float around her, old yellow ones with spidery lines.

Michael told her once, "You are your father's daughter, Ursula. You see a map as the layout of a journey, and you want the map to tell you why and how and when and what happened. But a map is not a narrative. It represents information. It marks distance and represents contours. It may project area, height, slope. In geology, it reveals formations. The questions it answers are physical and scientific. Its abstractions are those that allow us to perceive what is too large to see in actuality. The other abstractions are in the reader. The reader makes the map more than what it is." And Ursula said, "But if someone has made a map, then someone has been there, and if someone has been there, the land has been claimed. It is possessed." And Michael said, "Not by the map, Ursie."

Michael is awake. "You'd make a good ley hunter, Ursie," he says, turning onto his side to look at her. "You'd love the idea that there's a system of intersections among prehistoric sites, and that you can walk that system. It's a way of mapping that is all tied up with lost knowledge and values. It's so full of *significance.*"

"Why does it interest you?" she asks. She is thrilled that he is awake after all. His intriguing notions are incredibly sexy. "Do you believe a ley network exists?" She tries desperately to remember what she knows; he left something lying around, a book, a long time ago. All she can recall is the look of the map, dense with intersections. She doesn't know what land it mapped. Somewhere in England.

"I just like the idea of the symmetry and pattern, even if it is only an idea. I like it that it is there before I walk it, and after I walk it, it is there even if *I* never am. I don't care about the sites, you know, only the connectors."

Ursula thinks a moment. It is very difficult to lie still. She would prefer to have this discussion out of bed, where she could pace, or at least gesticulate. Then something occurs to her. "We could be in different places, and intersect, because where you are would be an extension of where I am." She smiles hugely. It is all she can do to keep from clapping her hands.

"You've got it," he says.

"I like the ley system much better than the idea of Andean lines as UFO landing strips. I mean, I think the smaller English scale suits me." She can see them now, strolling over green meadows, crossing paths with old codgers in wool jackets with walking sticks. Wind on the heather, all of it.

Michael strokes her shoulder. "You like everything that means more than can be explained. You like to go away from a conversation with a nut to crack, a cud to chew. That's why I could never tell you everything, wife of mine. I would fail you if I did."

"I love you, Michael."

"I'll show you a ley line," he says. He takes her hand and moves it lazily from his chest, over the rise of his hip bone, a sharp turn and down. He touches her chin with his lips. "It's all connected, you see. There's no need to understand. Trust me. This is our corner of the world. We're bound to find one another."

Ursula is able to lie still for a moment longer only because she knows the next moment will be so good. She tells her surprising, secretive, teasing, remarkable husband one more thing before she has run out of words to speak. "What I like," she says, "is when we get where we're going at the same time."

# THREE: SURRENDER

Katie is lying on the king-sized bed in a motel near the San Francisco airport, watching *The Buddy Holly Story* on tv. Sprawled on the same bed, asleep, is her daughter. Across the other bed, by the window, her mother sits under the lamplight, reading Studs Terkel's *Working*.

One of the Crickets just knocked Buddy's front teeth out, but he sticks them back in with gum and plays on the *Ed Sullivan Show* anyway. Katie loves the songs in the movie, and she loves the character. She wonders if Buddy Holly really was as sensible and kind as the movie makes him out to be. She can see why the Puerto Rican girl falls in love with him. She loves the way he takes charge of everything. Nobody puts anything over on him.

Her mother looks up from her book and says, "Is that that boy from Lubbock who got killed years back?"

Katie says it is.

June looks back at her book. "It's really sad how many people hate the work they do," she says.

"Mother," Katie says, "did you ever like music?"

"Why dear, I still do!" June says. She tucks her bookmark into place and puts the book down on the table. "One of my little notions has been that I would go and live in a city for a while, just so I can go to symphonies and ballets, and operas, too, though I really don't know if I would like them."

"You should stay over and see something here."

"I didn't think of it. Well, there's always the radio."

"Did you ever like Frank Sinatra, people like that?"

"My yes. When we were first married, your father and I used to love to go dancing. There was so much good music for dancing then. The jukebox was full of good songs. You danced close a lot, not like kids today. Sometimes your father would say, 'Ready, dip,' and I'd lean back on his arm."

"I never hear you say Daddy's name. You always call him 'your father.'"

"It's just a convention, Katie."

"But how do you think of him? When you remember him, do you think, 'Katie's father'? Do you think, 'my husband'? Or 'James'?"

June looks somewhat startled. She wrinkles her nose and sniffs nervously. "I don't really think about him," she says.

"But you lived with him so long."

"You don't know things, Katie. You don't know how you adjust when your life makes a big change, like when your—when James died."

"I know I seem to have Fish in me as much as ever, and I can't just set him aside." When her mother called about this trip, she told her the divorce might not go through. Her mother said, "You'll have to decide." She didn't ask Katie one question. Katie thought it was peculiar.

"It's not the same."

"Why not?!"

"Shh, Katie. Rhea's tired. She was so excited, she couldn't sleep last night. She was awake when I got up at five-thirty, raring to go. She used her little curling iron."

"What about me? Why is my being married nothing like you being married?" She is the age her mother was when Katie left home for good.

"Just think about it for one minute. Your father and I lived a conventional, ordinary life, with you, a house, his business—and I never even thought of divorce."

"And Fish and I are flakes."

"Darling, please let's not quarrel."

"When did you stop dancing?"

"When I was pregnant." June fiddles with her book, sliding her fingers in between pages, then going on to another place in the book. She doesn't pick it up, or look at it. Katie wonders what sorts of people like their work. Besides the obvious ones like movie stars and doctors and judges. She thinks Fish likes working now, more than any time she's known him, except maybe when he worked in the Richmond shipyards. He said the black guys always had dope on them,

and they would go deep into the ship and get stoned. He said
he hoped the people who built airplanes were more together
than the ones who repaired ships.

"But you could have gone afterwards. After you had me."
She tries to make a picture in her mind of her mother flung
backwards over her father's arm, her skirt flapping, her hair
swinging out from her neck. Her father used to get red boils
on the back of his neck. He would soak a towel in scalding
water and lay it across his neck. Her mother would come
along behind him, wiping up dripping water with a sponge.

"Everything changed then. James had his business to
build." June slides the book away, almost out of reach, and
crosses her hands on the glass.

"Did he like what he did? Selling tires?"

"My, you are in a rare mood," June says. She pushes against
the back of her chair and stretches her arms out for a moment.

"You mind?"

"I don't want to fuss with you."

"Mother, I'm glad Rhea's coming. I promise you I'll take
care of her. She'll have a good time." Katie speaks to reassure
her mother. She would die if her mother changed her mind,
after Katie has told everyone Rhea is coming. She certainly
plans to do the best she can, though the truth is she is
nervous about what that ought to be. She doesn't really know
how you entertain a nine-year-old girl. But when she told
Ursula, she admitted her fears, and Ursula was very sweet
and said they should spend all the time they want at her
house. She said, "You know how it is in summer, someone's
always around. She can sleep over if she wants, you both can,
in the spare bed. When my mother comes for the ballet, you
can make a bed on the floor in Juliette's room, or the living-
room."

Her mother shakes her head. She doesn't know anything
about Katie's sleeping arrangements, except that Katie said
she was in an apartment, at least until Fish's house is vacant at
the end of the month. Her mother has to believe Katie will
take care of Rhea, or else change her mind, and this is
already an expensive operation, meeting in San Francisco
and all. "I know you will. I'm glad, too, now that it's decided."
What she really means, thinks Katie, is that now that it's

decided she will live with it and convince herself it's best. It has to be best, because it is June who thought of it.

"I don't really understand why you're doing this."

"I told you, Katie. She came home one evening from her little friend's house. Emily's family was having a reunion. They said she could come over for dessert the next day. She wanted to know what a reunion was. Then, after she had been there, she came home and said, 'Why is it I don't have any relatives?' Your Aunt Christine gave me this look, all the way across the room. She didn't have to. I realized that Rhea does have relations. She has other grandparents. An aunt and uncle."

"She has a *father,* too."

"Of course."

"When I told Fish she was coming, he got very excited. He wants to take her to the beach, up to Crater Lake, and there'll be a parade on July 4th. It's important to all of us."

June leans so far forward, she puts her hands on the bed for support. "Please, Katie. Be careful?"

"Sure. Seat-belts, cut her meat into tiny bites—"

"Don't be silly!" June's face has tightened. The creases in her forehead deepen, her mouth is smaller. Katie's own face is flat and untelling, she hopes. Her heart is pounding.

"Being in prison did something to him, Mother. He's changed." Now her mother will say *in what way?* and she won't know what to say. It's just a feeling she has, a feeling between her and Fish. It's just a hope. *Katie and Fish.*

"I haven't ever spoken to Rhea about that. I don't think she has any way to understand."

"We don't go around discussing it. He doesn't wear his old uniform."

"Katie, listen to me a moment. This is your child, yours and Fisher's. And she is good and sweet and innocent and bright and full of love. I'm anxious about leaving tomorrow, about seeing you and her get on a plane going in the other direction. But when I thought about it, I realized that the risk now—of disappointment, of surprises, of an uneasy fit with the Fisher family, with Fisher—I realized that risk isn't as great as the one that she will grow up blithely, and then one day feel she was cheated. That she won't know who she is because she only has me and Christine, and what has been so little of you. I'm not doing this for you and Fisher, though my heart extends to her grandparents, for what they've missed for nine years. I'm doing it for Rhea, and I want her to be uppermost in your mind, too. I don't want her hurt by this."

"Mother, you ought to know that I'm not capable of operating my life with a subtext. I understand what you're telling me, but all I can do is be with her, take her around, and—love her. I can't give her her identity in ten days."

"Fair enough."

Katie watches her mother as June walks across the room to the bath. She turns the television up again, and watches Buddy Holly's story turn inexorably toward tragedy and immortality. Rhea turns over and rearranges herself under the covers. Her little butt sticks up, making a mound in the middle of the bed. Katie can't think just what Rhea looks like in the face. She wonders what she'll look like, older. It's funny how you look at the childhood photograph of someone you know grown and you can see the adult already there, in the face. But then you look back at the grownup—not all the time, but with some people—and you think it's really too bad the person changed so much, turning out lumpy or scrawny or hard in the face or whatever. Like Gary Busey. She saw him a while back on a late night tv movie about some guys who go to a South American country to rescue two hostages. Gary Busey is this banker who goes along to pay for things, and he is fat and disgusting, nothing like he was when he played Buddy Holly. If he had died he could have been remembered for that terrific movie, the way Buddy Holly is remembered for songs that are thirty years old.

When Katie told Fish that Rhea was coming, he said, "What got into your mother? She got cancer or something?"

When June comes out of the bathroom dressed for bed, Katie turns the tv off and crawls under the covers herself. All the lights are off except the one over the table where June was reading. June sits in the chair again, and props her feet on the bed. She squirts lotion on her hands and starts creaming her face.

"The college did a very provocative play last year," she says. "It's called *Equus*, have you ever seen it?" Katie grunts to say she hasn't, and June goes on. "It's about a very sick boy, emotionally sick, and about the doctor who's working with him. One day, when the doctor is doubting what he's doing, wondering about a decision he has to make, his friend says to him, 'One must hold on to priorities. Children before adults.' That's how I'm trying to mother your child, Katie. I wish I had done it more with you."

The silence is palpable. Each waits on the other, Katie thinks. She would like to say something to put her mother's mind at ease, or at least respond intelligently to her quoting a play, but she and her mother aren't operating in the same galaxy. They don't see the same constellations.

"When you were born," June says quietly, "my whole life changed. I wanted to do everything right. It took all my attention. Then when I looked around I realized that James was gone. He had the store to build up. Not that he liked or didn't like tires, dear. He would have scoffed at such a notion. He was doing what needed doing, in a way that allowed him to run his own life. But he was unhappy. I think he was unhappy almost from the moment you were born. Oh, what a terrible thing I've said to you. Don't think about it, it's the past." She coughs and covers her mouth with her hand. She looks quite distressed. So, Katie thinks in wonder, Mother has done this kind of horse-trading before. I was the prize. Poor Mother. "I've been trying to understand the past," she says.

"By the time I realized I'd had a child and lost a husband, I was desperate to make you worth the cost. So I boxed your ears your whole childhood."

"You never touched me."

"Not with my hands."

Katie feels tears brimming in her eyes. She looks at her mother in the lamplight, and her mother blurs, because of the tears. Her mother has confessed something and she knows she could hurt her very much if she said the wrong thing. If she said, for example, you've never stopped hurting me. But what would be the gain?

June turns off the light and gets in bed. In a little while, Katie says, "Remember when I broke my arm out in the yard?" June says, "I remember it well." "Well," Katie says bravely, "remember we went to the hospital in a taxi? It was the first time I'd ever been in one, I was excited about it and almost forgot about my arm." June says nothing. "I remember you were very angry. I don't know why it's been on my mind. But I keep wondering, was it because I fell down? Was it because I was so much trouble?" Katie thinks her mother is crying now. Her nose makes funny noises, and her voice, when she speaks, is thick and sad. Her mother says, "I was angry with your father because he wasn't there when we needed him. I was angry because he wasn't there and I had no idea where he was."

Katie doesn't know if she loves her mother or not, but in that moment she understands clearly that she does not hate her.

—50—

Rhea hugs her grandmother and kisses her loudly on the mouth, hugs her some more, and laughs, almost jumping. "OryGONE," she says. Katie bends down to her. "Oregon," she pronounces. Rhea is wearing a bright pink dress with a short pleated skirt and white piping on the collar. She also wears lip gloss, a ring with a fake pearl, a red Swatch watch, and black patent Mary Jane shoes. Katie thinks she and her daughter bear no resemblance whatsoever, except for the color of their eyes (brown) and the slightest upturning of their noses. Rhea's lips are full, a lot like Fish's lips, and she has long, nice legs, like Juliette, her cousin.

June is immaculate and serene at the gate. She kisses Katie's cheek and says, "I won't worry. Have a good time."

Katie smiles at her mother. "Sometime you should come, too. When we have our house again."

June is flustered. "How nice of you to ask," she manages to say. "I know it's a lovely state."

"Do you have a dog? Do you have a cat?" Rhea asks. "Do you have horses?" She puts one finger in her mouth and sucks on it loudly. When she sees her grandmother looking at her, she jerks her finger out, rubs her ring against her dress, and tucks her top lip down over her bottom one. Katie thinks she has the natural charm of a child in a movie. You look at her, and you know she is going to be in a lot of scenes.

June and Katie, grateful for Rhea's interruption, laugh uneasily. "Just people, honey," Katie says. She pulls Rhea by the hand, away from June. The agent announces boarding. "Safe trip, Mother," she says. Rhea breaks away and runs ahead.

"Who's going to meet us?" she asks when they're settled in their seats.

"I think Fisher and your Uncle Michael will both come."

"What about my cousins?"

"Carter has a job, and Juliette is rehearsing for her ballet. She has her first summer performance tomorrow night. So you see, you're just in time!"

"I've never been anywhere," Rhea says solemnly.

"Well, now you will have."

"Are there mountains?"

"Yes, little ones. And lots and lots of trees."

As the plane accelerates down the runway, Rhea takes Katie's hand and holds it tightly. "It's so noisy," she whispers.

They don't speak until they are in the air and the ride is smooth. Rhea says, looking out the window, "I can see the ocean."

Katie asks her if she wants gum. Rhea takes a stick of Juicy Fruit, which Katie bought specifically to have for now. She thought about getting bubble gum, but she knew her mother would die if she thought Rhea blew bubbles on the plane, and though her mother would have no way to know, Katie quickly changed her choice. It made her realize that her mother would be more or less looking over her shoulder all through the visit, and though the thought initially bothered her, it didn't take very long to realize it was helpful, in a way, to hear June's voice in her ear, like an angel. It would help her decide whether it was okay to do something or not.

Rhea rummages in her pink cotton drawstring bag and comes up with a bright yellow book with blue letters. "The girls in this series are always getting in trouble," she says. "I love it."

"That's what books are good for," Katie comments. "Much better than real trouble, don't you think?" She can't think of the last time she enjoyed a book. Books on how to live your life aren't a lot of fun.

Rhea is puzzled. "I don't know, Katie. I've never been in

trouble, I guess." There is a tiny fleck of jelly at the corner of
her mouth. Katie reaches over and carefully wipes it off. "A
little bit of breakfast," she tells Rhea. She hopes Rhea didn't
mind.

Rhea grasps her mother's hand. "Flying is just like being in
a dream," she says. She lets go and leans to stare out of the
window again. "I'm going to watch all the way."

Katie closes her eyes. "Wake me when we get there," she
says. "Or when you see a big mountain." On second thought,
she opens her eyes and leans over as far as she can to look out
of the window, too. "Rhea," she says. "What's your favorite
color, honey?"

Rhea puts her finger against the window. "That out there,"
she says. "The blue of the sky. Like when you sleep late in the
morning, and you look outside and the colors from early are
gone, and there's just sky. There's just blue."

Katie absolutely cannot believe it. She and Rhea come in
from the plane and Fish is not there in the throng of people
waiting. "They're probably parking," she tells Rhea, and says
probably they should wait over by luggage. "We'll take a
quick look down the other way first, and then go to the
carousel," she says. They trot down past the airline counters,
out to the sidewalk, but Katie doesn't see Fish there either.
When she goes back in she recognizes a woman coming in
ahead of her. The woman is wearing a baggy "dropped-
waist" dress in a blue and black print, and her short black
hair is wet and pulled back in a one-inch-long pony tail. She
turns a little and Katie sees that it is Joyce, who works for the
theatre and who was at the Al-Anon meeting.

Katie still hasn't decided if it is okay to say something to
Joyce when she sees her, if that violates the anonymity principle of the meeting. Of course they get their paycheck over
the same signature, so that's a bond of sorts. Thinking about
this quickly, Katie is frozen just inside the door, and Rhea
waits, looking all around, as if she would know her father
when she sees him.

Joyce spots Katie and rushes over to her. She squeezes
Katie's arm above the elbow, with both hands. She says, "I was
hoping you would come again," so that they could be talking
about tennis lessons or anything. Katie smiles and says, "I just

got here with my daughter." She remembers that Joyce spoke
at the meeting, but she can't remember what she said. Joyce
said, "If you didn't like group, but you'd like to talk sometime, you could call me anyway." She smiles at Rhea. "I'm
Joyce Devlin," she says. She looks back up at Katie. "I'm in the
book, initial J."

Rhea rubs the front of her shoe on the back of her other
leg. "My name is Rhea Fisher," she says politely. Then she
looks at Katie, as if for approval.

"I've seen you at work a couple times," Joyce says to Katie.
"I thought maybe we'd run into one another, but I guess the
costume shop is closed now."

"Yes," Katie says. She scans the room over Joyce's shoulder.
"Are you getting a plane?" she asks her.

Joyce looks sheepish. "I'm meeting my boyfriend, he's been
in Seattle, job-hunting." She drops down to Rhea's height, so
quickly that for an instant Katie thinks she's fallen. "You look
a lot like your mother," she says, which Katie thinks is only
true on the nose. Look at Rhea's light, curly blond hair, with
its permed wings brushed back above each ear. Katie has
never had such hair in her whole life.

"I look like my daddy, too," Rhea says, at the same moment
Katie spots Fish and Michael coming in the far door.

"I've got to go, there they are," Katie says. She thinks she
still feels Joyce's handprints on her arm. Impulsively, she
reaches out and touches the back of Joyce's hand. "Thanks,"
she says. "I hope your boyfriend had good luck." At that,
Joyce looks so forlorn, Katie remembers the meeting and
how Joyce was unhappy because her boyfriend didn't want to
stay in the valley, and she feels foolish and sorry to have said
anything at all, but she has no idea how to smooth over what
she said. "Que será será," Joyce says, and turns briskly away.

Katie wants to call out, Come back, come back. Tell me
what to do now. I don't know how you introduce your daughter to her father. I don't know how I could make my mother
think we won't all be sorry.

—51—

"What is it they're doing?" Ursula's mother asks. She is
standing in the breakfast nook, watching the girls through

the window. Ursula wishes she had thought to clean the panes.

"Baton work," Ursula answers. "Rhea was here about twenty minutes yesterday before she had it out." She moves closer behind her mother and watches her daughter as Juliette puts her hands on Rhea's chest and back and says something that makes the child raise her whole body, rather nicely. Then Juliette puts her own arm in front, lifts a leg slightly, and tips her head. Though she isn't holding a baton, Ursula thinks she can just see her at the head of a band. "I guess it's a big deal in Texas," she adds.

Clare turns back into the kitchen. "I like your new kitchen floor, Ursula. The fellows did a fine job. It looks quite European."

Ursula pours them coffee and they go back to the nook and sit down. Michael has gone for a bucket of chicken, Ursula has made salad. She only needs to pack up for their picnic at the park. She checks her watch. "I need to run Juliette up to the park in a little while. We'll go back at six-thirty, so we get a nice spot."

"Where is the child's mother?" Clare asks.

"She's gone to work a matinee. She'll join us at the ballet." Ursula sees her mother's brow knit ever so little above her nose. Out under the sycamore, Fish dozes in the lawn chair. The girls begin to strut about the yard and then, laughing, sprawl on the grass.

"They get on, don't they?" Clare says.

"Rhea slept with Juliette last night. I'd made up your bed but she never got that far." Katie went home before Ursula went to bed. "Rhea wants to stay," Juliette insisted. Ursula wondered if her daughter had some fine-tuned sense, to pick up Katie's nervousness. Katie agreed that Rhea should stay, with such obvious relief.

"The little girl lives in Texas?" Clare says.

"Since she was a baby. Katie took her down for a visit, we thought, and came back without her. I thought I'd die, almost like it was my child."

"She must have had her reasons," Clare says.

"We'd have taken Rhea, you know. We'd have been thrilled to have her."

Clare looks at her daughter. "But how awkward it would have been, think of it. It would never have worked." She pushes her cup away from her. "Did you and Michael want another child?"

Ursula, surprised at the intimacy of her mother's question, says, "Not really." She smiles. "We had a boy and a girl, isn't that supposed to be perfect?" When her mother doesn't comment, she goes on to say, "I've always wondered why I didn't have a set of twins. Katie, either."

"What a handful that would have been!"

"But special."

"I'd say you did very well, Ursula."

"Of course! I'm only speculating. And sometimes twins have twins."

"Has it been special, being married to one?"

Ursula's breath seems to burst out of her chest. "Oh heavens yes!" she says. "Sometimes I've felt I was married to both of them!"

Clare puts her hand over Ursula's on the table. She says, "You've been a good and fortunate mother, Ursula. To be together, and healthy, all of you." Ursula fears for a moment that her mother is going to cry. Clare says, "Juliette is quite lovely. I feel a very special bond with her."

Ursula thinks it may have something to do with Juliette's age. After all, Ursula was fifteen when her mother left. Maybe there's a sense of unfinished business. She rises and calls through the window. "It's time to go, Julie!" Both girls look up from the grass. It takes them a moment to find Ursula's face at the pane. When they see her, they both stare, locked for a moment in stillness, like a photograph. Ursula looks at the younger girl's unsmiling face and feels a shock of recognition. What is it I see? she wonders. Maybe it's only Fisher blood, or the loveliness of a girl at nine. Tears spring to Ursula's eyes. Maybe it is longing. Do Michael's ley lines extend to Rhea? Ursula puts her hand up against the window, as if to signal to the girl. As if to send something to her, to make the connection.

Brian makes an awkward speech about his decision to use some contemporary music this year. The program is "a mix of epochs." There is to be a ballet scene inspired by *Giselle* and choreographed for the small stage, and another especially choreographed for the four young ballerinas. There is a dramatic interpretation of a French poem about the illicit love of a knight for his lord's lady; Ursula fears for a moment that Brian is going to recite the poem, but the allusion is only for the audience's enlightenment. And there is a bit of Gershwin, and a rock number borrowed from U2.

Ursula has packed away the remains of their supper, and they all settle down for the performance. Rhea leans against Fish, and Katie sits close by. As the music begins, the audience hushes, and Ursula feels pride and anticipation rush through her on a shot of adrenaline. Her chest aches. She grasps Michael's hand for a moment, and he leans over to say, "Remember how long they've been practicing." Then the ballerinas flutter onto the stage, and as soon as she sees Juliette, she relaxes, for her daughter is so obviously at ease, it would be unjust to worry for her. She does not need her mother's vigilant apprehension. She can manage quite well.

At intermission, Clare asks Ursula if she wouldn't like to walk for a few moments. They go past the edge of the audience, toward the parking lot and onto a path. There Clare takes Ursula's hands. "Do you know how much talent Juliette has?" She seems so solemn, Ursula is relieved to hear the question. She thought for a moment her mother was going to tell her something terrible. She doesn't know how to answer her mother, so she smiles and shrugs, the picture of the falsely humble mother. Clare says, "You should think how you can get her better instruction. She can't be getting what she needs here."

"She has rehearsal every day, and performances all summer, now, once a week."

"Of course. And in the fall?"

"She dances every morning, four days a week, and she has a class on Saturday. My God, Mother, she's only fifteen."

Clare puts her arm across Ursula's shoulders. "We'll talk about it later. Let's go back."

"No. What is it you're telling me? What do you think I ought to do?" Ursula hears a shrill note of self-defense in her voice.

"I think you ought to quit worrying about what Juliette says to you, and worry about her talent."

"God, Mother, what else am I supposed to DO?"

"I have some ideas. Come along."

Ursula tries to watch Juliette with a stranger's eyes, but of course she cannot. What she can see is that her daughter seems to float where the others dance, that her legs and arms go on forever, and that she seems utterly without hesitation. There are no false steps. It becomes apparent that Brian has choreographed rather wisely, to keep Juliette from dominating the company. His wife is the prima ballerina, and he has kept Juliette well away from her, mostly offstage when she is on. He has saved all the dramatic, large movements for his wife, and given the younger women the lively, cat-like moves. Two of the women are in their twenties, dancers who have come from San Francisco for the summer. They are more expert than Juliette; they have the steps that cause the audience to break into applause when they pause, as if to say, "Didn't you like that?" But Ursula sees what her mother sees, even with Juliette's restricted role. Juliette is the company's angel. She is a dancer. The girl who has been whining and fussing and drooping around the house for two months is the picture of radiant confidence.

Ursula thinks she knows what her mother has in mind, and as she watches Brian's aging wife wilt before her young lover, she feels tears on her cheeks. She wishes the dancers were more convincing and able. She would like to weep.

—52—

At the house, there is a celebratory air. Rhea dances around on her toes, attempts an arabesque, and falls laughing onto Katie's lap. Michael pours wine for everyone. Carter and Annabel arrive, too. Ursula is amazed when Annabel says, "Where's Juliette? I want to tell her how wonderful she was. We loved it!"

"You went to the ballet?" Ursula asks Carter.

"Sure. I traded nights at work."

"Why didn't you come down to our blanket, son?" Michael asks. "We had chicken."

Annabel replies, "We got there a little late and sat up on the hill. It was nice from where we were. Where's Juliette?"

"She's bathing," Ursula says. "Carter, there's soda in the frig. Have you introduced Annabel to your Texas cousin?"

Carter's girlfriend is lovely, Ursula thinks. She kneels beside Rhea and talks to her in hushed tones for several minutes. Rhea giggles, Annabel squeezes her hand, and goes back to Carter. "We're going swimming out at the lake tomorrow," she says. "Maybe Rhea and Juliette could come."

"I don't know," Ursula says, because Annabel is looking at her. "Katie and Fish may have plans."

"I've got to work," Fish says.

"Whatever," Katie says.

"Oh boy," Rhea says.

Clare stands up. "I'm going to look in on Juliette," she says. In a little while she returns and says, "Ursula, you'd better come up."

Juliette is on her bed in a nightgown, her knees drawn up and a sheet pulled over her feet. She is sobbing.

"Darling, what is it!" Ursula cries and sits on the bed. She tries to take Juliette into her arms, but Juliette stiffly pulls away.

Clare comes close, and Juliette moves over to make room for her beside her. "It's all right, Juliette. But I want you to show your mother, so she won't see accidentally and get all upset."

"See what!" Ursula asks. "What is going on?"

Slowly Juliette peels back the sheet and reveals her feet. She turns one to the side, and Ursula gasps. The foot looks as if it has been chewed.

"What in the world!" Ursula says.

Juliette sobs more loudly.

Slowly Ursula touches Juliette's feet. All along the sides, the skin has been peeled away somehow. There are large raw pink spots. She slips her hands under the heels and feels the rough broken texture there, too. In places along the tender center of the sides of the feet, there are a few scabs.

Clare puts her arms around Juliette and pulls her against her. "Shhh," she says. "It's okay now."

"I don't understand," Ursula says. Her hands are trembling.

"I just—I just scratched them a little," Juliette whimpers.

"A little!" Ursula cries.

"Shh," Clare says.

"It's all OVER." Juliette says. "They're HEALING."

"All over?" Ursula looks at the feet again. She cannot imagine that they were once worse. "How did you do this, baby?" she whispers.

"Sometimes—I—picked—at—them."

Clare reaches down and pulls the sheet up. "There's no infection," she says to Ursula. "And Juliette is telling the truth, they're healing. She's just peeled the skin, picking at it."

"So that's why the socks, the feet always hidden." Ursula touches her hand to her forehead and shuts her eyes for a moment. "Why?"

"I don't know."

"What do you mean you don't know?!"

Clare reaches out to touch Ursula. "It's all right now, Ursula. In a way it's too bad you have to see, because it's all over, isn't it, Julie?" The child nods miserably. "So please, go back downstairs. I'll see to Juliette and be down shortly. She's exhausted. She just needs to sleep."

Ursula cannot move for a moment. "Oh Julie," she says.

Juliette bursts into fresh sobs and turns to put her face in the pillow. Ursula finds it heartbreaking not to touch her, but she can see it would make things worse. She stands up. Something occurs to her. "Has Brian seen your feet?"

Muffled by the pillow, Juliette says, "Yes, tonight. He said he is going to call you tomorrow. He said if I didn't tell you he would."

"Good for him," Ursula says, and marches out of the room.

It is relief to find that everyone has declared the evening a success but a tiring one. Carter has left to take Annabel home. Rhea has fallen asleep on the floor. "I could put her on my bed," Fish says, "and sleep on the couch." Ursula nods. Katie gathers glasses, takes them to the kitchen, and exits without saying much of anything. Finally, Ursula, Michael, and Clare huddle on the couch to talk about Juliette.

"I went up to tell her goodnight," Michael says.

"Did she show you her feet?" Ursula asks.

"No. She was awfully tired. She gave me a big hug and I think she was asleep before I left the room."

"Good," Clare says.

"I told you she needed a therapist," Ursula says.

"Don't be so hasty," Clare says.

"Hasty! How long has this been going on?"

"A few weeks, I gather. And that was a few weeks ago. If Brian hadn't noticed, probably none of us would have, either."

"God," Ursula says.

"Her *feet*?" Michael says.

"She's only mutilated them," Ursula says.

"She's been picking at them," Clare says. "It looks worse than it is."

"Hmmm," Michael says, unalarmed.

"You didn't see," Ursula says. "I think I should call someone tomorrow."

"Maybe," Clare says, "you should talk to someone yourself."

"Me!"

"To get a handle on your anxiety."

"Mother!" Ursula looks to Michael, who maintains a clearly neutral expression. "Michael!" Then she crumples and begins to cry. Michael puts his arm around her.

"Darling," her mother says, "take a tranquilizer or something and get a good night's rest. Go to work tomorrow and let me spend some time with her. Now her little secret's out she won't feel so guilty and confused. You know, as bad as it looks, I don't think she's hurt herself, really. Sometimes when you're worrying too much about something, and you don't have the coping skill, you do something else to distract yourself. Chew your nails. Drink. Tear paper. Julie scratched her feet."

Ursula feels as if she has already taken a sleeping pill. "I can't hold my head up much longer," she says in surprise. It seems negligent, to go off to sleep now.

"You go along," Michael says. "I'll be up in a while." He kisses her forehead. "If Clare is interested, I'll open the wine from the back of the frig. The good stuff."

Clare gets up too. "I'll wash us some glasses, Michael."

—53—

While the men help Mr. Melroy pack up his stuff from the flea market table, Rhea lies in the back of Gully's truck on his makeshift bed. It is rumpled and it doesn't smell very fresh, but Rhea has never been in any kind of camper before, and she loves the cozy feeling. She is reading a book her Uncle Michael gave her about birds and birding. She never heard about "birding" before. Uncle Michael and his students make nesting boxes for bluebirds, and take them out into the woods every year. He says she can put out water dishes and hang fresh fruit in the yard tomorrow, to make more birds come; he says his kids weren't so interested in birds, so he didn't think right away to tell her about them. Juliette does love the hummingbirds that come around the back of the house where the feeder hangs. Rhea loves to sit out there with Juliette, who is beautiful and smart and a wonderful dancer too.

Rhea recites the names of birds. She isn't sure how you say some of them, but it doesn't really matter. It's like saying a poem or singing a song: mourning doves, ring-necked pheasants, grackles and catbirds, tufted titmice, slate-colored juncos and redpolls, finches and grosbeaks. When Rhea gets home, she is going to tell Granny that they should feed birds in the winter, and when she has a project at school, she will do it about birds.

Or boats. Her father likes boats the way Uncle Michael likes birds, except that Michael does something about birds, and Fish doesn't actually have a boat. He says that after he moves back into his house, he is going to build a little fishing boat to take out on the river, and next summer when she comes back, they will go out in it together. She likes the idea of next summer already.

It is amazing to Rhea that she has so many relatives. It seems to her that if you are at Uncle Michael and Aunt Ursula's house, it is like a reunion just about every day. There are so many people in and out of the house, she wondered if she would have to write their names down at first to remember. But she knows everybody now, even several of her cousin Carter's friends.

"Hey sweet thing," she hears her Uncle Michael say. Her birding book has slid off her chest onto the quilt beside her. Her eyes are puffy and blurred; she has been asleep. "You can ride up front with Gully, or ride with Fish and me. Gotta have a seat-belt."

She sits up and rubs her eyes. "You all done?"

"Sure are. Melroy had a good day and he's invited us to come up and see the dogs and drink lemonade. Would you like to do that? We've got a little time before we need to go home."

"Oh yeah!" Rhea says. She crawls down out of the canopy and goes around to ride with her grandfather. Fish leans in the window. "You hungry?" he asks. She wasn't thinking about it before, but now she is. "Kinda," she says, and Fish produces a bag of popcorn.

When they are on the road, Rhea says, "I don't know what I am supposed to call you. You're my grandfather, but everybody says Gully."

"Well now, we didn't talk about that, did we? What do you think?"

"I don't have a grandpa in Texas. Could I call you Grandpa?"

"You can if you want to."

"What does Juliette call you?"

"Gully."

"My father calls you Pop."

"And you call him Fish!"

"Yeah." She thinks about that for a few minutes.

"What's that book you've got there?"

"It's about birds. Uncle Michael gave it to me."

"He does love them. Both boys had birds when they were kids. They had canaries and wild birds both. Once we had a goose we were going to cook for Christmas, they must have been five, they were in kindergarten. You know, that goose died a natural death the year they started high school? I couldn't believe that some critter didn't chomp its neck off. Course half the time the boys put it in a shed or the garage at night, and it slept in the doghouse, too."

"Did it have a name?"

Gully laughs. "Goose." He's a funny man, thinks Rhea, in his coveralls, with long white hair.

Rhea thinks her grandmother would wonder if he was all right, but he is. He's very nice. She laughs too. "I never had a pet."

Gully says, "One year they brought home a whole nest of orphan crows and kept them for months. Their Ma liked to died of the racket, but when we tried to get rid of them, they found their way back. They pecked at the boys' windows in the morning, real early."

"Did you like birds when you were a boy?"

"I was always a dog man. And I had a pet raccoon, a pretty tame squirrel, a rat or two. Never liked cats, like Michael does."

"But you don't have a dog now, do you?"

"Naw. My dog died. But I might take one of Melroy's. You want to help me pick one out?"

"Sure!"

"Look at that silly Fish," Grandpa says. He points to Michael's truck, in front of them. Fish has turned around in his seat and is making faces at them. Rhea giggles and waves and sticks out her tongue, back at him.

"I don't know when I've seen him have such a good time," Grandpa says. "He's real happy you came to see him."

"Me too." The funny thing is, she's hardly seen Katie at all. Katie works sometimes, and she sleeps someplace else and leaves Rhea at Uncle Michael's. She says she doesn't like to go out to Gully's house. Rhea feels funny about her mother. She thinks there is something she ought to do to make her mother like her more, but she doesn't know what it is. At least she knows she will see her again, in Texas, but even if they do talk about next summer, she isn't sure she will get to come to Oregon again, so it is really important to get to know everybody. There will be so many things to tell Granny and Aunt Christine.

"I've been thinking maybe I could keep a diary," she says. "In case I would forget the things I'm doing now. Our teacher says even when it's really important stuff going on in your life, you grow up and forget, because your mind gets stuffed up with new things."

"That's a fine idea. Would you like me to buy you one?"

"Yes, thank you," she says, "Grandpa."

"I think it's a fine idea, keeping a diary. Sometimes I write little things down, myself. But it isn't true that you forget everything. When you get old like me, you start losing stuffing, and lo and behold those old memories are under there waiting to come out again."

"Like what? What do you remember?"

"Well, like your dad's first boat he built. You ask him about it sometime, I bet he remembers. He was twelve, and he spent a whole winter building it. He had a grand summer with it, too. Then there was a big storm. He had it tied up at the river, and it broke loose and got pulled away. Months later he was walking and he saw this boat in an old man's yard, turned over and propped up against a shed. He went up to the old man and he asked him would he sell it, he'd like to have it real bad. Then he ran home to get money from me. Paid fifteen dollars for his own durned boat."

"Why didn't he just tell the guy it was his?"

"He didn't have any way to prove it. And maybe he figured the old man had rescued the boat, you know, kept it from smashing up? It was kind of like a reward."

"You tell good stories, Grandpa," Rhea says. "You should write them down."

"You think? Who'd care what an old goat like me had to say?"

"I would."


—54—


Rhea and Juliette sit up in Juliette's bed after everyone else is asleep, whispering in the dark. Rhea tells her cousin about Melroy's place. "You've got to go sometime," she says. "It's really fun." There were dogs everywhere, and all of them nice ones you could pet. Melroy showed her how he makes a dog do a trick, and if he doesn't do it right, Melroy shakes a bean can at him. "They knew lots of tricks," Rhea tells Juliette. Melroy lay down right in the middle of the yard, and the dogs jumped over him like a hurdle. It was the funniest thing Rhea ever saw. She loved that dog Bounder. Everywhere she ran, Bounder came too. And when she got tired and sat down right in the dirt, Bounder raced around her and licked her legs and jumped up to put his nose in her face. Grandpa said he liked Bounder, too, and Melroy said, anytime you want, the dog is yours. Easy as that.

Juliette says she doesn't like to go out to Gully and Geneva's. "Geneva doesn't like kids, didn't you notice?"

"We didn't stay there. We just went in for a few minutes, and she gave me a cookie out of a bag. An Oreo. It was okay.

She wanted Fish and Michael to stay for supper, but they said they had to come back because we were all going out Chinese, and she said, I don't know why anybody eats things in little pieces like that." Granny says sometimes old people just get a little sour, and you have to be polite and not mind, because you might be that way too someday. Rhea doesn't think she will ever get sour. After all, Granny is sweet and so is Aunt Christine. And Gully/Grandpa isn't sour, either. Maybe there is something that made Geneva really sad a long time ago and she didn't get over it. Maybe she wishes something about her life she can't change. If there was anything Rhea knew to do, she would do it. Geneva is her grandmother.

"I'm going to go to Seattle after my dad's birthday party," Juliette says. Rhea can tell she is excited. "I hope you don't mind. I'll only be gone a few days."

"I think I go back to Texas pretty soon after the fourth anyway. Time is going by fast. Fish said he would take me to Crater Lake, too. I think that must be far away."

"Not so far. A few hours."

"You're going to Seattle because your grandmother lives there?"

"She works for a school that trains artists and actors and dancers. They let high school students come half-days if they are good enough. I'm going to go up and audition, and see about where I'd go for the academic stuff."

"And not live here?!" Rhea doesn't see how Juliette could think of that. This is the nicest house Rhea has ever been in. It is full of things and people. Something is always going on.

"My mother hasn't said yes, but Dad says, we'll see, in a way that I know means yes if it works out. I just want to dance. I don't care about school."

"Is that what you're going to be when you grow up? A dancer?"

"Oh yes."

"I don't know what I want to be when I grow up. But right now I'd like to get to be good at baton twirling. I've been practicing the hand roll for the longest time. You try to make the baton roll around in your hand, while in your head you say, roll and grab, roll and grab. Only most the time it falls off my hand. It's a hard roll."

"What have you shown me? I mean, what do you call those things?"

"I can almost always do a Pinwheel. Sometimes with my left hand, too. I have to practice that. I know how to do the Baton Salute, and some poses."

"I can help you with that arabesque one. If you hold your head up higher you'll keep your balance."

"I can strut and keep time doing it."

"That's great."

"Juliette?"

"What?"

"Do you think I look like anybody? Like I belong in the family?"

"You look like your mom and dad both, Rhea. You look like a kid, I guess. Like you. Listen, we all like you lots."

"I've always wondered. My name is Rhea Fisher and I wondered if I looked like one. Like a Fisher. Or if I act like one."

"Don't do that!" Juliette laughs. "We're all crazy!"

"I don't think so."

"I gotta go to sleep. I have ballet class at nine."

"I'll go down to the guest bed. See you tomorrow."

"Night."


Downstairs, Michael and Ursula are sitting on the couch side by side, reading. The child peeks around from the stairway and says, "Goodnight." Michael says, "Come get a hug," and she does.

They hear her scampering along the hall upstairs. "She's a cute kid," Ursula says. She has Juliette on her mind, of course, but Rhea is sweet.

"She's a great kid," Michael concurs. "But why do you think they named her Rhea? Why would they give her the name of a flightless bird?"

"Don't you breathe a word!" Ursula says. "I'm sure Katie has no idea."

"The funny thing is," Michael says, "it'll probably be Rhea who finds out. She's smart and curious. If you ask me, she's very likely to have wings after all."

They go up to bed together and it isn't until they are in the dark that Michael says, "We probably ought to talk about Carter soon."

"What now?"

"I don't think he's going to go to school this fall."

Ursula jumps up and turns the overhead light on.

"Hey, that's not necessary!"

"It is too. I want to see you while you explain what you just said."

"He wants to open a pizza parlor. A jazzy one, he says. There's going to be a space in that cluster of shops across from the college, it's perfect."

"You have to have money for that. He's eighteen years old!"

"Annabel is putting up some of it. I don't think she's going off either. Not this year."

"But she's accepted at Bennington! She can afford it!"

"She wants to run a pizza place with Carter."

"They're BABIES."

"It's a lot better than having them."

"Oh God." Ursula can't think of that. "What do you mean, Annabel's putting up some of the money? Who's putting up the rest?"

"I gave him a thousand dollars to lease equipment."

"Michael. Without talking to me."

"You've been so wrapped up in this Juliette thing. And he had to make a decision or miss his chance."

"Our son is going to make PIZZA?"

"Just for now, Ursula. It's not a bad idea."

"And stay HOME?"

"He says he's going to move to the basement when Fish moves out."

"What about his school plans? What about his FUTURE?"

"He can get deferred admission. He says he's not ready to be serious. I think he's being pretty mature, frankly. And the worst that can happen is he'll lose his thousand dollars."

"HIS thousand?"

"It is now. Ursula, I think you should take time off and go to Seattle with Juliette. I don't think you should turn this whole business about dance school over to Clare. You'll be in a stew if you do."

"What good will it do for me to go?"

"Maybe you'll see what Clare sees. Maybe you'll see Juliette like they see her. Maybe you'll feel better."

Ursula starts to laugh. She stumbles over and turns off the light.

"What's funny?"

"I just realized. You've hardly snored at all in weeks. It's like, maybe you were snoring because you were bored."

"Maybe my nose has cleared."

She laughs until the tears run. "Oh Michael," she says, "I thought snoring was the only thing going on. I thought we were becalmed on a still, still sea."

"You know what you forgot? You forgot you had a family. You forgot you had kids."

"Did not!"

"You forgot the rule: calm before the storm."

"That one, maybe I forgot."

"It just goes on all around us, Ursie. It's what our lives are about right now. In the middle, though, it's you and me. And there's nothing wrong with us."

"Have you noticed?" she asks. "The only place we seem to talk is in bed."

"It's one place to catch each other. And it isn't all we do."

"Oh Michael, if you ever stop liking me—you know what I mean—if you ever stop wanting me—just shoot me, okay?"

"I'll do better than that," Michael says. "I'll move you to the basement."

<h2 style="text-align:center">—55—</h2>

The end of June falls in the middle of the week. Katie goes with Fish to the house to see if the renters are out. When Michael called to talk to them about returning the deposit, they said they'd be in touch, like they didn't have any plans. Fish is very edgy. He wants out of the basement and into his own place again. He has been wanting to go out there for days, but Michael says that since the lease is through the last day of the month, Fish doesn't really have the right to enter the house. Be patient, Michael cautions. Even if it is your house.

The family has a supper of cold cuts, and then Fish insists that Michael call to see if the house will be ready for him the next day. There is no answer. "I'm going out there and see what's going on!" Fish raves. Rhea listens, wide-eyed. "Can I go?" she says. "I haven't seen your house."

Katie can see Ursula chewing the inside of her cheek, but

she says, "We'll all three go," anyway. What can happen? She'll be there to tug at Fish's sleeve if she needs to.

The weather has been very hot, and at seven in the evening the day has not even begun to cool. The hills are parched and brown, but as they near the area of the house, they pass property thick with vines and bushes, and graced with trees, kept green by ample underground water. The house itself sits back enough that it is shaded through the summer, a pleasant bonus in hot weather. In winter it can be dreary.

They find Carol Lee in the front yard with a hoe.

"What the hell is going on here?" Fish yells as soon as he is out of the truck.

Carol looks up rather blithely. "I'm cutting weeds," she says. There is a large round patch in front of her, staked with tomato vines, and a couple of hillocks with squash or melons.

"What's the point of planting what you can't pick?" Katie says. Fish is looking about wildly, stomping a few steps in one direction and then another. Rhea stays behind them, near the truck.

"I've been out here a lot," Carol says. "I had this real need to get my hands in the dirt, you know? Like, it's you guys moving in, why not? You don't like tomatoes? Zuchs? Sugar babies?"

"Are they spending the night here?" Fish asks.

"Oh sure," Carol says. She motions over her shoulder. "They're in the back yard."

Fish heads off around the house. Katie knocks on the front door, and when there is no answer, slowly opens it to look inside. There isn't any sign of an imminent move. There isn't a box in sight. She turns and says to Rhea, "Maybe you should wait in the car, honey." Rhea looks at her, starts to say something, then turns around and goes back to the truck.

"They haven't even started packing," Katie says to Carol Lee, back in the yard. Carol Lee shrugs. "You *all* have to move," Katie tells her. "It's my house, too. I'm moving back with Fish."

"Cool," Carol says nonchalantly.

Katie goes to the truck and tells Rhea, "I'll be back in a minute. I'm going to go get Fish and we'll leave. You stay here." The child nods solemnly.

In the back, Prudence is on her knees on a blanket, pulling

a basket toward her in which a baby lies. The other baby is on Prudence's shoulder. Sky and Fish are over under the light at the back door.

"It's the fucking END OF THE MONTH!" Fish yells.

"Man, you SAID that!" Sky yells back.

"Man, you're supposed to be OUT." Fish throws open the shed door and pulls out a bottle. He turns around menacingly. "Out!" he says.

Sky takes a step back. "Put the bottle down. Hey, there are babies here."

"Fish!" Katie cries. She's never seen him in a fight. He is more inclined to flee.

Fish throws the bottle against the back fence. It cracks and falls to the ground. "You be glad I don't have a gun," he says, but he has lost his momentum.

"My mom's house isn't ready," Prudence whines.

"Why didn't you say? This isn't fair," Katie complains.

"You've got a month's deposit!" Sky says. "We'll get out as soon as we can."

"A deposit isn't rent," Katie says. "If you're here tomorrow, you owe us rent."

"Sky called the county. It'll take you a month to get us out," Prudence says. She sits back on her heels.

"HELL YOU SAY!" Fish screams. He grabs Sky's arm. Sky seems to go limp. Maybe, Katie thinks, he imagines Fish is a bear. "I'm moving in on Saturday," Fish says. "It's my fucking BIRTHDAY."

"Where are we supposed to GO?" Prudence wails. Both babies start screaming. Prudence lays the baby from her shoulder to the blanket, and just looks at it turning red and howling.

"Go to your mother's," Katie says.

"Go to fucking HELL!" Fish yells.

Sky pulls away from Fish. "Get off this property or I'll call the sheriff."

Fish laughs an ugly laugh. "It'll take him a fucking long time to get here, wimp."

"Let's go, Fish," Katie says. "Rhea's in the car."

He looks at her and his expression changes from anger to bewilderment. It isn't fair at all, Katie thinks. It's just what you could expect, but it isn't fair.

Fish bangs the steering wheel with the flat of his hand. "MotherFUCKERS," he mutters.

Rhea starts to sniffle.

"It's all right," Katie says. She sits on the floor behind the seats. "We'll go get some ice cream. Okay, Fish?"

He starts the truck and backs out, tires screeching. "Michael's supposed to be taking care of this," he says.

"I doubt there's anything Michael can do. But he'll know. Ask him in the morning, Fish. Let's go to my place now. We're tired."

Rhea turns in her seat to look for Katie. "I didn't get to see the house."

"No baby, the people aren't out yet," Katie says. "In a few days, maybe." She hopes Rhea isn't going to cry.

"When are we going to Crater Lake, Fish?" Rhea asks.

Fish lights a cigarette before he answers. "Sometime," he says.

"When do I go back?" Rhea asks Katie. She leans toward Fish. "It's soon," she says.

"Tuesday, baby," Katie says. Her throat aches.

Fish takes a couple of long drags and then he says, "I've got work to do the next couple days. We'll go Sunday or Monday. We'll go." Although Katie doesn't think Fish means to be unkind, he speaks harshly, and she reaches up to pat Rhea's arm. She thinks it is too bad Rhea came along. Ursula should have spoken up.

Fish gives Rhea and then Katie a disgusted look and pushes the accelerator. "It's just a hole in the ground," he says.

By the time they are back in town, Fish has cooled off. He stops at a store and buys a half-gallon of burgundy, then goes to a drive-in and buys Rhea a soft ice cream cone. Rhea licks at it unenthusiastically.

"Hey Fish, let's go to my apartment," Katie says. "I want to show you something." She leans over and takes a lick of Rhea's ice cream. "But *you* can't look, because it's a surprise," she tells her daughter.

"What is it?" Rhea asks. She brightens immediately.

"If I told you it wouldn't be a surprise. It's not quite ready."

"When do I see it?"

"Saturday. After the parade."

"Oh boy." Rhea begins to eat the ice cream.

They pull into Katie's parking lot and Fish leaves the truck idling. "Aren't you coming in?" Katie asks. "Aren't you going to stay?" She thinks it is very important that they stay together to make Fish feel better. She doesn't want him to go off and get drunk. She wants him to work it out with her.

"Michael and I are going to the house at six, before it's so hot. I'll sleep over there."

Katie feels a hot blast of anger. He's going to go pout, she thinks, and never mind about Rhea and me. If every time something goes wrong, Fish wants to be alone, what will become of them if they have real trouble?

She follows Rhea out of the truck, and then goes around to Fish's side to speak to him. "Turn it off and come in. Please?"

He turns the Econoline off. "I'm in a foul mood now."

"Katie?" Rhea whispers urgently, from a few feet away.

"Wait, okay?" Katie says to Fish. "Let me talk to her. Maybe we'll come back with you. Maybe she'd rather sleep there." There's a bed for Rhea at Ursula's, Katie thinks. How can she be with Fish if Rhea stays?

Fish reaches for his sack with the wine bottle. "I'll wait," he says, and unscrews the cap.

At the apartment door, Rhea holds up the remains of her cone. "I don't want anymore," she says.

"Just a minute and you can throw it away."

"I feel kinda sick."

Katie swings the door open. "Here," she says, and takes the cone. "You want to go use the bathroom?"

Rhea goes into the bathroom and shuts the door. Katie throws the cone away, stands in the kitchen a moment, then goes through the apartment switching on lights. She opens the front door and steps across the hall to tap at Maureen's door.

Maureen is watching *Three Men and a Baby* on her VCR.

"Oh good, you're home," Katie says. "Can you come over for just a minute and watch Rhea?"

"While what?"

"I just need to talk to Fish. He's in a bad mood and he'll scare her, but I need to talk to him." She sees Maureen's critical look. "He's not drunk or anything."

Maureen switches off her tv and follows Katie back across

the hall. "Rhea," Katie says at the bathroom door, "you okay, honey?"

Rhea's small voice says, "I think so."

"Maureen from across the hall is here. I'll be right back."

"Don't go, Katie!" Rhea says. "Oh," she says. "Ohhh."

"Do you want me to come in?" Katie asks. If Rhea throws up, it'll make Katie sick, too.

"No!" Rhea answers. Very quietly she says, "I'm okay. It stinks."

Katie grins and looks at Maureen, but Maureen is unsmiling. "So go see Fish," Maureen says.

As soon as Katie is in the truck, Fish says, "I'm sorry if I scared her. I'm sorry. I just want my house back. I want my life back."

"I know," Katie whispers. "Me, too."

"Do you?" he asks. He puts the cap back on the bottle and sets it behind the seat. "Do you want our life back?"

"Not the way it was."

"How was it?"

"I didn't ever know what was going to happen next."

"Who ever knows?"

"I didn't know if you'd leave, if you'd come back."

Fish reaches over and pulls her to him. He puts his hands in her hair, on her neck, on her breasts. He touches her like a man who's been away. It makes her want to feel the whole length of him against her. "I'm not going anywhere," he says.

She puts her arms around him, awkwardly straddling the gear box. Fish says, "Let's get in the back."

They lie close together on the bed. "Michael and I are going to build a house to sell," he says. "Later in the summer, after we finish this job." Katie doesn't much care. "And we'll move back in our house, and out from under Michael and Ursula."

She kisses him. She says, "I've got to go back inside and see about Rhea."

"Could she stay? Could she live with us?"

"No way," Katie says. She feels about to cry. The only thing to stop the tears is Fish. "Touch me," she says. She tugs at his waistband. "Stay with me the night."

"What about Rhea?" he says.

"You and me," she says. In a moment both of them have their jeans around their knees. In a tangle of clothes and legs, they come together. Katie holds on tight, her hands hard on his back. "Fish and Katie," she says when they're still. "You and me."

She goes back inside but Rhea and Maureen aren't there. She walks over to Maureen's. Rhea is curled up beside her on the couch, asleep. The movie is on at very low volume. Maureen glares at Katie.

"Gosh, thanks," Katie says. She puts her arms out toward Rhea.

Maureen brushes Rhea's hair back off her forehead and ignores Katie's outstretched arms. "Let her sleep. I'll bring her over in a while."

"Is she okay?"

"She had one hell of a case of diarrhea, which I'd bet was brought on by something the two of you pulled. She cried for ten minutes, without saying anything. Can't you keep it together for the time she's here? What's wrong with you, Katie?"

"Maybe she was sick because of something Ursula COOKED." Katie trembles with anger. "What business is it of YOURS?"

"I'm the neighbor you handed her to, remember? I'm the one you parked her with."

"God, it was just for a few minutes, I didn't know you'd mind."

"Were you fighting? Is that it? Don't you know kids KNOW?" Maureen says furiously.

"We weren't fighting! We went out to the house and the renters were still there. Fish got into a scene with them. It's THEIR fault."

"She's just a little kid, Katie," Maureen says. "She's just a baby, in your way." She doesn't sound so angry now. She just wants to lecture a little.

"I've made her a twirler's outfit," Katie says. "With fake fur on the skirt. It's a surprise."

Maureen looks at Katie as if Katie were speaking another language.

"She's had a good time!" Katie says.

Maureen slides her arm out from behind Rhea. Rhea slumps against the side of the couch, sound asleep. Maureen comes over by Katie. "Until she's gone, you have to put her first, do you understand?" Katie nods. This is humiliating. Maureen has turned into Katie's mother! "If you've got some trouble with Fish, it can wait."

Katie raises her chin. "I don't have any trouble with him," she says. "The trouble was with the creeps who haven't left our house."

"Listen, kid," Maureen says. "I think the trouble may be with you."

Katie turns on one heel and returns to her apartment. It's two or three minutes before she realizes what she should have said. She should have said, "I didn't leave her by a lake, did I?" but now it's too late, the moment is past.

Besides, she can hear what Maureen could say. Maybe you didn't leave her by the lake, but you sure were in the bushes, weren't you?

—56—

Ursula comes home from the parade before the last float has made its torturous way down the boulevard. The others will go down to the park to the booths, and eat lunch there, but she wants to get the food ready for the afternoon, before the day grows hotter.

She tells herself hot weather beats rain on the Fourth of July. She wonders if Michael minds turning forty-five. Probably not. It's Fish who might ponder what it means.

Gully and Geneva will come later to join the family, and Ursula has invited Angela and her husband, a couple of teachers from Michael's school, Teresa and Teresa's brother, who is visiting from New York. The yard looks good; Michael must have leaned hard on Carter to get all the brush and trash picked up and hauled off. Ursula bought eight metal lawn chairs, some white, some black, on sale at Bi-Mart, and the pleasant shade on the deck will be a blessing. Michael has cleaned out the two barbecue grills and set them up, and Ursula has set several pots of flowers on the deck, for color.

She makes herself a large glass of iced tea, cuts open a

cantaloupe, and begins scooping out balls. She will wrap them with lengths of prosciutto, as Carter reminded her not so long ago. Last night she made cream puffs. She has vegetables to trim and slice, a dip to make, four kinds of cheeses, hamburger to which she'll add teriyaki sauce and a lot of garlic, chicken to marinate in her lemon glaze, and loaves of French bread she brought from Safeway on the way home.

She is upstairs changing into shorts when she hears a car at the curb. She hears voices in the basement, and then the door down there slam, then the car again. It sounds like Fish's truck. Maybe he and Katie have something to do before they come back, she thinks.

It isn't until a couple of hours later, when Katie, Michael, and the kids arrive, that they realize Rhea and Fish have gone off without telling anyone where they are going or for how long. Ursula asks Michael, "Could he have gone to get your folks?" but a phone call confirms that Gully is planning to drive out about four.

"It could be anything," Katie says impatiently. "What's everybody so uptight about? It's not like Fish can't drive. It's not like they're strangers, is it?" Two hours later she says, "He got some feather up his ass to do something and couldn't bother to tell us." By six, she's threatening to call the police. Michael says if they're not back by dark, he'll start looking. Katie sits in the breakfast nook, drinking one beer after another, slowly. Ursula goes through the motions of the afternoon, uneasy and bitter, but determinedly cheerful; her guests don't have to know that something is wrong. They can think Katie is sullen. They can think she likes to drink alone.

Fish leaves the freeway and drives fast past two shopping centers, car lots and warehouses, fast food places, and then fields of grass and scrub, with stands of huge trees around old farmhouses. On a rise someone has built a new log house, the color of cinnamon, and here and there trailers sit on bare ground, looking hot and lonely. Fish doesn't slow down or talk until the road narrows to two lanes and takes them through little towns along the river. Rhea is admiring the shimmer of light on the water, and the places where the water ripples and foams white when Fish says, "We're almost at the folks' house, see, up around that curve." He points.

"Are we going to their house?" Rhea asks, disappointed. Fish said at the parade, "Want to get out of here? Want to go somewhere cooler, away from all these people?" Rhea was eager to go down to the park to see what the booths were; that's what Juliette was going to do. But she didn't want to turn down a chance to be with her father, either. If they went somewhere in his truck, just the two of them, maybe she could get him to talk about boats. She wants to know where he will go when he has one. She wants to know what she needs to learn if she wants to go, too. She'll be older then. She can learn to sail. She can imagine the sea breathing under her, out on deep water. She can imagine the three of them, her father and her mother and her, brown as berries and strong, landing on an island that is very beautiful and staying there a long time.

"We'll stop on the way back," Fish says. "I want to pick up my fishing stuff, and my gun. I'll bet my ma's got my gun under the trailer. She can't stand guns in the house. Fifty years with Pop, and two sons, too, and she still hates guns."

"There's this girl in my class, Vicky Anne? Her brother shot their parents last year with a shotgun. He's seventeen. I guess he really hated them. Vicky wasn't home, so you don't know if he would have shot her, too." Fish gives Rhea such a look, it makes her wary. She doesn't mean she thinks he'll do something bad. She doesn't mean to complain about his gun. He made her think of Vicky, that's all.

"No shit," Fish says.

"They put him in a hospital, Granny says. He was sixteen when he did it, and Granny says he'll probably get out."

"What about the girl? Becky?"

"Oh, Vicky. She lives with her aunt. She lives close to me now. I could play with her after school but Granny hardly ever lets me."

They come around a curve, and the river seems to split for a moment, around a chunk of land, and then it comes together again. Rhea thinks it would be more fun to drive the other way. It is confusing, going against the river. She can see that it runs fast, but she can't get a feeling for its flow.

"I never saw a river like this before," she says. She wants to ask her father what he thought about the parade, but she thinks he didn't like it, and she's afraid he'll say it was silly.

"You ever see any rivers?"

"Once, when we went to Plano to see a cousin of Granny's. The cousin died, it was her funeral. My grandmother grew up with her. Coming and going, we had to cross a river. It was brown and wide and slow. Granny said there are snakes in rivers. You can't go in them just anyplace."

"Not in the Rogue. There are rattlers, though, along the banks, when it's hot. In rocky places. Sometimes a hiker gets bit, but it's because he's stupid. You have to pay attention to what you're doing."

Rhea wants to talk about the river and not snakes. "It's pretty, the river. It's so blue."

"You wait. You haven't seen blue yet," Fish says. They are driving between high trees, like a ribbon blowing through a canyon. The trees stretch on and on now. After a while the thick firs and pines give way to skinny, bare trees. "Those are lodgepole pines," Fish tells her. "The Indians used them for the frames of their teepees." Rhea is fascinated by this, though she isn't completely sure he isn't teasing her. Everything about Oregon is new. She expected more hills and trees than at home; everybody knows West Texas is flat as anyplace on earth. But she didn't realize, when she was looking forward to the trip, that there would be so many trees and hills that sometimes they would fill the eyes and block the sky.

Strips of sun fall through the trees across the pavement, like slats on a window. Rhea closes her eyes. Still she sees bright stripes. She sleeps.

"We're getting close," Fish says, to wake her. The drive is exciting now, as they climb higher. There is snow in patches, on banks above the lake. They pull into the parking lot at the rim, and Fish complains hoarsely. "Look at this. Goddamned Fourth of July here, too." Rhea thinks it is exciting to be where there are so many people. All around, people in shorts or jeans or wraparound skirts are looking at brochures, checking their cameras, pointing at the lake and talking Everyone seems about to do something; they are all enjoying getting ready.

She remembers it's Fish's birthday but it doesn't seem the right time to bring it up. She wishes she had a present for him. She asked Katie about it, and Katie said they always had the barbecue for Michael and Fish, and that was all they wanted. It sounded like presents are something for kids, something you outgrow. She wishes she thought to buy a kit and make him a boat for his birthday. Uncle Michael would have helped her.

A lot of people are milling around the cars, between the rim of the lake and the big lodge with the cafeteria and gift shops. Rhea follows Fish down to the stone wall at the edge of the lot and stands staring at the lake. She squeezes her fists as hard as she can to keep from crying. It is more beautiful than anything she has ever imagined, and at the same time it is the most terrible disappointment. There is no beach, no water in which to wade. It isn't anything like a lake; it's much more like Fish said, a hole in the ground. The lake fills the crater of an extinct volcano. Its sides are sheer and high. It is far away from where they are standing.

"Can you get down by the water?" she asks. She remembers seeing a pretty lake on the way, where there were fishermen on boats. She thinks she would like that lake better.

"If you fall down the side, it's so steep, you plunge so deep you can't come up again."

Rhea bursts into tears.

"Shit." Fish kicks the stone of the little wall. He sits down and puts his head in his hands. "Shit."

"I'm sorry," Rhea says. Her nose is clogged and her face is all wet. She thinks people must be looking at her. They're probably saying, what's wrong with that little girl. She takes a step closer to Fish, but she doesn't know what to do next, so she sits down, pulls up her tee shirt and wipes her face and nose. "You know what I used to think your name was?" she says. She holds her breath until Fish looks up at her.

He grins at her. "Tell me," he says, and he looks like he would really like to know. As suddenly as she was sad, Rhea is happy.

"I thought your name was Fisher Fisher. Granny told me Fish was short for Fisher, and I knew your last name was Fisher, because so is mine." She doesn't think she has done a very good job of explaining the mistake. Out loud, there isn't anything funny about it. She used to think there was magic in saying it over and over, Fisher Fisher, that it might make him appear. Maybe it did work, another way. Maybe it made Granny give in and let her come to Oregon.

"You're a kid with a lot of spunk," Fish says. Rhea has seen that word in books, spunk, but she has never actually heard someone say it. "My name is Gulsvig Fisher, just like my pop. Gulsvig used to be his last name, but they changed it to his stepfather's name, Fisher. So he kept both names, see? And then he gave me the old name, and gave Michael *his* name." He shakes his head and laughs. "Pretty confusing, huh? Pop used to call me Gully, like him, but by the time I started school everybody called me Fish."

"Because you liked to!" Rhea guesses. "Like Grandpa. He told me he'd rather fish than eat. I've never been fishing. He said maybe we could go sometime, but I go home in a few days. And we didn't go to the beach yet, either. But I liked what we did do! I love Mr. Melroy's dogs. Do you like Bounder? Grandpa asked me which dog I liked best, and I said Bounder."

"Are you hungry?" Fish asks. She wishes he would say something to show he was listening, but what could he say. She didn't mean to make him feel bad about the beach. Ursula said sometime when she comes they should rent a house at the beach and they can all go stay for a week. Everyone seems to assume she'll come back next summer. Granny didn't talk about that. She said, We'll see how it goes. She should be here, to see Rhea at the rim of a giant lake. She should see it herself.

"I am hungry," she says. "I really am."

Fish leads her to the cafeteria inside the huge stone building. He doesn't watch to see if she keeps up with him. She likes that. While they stand in line he checks his wallet and counts his change. "We're in good shape," he says. "What looks good?"

She studies his face. "Macaroni and cheese?"

"Macaroni and cheese for the Texan," he says to the boy behind the food line. He takes a bowl of chili. "I hate macaroni and cheese," he says when they have sat down and Rhea is eating. She stops, mid-bite. "My ma made it every week, sometimes twice. And I had it about a thousand times in the navy." He notices that she has stopped eating. "I'm not having it, you are," he says, and she takes another bite. "You have to know what you like," he tells her. "You have to not care what somebody else thinks you ought to like."

He finishes his chili and smokes a cigarette. Rhea feels

content in the bustle of the cafeteria. If she calls her grandmother tonight, she'll tell her, you wouldn't believe all the
people who came to see a lake. Coming up in the car, Fish
told her the lake is as deep as from Michael's house to the
Safeway store. She tries to lay her mind on its side, to see how
far that would be. She wants to walk it when she gets back.
Suddenly she has an image of her crayon box from last year,
the one with crayons in tiers, like a choir. All the blues:
cobalt, robin's egg, turquoise, azure. All those colors, in one
lake.

"Did you ever wonder what I looked like?" she asks. He
doesn't quite look at her. He draws deeply on his cigarette
and blows it out slowly. He always smells like smoke. It
worries her. When he smokes, he takes it deep inside and lets
it out in a slow stream. She can see how much he likes it. She
knows smoking kills you, though, and she wants to warn him.
She wants to tell him about smoking and cancer, and about
the food groups, about how not to get struck by lightning,
and not to put butter on a burn. She has never assumed,
when she learned something, that everyone else already
knows it. She has always considered the possibility that she
might be paying more attention. Granny says someday Rhea
will know more than she does, that this is natural. She says
children get smarter than their parents, but Rhea doesn't
think Granny would say that about Katie. Whenever Rhea
asks about Fish or Katie, Granny takes a while to think before
she answers. Even simple questions. It makes Rhea think that
anything you ask about them has more than one answer, and
Granny needs a little time to choose the one that suits her
best.

Fish stubs out the cigarette. It bothers Rhea that he hasn't
answered her. She says, "I brought a school picture for you.
It's in my suitcase at Michael's. I'll give it to you if you want."
She feels dumb, saying that. Why does he need a picture,
when she is sitting right in front of him? If he would look at
her, he could see her perfectly well. Her blond hair is all
scraggly from not blow drying it or using a curler or anything. Granny warned her that a perm wouldn't look good if
you didn't mess with it, but she said Rhea could find out for
herself. She said they could cut it later and let it grow back
straight. She said you have to make mistakes to learn. It
almost made her not want to get the permanent at all.

Fish sucks in his top lip, and a lot of moustache with it. She wants to laugh but she doesn't think he knows he is funny, or that he means to be. He sometimes laughs when nobody else does, or he waits and laughs after everyone else is done. At night she hears him talking when she is falling asleep. He stays up late with Michael, and Carter when he gets home from work. They drink wine and talk and talk, after Ursula and Juliette and Rhea go to bed. Sometimes Katie is there and sometimes she isn't. She has worked at the theatre three nights and two afternoons. She promises she will take Rhea down to see where she works, but she hasn't, and now the time is almost all gone. Rhea hoped they would move into Fish's house before she left. She would like to stay in a house with both her parents at the same time.

"I knew what you looked like," Fish says. "Katie and I came to see you when you were three. It was winter. The wind was blowing snow when we got to your house. A few days later we were in Mazatlán, hot as toast. Your grandmother wouldn't let you go. It probably wasn't a good idea, but I thought you'd look cute running around naked on the sand."

Rhea used to dream about Fish. She has a snapshot Katie gave her of Fish standing against his truck, one foot propped up, his hand up to shade his eyes. She thought from the picture that he would be taller than he is.

"And the year after that your mother took a lot of pictures when she went to visit you." He pushes their dirty dishes aside and opens his wallet. He lays out slips of folded paper. Some of them have lists, and some have lots of numbers. Some are yellow slips, receipts from things you buy. "Fuck," Fish says. "It's got these little dopples on it, I got it wet." He is holding a photograph and smearing it with his finger. "But here's one. Katie has the rest in a box somewhere." He hands the photograph to her. "See that cloth tied around your head? A bandanna. That's the way I used to wear bandannas on my head in Vietnam. It was like a joke your mom made for me, dressing you like that. That's her scarf tied around your belly. I always figured you would be scrawny, but look at that belly and those legs. It'd take a truck to knock you down."

The girl in the picture doesn't look like her. She knows you look different as a baby, but she can't imagine she ever looked like that. She doesn't think her grandmother would have agreed to her being dressed in a scarf.

"It's pretty old," she says, and hands it back to Fish. He stuffs all the papers back in the wallet in wads, then slides the picture in last.

"Let's drive around the rim," Fish says. "You might never see it again, or anything like it." Rhea's mouth is dry in an instant. She can't believe he would say that. "You might never come to Oregon again," he says, getting up. He isn't even looking at her when he says it.

As they come down off the mountain and drive along the river, she starts to cry. "I don't want to go home," she says. She wishes Granny and Aunt Christine would move to Oregon.

Fish pats her leg. "It's not late. We can do something else." He thinks she means now. "Let's see if Pop is still at home. Let's see if we can catch you a fish."

## —57—

After they pick up what they need from Fish's parents' house, he drives a few minutes and then pulls off the highway onto a graveled shoulder above the river. Down a steep, rocky bank, the water breaks over rocks, and then surges toward the opposite bank in a deep arc. "Salmon rest in deep water before they struggle up the next shallow, faster water," her father says. He shows her how he ties the preserved eggs into a little cluster surrounding the hook at the end of the line, and how the weight above the hook will pull the eggs down deep, yet let them drift with the current.

They walk partway downstream, below the head of the deep water, and he casts the egg cluster upstream and slightly across the current. He turns the handle on the reel and gradually winds in line. "You've got to keep a little tension on the sinker," he tells her. "You have to feel the weight as it drifts, bouncing along the bottom, so that if it suddenly stops, you can set the hook zip! just like that, when the fish snaps at the drifting eggs." *Bait,* Rhea thinks. That's what bait is.

She does not know how much time goes by. *It must be an hour we've been here,* she thinks. In the steep canyon of the river, the sun is already setting. She has watched Fish carefully, but she is growing tired, and she is disappointed that he hasn't had a strike. He tells her that sometimes he has fished for days without catching a salmon. "The uncertainty is supposed to be part of the fun," he says. Even as he says it, he lifts the rod in a sudden arc, both hands high over his head. At the same instant a high-pitched whine comes from the reel as line is stripped from the spool and pulled rapidly up the current toward the shallow water. "We've got a good fish if we can land it!" he shouts to her.

Rhea can't see the fish, but she watches the movement of the line as it swings upstream, and she sees her father's arms cocked against the buck and throb of the straining rod. He tells her, "Hooking a salmon and landing one aren't the same thing. I wish I'd thought to bring the landing net."

In a moment he says, "Wily bastard's switching strategies on me." The fish turns and races downstream so quickly that Fish can't wind in the line fast enough to keep it taut. "Holy shit!" he yells. He looks mad and happy at the same time. "That sucker is going to get off the hook if I can't catch up with its run," he says. She sees the line tighten. The fish is stripping line from the reel faster than before. "It's got the current on its side," Fish says. "If it gets into the rocks at the bottom of the hole, it'll break the line." She steps closer to him, puts a hand on his hip as he arches. "I've got to stop its run," he tells her. "It might break that way too, but I don't know what else to do." He fumbles with the drag until the whining sound drops and then stops altogether. His face is set and she can see the strain in his arms and shoulders. If she were taller, she would put her hand up across his shoulders to feel how strong he is. She peeks out from around his body, and suddenly sees the fish churning at the surface in a flash of spray. She had no idea a fish could be so large. In an instant it dives and disappears. Her father holds the fish against the current for a long time. She hopes it will come up again so she can see it, and says so. "Let it sulk," Fish says. "It'll tire itself out."

She feels like she cannot wait another moment for something to happen, and then Fish begins walking slowly downstream, almost as if he is stalking something, holding the tension in the line, winding it in as he moves. She can tell they're getting closer to the fish, but the fish doesn't move.

Suddenly it is there again, rolling at the surface, larger

than she thought before, its back a dark green with a bright, silvery side. Again it disappears under the water, and then she sees that it has turned and is heading upstream again.

"Hot damn!" Fish says quietly. "Hot fucking damn! The current is going to be on our side, honey." He is now able to gain some line as the fish struggles against the water. Rhea can see it just below the surface. It is coming closer, almost out of the current. It makes a lunge, shaking its head, then pauses and rises slightly under the strain of the line. He speaks almost in a whisper, bending his head a little toward her. "We can land it if it won't panic," he says. "If it just won't move and snap the line."

He gestures with his head. "Stand behind me so the fish won't see you." As she does, he swings the fish slowly inward toward the bank until the water is so shallow the fish's back comes out of the water as its belly touches the gravel. The fish seems to explode with panic. She hears a pop as the line parts, and her father steps aside, nearly losing his balance. For an instant the fish is motionless. Without thinking about it, she runs toward it, the water suddenly cold on her feet and legs.

She is astride the fish in the shallows. It twists and bucks, and she hears her father yelling. She tries to grasp the fish, but it is too slick and large for her hands. Then one hand finds a gill and she gets a hold on the fish, just as her father reaches her. He works a finger into the other gill and together they scramble onto the shore, pulling the fish between them.

"I didn't know," she gasps. "I didn't know about fish."

At the house he says, "You better go in first." It is almost dark. At the door he gives her the fish. She grasps it at the gills, straining to hold it in front of her. Fish opens the door and lets her in. She hears a dog at the back door, whining and scratching. The cat streaks across the hall floor and into the front room. Then Rhea stumbles into the kitchen. Michael and Ursula and Katie are at the table in the breakfast nook. Gully and Geneva are at the table to the left, in the dining room. She stops in the kitchen and tries to hold the fish higher. Her chin touches the fish's head, and its tail slaps against her thighs. "Look at my fish!" she says, panting, as she loses her hold and the big fish falls to the floor, revealing her wet and bloody clothes.

Rhea sees that her mother is glaring at Fish over Rhea's shoulder. She feels her father come up behind her. He puts his hand on her shoulder. "Do you believe this kid?" he says. It makes her chest ache with joy. Ursula says, "How could you, Fish?"

Katie says, "You son of a bitch."

—58—

Geneva says to Gully, "So can we go now?"

Gully says, "Give me a minute, Ma. They just got here."

Fish says, "Salmon in an hour! Gonna cook our fucking fish!" He ignores Katie and goes to the back door, hauling the big fish. His shirt is smeared and wet.

Juliette comes in and says, "So you finally got here?" She gives Rhea a light pinch on the arm. "Come upstairs with me and I'll get you cleaned up, Rhea."

The dog races in behind Juliette. Fish makes a show of jumping aside for the dog. Rhea says, "Bounder!" and falls to the floor to hug the dog and send him chasing off through the house at top speed. Then she follows Juliette upstairs. The dog reappears in the kitchen and skids to a stop at Gully's feet. "Good dog," Gully says. "Good Bounder."

Ursula says, "People have been and gone, Fish. We ate. There's still chicken left, and some stuff in the refrigerator." Katie thinks Ursula looks and sounds weary.

Katie says, "I hate you, Fish," though without vigor.

Gully says, "Happy birthday, son."

Fish takes the salmon to the back yard to clean. Katie follows him. Her head is throbbing. She would like to sock Fish in the throat. She would like to scream and jump around. She brims with anxious energy, and she doesn't know what to do with it. She has a momentary flash of Fish and her in the back of the truck, arguing and sweating and making love. The image makes her angry at herself. She has been mad at him for hours.

Michael says, "I'll need to stoke the coals if you're going to cook that fish. You want to cut some filets and freeze the rest?

Let me know if you want some help." Katie thinks Michael's placid neutrality is as aggravating as Fish's delinquency. Peas in a pod, she thinks. Acting like the fish matters, like the fish can make everything all right.

"You couldn't call us?" she asks Fish. Now she has this picture of Fish and Rhea standing hip deep in the river, using a walkie-talkie.

He takes his knife out and slices down the belly of the fish. It makes her want to throw up. "You couldn't come to your own party? You couldn't wait until TOMORROW?" Her voice grates in her ear. Fish doesn't look up.

Ursula calls to her from the kitchen door. "You want to make a plate for Rhea, Katie?" Katie sighs and leaves Fish and Michael with the salmon. She can't think of any more accusations anyway.

Rhea comes back downstairs in clean shorts and a shirt.

"Aren't you hungry, darling?" Ursula says. Katie says sharply, "I'll find her something." She wants them all to recognize who's in charge of this child, whose child she is. Maybe she hasn't been in charge before, but she's going to be now. If her mother knew Rhea went off with Fish alone, she would scream until Christmas.

She finds Rhea a shrunken strip of chicken breast on a plate of meat; Michael has cleared the grill and added coals to it. Rhea takes a pickle and some carrot sticks from another plate in the refrigerator and sits at the table, careful to move her chair quietly. "You want some pop?" Katie asks her. Rhea nods but still doesn't say anything. Katie gives her a Sprite in a can and she takes a little sip. She eyes her plate as if something might be moving around on it. Katie knows Rhea is avoiding her eyes, and it is wounding and frustrating and unfair. Katie isn't the one who went off and ruined the day for everyone. Katie isn't the one out in the yard making a lot of noise and commotion and not even bothering to speak to his parents, who have waited hours and hours to see him.

Gully pulls up a chair and sits down near Rhea. "Where's Bounder?" she asks him.

"I put him in the back yard," Gully says. He looks at Katie and says, "We'll take the dog back with us. Rhea likes him so much, I thought she'd want to play with him today." He's so tired his face seems to have shrunk, like the chicken on

Rhea's plate. To Rhea he says, "Maybe you can come out and play with Bounder tomorrow."

Ursula boils water and rinses the teapot. "I'll make Geneva a cup of tea," she says to the wall. "I know she's feeling wrung out. Ha. Who isn't?"

Katie's observation is that Geneva is close to exploding. She hasn't moved from her post at the dining room table. Through the double doors Geneva can see Gully at the table with Rhea, and she stares at him as if he were having a tête à tête with another woman.

Fish bursts through the room and down the stairs, letting the door slam hard behind him. In short order he is back up and out again, carrying his tape player and a handful of tapes. At the back door he turns and says, "Are you all asleep? This is DEAD CITY around here!" He sticks the player under his arm and grabs a beer out of the refrigerator.

Michael crosses paths with his brother on the deck and comes into the kitchen. "Have we got lemon?" he asks. Ursula says yes, and spoons loose tea into a pot. Michael says, "I can eat again by the time the fish is done. Fresh salmon. What a surprise." He leaves again.

Rhea looks at Katie. "I didn't catch it," she says. "I was just there." There is a blast of Janis from the yard.

"Nobody's blaming you," Katie says. "Eat up. I have something for you upstairs."

Katie goes to the window to look out on the yard. Ursula switches on the yard lights and returns to the sink to rinse dishes and stack them in the dishwasher.

"I'm not really hungry," Rhea says. She is leaning on her arms.

"Come up," Katie says. "Come see what I've done."

"Gully," Ursula says. "Here's a cup of tea for Geneva. Why don't you take it to her? We'll sit down."


When Katie and Rhea come back down with Juliette, Ursula is at the table with Geneva, and Gully has gone outside with his sons and the dog.

"You better come see, Aunt Ursula!" Rhea says. She is feeling much better.

The twirler's outfit is baggy in the seat of the pants, but otherwise it fits nicely. It is pale blue satin, trimmed with

white false fur. It has a short pleated skirt, a close bodice with
a scoop neck, and cap sleeves. Katie has attached yards of
shiny rickrack around the neck and sleeves. It was worth it all
for the look of astonishment and delight on Rhea's face when
she saw it. Rhea said, "*That's* where you were!"

Rhea carries her baton into the yard, followed by Juliette.
Katie sits at the dining room table, facing out through the
nook and the windows, into the yard. She can see the two
girls prancing and strutting, Rhea holding the baton up high.
The dog is barking and racing about.

"I don't know what I thought happened," Katie says wearily to no one in particular. "It was like he'd gone off with
her. Like to Canada or Mexico. Like he robbed her from us.
And they were having a good time, that's all. Rhea is full of it.
She had a great day. I've made a scene about nothing."

Ursula says, "Fish was thoughtless and stupid to go off
without a word, but maybe it would be better to shut up
about it for now. We don't want Rhea feeling guilty. Kids pick
up on these things."

"Doesn't she seem like a really happy child?" Katie asks.

Ursula says, "I thought that right away."

Geneva says, "In all of Evelyn's nineteen years, I cannot
remember a single time Gully went anywhere with her
alone."

The other two women stare at Geneva.

"The boys had dogs. The boys had birds. But let Evelyn try
to pet one, and it bit or scratched or pecked or barked. One
year they had a pigeon and it dropped doo-doo in her hair."

Katie and Ursula look at one another.

"He stays up late like this, he'll have an angina attack
driving home."

"Michael can take you," Ursula says quickly.

"He won't be able to sleep, and he'll roam around the
house and I won't be able to sleep either," Geneva keens.

"You could sleep in the spare room upstairs if you want.
You could go up there now," Ursula says. Her eyes are drooping and dark, her hair sticks out in tufts, her kelly green tee
shirt has several stained spots on it. Katie thinks it was worse
for Ursula than for anyone today. She expected the most.

She stands by the window and looks out on the yard. The
girls are chasing the dog, catching him and sitting on the
grass, letting him run back and forth over their legs and

around them. Rhea lies flat on her back and the dog jumps across her belly, but lands halfway on her chest. Fish is playing a Grateful Dead tape. "Ripple in still waters . . . When there is no pebble tossed, no wind to blow . . ." Why, this should be a good time we're having, she thinks. "Where's Carter?" she asks without turning around. They wouldn't get him down.

"He's working tonight. Two more weeks till he quits and gets his place ready. They're going to call it 'Annabella's Pizzaria.'" Ursula drums her fingers lightly on the table.

"He's a funny kid."

"Don't I know it?" Ursula sighs.

Fish comes in fast and takes a six-pack out of the refrigerator. "Fish is almost done!" he yells as he exits. Geneva slumps with her midriff against the table. "His last dog died ten years ago. Why does he get one now?"

Ursula stands up. "I'll get Gully, Geneva. Michael can drive you both home and he and Fish can bring your truck out tomorrow."

Geneva lays her head on the table.

Katie follows Ursula into the yard. Fish has changed the tape to the Rolling Stones. The girls are back to their baton twirling act, with Rhea leading Juliette as they march from one end of the yard to the other and back. "Watch, Katie!" Rhea calls. She twirls in place, and her pleated skirt flies out around her. When she stops, she does a bump with her butt.

Fish has a beer in his left hand and a long fork in the right. He is poking at the fish on the grill. Smoke is billowing.

Ursula says, "Michael, Geneva's tired and wants to go home. Maybe you should drive them."

Gully says, "I can drive when I want to, I want to try the fish first."

Michael says, "I'll talk to her in a minute, Ursula." He pops the tab on a can of beer and sips it. Fish takes a long noisy drink from his, and burps loudly.

"If you're going to get drunk, you can go to hell," Katie says.

Michael says, "It's our birthday. Both of you could stand to lighten up."

"What have I done?" Ursula protests. "Cook and talk? Serve and clean?"

"I wasn't talking to you, Michael," Katie says.

"I'm drinking beer too," Michael replies.

"Never mind, Michael," Ursula says. "Your mother is *tired*."

"Everybody's TIRED," Fish says. He jumps up on the lawn chair near the grill and swings the fork around. "They're all WORN OUT. Somebody didn't DO RIGHT and it's got them all DOWN. Katie's afraid Fish won't stay SOBER. Katie's afraid Fish will FUCK UP and DESERVE DIVORCE. Fish might lose his keys, drive the wrong car, break a plate, piss in his pants. HAVE A WRECK! FUCK A HIPPIE! FISH MIGHT GET THE HELL OUT OF HERE AND INTO HIS OWN MOTHERFUCKING HOUSE. FISH MIGHT SHOOT THE ASSHOLES WHO ARE STILL IN IT." He burps again.

Gully says, "Son, I know just how you feel, I've been there too."

"High and Dry" comes on the tape player. Fish bellows the song out along with the tape. He swings the fork, kicks one leg out and back, sways precariously. "You left me with no warning . . ." The girls are giggling and racing with Bounder now. They rush by and away again. Gully says to his son, his voice crackling, "You don't think that fish is done?" Fish is screaming the song. "High and dry, well I couldn't get a word in . . ."

"I better go," Gully says. "I don't feel so good." He reaches out toward Michael.

Rhea and Juliette are shrieking, running after the dog.

Fish screeches, "What a way to go . . ." He swings his head and shoulders around. The chair tips and then topples. Fish falls as the chair hits the barbecue grill and sends it onto its side, fish and coals flying. Everyone jumps back. Michael misses Gully's hand. Fish sprawls on the far side of the chair. As Gully steps backwards, Bounder bounds behind him, and Gully stumbles and falls with a thud. He moans once and lies still.

Katie grabs the tape player and throws it all the way across the yard against the garage.

Rhea cries, "Grandpa," and Juliette, "What happened?!"

Fish says, "Now what have I done? Shit, what have I done?"

Michael and Ursula are on the ground by Gully. Gully says, "I think it's broke."

Rhea begins to cry loudly. "It's my fault," she wails. "I made

Bounder do it." Juliette puts her arms around her and starts to cry too.

Katie starts hitting Fish on the chest and head and arms. She doesn't say anything; she grunts and hits and starts to weep. Fish stands with his arms hanging at his side limply.

Ursula says, "Thank God nobody's burned."

Geneva appears and says, "I hope everybody's happy."

## —59—

Ursula sits with Katie at the dining room table under the soft glow of the hanging lamp. The rest of the house is dark, except for a night light on the stairs and in the upstairs hall. Ursula managed to find some gin stashed in the cabinet above the refrigerator, along with an inch of cheap cognac and half a dozen miniature wine bottles from airplane rides. They have killed the gin, drinking it with Sprite, and Ursula feels not so much high as slightly numb. She probably would feel the same if she drank water, she's so tired.

Michael calls a little before midnight and says it's going to be a while. Gully's heart is acting up, it's his angina. They still haven't set his arm. "Mom's asleep on a couch," he tells Ursula. "She's half-dead, I wish I could check her in too."

"And you?" Ursula asks. "Are you okay?"

"Sure I'm okay," Michael says. "Why wouldn't I be? Is Fish there?"

"No, he left right after you did, in his truck. We haven't seen him."

"Maybe he went to a bar. Or driving around."

"Katie says maybe he went to Mexico."

"Too hot this time of year. Listen, I've got to go. Don't wait up."

"We'll see." She hangs up and recounts the conversation for Katie.

Katie says she doesn't know if she can stay awake much longer.

"You don't need to. Go up to the spare bed. Rhea's with Juliette."

"I was hoping Fish would come back. I was hoping he wouldn't go out and get drunk, or drunker, and do something stupid."

"It's up to him, I guess," Ursula says. She wishes she had more gin, or liked cognac.

The phone rings again. "Just a minute, just a minute," she says. She puts her hand over the mouthpiece. "It's the renters. They say Fish is sitting in his truck in the driveway. What do they think we can do about that?"

"Give me the phone," Katie says. "Who is this?" Now she pulls the phone away from her face to tell Ursula, "Sky the dipshit. Okay, Sky, he's had a very hard night, and he is very pissed at you. You go out there and tell him Katie says come home, it's cool here. You don't make it worse, you hear? And in the morning start packing your shit." She bangs the phone down.

Ursula feels guilty, though she has nothing to do with it. "Michael was absolutely scrupulous about references, deposits, all of it. But all the people who wanted to live in your house were a little—*alternative*. Know what I mean?" Katie knows. "Michael did go file for an eviction notice, you know. They're wrong, but they're there. It could take a while."

Katie waves her hand in front of her face. "I hope Michael knows what he's doing, starting a house with Fish."

Ursula props her chin with her fist, leaning on her elbow. "I don't allow myself to think about it. Michael is going to teach half-time this year, Global Studies, mornings at the high school. He's completely changing what he's doing so he can work with Fish."

"Fish is lucky."

"Michael says he feels like he's a big winner, doing this. He was in a rut. And he likes working with his brother. For all of Fish's troubles, he doesn't have many with Michael, as far as I know. Michael says, the time is right. I think he senses some changes in Fish. The turn at forty-five. Ahh. What a birthday this turned out to be."

"Oh Ursula, why do I have trouble?"

"Maybe because you expect trouble."

"They tell you, learn from history."

"What Fish did today—going off harebrained as a seventh-grader—it really wasn't big enough to merit all this that came out of it. From Rhea's point of view, it was a damned good day, evidently."

"So who's fault is that? Didn't Fish knock over the grill? Didn't he make the scene?"

"Not by himself. I don't think he could do it by himself."

Katie pulls herself up tall in her chair. "I didn't do it. I didn't tell him to get on a chair and sing like Mick Jagger. God DAMN it, Ursula, don't do that to me."

"I'm worn out, Katie. I don't mean to blame or criticize. Don't you know I love you?"

The phone rings again. Ursula answers, tells the caller to wait, and hands the phone to Katie. "Carol Lee?" she whispers.

"Carol?" Katie says. "What's going on?"

She listens for a minute, looking more and more alarmed, and then tells the girl to wait. She explains to Ursula. Fish has stormed into the house and started throwing stuff out on the lawn.

"Damn."

Katie is back on the phone. "Michael's not here, Carol. I don't know anything to do. I think you ought to stay out of his way. He's not crazy, really he's not. He's mad. He'll stop for a breath and realize what he's doing, and go tearing off in his truck. Stay out of his way. Keep the babies out of his way." She hangs up and begins kneading her fingers, wringing her hands. "Don't do this," she whispers. "Please don't do this."

Ursula moves over by Katie and puts her arm around her. "You want to take my car and go out there?"

The phone rings again. Ursula answers and the same girl, Carol Lee, says, hysterically, that Fish has gone to the back yard and is shooting bottles out of the shed. Ursula repeats, "Shooting bottles!" She hands the phone to Katie.

Katie listens a minute, looking at Ursula miserably. Tears are streaming down her face. She reaches over and takes Ursula's hand. Then she tells Carol Lee, "If I were you I'd call the sheriff. There's nothing I can do. Call the cops." And she hangs up, turns and leans against Ursula, and sobs steadily for five minutes. When she stops, she says, "They'll haul him off, won't they?"

"I'd think."

Katie speaks intensely, almost leaning into Ursula's lap. "I can't bail him out or make him be good. He doesn't want me to, anyway. We never ask him if he wants us to." She sits up straighter. "I can't take care of myself worth a damn. And you know what Jeff told me? The guy who made the scene about my car? I saw him in the grocery store the other day, I was ahead of him in line at the register. I waited to walk out with him. I said it was nice to see him. I thought that was a nice thing to say. He walked me to my car, and you know what he said? He said he felt so crazy for having liked me, he was going to see somebody. You know, like a shrink or somebody! He said something about me had appealed to the part of him that hadn't grown up. I'm standing by my fucking car with egg on my face. I made him crazy, he says. Is that what I do to Fish? Is that what I do to Rhea? To my mother? To everyone?"

Ursula isn't going to listen to this nonsense. The rationality of the caseworker comes back to her. "Whatever your friend's problem is or was, Katie, is or was *his*. He probably does need a shrink, a Yuppie shrink for his Yuppie problems. As for you, you did pretty damned well this winter. You put yourself together in a whole new way, including holding a good job. Make Fish crazy? I don't know how that can be. Who ever loved him as much as you? Who's stayed with him for damned near twenty years? Who has he always been crazy about, whatever he did not to show it? Fish and Katie. It's like moon and stars, bread and butter, shoes and socks. I don't know what to tell you, I don't know why Fish fucks up, but I don't think he's going to hurt those people out there. Maybe he's shooting bottles because he's through with them, did you think of that? Maybe it's his message to the world. Maybe you ought to wait and ask him in the morning. Maybe you shouldn't give up on the basis of how you feel in the middle of a very long night."

Katie says, very quietly, "Thanks, Ursula. You're always here. I know I haven't talked to you in a long time. I don't know why, but I think maybe I had to—leave home, you know? I had to try living outside the Fisher circle."

"I don't think of it that way, as a circle," Ursula says. "I think of it more as people whose paths all cross. People who are connected. Family, Katie." God, I love Michael, she thinks.

Katie gets up. "I do love you, Ursula, and I know you want to help. But would you mind very much if I used your upstairs phone? Would you mind if I called a friend who's been as messed up as me? And then could I call my mother?"

After Katie has gone to bed, Ursula lies on the couch in the living room a long time, thinking about Katie and Fish. Her tired mind plays with a sequence of terrible scenarios, a set of might-have-beens, in which Fish and Katie, isolated and hapless, try to raise the baby Rhea. What would they have done with her? Would the child have raised them to a higher level, to better themselves? Or would they have hurt her?

How many of the children Ursula has seen were from couples no more pathological than this, but twisted, stressed too much, by parenting?

Her heart feels flooded and painful. She feels for certain "bad" mothers as she has not before, mothers who could not keep their babies out of the road, so to speak. And she feels a large love and respect for Katie, who in choosing Fish, nine years before, may have been choosing Rhea after all.

She knows she can't sleep, so she decides to do laundry. She turns on the hall light and collects some clothes from both Carter's and Juliette's rooms, without disturbing them. She carries them in a basket down to the basement, sorts them with clothes stuffed at other times down the chute, and starts a load. She switches on the tv and sits on the lumpy couch. An old Natalie Wood film is on, *Splendor in the Grass.* Jesus, she thinks, don't let this mean something. She watches Natalie leave a dance to throw herself in dangerous waters. The wash cycle ends. She switches it to the dryer and starts running a load of colored clothes, then goes back to watch Natalie in the hospital, painting and talking her way to sanity. Why do so many women give themselves over to Warren Beatty? she wonders. What secrets does he possess? What does he promise them, and does he deliver? Why do they never seem to be bitter?

She folds the dry clothes and lays them neatly in the basket, switches off the television—Natalie isn't going to go back to Warren, who has married someone else anyway—and heads back up the stairs, hoping Gully is okay, wishing Michael would come home. At the top of the stairs she turns to push the door open with her backside, and as she turns again, to head into the kitchen, she sees Pajamas darting toward her and the door. The cat is a second, half a second too late; though she drops the basket and grabs for the door, she is past it, and with its tight spring, it snaps shut too quickly for her to stop it.

It doesn't actually snap. It is stopped from the precise click of closure by the head of the cat. It happens too quickly for the cat to know; it doesn't have time to make a sound.

Ursula opens the door and scoots the cat back with her foot. Then she rushes to the stairs, sits on a low step, and howls with grief.

Katie comes tearing down the hall and the stairs. Juliette creeps along in a few minutes. Together, the three of them bury Pajamas in the yard, around the back of the garage, between the old kiln and the fence. It is harder work than Ursula imagined, but with three of them they are able to accomplish it.

She tucks Juliette in, and kisses her and the sleeping Rhea. "I dread Dad finding out," Juliette says. "He's going to be so sad."

"He is, sweetheart," Ursula says achingly. Juliette seems to fall asleep in that same instant.

Ursula goes down to Katie and asks her if she needs anything. Katie says, "I think I can sleep, believe it or not. Let's see how it all looks tomorrow." She turns over toward the wall.

Ursula takes her pillow with her back down to the couch, curls up, and falls asleep.

She wakes to find Michael sitting beside her. He strokes her hip gently. "What time is it?" she asks.

"Nearly dawn."

"Poor Michael."

"Pop's okay. He'll spend another night there, for observation. He's going to have a helluva time, though, with a broken right arm."

"That's what wives are for, I guess," Ursula says. She hopes she sounds appropriately fond, or wry, and not sarcastic. She doesn't mean to mock Geneva.

"There's a problem there."

"Where?"

"With Mom."

Ursula rubs her eyes. "I'm not following this, Michael. Where is your mother?"

"She's home. But I listened to her rage for two hours. She's mad about the dog. For some reason she's mad about Rhea—"

"She's jealous. I figured that out tonight. Gully likes Rhea, but he was mean to Evelyn."

"Christ. That's nearly thirty years ago!"

"I think your mother has quite a file on Gully, honey."

"I got a glimpse of it tonight. She says she's going to call Ruby tomorrow, and if Ruby will have her, she's going to fly to Spokane as soon as she can get on a plane. I think she's serious. She says Ruby has invited her to go to Arizona with her for the winter. I don't get it, but I think she's serious."

"Who'll look after your dad?" She laughs and puts a finger to his lips. "Stupid question, huh?"

"He's had her taking care of him for fifty years."

"We'll have plenty of room, won't we?" She doesn't mean to feel sorry for herself. It just happens to be true. "Actually, I think I could get along with Gully here, Michael. It's your mother who gets to me."

"Thanks, Ursie, I've got to do whatever I've got to do."

"What about Fish?"

"With Pop?"

"Why not? They're related too."

"You know how Fish is about Pop. He won't stay around him any length of time. He has this stupid picture of Pop the way he used to be. I don't know how Fish remembers it, but I'll take Pop now. The way he was going, he wouldn't have had an old age."

"I know. Come here." She puts her arms around her husband and kisses his forehead, then his cheek, and, softly, his lips. "I have to tell you something awful," she says. She chokes up, but she tells him how she killed his cat.

He doesn't say anything. He quietly goes out the back door to the yard. The light is off, and when she looks out the window she can't see him. In a moment, though, she hears him vomiting, and, she thinks, crying. She steps out onto the deck to wait for him. "Michael," she calls. "Michael, let me help." Ohh, she thinks, how stupid that sounds, when she is the one who did the deed. But the thought of her sad husband out in the dark retching is so painful. She doesn't know how much more she can stand in one night. How many tears are they going to shed?

She hears Michael, then sees him, at the side of the house, washing and rinsing out his mouth at the hydrant. When he reaches her on the deck, he takes her hand. "Let's sit out here a few more minutes," he says. "I'm so tired I'm past it."

She leans against his shoulder.

"There's something I've wanted to tell you for a long time," he says. The stuffiness of his nose muffles his voice.

"Are you sure you want to tell me now?" she asks. She hopes it isn't something bad.

"I should have told you," he says, but then he starts to cry. His shoulders heave and his body rocks. She slides her arm away, to give him peace.

"I'm so sorry," she says. "I'm so sorry about the cat."

It takes him a while to get calm again. "I'll miss her a lot, but she's not a child. I'll get another cat," he says. He turns and kisses Ursula, catching her quite by surprise with his damp face and ardor. Then he says, "Listen to me. It's about when I went away to the Peace Corps, and came back before the training was over, so they wouldn't send me overseas."

She can't imagine why he brings this up now. She has given her support to him and his parents, hasn't she? She's said it's all right if Gully comes to live. She doesn't complain about Geneva except once in a great while. Why does he have to tell her again how he had to give up the Peace Corps for his mother?

"I left the Corps for you," he says.

"What? I thought it was Geneva—"

"That gave me an excuse. I don't know why I thought I couldn't tell you the truth. I realized that Fish would get out of the navy about the same time as I would get out of the Peace Corps, and I was absolutely seized with terror that you'd—you'd want to go back to him, and not to me."

"I don't believe this." She feels a surge of anger, but she isn't sure why. That she swallowed so hard, marrying him when she thought he came home for Geneva? That he has known something for twenty years that she did not? Then she realizes what he has said. "You came home for me?"

"I almost convinced myself it was to save you from my

brother. But it was for me. It was my chance to be happy. Remember you picked me. You showed up at my door with your clothes in a box. I'd never have known I could win you. I was the luckiest man in the world, and I could not leave the country and give it up. Besides, I didn't want to be away from you for two years. I sat in my little dorm room at night, sounds of French Africa dialect in my head, and I thought, Ursula, Ursula."

"But you never said!"

"I was too shy, I guess. Then time passed and it seemed a silly thing to tell. This summer I realized I needed to tell you, that you needed to know. That I loved you. That I love you now."

The light turns pink and then the blue of the sky begins to filter morning through the dawn. "I love you too," she says. "And I want to go to bed. But I think I better tell you one more thing."

She tells him where his brother is.

—60—

When Katie doesn't find them at the trailer, she walks across the road and picks her way along the riverbank. She is wearing khaki pants and tennis shoes, so she feels sure-footed. She sees Gully first, sitting on one of those fold-up chairs people take to outdoor concerts, to give his back support. He is writing in a notebook. Nearby, Fish sits on the bank with his knees up, reading a tattered paperback book. It is a glorious Indian summer day in October, and the scene is so peaceful and colorful and tender—Fish and his father above the water—she feels a catch in her throat.

"Hi guys," she says, standing just above them. Both turn and see her, then jump to their feet. She scrambles closer. "Gosh, Gully, don't get up," she says. She embraces him, smells his sweat and the earth on his overalls. He rubs her back with his hand. "Katie, Katie," he murmurs, then steps away. She turns to Fish, hesitates for a fraction of a moment, and then hugs him too, more shyly, more quickly.

She sits on the ground between them. "What are you writing, Gully?"

He smiles and waves his notebook at her. "I'm writing the story of my life, can you believe that?"

"That's great."

"That little girl of yours, she had all these questions. When did I catch my first fish? What kind of car did I learn to drive in? I told her my mother took us to live on the reservation near Missoula when I was a tyke, and she wants to hear all about that. I decided to get it all down once and for good." He slaps his notebook. "By golly, it's getting to be a long thing."

"Michael and I are going to have it typed up," Fish says. "Pop's a good storyteller."

Gully gets up again. "Makes my arm ache. I can't go at it too long, but what else have I got to do? I'm going to go take a little nap before supper. What's for supper, Fish? Katie's here in time for supper. We could drive into town. That'd be better, we'll go in somewhere and have a good meal."

"That's okay, Gully," Katie says. "I'm going to have pizza with Ursula and Michael later. At Carter's place."

"You come over before you leave? You come to say good-bye?"

She kisses Gully quickly. "I don't need to. I'll be seeing you. I'm back." He breaks into a smile, moves his chair over, and tells her to sit down. "This boy of mine has been taking good care of me," he says, and leaves.

She sits on the chair, which is surprisingly comfortable. "What are you reading?" she asks. Fish is still holding his book in his hand.

"Ray Bradbury stories," he says, laying the book on the ground. "A quarter, used, at the bus station. Not much to do around here on a Sunday."

"Where's Geneva?"

"Flagstaff. They've got a distant cousin there or something."

"I'm surprised at you, living with your dad. What does he do while you're working?"

"He has his little outings, now that he can drive again. He spends a lot of time with his friend Austin Melroy. We kept Bounder, he's in the shed at the house."

"I saw him. He seemed a little better-behaved."

"He must have been sleepy."

They look at one another, shy as schoolmates.

"He likes to come out to the site where Michael and I are building, too. He can nap in his camper, or sit out in a lawn chair and watch. Supervise, he calls it. He's a nice old man, Katie."

"He's not soaking you in remorse and moral fortitude?"

"Not really. Though I've learned my share of his affirmations. How about, 'Victory is won not in miles but in inches.'"

"General MacArthur? Robert E. Lee?"

"Nope. Louis L'Amour."

"I went out to the house. I was surprised to find Carol Lee there."

"Sky and Prudence didn't get out until the end of August. No way am I renting the place again. She said she'd keep an eye on things until I move back. I thought, why not?"

"I'd like to keep an eye on things, myself."

"Live out there, you mean?"

"If that's okay with you."

"You're not—you're not back with the pear man?"

She hoots. "I don't know if he's back from Italy or wherever he went, but no, I'm not back with the pear man. Now or ever."

"Are you back with me?"

She has thought of a hundred answers to that question, knowing it would come, and all of them fail her now. "In some way, I am," she says simply. "We're not divorced." She smiles at him. "I'm out four hundred dollars for nothing."

"I've been careful to stay dressed, thinking there might be more papers served." He seems good-humored about it.

"I'm sorry I didn't write, didn't tell you what was going on. I was at my mother's. I wanted to be with her and Rhea."

"That's a long time to be with June."

"It was all right this trip. I'll tell you about it sometime. Listen, I'll stay at Michael's a couple of days, but can you get that girl out?"

"Sure. She's got her brother to go to. She's nothing to me, Katie. Not really even a friend."

"Are you going to stay here until Geneva comes back? Do you know when that will be?"

"I could come and go now. I don't have to stay all the time. It was a lot harder on Gully when he had the cast."

She stands up and folds the chair. Fish moves closer to her. She starts up the bank.

At the road she says, "I don't feel so desperate now."

He says, "I don't know if you'll believe this, but neither do I. Except I wonder all the time about Rhea. Whether I'll see her. I guess I fell in love with her."

"You've written her. That's nice. It means a lot to her."

He grabs her arm. "Aw, Katie, don't be mean." She goes inside the circle of his arms, feels his warmth. She lays her head against his chest, and doesn't raise it for his kiss. In a moment she pulls gently away.

"Give me a fucking list," he says earnestly. "Tell me what you want me to do."

"I don't want to tell you. I want you to find out for yourself."

"Find out what!"

"You just have to grow up, Fish."

His cheek twitches. He looks away. "But you're here."

"I'm here. Come on, I brought something for you." She leads him to her car. In the front seat is a box of pears. She takes one out and holds it up between her and Fish. It is the exquisite red of a peach, but smooth, with a ruby undertone. "Take a bite," she says. "It's wonderful. I went to a lot of trouble to get these."

She holds the fruit and he eats it. She turns it as he takes the next bite, and the next. Juice drips onto her hands. She draws the pear up to her own mouth and sucks the juice at the edge of the tears his teeth made. Then she holds it up to him again, standing a little closer.

## END